CORNERED

A HOLLOWAY PACK NOVEL

BOOK 5

J.A. BELFIELD

CORNERED
A HOLLOWAY PACK NOVEL

Published by J.A. Belfield
www.jabelfield.com

Copyright © 2019 Julie Anne Belfield

Cover art by Aimee Laine.

First Printing: 2016
10 9 8 7 6 5 4 3

CORNERED

For my own pack of wolves.

1

Thud. Thud. Thud.

The rhythmic pounding from Kyle's bedroom sent a twitch to the muscle just beneath my left eye.

Thud.

I grabbed my pillow and attempted death by self-asphyxiation.

Thud.

I guessed, if being completely honest, I could've ignored the incessant beat that I had to listen to on a daily, nightly—sometimes even *hourly*—basis … if not for the growls and the gasps and the screeches and—

With a groan, I flopped over onto my stomach and dug my right ear into the mattress, while plugging my left by squishing my forearm against it.

Thud, thud.

It wouldn't have been so bad had there been at least one corner of the house they couldn't be heard from.

Thud, thud, thud.

It also wouldn't have been so bad if my own dick didn't twitch in response—a result of too much pickiness and too little action of its own.

Thud, thud, thud, thud.

With a growl, I pretty much threw myself off the bed, knocking my pillow flying across the room and a picture frame slamming down face-first against my nightstand. On my stride to the door, my feet hit the carpet so hard, I might as well have been yelling *'Fee-Fi-Fi-Fum'*, like the giant in Lia's fairy tales Jem made me read to her.

The bedroom door clattered off the wall as I swung it wide, and I stepped out onto the landing, where the snarls and wails built into a deafening crescendo, smothering my ears before I passed Kyle's bedroom door.

Sometimes, having enhanced hearing sucked.

My descent to the hallway drummed the stairs, and, at the bottom, I snatched up my boots and began yanking them on, balancing on one leg at a time as I did so.

Dad's massive form appeared in the living room doorway to my right, as I straightened and reached for my leather jacket off the banister.

"Pay-per-view's quieter than those two," I said to him, shrugging on the jacket. "'Least you can mute the bloody screen."

He sent me a nod, the simple gesture seeming to confess he knew exactly how I felt—though I doubted he did. "Going somewhere?"

"Yeah." I scooped up my helmet and keys off the hall stand. "Out." As I took a step for the front door, he gripped hold of my arm.

When I turned back to him, his green eyes regarded me from beneath his thick ginger waves. "You can talk to me if you need to, Dan."

"I just did," I said, trying to shrug loose.

A hint of hurt entered his eyes, as he frowned. "You've been out every night this week."

"Perceptive of you."

"You're not the only one who's had to adjust to Brook being here."

"I know that. But sitting here listening to the show day after day is your prerogative, Dad. Just as getting the hell out of here, so I don't have to, is mine." I jerked my chin toward his hand wrapped around my bicep. "My arm?"

He released me, but only after he'd stared me down with his probing attention for a few beats, and I marched from the house and into the cool evening air.

At some point, rain had kicked in for about the fifth time that day, dulling what should've been a pink dusk to a wishy-washy grey. I rounded the house to the carport, and in the dusty shadows, tucked between Dad's pickup and the house, my new wheels called to me like the escape I'd bought it to be.

Ethan and Shelley'd had my old Hi-Lux for Gabe, a couple months before, and the pack'd been shocked as hell when I'd taken their money, gone out alone, and returned with a matt black Triumph Speed Triple. One with a single seat. It'd taken some explaining for them to 'get' that sometimes a guy just needed to be alone.

Swinging a leg over the seat, I straightened the bike and slotted in the keys. A press of a button brought the engine grumbling to life, and I gave a little twist of the throttle for good measure. With it idling between my thighs and loving every single vibration it sent through me, I slid my helmet over my mess of hair and fastened it in place under my chin.

Five seconds later, I'd rolled out into the faint mist of rain, down the driveway, and had hit one of the few roads that cut through the forest of Wild Woodington in Derbyshire.

The Hang & Hide had become my regular hideout around five weeks back, when I'd stumbled across it in need of somewhere to dry off, and definitely in need of a drink. About a half hour from home, the flat but broad shack of a building sat just before the cusp of the town of Derby on a weed-riddled, uneven car park, and resembled a rundown, wood-fronted shack, but on a grander scale.

Four older teens clustered near the entrance, beneath a bug-spattered lamp that cast a less than weak glow over the lot once sundown arrived. Heading for the opposite side, I bumped across the potholes to my usual spot for parking, just to the right of the windowless door. After cutting the engine, I climbed off the bike and trod toward the entrance, slipping my helmet off on the way.

The kids near the door spared barely a glance when I passed them, and I ignored them right back. I'd never gone there to make friends, never gone there to create new roots.

I'd only ever gone there for a break from the stress-hole my house had become.

Stepping through the decrepit wooden door didn't bring with it much more light than that cast outside. Every strip along the ceiling worked, if one listened to the gossip, but the owner never flipped them on—some said it was because he didn't like the bills that created.

Inhaling offered up sweat and perfume, dust and spilled lager, and I chased the latter with a glance to the left.

A couple of folks hogged the stools at the bar, behind which Joe, the bar manager, poured from a tap. Farther long, doors led out to a long corridor that ended up at an emergency exit past the loos, and at the back wall, a couple of pool tables were in use—the highlight of the place and probably what brought in the younger crowd.

I knew the situation of everything—had since my first visit—and, as I'd grown used to doing, I checked every corner over, from left—skimming over the ID's of those at the bar, the two twenty-something's shooting balls.

The right wall was mostly filled by elongated booths, all of them with haphazardly placed circular tables, like someone'd just tossed them to see where they'd land. The seating had fared little better. Helping to clutter up the space, padded stools of all designs sat in disorder around the tables, pressed up against the threadbare bench seats that stretched the full length on opposing sides of the booths.

On one of those benches, in the booth nearest the door, a head of red hair was bent over some notes on a table, and I smiled to myself. I didn't head that way, though, but went straight to the bar.

Slotting myself between the two occupied stools, I waited for Joe to notice me—or to quit pretending he hadn't noticed me, anyway. It took a full four seconds before he nodded my way. No words, just the nod. From my short time visiting the place, I'd noticed Joe never seemed to have a lot to say to his patrons.

"Pint, and whatever Liv's on tonight," I said, leaning my elbows on the bar.

The grunt he gave was the equivalent of a full blown conversation, coming from Joe, and as he turned away to grab glasses, I glanced in the mirror behind the him. Right into the dark eyes of the blonde on my left.

I'd seen her before; she sat in the exact same spot every time. Seen her smiles before, too, because she sent me one whenever she thought I was looking. I rarely returned them, though. I hadn't gone there to pick up, and if I had? Well, something just seemed off about her. I didn't like a female to be too eager.

Joe's bulk blocked the view again, and he slammed the drinks down in front of me and held out his hand. He rarely even bothered to let customers know how much they owed him. If they gave too much, he returned with change. If they gave too little, his hand just didn't move until the error had been corrected.

I dropped a folded fiver onto his palm and told him to keep the leftovers.

With both drinks in hand, I turned for the booth, lifting the smaller glass and taking a sniff. Coke. Usually meant Liv had too much work to get through.

Liv studied at Uni and often landed at The Double-H—as the locals called it—to work on assignments. Said the atmosphere helped her to slip into a zone her wall-facing home desk tended to kill.

Not wanting to break her stride, I placed her drink down on her table and took a seat on the opposite bench without saying a word. Didn't mean I didn't cock my head to the side to see what she worked on, though.

At the top, in her neat handwriting, she'd penned 'Olivia Fanella', and beneath that, a load of gobble-de-gook I didn't understand. She'd once tried to explain what all the codes meant, the one time I'd asked her. It hadn't sunk in, and rather than ask again, I scanned the room for the second time since arriving.

One of the teens, a black kid, lounged over the pool table as he lined up a shot. The other, a pale blond, kept shaking his head, muttering for him to '*miss it*', despite the wonky smile on his lips.

I watched them a moment, almost wondering what it might've been like to grow up normal. Human. To have continued on through school until the very end. Through college. Uni, even—like Liv. Instead of hushed phone calls and donations made to school, the day Nate—our Alpha, and Dad's best friend—decided I couldn't go back, because I'd experienced my first full body muscle spasm.

I'd been popular in school. Popular with the sporty kids. Popular with the girls. It'd been weeks before I quit sulking over the loss of that popularity. It'd been longer still before I'd been given a new outlet for my energy, because not only did I have to wait until I reached eighteen before Dad and Nate would let me join them at the family construction business, I also had to wait for my first few changes to pass. They'd been some seriously, *seriously* boring months.

The black kid must've potted his ball, because, as he straightened, he outstretched his arms, his face full of smugness. "Man, you've either got it, or you ain't," he said to his friend.

From the other side of the floor, his volume shouldn't have been audible. It likely wasn't, to anybody else near where I sat. I didn't fall into that category, though.

Studying the guys a bit longer, I took in the fitted cut of their shirts, the neatness of their hair. Despite only wearing jeans and boots, everything they wore seemed to have been chosen with precision. The blonde at the bar looked designer dressed from head to toe, too, and even the bloke on the other stool had on a pressed shirt and trousers, his tie from whatever job he'd left behind still secured about his neck.

Nothing like my stained jeans and scuffed boots, my hair overgrown and a bloody mess. I probably stood out like a tick on a bald cat.

Except for the girl sitting opposite.

I turned my attention back to Liv. The way that red hair of hers hung in her face had a roughness about it, making it—*her*—seem wild and untamed, despite her quiet demeanour. The hand not holding the pen clutched onto a bunch of the strands, like she needed the anchor to keep her grounded while she worked, showing a glimpse of the black-framed glasses she always wore. Beside her on the bench, her usual parker sat scrunched, leaving her in only a white T, with rolled up sleeves and a Rolling Stones logo on the front, a pair of ratty skinnies leading to the green Converse on her feet. Seemed to be her usual 'work' gear—she'd barely deviated from the outfit since the first time I'd seen her.

The pair of us looked way out of place, when compared to the rest of the patrons, even if, all things considered, we probably were the only ones in there who actually suited The Hang & Hide, in all its ramshackle glory. Probably what'd drawn me to sit near her in the first place—that, and the way she seemed to want to talk even less than me.

Still, I couldn't help but lean forward and open my big mouth. "You know, you don't really look like the kind of female who'd hang around a place like this all the while." As soon as I said it, I knew I'd sounded like a twit.

"Why's that, then?" She nudged her glasses up her nose as she lifted her gaze. "Or maybe you just think the place should be full of more like *Barbie* over there?"

I followed the jerk of her chin, to the blonde at the bar. Like she sensed the scrutiny, the female twisted in her seat, giving me another of her smiles. Another one I ignored. With her movement, her thick waves of hair swung over her shoulder, the colour of popcorn flavoured jelly beans. Her eyes, on the other hand, resembled the liquorice ones.

Personally, I preferred the orangey sorts.

I downed a fat swig of my pint and turned back to Liv, resting my elbows on my knees.

15

Liv's attention had already returned to her pad, her coarse wispy strands falling around her face, as she tapped her pen against her bottom lip, creating a smudge of blue there I instantly wanted to wipe away.

"Your hair reminds me of satsuma jelly beans," I said, before I could stop myself.

"That supposed to be sweet talk, Danny?" she asked, looking up again. "Because you're seriously crap at it."

"Just saying." I shrugged. "I like satsuma jelly beans."

Breathing out a laugh and shaking her head, she went back to hunching over the table. "Thanks for the drink," she muttered. "But work on your chatting up skills, yeah?"

Straightening, I lifted a foot and flopped it onto a stool, slouching back as I necked the rest of my lager in a few long swigs. "Who says I'm chatting you up?" I asked when I came up for air.

She dropped her pen long enough to take a drink. As she lowered her glass, she said, "There are always plenty of girls in here you can talk to, yet, you always talk to me. So, either you're chatting me up ... or you're gay."

"Self-flattery." I let out a low whistle. "That's ... quite a skill."

"I'm not going to sleep with you, Danny."

That got my attention, and I studied her serious expression, the tightness between her brows, the way she fingered her pen like she needed the distraction. My own frown moved in. "Feel better now you have that out there?"

I heard her swallow as much as saw it, before she gave a small nod.

Leaning forward in my seat again and dropping my foot back to the floor, I swiped up my glass. "Good." I pushed up from my seat, but paused before taking more than a few steps and twisted back to find her gazing my way through her lenses. "I'm not gay," I said, like that was somehow important. "And I sit next to you each week because I come here for some peace, and you happen to be pretty good at providing that. Just so we're clear."

Without waiting for a response, I headed for the bar and slid my glass across the counter. "Another, when you've got time, Joe—JD and Coke, too. I'll be back in a sec."

Black scuffs marked the walls of the corridor leading to the loos, like boots had been planted along there and God knew what else, and I shrugged my shoulders in to avoid contact. On reaching the Men's door, I took a deep breath and held it, then nudged my way in using my elbow. My eyes stung at the stench in there, and I strode for the urinals and made light work of relieving myself, before zipping back up and ducking back out in record time. As soon as I entered the corridor and the door swung shut behind me, I sucked in the breath I'd held and headed back out to the bar.

Liv hadn't moved, though the twitch of her head told me she might've been watching for my return. Slapping money on the bar, I nodded toward Joe and scooped up my drinks.

Liv wiggled her pencil back and forth, meeting my eyes as I sat down. "I'm sorry I made assumptions about you."

Sliding my pint onto the table beside me, I took a sip of the JD&C and sank back into my seat. "Okay," I said, once the liquid had travelled to the spot I needed it to hit.

"It's just ..." She dropped her pencil down and flattened her palm atop her papers. "Look, most guys, in my experience, only bother to spend time with a girl because they want to get into her knickers."

As soon as she said it, my focus instantly dropped to where those knickers would hug, and my eyebrow twitched before I could stop it. "Okay," I said again, because up until she mentioned them, I hadn't even given them a thought. At least, not outside of my bedroom. It took effort to force my eyes back up to hers.

"So, you're saying you're not like that, then?"

I smirked. "I'm not trying to get into your knickers, no." At least, not then, anyway.

She didn't look convinced. Not that I blamed her. I didn't dare tell Liv she'd been my inspiration a few times since we'd met. She'd probably never talk to me again, if I told her what, exactly, she inspired. Even so, she picked her pencil up again and turned back to her work, offering up her own, "Okay."

Chuckling, I lifted my glass back to my lips.

2

I didn't leave the bar until after closing, but the living room light still glowed behind the closed curtains as I swerved through the gates of home. The rain had kicked up a few notches since earlier, and idly splashing over the block paving, I guided the bike to its spot beneath the carport, beneath which the rain beat out something akin to a Rammstein track, more so once I'd cut the bike's engine.

Beside me, Dad's truck sat like a hulking dark beast, thanks to the cloud coverage blocking any natural light. My elbow scuffed against the house bricks as I kicked down the stand and swung my leg over, tugging at my helmet straps the second I'd set the bike down. Cool, damp air swamped my face as I freed my head, and pocketing my keys, I crabbed out from the carport toward the rear of the house.

I'd barely rounded the corner when I caught the low laughter over the rain drumming my shoulders, and peeking through the kitchen window confirmed what I'd heard.

With her back to me, Brook sat planted on the worktop, her knees spread wide enough to accommodate my brothers bulk. Thanks to his face being buried into her neck, only his thick auburn hair could be seen, the curled strands sticking up all over the joint like they'd had Brook's fingers in them a few times too many.

My teeth ground at them invading a shared space of the house, and I glanced toward the back door, but only for a second before I about turned and ducked back beneath the shelter beside my bike. As I worked off my leather jacket, I slid my mobile from my jeans pocket and scrolled through my contacts to *Dad*. After typing out a quick message: DOSSING AT NATE'S, I clicked 'Send'.

With my mobile zipped safely in the inside pocket of my jacket, I undid my jeans button and made fast work of shunning the rest of my clothes until they all lay strewn over my bike seat, with my boots hiding just beneath.

Raindrops attacked my bare flesh as I stepped out from beneath the shelter, and I cut a diagonal path right into the trees of the forest surrounding our home. The woodlands had belonged to Nate's family for too many generations to keep track of, and a fast run north-east across the five-mile gap, to the home belonging to our Alpha, would be a whole lot faster than the round-about route by road.

Despite the overhead canopy being lush with foliage, fat blobs of wetness still broke through, spattering my head and thudding quietly upon the dirt path cutting between the trees. Goosebumps sprang up over my chest from each hit I took. With it being May, it should've been warm, not freezing my hide off. So much for it nearly being summer.

It took only a few minutes to trek through to my changing spot. I'd initially selected it because there'd been a horrific downpour the evening of my initial change, years before, and I'd hunted for somewhere dry. I must have liked it, because I'd returned there ever since.

Old fern and bracken crumpled beneath my soles— beneath my palms, too, as I hunched down and braced myself. After a quick scan through the sooty darkness to ensure my solitude, I closed my eyes, drew in a deep breath and forced concentration.

The change hit my nape and scalp first, no more than a prickling sensation. Within seconds, it'd intensified to needling, then stabbing, rolling along my vertebrae to my shoulders, before dipping forward to seduce my chest.

Tendons in my thighs and shins tightened. Muscles either side of my spine began to condense. A splinter of pain pierced through my left leg, as an inferno roared the length of my arms, and my chest heaved beneath my hastened breaths.

With each inhalation, musty oak-wood got sucked in, along with mulch and cleansed greens, soggy soil, matured fruits, and I focused on those instead of the fire raging through me.

Catching a whiff of stoat, I held onto it a moment—before releasing a groan as a fist-like agony clenched at the base of my spine and knotted the cords there. When every muscle in my body seemed to implode, before being branded by the flames raging through me, that groan expanded into an outcry.

Allowing me scarcely a pause to absorb new breath, my entire spinal cord snapped out of alignment, one debilitating vertebra at a time, and my back bowed low, far too low to be considered 'safe', kicking my chest high like a ship's figurehead. If my fingers still existed, I'd have clutched at the soggy earth, but I knew only stubby lengths would be there, mid-mutation, and that hairs would be lengthening, claiming my skin.

Stuck there for a few long beats, trapped within a prison of agony, I blinked, then blinked again, finally accepting my altered sight, the dimmed hues, the skewed tones.

As the next stage brewed, my tendons winched tauter still, and my breaths steamed the already clammy air. The instant I felt my first vertebra unlock, I unleashed my moan, the sound like a crescendo through the dark as the pain ran the gauntlet on a direct route for my coccyx, before settling down again as flesh forced itself forth from there.

For only a beat, my body swayed on trembling limbs—limbs that, I knew from experience, no longer resembled those of a human—and I barely had time to ready myself before my skull split, the noise of it blasting through my head loud enough to drown out my growl of dismay. Equally as deafening, my cranial bone shifted, each slight movement, each modification hitting my hearing like fucked up popping candy—like getting pelted by a wrathful storm of hailstones tailored made for myself. As it rushed forward against my facial bone, it was like I'd pissed someone off enough to stab me. Repeatedly. With a billion toothpicks. Sending my growl rumbling up a notch to a full out attack snarl.

As harshly as the assault on my nervous system began, it stopped, but the thunder in my chest continued rolling for unnecessary seconds afterwards.

Shoulders high, and snout low, each exhalation coming out fast and sharp, I didn't want to think about how long my change took. Prior to the stress with Kyle—with Brook moving in—I could've been done and dusted on the good side of twelve minutes. Since then? I didn't know exactly. I just knew the rest of the pack easily left me behind. If I listened to Dad, though, he'd argue Kyle had nothing to do with any of it. He preferred to blame it on my nightly tendency to drink.

Shaking my thoughts off, I listened for sounds beyond my own, the twitch of my ears sending too long tufts to tickle my jaw bone. Finding nothing concerning, I stretched out my limbs and, with a kick off of my hind paws, ran the path to Nate's.

Lingering sweat clung to my body and merged with the fresh rain, as I stepped from the forest and beneath the arches to Nate's property. The lawn appeared almost black, thanks to the weather, stretching all the way to the block paving that surrounded the house. The grass both soaked and tickled my soles as I strode toward the conservatory, where light from the kitchen offered a warm glow.

As I grew nearer, Nate's broad shoulders, bunched over the kitchen table, came into view through the windows of the French doors into the main house.

His head lifted when I opened the conservatory door, exposing the laptop he sat in front of, and his gaze tracked my movements across the cool tiles, my entrance into the warm room with him.

A quick glance around the oak-designed kitchen showed no one else. His wife, Beth, must've already gone up to bed, as no sounds came from the rest of the house, either.

"Figured I'd crash here tonight," I said, twisting back to Nate's appraising stare.

His blue eyes seemed filled with questions, but the only one he asked was, "Again?"

It was a fair question, considering I'd intermittently shown up over the last few months—sometimes even sneaking in after a long run, well into the night, to a house in darkness.

I nodded.

His gaze swept over me, before he lifted his fingers from the mouse-pad of his laptop and brushed them over his dark, recently-cropped hair. "Better find a towel and dry yourself off, then."

"Thought I'd take a shower first," I said, trying to gauge his mood. I would've tried to figure out his late night, too, if the behaviour wasn't common for him. Maybe I wasn't the only one who enjoyed a bit of alone time.

"Go ahead—but let Connor know you're here first."

"Already did," I said, moving toward the hallway. "Sent him a text before I left."

"Danny," he barked, stalling me, and I turned in time to catch his mobile as I flew at me. He jerked his chin upward a notch. "Do you good to just *speak* to him, once in a while." He lowered his attention back to his laptop screen. "You can leave that in the living room once you're done."

Typical Nate: Giving me an order, along with semi-privacy to carry it out. Palming the phone, I cut a quiet path over the hallway tiles and, after sending a longing glance toward the stairs on my left, took a right into the living room, nudging the door to behind me.

With the curtains drawn, only the outlines of the plush sofas and armchair showed up against the pale backdrop of walls. As I found Dad's number, I slumped into the nearest

23

one, rubbing at my face while I waited for the call to connect.

"Nate?" Dad's deep bass sounded weary. "Dan get there okay?"

"It's me," I said."

He sighed. "Dan, you could've at least called when you got here. It's worrying, having you running out there alone so often."

"Well, I would've, but there was an obstruction," I said, fisting my fingers in my hair.

His second sigh came through louder. "How long is this going to go on, Son? Something's got to give soon."

"How long will their taking over the entire house go on for?" I said back.

He didn't answer, only his breaths blew down the line.

Dropping my hand to drape over my knee, I said, "I just want things back to normal, Dad. I just want our space back."

"So, you'd ask Kyle to give up who he's fallen in love with, just to keep the rest of us happy? Would you give her up, if it were you in his shoes?"

My teeth ground at the same argument we'd had a few times of late. "I wouldn't be with a *cat* to start with."

"He didn't plan it, Dan."

"Doesn't make it any less weird."

"Doesn't make it any less real, either," he said, conviction in his tone, and I knew—as I always knew—I'd be arguing an already lost case if I continued.

"Look, I'll be back before work. I'm gonna go grab a shower before bed."

"I love you, Son," he said, his voice deepening.

"Love you, too, Dad." Before he could get sappier, I hung up the phone and, pushing up, placed it on the coffee table.

The shadows of the hall stretched up toward the upper landing, as I made my way upstairs. Soft breathing drifted through the door of Jem and Sean's room on the left, and I poked my head through the ajar doorway opposite, took in the made bed, bathed in a soft blush made by the nightlight, and, at its foot, the small sleeping form between the bars of the cot.

A combination of soft and gruff snores came from the remaining two bedrooms on my continued pad toward the end of the landing. I didn't have to tax my brain too much to figure out which belonged to Ethan, which to Beth.

The last door led to the bathroom. Rain splattered against the un-frosted window that overlooked the rear garden and forest beyond. A freestanding bath took centre stage, pretty much like our own bathroom at home. In fact, the entire house resembled our own, if I discounted the added conservatory at Nate's.

Not bothering to flick on the light, I went directly to the shower in the rear corner, and after knocking on the tap in there, I shut myself inside. The initial shock of water hit my back like a blast of ice water, jolting me forward, and I braced my hands against the glass panel as I waited for the heat to kick in.

It took only minutes to soap and hose myself down. Might've taken longer had I let my mind linger on the recollection of Liv's knickers—mostly what kind she probably wore—but I'd ordered my thoughts forward. Hard-ons had no place in a bedroom decorated with butterflies and fairies.

With my hair rubbed dry enough, a towel secured about my waist, that bedroom was exactly where I headed.

The same steady breathing and snoring patterned my walk along the landing, but tiny grunts and shuffling greeted me when I let myself into Lia's bedroom. Trying not to make sound, I crossed to the cot.

Little legs wriggled beneath the pink and green blankets, while her chubby fists brushed over her head. I'd stayed over enough times to know what her struggles preceded, and not bothering to wait for the inevitable, I scooped her up against my chest, her face instantly snuggling into my neck as I carried her across the room.

It didn't even take me as far as the bed, though, to notice the warmth pressing against my ribcage, and I detoured us to the changing table.

Sleepy blue eyes blinked up at me when I set her down. "Hey," I whispered, giving one of my best smiles while popping open the legs of her 'gro. At the tired smile I got in return, I chuckled. "Yeah, I know how you feel."

Having done the deed a couple dozen times before, it didn't take me long to switch up her soiled nappy for a clean one. As I was clipping her clothes back together, a door opened out on the landing and footsteps trod toward and down the stairs.

"You're in luck." Her dark mop of fluffy hairs tickled my chin when I picked her up again. "Sounds like Mummy's gone to fetch you some nosh."

When Jem'd been carrying Lia last summer, Sean had switched out the old king-size in the spare room for a double bed. Ensuring I had a good grip on the fidgeting bundle, I pulled back the covers and plumped up the pillows. Once I'd climbed inside, I tugged the covers up and tucked them around Lia, drawing up my knees for her to rest against.

"There," I said, sinking back and letting the pillows support me. "Now, how about you tell me why you're awake at this hour, and then I'll tell you why *I'm* awake at this hour."

The growly gurgle she made could've passed as a laugh. Understandable really. I made the same deal with her every time I ended up there for the night, and neither of us ever played the game right.

"Looks like it's gonna have to be *Row-the-Boat* again, then."

"Only because that's the only song you remember all the words to," Jem said, looking half asleep as she trudged into the room with a prepared bottle in her hand.

"Already have enough going on in my head, without having to contain more shit, too."

"Language." She sent me one of her disapproving frowns, coming closer and setting the bottle on the bedside table. "You want me to take her?"

As usual, she didn't bat an eye at my being there— though, it'd probably breached a point where my absence would surprise her more.

I reached for the bottle and waved it toward the parted lips waiting for it. "I can do it. Me and Lia here were planning to do some talking, anyway."

"Talking or singing? And there're plenty of us you can talk to, if you've stuff you need to get off your chest."

"Yeah, but Lia doesn't judge. Nor answer me back," I added, before she could argue.

"How many did you drink tonight, Dan?"

I shrugged. "Handful of pints." *Maybe a half-handful more.*

Leaning in close, she inhaled. "And how many JD's did you add to those?"

"A few."

She sighed, and before she could get too serious on me, I planted a kiss on her cheek.

"I'm good. Promise." Giving my attention back to Lia, I grinned like an idiot until she reciprocated. "See? It's all good. Go back to bed, Jem. I got this. Stupid for you to be awake when I already am." I plugged the bottle teat into Lia's mouth, pretending I hadn't noticed Jem's hesitation. When she finally kissed Lia's cheek and turned toward the door, the brewing tension in my shoulders unknotted.

"'Night, Danny," she said, as she passed through the door and went back to her own room.

"Now, where were we?" I asked, but Lia had already moved on to filling her belly. And there I'd been about to tell her about my riveting night out, how I'd been drop-kicked to the kerb without even having opened my mouth.

Which brought my thoughts right back to a certain redhead. With smoky blue eyes. And knickers. Definitely knickers. Of some kind, or another.

The teat of the bottle fizzed and popped as Lia released it, slamming my brain back to the moment, the room. The task.

After sliding the bottle onto the table, I used my thumb to wipe away a stray dribble of milk from the corner of her mouth and took in the wide roundness of the eyes staring back at me. An added kick up of her legs and wave of her arms told me she wouldn't be falling back to sleep anytime fast.

Letting out a sigh, I wrapped my fingers around her wrists and clapped her hands together. "Pat-a-Cake it is, then."

The rain had eased some during the night, but in its place, a gale force wind battered my coat from all angles on my six a.m. run home.

Added to that, Sean's words echoed around inside my head.

He'd caught me as I'd gone to jog down the stairs, his voice deep and serious as he'd said, "Next time you want to share Lia's room, you better turn up with less alcohol inside you. Otherwise, I'll be ignoring Jem's request to leave you be and kicking your arse down to the sofa to kip. Are we clear?"

I'd had no choice but to nod—mostly because Sean'd looked like he wanted to shred my hide. Just another peg on the board of things pissing me off.

Working off my irritation, I pushed my muscles hard on my run, stretching out kinks caused by a night spent with Lia snoozing on my chest. She'd finally drooped there a little after three, and too knackered to move her, or myself, I'd managed to switch off enough to get some shut eye.

With the shitty start I'd already had to the morning, a part of me wished I'd just stayed asleep.

My body still ached by the time I hit our side of the forest. Changing form only made that worse. Sweat stuck to me, as I balanced there in my crouch, the dampness fast becoming frozen once hit by the chilly blasts of air.

Head dipped low and eyes closed, fingertips still digging into the earth, I stayed there a moment, regaining my breaths, replaying Sean's warning ... hoping the kitchen would be unoccupied when I went through.

I'd purposefully made the journey a half hour earlier, just as I'd been doing for the past few weeks. Everyone at home tended to wake by their internal clocks, though, meaning the strategy didn't always work.

Pushing up off the ground, I straightened my legs, ignoring the tightness clenching my calves. Stretching out my fingers took conscious effort, as did up-righting my spine. My neck cracked when I worked it side to side, my shoulders crunching when I rolled them.

Once as un-tense as I could make myself, I finally opened my eyes to a confusion of colour.

The funky weather had begun a good couple of months earlier—giving us snow mid-April, floods down south, land-invading seas along the coast. At least it'd been a couple of weeks since the last hailstorm. Those were a killer on my bike.

As a result of the weirdness, nature didn't seem to have a bloody clue what season surrounded it, and aside from the wilting plants and bad crops, prey had been yo-yoing in and out of hibernation, and the trees had become a collage of greens, browns and pinks.

Sadly, the colour didn't extend much beyond the forest roof. As I trod through the remaining timber to home, only filthy-looking greyness toned the sky.

On my squelch across the lawn, I scoured the rear windows of the house. Curtains obscured the right-hand upstairs window—my room—but the one to its left showed shadowed movement within the bathroom. Hopefully Kyle. Or Brook. Better yet: both. Anything that meant eating my breakfast in peace.

A couple of metres from the back door, though, I knew it wasn't them upstairs, because they both sat at the kitchen table, chewing on food.

Not ready to deal, I veered off toward the carport to collect my gear.

The dampness of night had made my clothes limp and cold, but I still tugged them on, just to kill time. Retrieving my mobile from my jacket, I relocated it to my jeans pocket, and after grabbing up my helmet and boots, I made the too-short walk to the house.

So much for luck, though. Kyle and Brook still sat exactly where they had been. Sending out a silent prayer for patience, I tugged down the handle and stepped inside the warm kitchen, to the scent of eggs, sausage and cat.

Kyle raised only his eyes at my arrival. "'Morning."

I jerked my chin his way with my quiet, "Hey," my stomach growling as I eyed what they had left on their plates.

If either of them were surprised by my early entrance, neither showed it. They were probably as used to my comings and goings as the rest of the pack.

"There's some left," Brook said, scraping her chair back. "I can fix you some, if you would like."

My jaw tightened as I took in the wariness in her movements. "I'm going for a shower." Kyle's head made a slow upward rise, his stare darkening, and swallowing down my attitude a little, I added, "Thanks, though," before cutting through to the hallway.

I reached almost the top of the stairs before they began talking about me, and I caught the low grumbles, followed by, "Give him time," from Brook.

As Kyle's, "He's had four months," carried up, I strode the length of the landing and shut myself in my room.

Rain made it harder to see the road, as it splashed against the visor of my helmet. Like the country was being punished for some misdeed, the downpour had started up again while I'd taken my shower. The dull headache that'd taken up permanent residency inside my head didn't help matters either. Nor the almost empty tank of my bike, adding to my already low mood.

The trouble with building work was the law stating we couldn't begin making noise before certain hours. Meant we got stuck with the main run of morning traffic. Even though I'd left the house before everyone else, it still caught me. Luckily, my bike could squeeze through spaces cars couldn't, and on reaching a queue six-deep into the petrol station, I just weaved a line around the lot of them, between a couple of cars at the rear pumps, and straight next to a newly vacated pump at the front.

Not even bothering to look at what glares I'd earned, I slid off my helmet, hooked it over my handlebars, and climbed from the bike.

The overhanging roof kept the rain from me as I unlocked the tank and detached the fuel nozzle from the pump. Keeping one eye on the gushing petrol as I filled up, I glanced about the forecourt, taking stock of the cars at the four pumps visible from my angle, an additional one over near a hole-in-the-wall cash machine. Some guy checked the air pressure in his Subaru tyres, to the left of the main building, while a row of three vehicles filled the kerbside right in front of the shop.

As soon as the gaseous liquid neared the top, I clicked off the nozzle. After relocking the tank and collecting my helmet, I headed inside to pay.

Five others stood before me in a line to the counter, and I joined them like some kind of sheep. To my right, shelves of confectionary stretched the entire wall beneath the window, and I picked up a Bourneville. As I grabbed a second choice of a Fry's Chocolate Cream, fingers folded over my left arm.

"My God—Josh?"

Turning back, I found a female staring up at me. Though grey streaked her temples and parting, enough blonde remained in the rest of her shoulder-length hair to identify its colour.

It wasn't the first time someone had mistaken me for my little brother, but I didn't know the woman before me. Inhaling didn't stir any definite answers, either.

Giving a slight shrug, I shook my head, but she didn't let go.

Creases I'd noticed around her eyes deepened, like she studied me a little harder. "Josh Larsen?"

Okay, she had my attention. I still didn't know her, though, and held back any reaction as I took in her slender frame, made even more so by the pressed black trousers she wore, the pressed black shirt that matched.

When I brought my attention back up to her face, some kind of familiarity tugged at me that I couldn't place. There was a softness to her jaw, supporting lips she held slightly parted. Her nose seemed a little too long for her face, but it was her eyes that had me stalled, and I knew they'd been where the hint of recognition had come from, even if my brain didn't seem up to working out why.

"I'm not Josh Larsen," I finally said, but my voice didn't sound as sure as I'd aimed for.

She released me. "Sorry. I thought you were someone I used to know."

I twisted to track her as she walked away. Even her walk seemed familiar—everything about her bugged the crap out of me.

When she tacked herself onto the end of the queue, I spun away and took a couple of steps toward the counter before she could catch me staring. Even still, my mind strayed back to her. To those damn eyes. The way she'd looked at me—they'd held such hope, such anticipation, yet, at the same time, a whole lot of anxiety had given a frantic edge to their hazel tones. Damn, even her voice had my head shot.

Though, neither of those bugged me as much as her calling me Josh. Not just Josh, but his full name, too. Like she knew him. Really knew him.

I thought you were someone I used to know.

I barely registered the cashier as he reminded me of my bill, nor as I handed cash over.

As soon as I had my receipt, I swung back around and marched the length of the line.

As if she'd been watching my every move, her eyes tracked each step I took, right up until I reached her.

I leaned in closer until blocking her way forward. "How do you know Josh?"

Her gaze flickered across my face. When she lifted a hand and cupped my cheek, I should've jerked away, but something—something deep inside—kept me rooted. In less than a second, the uncertainty in her eyes shifted over for warmth. "Danny Boy?"

With those two words, I knew.

I knew why she knew me—us. Why she seemed so familiar. Why I'd gotten so stuck on her eyes.

Because I looked at those eyes every bloody day of the week. In my memory, as I fought to cling to the reality of the most important female in the world to me. In the photographs—all we had left—that we all had dotted about the house.

In Kyle, every time I glanced at him.

"Aunt Maghon?"

She pressed a hand to her lips as she nodded, and I had no idea how to interpret the tightening around my heart. Could've been that she was the closest thing I'd seen to my mum in almost twelve years.

"You're just like her," she whispered. "God, you're just like her."

"Next!" came from the checkout, and she snapped a glance that way before turning back to me.

"Wait here," she said, clinging to my arm again even as she stepped away. "Just ... don't go anywhere, okay?"

I think I might've nodded, but couldn't be sure. I just couldn't take my eyes off the female as she covered the few steps to the counter and paid.

Mum's sister. Mum's older sister who I hadn't seen in over eleven years. Since Mum's funeral.

Aunt Maghon didn't know 'of' us—our origins. Mum had kept that side of our life private from her whole family.

34

When Mum had died—*killed* by an outside pack—Dad'd had to concoct a believable story to keep them off his back.

He'd never told us what tale he'd made up. He'd never told us why her sister stopped talking to us, either. In no time, that estrangement had extended to her entire family—parents included. Dad said it probably made things easier for us that way. Josh and I were still teens and hadn't even had our first change at that point—so what did we know? We just did as we were told.

It'd been so long, I'd stopped thinking about Mum's family. I'd probably even forgotten they were about, somewhere, if I delved deep enough to be honest.

The moment Aunt Maghon pushed away from the counter and fixed those hazel eyes on me, though, it was like those memories had never gone anywhere at all.

The windows of the cafe we ended up in reached low enough for me to see my bike, where I'd parked it on the pavement outside. My position also gave me a direct view of the entrance, a clear shot toward the counter, a scope of about eighty percent of the other tables. Not to mention the female sitting across from me, as she fiddled with her tea mug and did a whole lot of staring.

On the opposite side of the street outside, around forty yards away, I could just about make out the pack moving about behind the erected railings that helped keep our work site secure. The phone call I'd made to Josh should've hopefully kept them off my back some, for when I showed up late—though he'd been grumpy as hell that I'd chosen him to break the news for me.

"How have you been?" Aunt Maghon asked after the pause had stretched.

"How do I look?" Instantly regretting my tone, the way it made her eyes crease, I sighed. "I'm doing okay." Wasn't like I'd break down and tell her all my woes, anyway. That kind of trust had to be earned.

She lowered her gaze before asking, "And your dad?"

35

"If you wanted to know that, you could have asked him directly, any time over the past twelve years."

"Don't judge me, Danny Boy, when you don't know the whole story." That time, her tone held bite that made me pay attention as a memory sparked. Of how she only ever used to use her full nickname for me in admonishment—or to calm me down.

Tapping a fingernail against the ceramic of my mug, I slouched back against the booth seat, glancing over as a young female rounded the counter.

A pink apron covered her entire front, down to her knees, over jeans and trainers, a short sleeved T. The platter plate she carried, piled high with sustenance my body badly needed, meant I knew to expect her before she even drew alongside our table.

"Mega breakfast for one?" At my nod, she set it down in front of me, along with cutlery wrapped in a disposable napkin, her strawberry blonde ponytail almost dipping in my beans as she twisted toward Maghon. "Sure we can't get you anything?"

"Thanks, but I already ate."

More than I'd done. Thanks to lack of sleep, once I'd locked myself in my room, I'd crashed back into the land of nod. When Dad'd banged on my door to see what I was doing, I'd had only twenty minutes to spare. Not wanting to play happy families around the table while Brook snuggled onto Kyle's lap like they hadn't just spent the entire night together—the entire week, month, last four months—I'd grabbed my stuff and left. So my stomach could be forgiven for growling at the sight of food.

The waitress unblocked my view, and Aunt Maghon stared at my plate. "You still believe you can eat all of that?"

Nodding, I picked up my knife and fork. "Watch me."

"Must have one heck of an appetite."

A laugh came out on my exhale. "You have no idea."

"Are you going to answer my question now?" she asked, as I bit a chunk from the whole sausage I skewered with my fork.

I watched her as I chewed. Spotted the stubborn set of her jaw—a trait of hers I vaguely remembered. A trait she'd shared with Mum. "He's doing okay," I said once I'd finished chewing.

"Did he ..." Trailing off, she took a sip of her drink, her gaze on mine as she set her mug back down. "Did he ever move on?"

She asked like too much hung on the balance of my answer. And what did she even mean, anyway? Move on with his life? Move onto another female? As if. "He's doing okay," I said again. Anything other than that, she could ask him herself if she wanted to know so badly.

She must have taken the hint, because she changed course with, "I'm sorry, okay?"

I lowered the forkful of black pudding I'd been about to shovel in.

"I'm sorry I didn't call all these years," she added.

"Why didn't you?"

"It's a lot to understand."

I frowned. "I'm not a kid anymore."

"I know. It's just—" She sighed. "I blamed your dad ... for taking her from me."

That much I already knew. "He didn't kill her," I said, in his defence.

"I know, I know," she said, shaking her head. "It's not just that, though. I mean ... for taking her from me in general. At all."

I set my cutlery down and leaned forward on my elbows. "I don't understand." I realised the words only drove home her point about it all but didn't care.

She turned away, stared out toward the window. "We were inseparable. Until your dad came along."

I shrugged. "That's life, Aunt Maghon. You meet someone and fall in love—your priorities shift." My brain instantly bounced to Kyle and Brook, but I shunted the thoughts away fast and hard.

"You don't get it," she said. "I wouldn't expect you to. But we did *everything* together. Neither of us had barely a friend of our own. We didn't *need* anybody else."

Kind of like the pack, popped into my head. "What about Beth?" I asked, knowing Nate's wife and Mum had been best friends at school, even before dating Dad and Nate.

She smiled, the expression seeming to hold as much sadness as fondness. "Beth was different. She simply became an extension of us—like a third sister. For a while, anyway."

Probably until Beth met Nate and found other interests, too.

A part of me wondered if some of the blame she sought to place had landed on Mum's best friend as well as Dad. To listen to tales of their younger days, it sounded as if Beth and Nate had helped my parents get together. Or maybe Maghon didn't know that part of the tale.

"Then Nadine met Connor," she continued, "and she started staying out late. Going places I wasn't invited—skipping lessons in school, too. She grew more and more secretive and closed off. Danny, your mother stopped *talking* to me almost from the moment she got with your father. She used to tell me everything, and all of a sudden she wouldn't tell me a thing. Not even Beth would let me in on what was going on. Tell me ..." Her brows bunched in the middle before releasing. "How would that look to you?"

Bad, I wanted to say—but I didn't. Because it could look as bad as it liked to anyone not in the pack, but I knew our side—Dad's side. The true side. That Dad loved Mum. He went to the ends of the earth to make her happy. If Mum ceased needing anything—or anyone—outside of what she had, it would have been because she already had everything she needed right there.

Besides, it hadn't been like she'd cut off all communications. "She still visited you," I said at the memory. At least once a month, Mum'd taken us to Aunt Maghon's. They'd spent the time chatting in the kitchen, and we'd gotten sent out into the garden to play with our younger cousin Clem. "She never gave you up," I added.

A gloss of moisture coated her eyes, making their hazel tones look polished. "Yeah," she said, her voice thick. "I see that now." Sliding her handbag onto her lap from the bench seat beside her, she rummaged in there. She produced a tissue and waved it toward my plate. "Your food's getting cold. You said you were hungry."

Averting my gaze, I grabbed my fork and scooped up some scrambled egg. "So, how's Clem, Uncle Bill?"

She sniffed hard. "Clem got married last year. She works for the council over in Leicester. She's doing well—I'm just waiting on her bringing me some grandbabies to love on now." She gave a watery smile and wiped the tissue beneath her nose. "And your uncle—well ... he turned out not to be the right man for me."

My frown moved back in. "You separated?"

"Divorced." She tucked her tissue back into her bag. "It's okay. I moved on from that about six years ago."

Not quite sure what to say to that, and not wanting to delve, I folded over a bacon rasher, coated it in tomato, and stuck it in my mouth.

As if the turn in conversation had stemmed her own flow, Maghon sat quietly, intermittently glancing at me but mostly toward the window. Or maybe she just wanted me to finish eating without interruption.

Around us, other patrons chatted, ate, drank tea or coffee, came and went. Each time someone entered or exited, a tiny tinkle sounded out above the door.

When it chimed for the fourth time, I caught the scent of the new arrival before I lifted my gaze to see the hulk of muscle twisting his way around the tables.

Pushing up from my seat, I almost dived into the aisle, talking a few strides in time to intercept him before he could reach our spot.

"Dad—"

"What the hell do you think you're doing, Danny?" he asked, keeping his voice low. "You think this is funny?" He thrust a finger toward the window. "If you're going to shun your responsibilities to your family, you could at least have the decency to not do it right under my nose."

I looked toward where he pointed. My bike. Explaining how he'd known I was there. "It's not like that, Dad," I said, turning back to him.

"So, you're hiding out when you should be working like the rest of us, just so you can schmooze some female you've me—"

"It's not his fault, Connor," Aunt Maghon said from behind me. "It's mine."

Mouth still poised for speech, Dad stared at a spot just to the left of my shoulder, and I watched as his expression altered, from shock, to hurt, to a darkness he rarely showed.

Without saying another word, he spun away.

My, "Dad, wait," clashed with Maghon's, "Connor, please don't go," and he halted.

"Give me one good reason why I shouldn't walk straight out that door right now," he said over his shoulder, not looking at either of us.

"Because I'm pleading with you not to," Maghon said. "And because I think it's about time we talked."

The clenching of his jaw sharpened his profile, as did the high tension along his shoulders, sending his frame into a rigid display of angles. He stood like that for seconds before his quiet, "Danny, get yourself to work," rumbled out.

Stepping back, I grabbed my stuff, sliding my arm through my helmet, but as I squeezed past Dad, he gripped my arm and pulled me close.

"Don't tell your brothers who you've been with this morning. Do you understand me?" His green eyes held only a serious concern, none of the anger his voice had portrayed when he'd first found me there, and I nodded. "I need to assess what she's about, after all this time."

"And Nate?"

"Tell him I'll be a while and will explain when I get there." His pat to my shoulder acted as dismissal, and I strode for the door, ignoring the stares our exchange had provoked.

The tinkle sounded out on my exit into the blustery wind, and as I rounded the cafe front, toward my bike, Dad came back into view through the window.

Closing his eyes for a moment, he rubbed a hand across his face, before spinning toward the table and taking my emptied seat.

As I reached my wheels, I just caught his words through the glazing.

"Okay, May, let's talk."

4

The driveway at Nate's was quiet when I drew onto it that evening. Beth's Lexus sat to the side of the house, and I knew Sean's Porsche, which Jem mostly used, would be in the garage, but neither Nate nor Ethan's trucks had made it back yet—which had kind of been my plan: get Beth to agree to feed me before Nate could object.

After parking up next to the Lexus, I headed around to the rear of the house, thankful for the ease up of rain since earlier.

The way into the conservatory stood open, as did the French doors into the house, leaving rich, spicy scents to waft outward. Through the kitchen window, Beth stood over by the cooker, and as I reached the glass enclosure and turned in, weaving between the basket furniture in there, Jem came into view at the kitchen table.

Beside her, in a highchair, Lia banged a couple of cubes of plastic against her tray with one hand, while mulching a chunk of banana in the other. Pale yellow gunk clung to her lips, too.

"Looking good, Lia bug," I said, stepping into the room.

Jem lifted her gaze like she hadn't known I was there, though she'd probably been expecting me to step through the door from the moment my bike got near the property. "Beats the strawberries from yesterday. They make her look like she's been massacring prey."

Chuckling, I turned to Beth. "What's cooking? It smells good."

"Chorizo and roasted veggies." She spun, spatula in hand, her eyes seeming loaded with meaning as she added, "You have some of your own at home. I sent a batch back with Brook."

Trying to control any facial tics at the mention of the cat, I drew in a long breath through my nose. "I thought I'd eat here tonight."

Her eyebrow twitched. "Does Nathan know this?"

My head tilted at a quiet rumble coming from the front of the house, and I smiled. "If he didn't before, he does now." The second he saw my bike, he'd know.

"Is this because of ..." She lowered her tone, still seeming to study me a little too hard. "Because of today?"

Dad had returned to the building site around twenty minutes after I'd left him that morning—probably to make sure nobody noticed it, beyond me and Nate, enough to question his absence. In fact, he'd spent more time in the Port-a-Cabin with Nate than he had with Aunt Maghon. Right after that, he'd called me in and told me he wouldn't be home for dinner—after which, both he and Nate had ordered me to stay quiet about who I'd bumped into. Apparently, Dad still didn't know her intentions, and, until he did, there wasn't any point stirring the others up.

Sucked, though. Sucked that I couldn't talk to my brothers about it. Sucked every time I looked at Josh throughout the day.

Our younger brother had barely been smacked with puberty when Mum got killed. When Aunt Maghon cut us off, it'd been another blow to his already crushed soul, and he'd gone through a stage of curling up inside some imaginary shell and pretending nothing had changed in the world—all while biting at us with every word spoken.

Luckily, at home, he'd had Dad and us clamping him tight into the family fold—while at school, he'd had his childhood girlfriend Blaise to catch his falls. He'd come out the other end okay.

What sucked most about dinner, though, was that Dad wouldn't be there. Not a single day had passed in my life without Dad there for dinner. His absence would be like some giant fucking elephant in the room. Especially to my bothers, who didn't even know the reason why.

43

I held my eyebrows in check at her blatant mention of it, though. "You know about that?"

Smiling, she turned back to the cooker, bending over as she pulled open the oven door.

It'd been a stupid question. Of course she knew. She always knew—everything. Even stuff nobody told her. Nate had probably been on the phone to her the second he'd finished getting the rundown off Dad.

As I headed out to the hallway to store my jacket and helmet, the smell of fresh bread had my mouth watering. "So, you have enough for me, then?" I asked over my shoulder.

"We always have enough for you." She sent me a smile. "But not before you've cleaned up."

The thud of work boots hit the block paving at the rear of the house, and I made light work of mounting the stairs, giving myself a few minutes' reprieve before the questioning began. Maybe Nate would have used all his interrogation energy up on someone else before I got back down there—spare me the intensity.

The window of the bathroom had been left ajar, letting in a slight breeze as I washed my hands at the sink and gave my face a good splashing. Even though the forest stood a decent sixty metres away, behind the high-walled garden enclosure, the strong barky scents held pungency on the carrying winds, creating a synergised concoction alongside gentle pine and wild rodent. If I hadn't only just ran that morning and the night before, and the days before that, I'd have been tempted to postpone dinner until after I'd headed out and built up an even bigger appetite.

As it was, my body felt too weary for exercise, and far too in need of food, so after towelling myself off, I headed back downstairs, nodding to Ethan on the way, where he stripped off in his room.

Down in the kitchen, Sean sat in a huddle with Jem and Lia like a circle of connection—Sean with his dark hair and eyes, Jem with her blonde and blue, and Lia between them like some gorgeous combination of the two. She might've had a thatch of hair as thick and dark as her dad's, but those sapphire eyes that had all of us melting came one hundred percent from her mum.

Like he hadn't seen either of them in a couple of months, Sean kissed their hair, kissed their cheeks. He'd been making jokes the past few weeks, about expanding his family—though the way he studied Jem each time he said it had me wondering if he always meant it as a joke.

"Danny?" Nate said, drawing my gaze round to where he brushed close to Beth. "You have a problem with eating at home tonight?"

The wording, the probing tone made it sound like *Nate* had a problem with me being *there*, but he didn't. He never did. Any day, any time, we were welcome, just as the Holloways had a permanent pass to our home. We mightn't have shared a surname, but we shared a bond as strong as any formed by blood—maybe even stronger.

The blue of my Alpha's eyes seemed to be drilling right through to my brain, like he could extract my thoughts himself if he only pierced deep enough. I knew he was probably waiting on a lie, was probably expecting Brook to be my reason for delaying going home, but he had it wrong.

Being far more honest than he likely expected from me, I told him, "Maybe I didn't want to spend my mealtime having to lie to my brothers' faces, while they speculate about why Dad's not home."

"Connor's not home?" Jem said from the table.

"He has some business to take care of." Nate still hadn't taken his gaze from me.

That seemed to pique Sean's interest, with the way he straightened in his seat—Ethan's, too, as he trod the tiles into the kitchen and asked, "What kind of business?"

Nate's eyes narrowed slightly—at me, as if in warning. "Nothing to concern anyone with. Just some personal stuff he needs to wrap up." He finally broke his stare down, leaning in to kiss Beth's cheek. "I'll go and wash up."

He'd scarcely got to the top of the stairs when Jem tapped the table and pointed to the opposite chair. Scraping it out created a screech, and as I sat, she leaned over the oak top. "Connor have a date?"

A soft laugh burst from me—because the idea of Dad on a date was fucking ludicrous. "No, Jem. Dad doesn't have a date." I laughed a second time at the frowned disappointment on her face, and a third time when Lia squealed and slapped a palm against her tray. "See? Even the kiddo knows how farfetched an idea that is."

With Ethan headed out to see Shelley, Sean and Jem putting Lia through some evening routine they'd adopted in the hope of helping her sleep better, and Beth taking a soak in the bath, only Nate and I occupied the living room around an hour after dinner.

Something resembling sleet splattered the window, the renewed onset of crappy weather adding dullness to what should've been a light evening. Feet kicked up over the arm of the sofa, I watched from my horizontal position as each wet splodge hit the glass.

The news channel ran at a low volume on the TV, while, every so often, a scrunched sound told me each time Nate turned a page in the newspaper he read.

"This weather's freaky," I said, wiggling my feet back and forth.

"Yeah," Nate said from his armchair.

"It's supposed to be May."

"Yeah," he said again.

"What the hell happened to spring?"

Another paper rustle, another page turn. "Beats me."

"It's not looking too promising for summer."

His sigh was quiet, but I still caught it. "What's really on your mind, Danny?"

I frowned, my feet action halting. "Nothing." Lying still a moment, I tracked the dragged path of a sleet drip before my feet twitches kicked back in. "You heard anything from Dad yet?"

From the slight lightening to his tone, I could've sworn he smiled as he said, "Nothing."

I glanced over, but the paper blocked the lower half of his face. "Maybe I should call him."

"Maybe you should leave him be and trust him to sort this out." He lowered the paper, his eyes aimed my way. "Your dad'll ring as soon as he's done—you know that."

He settled back in his seat, and I went back to watching the shitty weather. Above us, I could just hear the low murmurs of Sean and Jem. Whatever they were trying with Lia must've been working, because I'd not heard a peep from her in minutes. Also upstairs somewhere, a door opened—probably Beth done with her bath.

I could've used some extra cleaning up myself, if the stench from my armpits was any indicator.

"Maybe it's time you were heading home yourself," Nate said after about a minute of quiet.

Feet stilling again, I twisted my head and found his focus on me. "You kicking me out, Nate?"

He smiled. "Never."

I'd already known what his answer would be, anyway. Just like I knew why he'd suggested I go home—why he made any of his suggestions lately: go home, spend time with your family, talk to your dad ...

If Kyle had talked to us all, instead of blocking us all out of what he had going on, then maybe it wouldn't have reached a point where he turned on his family for a fricking cat.

Maybe it wouldn't have reached a point where we found out he was fooling around with her by stumbling over them in the forest.

Our forest. A wolves' forest. And he'd been screwing a cat in there.

It wasn't that I didn't get the connection, because I did. Kyle and Ethan had gotten nabbed by some vampire ring the autumn before, when they'd gone on a rescue mission after Gabe had gone missing. Turned out the vamps responsible were taking whoever they could from the supernatural pool and forcing them to fight—each other. For sport.

Biggest problem there was, vampire venom had a toxic and deadly effect on werewolves, and the ringleaders had needed to keep Kyle and Gabe alive for whatever twisted reason, so they'd injected both of them with some kind of anti-venom after their fights, and that juice had done something to fuck them up. Kyle more so than Gabe, judging by his behaviour since.

That had been where he'd met Brook.

Kept in a cage opposite, and having been forced to take part in her own share of fights, Brook'd latched onto Ethan and Kyle, and they'd taken her along when they got out. For a few days afterward, she'd even ended up staying at Nate's. Little did we know—did any of us know—even once she'd gone home, Kyle'd snuck around with her, behind our backs, from that moment.

Sure, we knew, or at least suspected, that he'd kept ducking off for a female—but for that?

I honestly hadn't understood what we'd found in the forest that day. I still didn't understand it, any of it—didn't understand *them*. My lip curled just thinking about it.

Definitely, not talking about shit created a whole heap of problems. Maybe Nate, and Dad, did have a point.

"You know, I think I will head off," I said, flipping to my feet.

Not removing his attention from his paper, Nate nodded.

I found my stuff out in the hall, laced up my boots, shrugged on my jacket. With my keys and helmet gripped in one hand, I reached for the front door catch, but stalled at Nate's quiet, "Danny?"

Ducking my head around the doorframe brought me face to face with his serious stare.

"Make sure you go home, okay?" he said.

I jerked my chin up in a half nod. "Sure."

"I mean it, Danny. Go home."

My lips curved. "I know." After sending him another nod, I stepped out into the plummeting degrees of air, rounded the house, and straddled the bike.

A few minutes later, my wheels rolled across tarmac shiny with melting sleet, while a biting wind lashed at my exposed throat as slushy drops of freezing rain hit my visor and marred my vision.

The main road through the forest wove amid greenery—usually, in the summer, anyway. Dense clusters of trunks stood to my right, a lighter offering to the left—both sides fenced off to pedestrians and voyeuristic traffic. Within the depths of each, shadows stretched tall, shifting with each sway of branches, each movement of nature. The accompanying scenery offered a calm contrast to the attacking temperatures, as well as to my speed as I raced along, probably a whole lot too fast for the conditions.

A few miles out, a lesser road jutted off to the right, and I slowed to make the turn, working my fingers on the clutch and brake against the stiffness settling in. Once straightened, I opened the throttle again for another few miles, banking for the nearside curves, flipping for the rights.

The upstairs glow of Kyle's bedroom light came into focus through the trees before the property itself did, and I kicked the gears down as I cruised to a stop outside the gates.

Up in the window, partially drawn curtains blocked inside, but the shadows—plural—of someone moving about in there could still be seen. A moment later, one of the curtains twitched, and a head draped in long, dark hair pecked out.

Even across the gap of driveway and road, I felt the weight of Brook's stare dragging me down. She'd obviously heard my bike, so she'd have known to look for me, and she confirmed the sighting with a lift of her hand.

Couldn't blame the cat for trying. Definitely couldn't blame her for that.

As much as I didn't want to, I waved a hand back, because I didn't want to be a total bastard. That, and the pep talk I'd given myself, right before leaving Nate's, still sat heavy in my brain.

Yet, staring up at the female who caused a rift in our family, every bit of resolve I'd built up seemed to just crumble away.

Twisting back, I stared down the emptiness of the road ahead of me. No other drivers about. No interruptions. No complications. No noises I didn't want to hear.

I knew, without doubt, I'd probably get my arse kicked if I went that route, but even hough I'd acknowledged Nate's order to go home, neither of us had specified when. In my mind, that made the open-ended choice I had an easy one to make.

Listen to a female I didn't want to listen to …

Or look at a female who was easy on the eyes.

Kicking the bike into first gear, I twisted the throttle, and sped toward The Hang & Hide.

5

The weekend tried my patience.

Saturday had Nate's family piling into ours, and more fucked up weather had us penned indoors. Other than dinner of the best damned stroganoff on the planet, during which Kyle and Brook's mouths were too occupied with eating to take up any tongue action, the day had gone along pretty much like any other day. As in, we all got to watch them making out. A lot.

To top it, when evening had come and I'd reached for my boots, and asked if anyone had seen my keys, Nate had ordered me to stay home for the night.

Bloody ordered me.

Which'd left me squashed in the living room for the remainder of the day.

On the sofa.

Right next to my brother and his ever-loving cat.

Hadn't helped that Josh had seemed to be laughing to himself every time he'd glanced my way. Baby of the family, or not, I intended to make the little shit pay for that.

Sunday brought a little more excitement. In the form of Dad's announcement that he wouldn't be joining us for dinner at Nate's.

My eyes narrowed on him, as both Kyle and Josh twisted in their seats toward him.

"Where are you going?" Josh asked.

"Nowhere special," Dad said. "Just to deal with some business." His gaze cut to me and seemed to hold some kind of plea—whether for my silence, or understanding, I couldn't quite figure out.

"Do we get to know what kind of business?" Josh asked, shifting in his seat.

Though he didn't say a word, Kyle seemed to be studying Dad. I wondered if he'd put two and two together and come up with 'female'. Even if he did, he'd still fall miles from the real answer.

Only one, beside me, who didn't go all out on the scrutinising was Brook—leaving me guessing at how much she, Jem and Beth shared when left to their own devices.

Dad glanced around at all of us before giving an almost non-existent shrug. "Of the personal variety."

Just like that, the curiosity and tension left my two brothers.

Dad'd been known to pay visits to town in search of relief for his libido. God knew, we all needed that relief if we wanted to stay sane—so, of course, the others would never question that excuse.

Except, as soon as he left the room, my younger brother turned and stared at me. "You believe him?" At my shrug, his green eyes pierced a little deeper, his mousey blond curls flopping with the tilt of his head. "You know something about this."

Looking from him to an equally interested Kyle, I shook my head. "I don't know shit." It was *almost* the truth—because, I suspected, a second visit meant there was a whole lot going on with Aunt Maghon that Dad wasn't letting on.

6

The H&H held about as much excitement as it did on any other Monday night, when I arrived there after a cold and wet day at work. Even the pool table stood abandoned, the cues secured like a spiked fence along the far wall. Hell, I could count the evening's occupants using the digits of one hand.

Joe leaned over the bar, glaring, like he could intimidate his customers into buying more rounds just to give him something to do. Unusually, the barstools in front of him were empty.

Some guy, who was possibly mid-thirties but looked closer to ninety, swayed on a low stool near the dartboard, like he was thinking about playing a game he didn't have the energy for. His hands nursed his pint glass between his knees, his head dipped as though in prayer to a sacred life source. I should've probably been disgusted by the muck outlining his fingernails and the sorry stench of soil and piss drifting over from his clothes, but I only felt sad. Sad that he didn't seem to notice his condition. Sad that he just didn't seem to have it in him to change what looked, to an outsider, like a lonely existence.

In contrast, the blonde chick, who seemed to be an avid regular, had changed her M.O. by swamping herself in an empty both with a dozen seats to choose from. Every once in a while, her eyes peeked my way, the coy smile I'd grown used to seeing plucking at her lips.

As she'd likely grown used to in return, I ignored it, choosing to focus, instead, on the red bush that twitched behind the lifted laptop lid opposite me.

Sipping on my pint, I tuned into the quiet-but-steady tap of keys, tracked the arm that occasionally snuck out to the side, the fingers that curled around the glass on the table beside her with their slightly chipped purple nail polish.

About once every ten minutes, my presence even got acknowledged with a lift of her head, though the glow from her screen smothered the lenses of her glasses, hiding her eyes.

"Hey," I said, and that head popped up, looking like Einstein'd been dipped in a vat of rusty water—except prettier. Definitely prettier. "Got any paper?" I asked.

"Like, writing paper?" Liv asked.

I shrugged. "Anything."

I half expected her to huff and puff at the interruption, but she didn't. She just closed her lid and drew a laptop bag across the bench toward her and peered inside, lip caught between her teeth.

For some reason, I focused right on that. Teeth. Lips. What might lie beyond those.

She stuck her hand inside her bag, tugged out a file, which she set on her pc. Tugged out a half-eaten packet of chewy éclairs, which she plonked on top of the file. The next delve produced a spiral-bound notepad, and as she swung it toward me, it hauled the strap of a lanyard with it.

Of course, my fingers snapped around the flat piece of plastic as well as the pad.

As I opened my hand on the card, she made a grab for it, but I snatched it away. "Ah, ah. It's caught. See?" I waved the pad at her. "Let me unravel it, and you can have it back."

The glare she sent me would've floored a weaker guy, and I chuckled. Unwinding the strap from the metal spiral only took a couple of seconds, and as soon as I had it free, she held out a hand.

"Okay, now give it back to me," she said.

Yeah, right. Fist closed, I turned my hand over.

"Do *not* look at it," she said.

I uncurled one finger.

"*Danny* ..."

A second finger.

"Please." She frowned. "I look horrible in it."

My own frown moved in. "Liv, you couldn't look horrible even if you were in fancy dress *as* someone horrible."

Her mouth opened, but no sound came out, and I used the moment to fully uncover the plastic card—and with it, a cheesy ID photo of Liv.

"I hate that picture," she said.

I studied the bored expression on her captured face—one that screamed objection over the photo being taken—the red splotch of a pimple on her chin, glasses with silver frames a granny might wear, and my lips threatened to curve.

"Dick," she muttered. "I s'pose you look all cute on your photos."

"Actually, I look pretty much like what you just called me," I said.

She rolled her eyes. "Whatever."

"Take a look if you don't believe me." I reached inside my leather beside me, sodden from the rain, and extracted my wallet from the pocket. Opening it up showed said 'dick' photo behind its clear sleeve, and I held it up to her. "See? *Dick.*"

She took my wallet from me, but instead of lifting it closer, she worked my driver's license out and studied it direct. "Wow. You *do* look like a dick," she said, doing a shitty job of hiding her smirk.

I clicked my tongue. "I warned you."

"Daniel *Larsen*," she said. "Lives in ... *Wild Woodington*?" Her gaze shot to mine beneath arched eyebrows. "Nobody lives in Wild Woodington."

I gave a mock smile and waved a hand.

"There's not even any houses in Wild Woodington. It's just ... trees."

"Sure, there're trees." I nodded. "There're also houses. Two, to be exact." Ours, and Nate's.

She stared at me a second longer before looking back to the license. "Birthday February seventh ..." She paused, her lips popping open on a soft exhale. "Jesus, Dan. You're, like ... twenty-seven." Her eyes lifted, and as she mouthed the age again, I laughed.

"What's so bad about that?"

"It's old," she said.

"Not that bloody old—anyway, why does it even matter?"

"It doesn't." She tucked the license back inside my wallet and handed it back. "I just thought you were younger. You *look* younger."

I gave a half nod. I got told that a lot. After sneaking a glance at more of her details beside her photograph, I relinquished her lanyard. "Seven years isn't that big of an age gap."

Her brow scrunched up like she didn't get my implication. Couldn't blame her. I didn't even know what I was getting at myself.

Sticking my wallet back in my pocket, I swapped it for a pencil I kept in there and, after downing another swig of my drink, hunched over the table and the borrowed writing pad.

For a few beats longer, I knew she still watched me, as I swept my pencil in a small arch across the paper. Then for a few ticks more, as I sketched an inverted arch that met up, point to point, with the first, and I wondered if she stared at me, or at the patterns I made.

On the verge of making me feel uncomfortable, all five foot five of her shadowed me as she leaned across the table and grabbed my glass.

I glanced up. "What're you doing?"

"Getting drinks," she said, collecting her own glass.

I dug into my pocket. "Let me give you some cash."

Not giving me a chance to cough up, she turned away and swayed over to the bar. Swayed. No other word could describe the way she moved.

Pale jeans clung to her rounded hips and a butt that swung side to side with each step like a damn pendulum.

Her ankles seemed skinny in comparison, where they tucked into her trademark Converse, whilst, topping it off, her frizz-ball of hair seemed to have a life of its own—like Medusa snakes waving about atop her head.

Reaching Joe, she plopped down the empties and lifted her arms to chest height, propping them against the bar-top. As her torso tipped forward, her butt perked outward. She tapped the toe of her plimsoll against the floor, making the cheeks of that arse twitch then jiggle, a pattern that matched each impact of her foot.

Joe took the empty glasses. Rather than switch them up for clean ones, he just filled those same ones back up, and as he did so, Liv pushed away from the bar and stretched up her arms. Over her head, behind her head, arching her back into the movement, shunting her butt out even more. In a way that made it wiggle. And jiggle.

And I really needed to quit staring.

As Liv picked up the replenished glasses and turned my way, I ducked my head down like I'd been focused on my scribbling the entire time.

Her scent arrived before she did, something subtle, something sweet, something *human*, and as my glass tapped against the table-top, I curled my fingers around it without looking up.

Taking a sip, I nearly spat it right back out again. My gaze shot to Liv's. "What's this?"

Lowering to her seat, she smiled. "Shandy."

"Why the hell would you get me shandy?" My lips still puckered from the taste.

Her smile dimmed a little. "Because you shouldn't be drinking so much when you're riding that bike all the time."

My lips parted. To tell her to shove the lecture—I had a Dad and Alpha for those. To explain that a pint for a human was like a swig for someone with the metabolism we had. To tell her not to bother getting me any more drinks, if she was going to insist on shitty shandy. I couldn't, though. Because studying her face revealed only concern. I didn't have the heart to beat on her for that. Shrugging, I said, "I have hollow legs."

Shaking her head *and* rolling her eyes, she reached for her laptop lid. "Whatever."

Before I could come up with further argument, or before she could fully lift her lid, vibrations buzzed her mobile across the table.

Pretending to be focused back on my drawing, I shaded an orb within the shape I'd created, while watching Liv out the corner of my eye.

Her thumb swiped over the screen, and a second later, her frown of concentration folded into something darker. Dropping her phone back to the table, she stared at it a little too long before her gaze moved away.

Sketching veins splintering outward from the dark circle, I asked, "Problem?"

A pause, then, "Just some party."

Lips pursed, I gave a small nod. "Party doesn't sound like much of a problem to me." Pressing down hard, I outlined a couple of spindly limbs, darkened the outer rim of the circle. When she didn't say anything, I added, "Parties are supposed to be fun."

In my experience they had been, anyway. Almost every other week, someone from school had thrown a get-together. All it'd taken was for someone's parents to be out for the night. I'd gotten my first taste of alcohol at a party. Learned how to use a pogo stick—showing everyone else up as I'd rattled my brain about. Kissed my first girlfriend. Shown Tommy MacCaller that I could punch, and punch *hard*, when he'd felt up that same girlfriend just to piss me off. It'd worked—and he never tried pissing me off again.

She sighed, the sound somehow both soft *and* heavy. "Yeah."

Twiddling my pencil between my fingers, I glanced over at her, took in the knot of tension between her eyebrows, as she still stared at her phone like it'd thrown an insult she didn't know how to come back from. "So, why d'you look like someone just stole your mojo and replaced it with a nojo?"

A small laugh breathed from her, but it was short lived as the knot moved back in. "Because my ex is going."

"Your ex is a problem." I didn't know if I meant it as a question or statement, and it came out sounding like neither.

"He's just a div," she said, shrugging. "Hasn't quite caught up with the *ex* part of our relationship status."

I cleared away a brewing growl before it could rise. "How long have you been split?"

"About eight months." She let loose another one of those laughs that wasn't quite a laugh.

"So, you'd let this dick stop you enjoying yourself?"

The tightening of her features told me he already had stopped her enjoying herself. Probably more than once. I wanted to hurt him. "It's hard not to, when he thinks he still has certain rights," she said, making that picture I had of him a million times worse.

My free hand fisted against my knee. "Tell him you've moved on."

Another non-laugh. "Sure."

"Then, show him. Take someone with you. Make him believe it."

"Except he knows everyone." She glanced away, waved a hand. "Forget it. It doesn't matter. I just won't go." She turned back to her laptop and, lifting the screen fully, ducked behind it.

I listened to the steady tap of keys as it started up, watched as her hand slipped out to the side and flipped her mobile to face downward.

I'd no idea who her ex was, but I knew he needed a good smack upside the head. With a fist. One swung really, really hard.

Not yours, I told myself, un-flexing the knuckles of my hand that'd curled tight.

I leaned over my sketch again, swept a couple of lines out from the shape, pressed on lighter to give some shading. Adding emphasis to the upper rim of the eye, I wondered how it'd looked if I framed it in black, coated it with the sheen of a lens.

I lifted my gaze once more to the frazzled strands of orange spraying out behind the laptop, noted the silence of the keys, the stillness of her movements.

I hated that someone had upset her. Hated that she'd change her plans just because of some knob.

"You should go to the damn party. Just show him," I said.

"Danny, I already told you—"

"You want someone to come act as boyfriend, I could do it." I'd scarcely finished the words when my lips clamped shut and accusations of stupidity screeched through my head.

The quietness on the other side of the screen made me want to punch myself, or something. I thought maybe she hadn't heard me, but then her fingers folded over the lid and pulled it down, leaving those smoky blues staring at me through her lenses.

"You'd come to the party?" she asked, frowning.

I nodded.

Her eyebrows jerked up. "As my boyfriend?"

"*Pretend* boyfriend," I said, though I didn't know why it felt important to reiterate that.

She nodded—but like she mulled it over rather than agreed. A small smile played on her lips. I'd take that any day over the frowning and tension and darkness in her eyes, but then she said, "'Kay." She held out a hand in a half-hearted gesture. "You have a number?"

My pencil flicked from my fingers and spiralled to the floor. "My number?"

"In case I decide to go. Then I can call you," she said, sounding a little less confident in the request.

"Uh ... sure." I bent over for the pencil and grabbed my mobile on the way back up, pointing to it. "It's—it's in here."

Rolling her eyes, she reached over and took it right out of my hand. Her finger moved easily across the screen, her thumbs joining in a moment after. Her mobile buzzed against the table, and she glanced over at it, picked it up. A couple of swipes and taps, and she handed me my phone with a nod.

Taking it back, I skimmed it past my nose, sniffed at the faint trace of female she'd left behind. As I fisted my hand around it, I hid my smile—it'd been a while since I'd given my number to a female. I also ignored my reservations, because the last one'd had some serious fucking issues.

"So, when is this party, exactly?" I said, tucking the phone inside my jacket pocket—to keep it safe, I told myself, not to preserve its new scent. "You know, just in case."

"Tomorrow," she said.

Tomorrow, I mouthed.

'Tomorrow might be bad for me,' I could've told her. *Should've* told her. Yet, when my lips parted to say the words, my throat refused to let them pass. Refused to give me a chance to let her down when I'd only just offered.

So, instead, I found myself telling her, "Looking forward to it," while in my head, I tried to convince myself, *Everything'll be fine.*

7

Taking the key from my bike, I slid off my helmet and looked to the empty space under the carport. The space where Dad's pickup should've been.

He'd been home when I'd left for The Hang & Hide.

Low light shone over the rear patio as I dismounted my bike and made my way to the back door. No one could be seen through the window I passed, and I pushed inside to the lingering odours of the dinner Beth had cooked, and what sounded like a warzone blowing up the living room.

I headed that way, pausing just outside the doorway to inhale.

Kyle and Brook.

For a beat, I considered turning away, going straight to my room, but if I knew they were in there, they likely knew I stood right outside.

On a sigh deep enough to raise my chest, I rounded the doorframe into a room lit only by the glow of the screen.

Kyle already looked my way, his eyebrows slightly raised as if in question. Snuggled against his side, her arm draped over his torso, Brook seemed to be making a conscious effort to continue staring toward whatever film they watched. Almost like she feared mere eye contact would piss me off. Again.

I guessed she had a point.

"Everything all right?" Kyle asked, after I'd just hovered in the corner for a couple of seconds.

I nodded. "Where's Dad?"

Something flittered across his expression—maybe irritation, maybe concern—but vanished almost as quick. "He didn't say."

Dad 'didn't say' a lot just lately—not about his disappearances, anyway. Not even to me, and at least I knew some of the story.

Almost like he suspected as such, Kyle continued to stare, so I offered up an, "Again?" though it sounded half soaked, even to me.

"Yeah, again," he said, his eyes narrowing in the shadows of the room.

Needing to divert his attention, I nodded toward the screen. "What's this?"

"*Lone Soldier*. You wanna watch with?"

Before everything had changed at home, I'd have been happy to slump down on the sofa and chill in front of the screen. Before, though, I probably wouldn't have just walked in from a solo trip to a bar. The cat wouldn't have been there. And Dad wouldn't have been absent.

I gave a small headshake. "Nah, I'm gonna go see where Josh is at."

Twisting away before I had to witness whatever reaction he came up with, I ducked back into the hall, where I deposited my helmet and keys on the hall stand.

The landing stood in as much darkness as the living room had when I made my way up the stairs. Ignoring Kyle's and Dad's door, I went straight to the second set that stood opposite each other, but rather than taking a left, I tapped my knuckles against the door on the right.

I could've just entered, I supposed, but past experience warned that some things my little brother got up to in here, I just didn't want to see.

At no response, I leaned in closer, just catching the soft sigh of movement and the tinny beat of a muted track. Prepping to back out fast, if need be, I tugged down the handle and pushed inside.

Josh lay in his boxers on his bed with his eyes closed. Propped up against his headboard by his pillows, his head shifted slightly, probably in line with whatever tune blasted from the ear-buds he had plugged in, while his knees tapped together a half beat behind.

Striding across the room, I took in the small pile of stinking work clothes in the corner, the water rings on the dresser from all the drinks he'd had in there, to the array of framed photos perched on his bedside. As soon as I plonked down on the bed next to him, he jolted with the movement, eyes flying open. Even his hands went from relaxing on his bare chest to clenched and ready for the fight.

"Relax," I said, chuckling.

He slipped out one of the ear-buds, Ed Sheeran spilling out with it, as his gaze darted toward the door. "They finished?"

I didn't have to ask who, just as I didn't have to ask what he referenced. "Haven't even started." At the downturn of his lips, I smiled, rubbing it in by adding, "They will, though. Just gotta give 'em time."

He muttered a curse as he settled back against his pillows.

"How long's Dad been gone?" I asked.

He shrugged. "About an hour." His gaze sliced toward me, his scrutiny loaded as he stared hard with a grim determination I could never take seriously on him. "He found himself a female, or something?"

My focus strayed toward his photos. "I don't think that's it."

"When was the last time he went out at this time of night?"

"Last time he wanted sex," I said, taking in the female who starred amid most of Josh's frames, her intense hazel eyes so similar to those of Aunt Maghon's.

Josh snorted, though the sound held little humour. "This many times in as many days?"

I shook my head, studying the dark blonde hair that almost matched mine and Josh's for tone, the arms of the female stretched wide in an obvious attempt to hug all three of her boys in one go. "I never said Dad was out for sex now," I told him.

"So, why the heck is he vanishing nearly every night, then?"

I turned to him. "I vanish nearly every night."

He gave the equivalent of an eye roll. "This is Dad we're talking about. Not you."

My gaze cut right back to that photograph. I didn't remember the day it depicted. Didn't remember the voice of the woman. I couldn't even remember the sound of my mother's laughter—and I couldn't help but wonder if Dad had forgotten those details, too. If that was why he'd seen Maghon more times than he needed. I just wished he'd talk about it, so I didn't have to keep pretending I knew nothing to my brothers. "I'm pretty sure he has his reasons," I said to Josh.

Head tipping, he glanced toward the door again. "It's gone quiet out there."

"Calm before the storm," I said, holding my lip in check as it went to curl.

Sure enough, footsteps hit the stairs, the slow and lazy rhythm seeming to prolong what both Josh and I knew was coming—literally. The deepness of Kyle's chuckle travelled in, followed by that husky laugh of the cat's. The opening of his door blasted out, slamming shut equally as loud a moment later, followed by a thud.

"The first of many," Josh mumbled and held out the bud he'd pulled from his ear. "You want? I've got two."

Chill with my brother a while, or sit stewing alone, in my bedroom, right next to Kyle's, getting mad again?

I shoved him with my knee. "Budge over, then."

By the time he'd shunted out of the way, and I'd flopped down beside him, the banging had kicked in from the other room.

"You got anything else?" I asked, taking the ear-bud from him. "Ed's not going to cut it."

He pulled up his mobile from his other side, scrolled through a list of tracks he had on there. "Should do it," he said.

As I wriggled the bud into my ear, Pendulum attacked at a louder volume. "Crank it up," I said, and with that killing the chance of anything else entering my left ear, I curled a pillow around my right and thought of Liv. Mostly of the invite I'd kind of given myself.

Pushing aside any concerns I had about that, I closed my eyes.

8

I'd tried getting Dad alone before breakfast, but he'd shunned me and headed downstairs.

I'd tried grabbing his attention during breakfast, but he'd looked anywhere but at me.

I'd even tried cornering him once we got to the building site, but he'd told me it would have to wait and practically run off toward Nate.

If I didn't already suspect there was more to his recent outings than I first thought, I certainly did after that lot.

Despite the sun making a decent ascent of the sky, a biting breeze snaked around the yard, prickling any uncovered pieces of my flesh it hit. Thankfully, the window delivery had been scheduled for mid-morning. At least once those were in they'd block out the worst of the cold for when I started on plastering the insides. Dad and Nate had done nothing but grumble about the erratic moods of the weather, blaming it on the climate change, or the ozone layer issue, or whatever else they could think of to toss insults at. The rest of us didn't really care so much, but then I guessed we weren't the ones stressing over the budget and deadlines. We just turned up when ordered, and then got paid.

The Porsche had followed in behind the truck when the Holloways had arrived, bringing Jem with it. Since then, she'd been inside the property that would become the showroom, checking her measurements. At least she had something to do. With little other to do than guttering and plumbing, half of us strode around looking busier than we were.

Donning my hard-hat, I headed for Jem's domain. As I stepped through the hallway into the open-plan of downstairs, I found Sean in there with Jem, the tail end of her laughter lingering on the air.

Jem always had a way of laughing that made her entire face join in. "Daniel."

My lips twitched at the formal greeting. "Jem."

"Anyway," Sean said, leaning in and brushing his lips across Jem's, "I'd better find a job before Dad gives me one I hate." He smiled as he strode toward me and brushed past on his way outside.

I tracked him for a moment, as he rounded what would become the front door and his steps ground against the gritty dirt of a path, looking back to Jem when she waved a measuring tape my way.

"If you're looking for something to do, grab the end and help me size up."

"Beats getting yelled at," I muttered, and pulled the metal-hooked end toward the far corner of the wall.

"How's it going at home?" she asked, peering at where she held her end of the tape.

I shrugged. "It's going."

"You've not slept over in a few days. That, to me, says it's going better."

"It's not—" I sighed. "Look, I'm trying."

"You can try as hard as you like ..." She tugged on the tape, and as I let it go, it zapped back into its reel. "But until you're ready to accept that it is what it is, you're wasting your energy."

"I didn't say I didn't accept it." I had no choice with how Kyle and Brook hung around each other's necks.

"And now you're in denial," she said, her smug smile moving in, which she only pulled when she decided she was right.

"Whatever." As she went to twist away, I asked, "Do you know what's going on with my dad?"

She paused, lips pursed as she turned back. "I do—but before you can ask," she added, as I opened my mouth to speak, "I suspect I only know as much as you do."

"And Nate?"

She gave a half shrug. "I get the impression he's figuring it all out, too."

Which told me absolutely nothing at all.

Jem didn't bother heading home once she'd finished what she came for, and around an hour after that, Beth's black Lexus showed up. From the driver's side, Beth embarked with Lia, hooking the little one over her hip as she shut the door.

From the rear climbed Brook. At least she carried a cool-box. A cool-box meant food.

As soon as he saw Lia, Sean took her from his mum, carrying her inside the building to shelter. Since the windows had arrived an hour before, we'd shuttered in the master bedroom of the showroom house, so at least she'd have somewhere out of the freezing wind.

I followed them in, finding a corner to nestle into, and a few minutes later, most of the pack had joined us, along with Beth carrying the food.

"Hungry?" she asked, and a bunch of grunts answered.

"Like you wouldn't even believe," Jem muttered.

Beth laughed. "Guess it better be ladies first, then."

She chucked a cellophane roll of something toward Jem, which she'd caught and half ripped open before Beth had even reached in for a second.

Around bundle number four came flying in my direction. Catching it, I studied the seeded bread, the beef poking out from between the roll.

"Hey!"

I glanced back up at Beth's shout.

"Because I know how much you love them," she said, and threw a second parcel toward me.

I smiled as soon as I caught it. Jelly bean cookies peeked through the clear plastic. Three of them.

As I unwrapped, bit down and chewed, I studied the way the pack slumped together, as they did most days for lunch.

Jem and Sean sitting close with Lia balanced between them, like they'd a giant elastic band wedging them together. Beth almost as close in her quiet mutterings to Nate. A couple of feet over from Gabe, Ethan stared down at his phone as his thumb moved across the screen. Josh's did, too, except I guessed he only played stupid games, whereas Ethan probably texted Shelley. Or sexted, judging by the ridiculous smile he did a shit job of hiding.

The pack all together was one of my favourite scents. Like a concoction of familiarity and safeness that reminded me of home, one I could never help absorbing and deciphering until I'd picked apart each individual ID. Except, doing exactly that only emphasised the missing pieces.

"Where's Dad?" I asked.

Nate glanced up first. "He had a call to make."

I stared at him. I really wanted to ask *who to* but the slight warning darkening Nate's bright blues held the query in check. Instead, I asked, "Everything okay?"

He paused, for a little too long, before nodding. I couldn't help but wonder how much Nate was being kept in the loop with Dad's behaviour. Maybe he had his reservations, too.

Shoving in the last of a cookie, I chewed hard as I pushed to my feet. Nate's attention followed the move. So did Sean's. And Jem's. And Beth's. Nothing quite like feeling under scrutiny, I guessed. Swallowing, I told them, "I'm going to grab a drink ..." ... *and if I just happen to bump into Dad and get some answers along the way, all the better.*

Nobody questioned me as I stepped from the property into temperatures that seemed to be plummeting with each passing hour.

The foundations for each garden had been mapped out, and I followed what would become the path to the end, before cutting across to the right, toward where the Port-a-cabin stood in the plot's corner. No more than a grey box

70

of panels, the cube was the epicentre of every build, the place to plan, the place to escape, the place to refresh. Climbing the couple of steps to the entrance, I reached for the handle, pulled down, and pushed inside.

The door hadn't even swung closed when I halted and wished I'd stayed with the others.

Kyle sat in Nate's office chair, Brook sat in his lap, and the two of them shared the food she must have brought in with her. In every way possible.

"Seriously?" I said before I could stop myself.

Brook started climbing to her feet, but Kyle tugged her back to him. "What's the problem, Danny?" he asked.

"Is nowhere safe without having to witness ... *this*?"

Eyes threatening to blacken—just one of the fucked up side effects of the vampires' treatment—his dark expression folded into an epic scowl.

I knew that look. I knew the tone he'd used, too. He only used either of them when pissed off. I'd witnessed him using them in the past. Most times had been aimed at an outsider. One time had been aimed at me. The start of all our problems.

"Forget it," I said, backing toward the door. "I'll go somewhere else." Just like you two should've done, I wanted to add, but didn't, because I couldn't be bothered with the fight—not then. I had other issues to sort out.

Shutting the cabin door behind me, I hovered on the top step and inhaled what the breeze told me.

Kyle's and Brook's scents had swept out as I'd left. The imprints left behind by the pack every time they visited there also swirled around in a mishmash of flavours. Nothing in there to tell me where Dad hid out, though. No visual or sound-hints from him, either.

Hopping down the last few steps, I headed toward the site entrance. If not on site, Dad had to be out there. I didn't care how much he wanted to keep shit from the others. If he expected me to keep secrets, he could at least have the decency to tell me what they were.

Traffic always thickened up until around ten, and a steady line of cars claimed the road outside. Pausing at the kerb, I checked both sides, inhaling for scent, but came up with nothing. The stretch of buildings to the right mostly comprised of residential properties, whereas those to the left housed anything from the cafe I'd eaten in the other day to a mini supermarket, baker, dry cleaners, and more beyond.

Deciding to go that route, I stepped into the road and just dodged being bibbed at as I jogged to the other side and onto that pavement. Another check of the street showed nothing, and I strode up toward the corner cafe.

On reaching it, I cupped my hands around my eyes and peered through the window. A bunch of faces turned my way at the intrusion. None of them Dad's.

Pulling out my mobile, I moved farther along the road to the supermarket. As I stepped through the auto-doors, I dialled Dad's number. Only the engaged tone hit my ear, and shoving it back into my pocket, I walked the width of the store and checked each aisle.

Still nothing.

Next shop along was the baker, small enough to see without having to enter that Dad hadn't gone in there. Same with the dry cleaners.

After passing a cobbler-cum-key cutter, a hardware store, a newsagents and a chip shop that smelled greasy enough to clog my arteries with a single inhalation, I hit the far corner, on which stood a local pub.

Oak-stained beams supported white-painted brickwork on the exterior, and after a final glance the full length of the road, I pushed through the outer door into the small lobby, and then through the second door into the lounge.

A scattering of die-hard regulars sat hunched over in a few of the seating sections, identified by the broken capillaries veining their skin and the red rimmed glassy stares they aimed into space. No Dad, though.

Following the sticky carpeting, I headed for the unattended bar. From there, I could see straight through to the bar section of the pub, where more die-hards did a decent job of holding up the counter on that side. Weird thing about those types—they all likely visited the same pub every day, could all likely identify each other by sight, but even when they sat within touching distance of each other, they didn't seem to give a shit for conversation. Like, despite the visit being some kind of obvious escape, they didn't even have it in them to escape any further than their own heads. Or maybe their heads wouldn't let them escape.

Standing on my toes, I scanned beyond them, to every seat I could see, but still didn't spot Dad. I'd no fucking idea where he'd gone. Guy was a master evader when he flipping wanted to be.

Removing my hard-hat, I set it down and rubbed a hand across my face, before propping my butt onto a barstool and leaning my elbows on the bar. Figured I might as well get that drink Kyle and Brook put the kibosh on.

A mature guy who looked as alcohol-weathered as the rest of the folk in there came out of a door on the left, nodding my way like he'd known I was there all along. "'Can I get ya?"

My gaze instantly shot to the pumps. Then to the JD bottle hanging with its pals. At the same time, my brain tuned into Nate and his strict rules when it came to work.

I sighed. "Bottled water."

He let out a laugh and shook his head. "Don't get many requests for that in the daytime."

As he turned away, I worked my wallet from my trousers and took out a couple of quid, which I placed on the bar-top.

"You want this in a glass?" he asked, bringing one with him when he returned.

Nudging the coins toward him, I nodded and, waiting until he'd poured the water, took a healthy swig of the drink. "Keep the change," I told him when he clunked my empty bottle in the bin, and he waved his thanks as he rang up the sale.

The door to the pub popped open like some kind of vacuum seal held it closed, and just like every other saddo with nothing better to do in there, I twisted my head enough to see who'd come to join us. My gaze landed on a mass of muscle and the dark eyes that scanned the room.

Smiling, the expression as crooked and smug and full of attitude as usual, Ethan marched my way.

"Nate send you?" I asked, as he hopped onto a stool next to mine.

"Maybe." He glanced over each of his shoulders, toward the other patrons. "Why here?"

If Nate had sent him, he had to know I'd headed out looking for Dad, because Nate would've put two and two together easily enough. He'd probably sent him after me the second I'd left the room. I shrugged. "Why not?"

Ethan dropped his forearms onto the bar next me. "Okay, so, what're we celebrating?"

Half shrugging, I pursed my lips and thought about it. "Independence?"

He smiled again. As much as I loved him like a brother, sometimes I hated that smile. "How's that going for you?"

"It was going okay." I sent him a sidelong glance. "And then you showed up."

He chuckled. Ever vigilant, his eyes tracked the movements of the barman as he wiped the far counter farther along, and again as he pushed open a hidden half door to the other bar, where he tended to customers on that side.

I took another swig of my drink, wiping my mouth as I lowered my glass.

"So, this is what you'd do if you had more independence?" he asked after a couple minutes. "Spend it in the pub?"

"Take a closer look. This *is* what I'm doing."

74

"Looks fun," he said, though his tone suggested anything but.

"It is."

"Might as well join you, then. No sense you getting into trouble on your own." He signalled to the barman, once more tracing every move he made on his way back around to us. "Fill me up with whatever you gave him."

Within seconds, a glass of the clear stuff appeared in front of Ethan, and he lifted it toward me in a salute. "To self-destructive independence."

Smiling to myself, I watched as he lifted it to his lips, grinning when he took the first sip and confusion creased his brow.

His eyes narrowed. "Water."

"Just being self-destructive."

Shaking his head, almost to himself, he folded his arms atop the bar. "Be careful, Danny. Next thing you know, you'll be watching reruns of *Happy Days* and studying The Fonz for tips on how to swagger your way through this early midlife crisis you have going on."

"Maybe *you* should be careful," I told him. "You're showing your age if *Happy Days* is the best you can come up with."

"Yeah," he said, rubbing at his face. Lowering his hand, he took a sip of his drink, nudging the glass around the bar-top once he'd placed it back down. "So ..."

I knew that *so*. It always preceded some kind of discussion. Keeping my mouth shut, I waited for him to continue.

"The deal with you and Kyle?"

I inhaled. Exhaled. Both actions long and slow. "What about it?"

"Think you're going to sort it out?"

"Do you think it *can* be sorted out?"

"Quit answering questions with questions," he said, twisting to face me again. "Look, I get that he pissed you off—damn, he pissed us all off. But he's your brother, and

75

what went down between the two of you was months ago. I think it's about time you let it go."

I shook my head, my laugh coming out like a scoffed sigh. "You think this is only about that day?" The day when we'd stumbled across Kyle and Brook in the forest and discovered their relationship development had resulted in a mess that included Kyle threatening me over the cat.

"Isn't it?" he asked.

"No. It's about every bloody day since." I tapped a fingernail against my glass. "You don't live there, so you don't get it."

He lifted a palm. "So, fill me in."

"It's like ..." I paused, already knowing exactly how I'd sound. "It's like he's rubbing my nose in it."

Again, he brought his palm up. "How?"

The way he said it made me feel like a sulky brat. Maybe I seemed that way to somebody else, but knowing that refusing to continue would definitely paint me as one, I drew in a deep breath. "They have no respect for boundaries. There's not one sacred spot left in that house, I swear."

His lips twitched. *Bastard.* "Danny, they're a new couple. What did you expect?"

"A break?" I said with a shrug.

He barked out a laugh. "Can't you tell you haven't found *the one* yet."

I frowned. "Thanks. Rub it in." Might as well have rubbed it in that I hadn't shot my load into something other than my hand in over a year, too.

"Quit being on the defensive all the damn time and listen to what I'm telling you," he said, his voice deepening. I didn't argue, and he continued, "When you find the right one—your mate—nothing else beyond that seems quite so important anymore. She becomes your whole world." His 'stupid' smile moved in, and I knew he was probably picturing Shelley. "When you're with her, all you can think about is touching her and getting as damned intimate as physics will allow." His expression sobered. "And when you're not with her, you're thinking about how soon you *can* be with her so you can do everything your body needs. Because that's what it is when you find your mate. A need. And when you're waiting to fulfil that need, something inside you ..." He tapped his head with a finger. "... goes a little crazy."

I studied him. The sincerity in eyes. "Sounds painful." Enough to make me wonder if I truly wanted to find a mate.

"That's the way it is." He shrugged, like it was all part and parcel of the deal. "And I've seen it from both ends of the spectrum, remember." His face ducked a tad closer. "You think I didn't go through what you're going through when Sean got with Jem?"

I jerked a shoulder up. "How would I know? You didn't say."

"I didn't say, because Sean's my brother and he was happy. That seemed worth putting up with it, in my opinion."

I glanced away. "Yeah, well, they could be less loud about it."

He chuckled, his stool squeaking as he twisted back toward the bar. "You want me to have a word with him. Ask him to keep it down?"

I made some sound that came out sounding like a snort of derision. "I doubt the cat is capable of being quiet with the way she hits decibels I didn't even know existed."

"The cat has a name," he said, the humour leaving his tone.

A heavy quiet settled between us, and I wondered if he expected me to say something. If he expected me to apologise.

After a few minutes, he broke back in with, "You know Kyle's thinking of moving out because of this."

I sliced my gaze to him, found him staring my way.

"If you don't work this out, he's gonna go," he said.

77

The words stabbed through me until my hand tightened around my glass and my brows knotted tight. *Kyle* and *moving out* in the same sentence just didn't gel right.

Not once had I considered we should split us up. Not once had it occurred to me that either of us would even want to. That he'd consider such an idea, over trying to work things out with me, pissed me off. A lot.

How the hell had it come to that?

Not to mention the fact that I'd auto be the one to blame. The one everyone looked at as the reason for his leaving.

Fucking brilliant. Man up and quit complaining, or tear the last stitches from the seams holding us together.

Knocking back the last of my water and slamming my glass back down, I slid from the stool. "Maybe I should just move out instead. Then everyone will be happy." I snatched up my hard-hat and strode from the bar.

9

I spent the rest of the day in a shitty mood. Every time I'd looked at Kyle, I'd tried to gauge his feelings. Figure out what was going on behind the stares he shared, the polite-but-no-longer-close tone he offered any time he had to speak to me. On top of that, Dad had been back on site when I got there and acting like he'd never left. He might have convinced me, if he hadn't seemed to only work for the rest of the afternoon on whatever I wasn't.

Nothing quite like being made to feel like a leper by one's own family.

Due to the dry weather, we ended up staying on an extra hour, too, and by the time I left the site, I'd had my fill of being avoided, of feeling like nobody wanted to be around me.

After speeding ahead of the others to beat them all home, I parked up my bike, removed my helmet, and sat on the front steps of the house awaiting their arrival.

As the truck turned in, Dad's and Kyle's eyes honed in on me, and Josh's from the backseat a moment later—likely prompted by the mumbling lips of the duo up front. I watched as the vehicle made the small incline and slipped under the carport, and pushing up, I strode around the side of the house until I reached the driver's door.

Dad stared back at me through the glass, plaster dust lightening his auburn hair. Not his eyes, though—I doubted anything could dull the bright sharpness of those.

Sending me a frown, Kyle climbed from his side of the pickup. "'Sup?"

"Nothing. Just need to speak to Dad."

As Josh hopped out, he and Kyle headed off toward the rear of the house. Leaving me standing there staring in. And Dad sitting there staring out.

"Why are you making this feel like a stand-off?" I asked through the glass.

He faced forward, his chest rising high before settling, and he switched off the engine. When his door swung outward, I stepped back to give him room. "I'm not trying to make it feel like anything," he said.

"You've been avoiding me."

He climbed down onto the block pavers and shut the truck door. "I'd say that's nigh on impossible, seeing as we both live and work together, Danny." He went to turn away, but I grabbed his arm and tugged him back.

"Talk to me, Dad. What's going on?"

"You ask of others what you're not prepared to give yourself?"

I scowled. "Don't turn this on me. Tell me what's going on."

"Nothing's going on." The unsteadiness of his eyes told another story.

"Bullshit!"

"Watch your mo—"

"No, Dad. I'm sick of this shit." I dropped my hold of him but didn't move away. "I find my aunt I haven't seen in years, and you kick me out of it and tell me to keep my mouth shut. And then you do nothing but disappear night after night, lying about where you're going. Don't try telling me these vanishing acts have nothing to do with Aunt Maghon, because I'm not buying it."

"Will you keep your voice down," he rumbled, his tone full of warning.

"No." I jerked closer. "Is she who you've been with every time you piss off?"

"*Danny*—"

"What the hell's going on, Dad?" I asked, flipping my palms out.

"It's not—"

"What's she got on you?"

He tapped a finger against my chest as his eyes narrowed. "It's none of your damn business where I go, or who I go with," he said, his tone deepening. "Remember who you're speaking to, boy."

"Fine." Chest heaving, I backed away, my nod a stilted action. "Keep your fucking secrets. But know this. I'm sick of lying to my brothers on your behalf, because that ..." I prodded a finger toward him. "That you have no right to ask of me." I spun away and strode for the house.

"*Danny*!"

Ignoring him, I kept going.

"Danny," he said, his voice softer. "Where are you going?"

"For a damn shower," I tossed back at him. "See if I can scrub off this shit wearing down my shoulders."

Water rolled along my spine as I stepped out onto the landing with my hair still wet. I could hear the movements of the others on my cross of the landing, smell the herby scents of the beef and wine stew Brook had brought home.

"You in tonight, or out?" Josh asked, his voice drifting up the stairs.

Knowing who he probably spoke to, I paused outside my bedroom, head tipped to catch the answer.

"I'm not sure, yet, what my plans are," Dad said after a small pause.

"But what about the ..."

Not bothering to listen to any more, I ducked into my room and tossed my towel to the far corner. I slumped down on the edge of my bed, wedging my elbows onto my knees. Forehead propped against the balls of my hands, I raked my fingers into my hair, closing my eyes and ears to the outside world as I attempted to un-grit my grinding teeth.

Had Dad even listened to a single word I'd said to him?

Fuck lying to my brothers. Fuck covering for him. Why the hell should I have to when he couldn't even be straight with me?

How the fuck did home-life become so stressful?

Vibrations rippled across the bedside table behind me, and I rubbed at my face before flopping over the bed and stretching up for my mobile. I didn't even bother sitting back up to check the alert on the screen.

YOU HAVE 1 NEW TEXT MESSAGE.

I tapped the screen to view it but didn't recognise the number that'd sent it. I recognised the message, though— because that could've only come from one person.

K I'LL GO.

7:30.

231 TOWNSLEY ST.

CU THERE?

The party. The fucking party. With all the amazing *chats* I'd had throughout the day, I'd let it slide to the back of my brain somewhere.

I thought of Dad.

I thought of Kyle.

I thought of everything Ethan'd had said in the bar at lunch.

I should've been planning to use the night ahead to build some bridges, except some voice in my head reminded me: *You told her you'd go. You were the one who fucking offered.*

I checked the time: seven o-three.

Go the party. Play my part for Liv. Be back in time to spend the rest of the night with the pack.

Tapping the 'reply' icon, I typed in

NP. CU L8R

and hit 'send'.

For a moment, I stared up at the ceiling, trying to gauge if I'd just made a good decision or a really, really bad one. Still none the wiser, I pushed up and headed for my dresser.

It took only about ten minutes to tug on some underwear, some jeans and a T, and dig out my non-work boots from the wardrobe. After rubbing the towel over my head a couple of times and dragging my fingers through to lose the knots, I deemed myself about as decent as I was willing to get for a party with a bunch of students.

Chatter from downstairs sounded like it'd moved to the kitchen when I stepped from my bedroom and jogged down the stairs. Pausing in the hallway, I tugged my boots on and headed in to them, halting in the doorway when all heads turned my way. "How long 'til dinner?"

Dad's gaze travelled from my head to my feet. "Going somewhere?"

I jerked my chin in answer.

"I don't think so," he said, turning to face me.

"Luckily, I didn't ask what *you* think."

"How many times today am I going to have to warn you to mind your tongue, Son?"

I narrowed my eyes at him. Did he really want to go there after our 'chat' outside?

He poked a finger toward the table. "Sit down. Your food's almost ready."

"Whatever," I muttered, twisting for the hall.

I'd taken only three steps out of the kitchen when Dad's boots tapped the tiles behind me. At the bottom of the stairs, I snatched up my keys, helmet and jacket, but as I reached for the door catch, Dad reached around my head and braced a hand against the door.

"Where do you think you're going?" he asked, so close his breath heated my neck.

"I told you," I said without turning. "Out. I have plans."

"Not tonight, Son. Cancel them."

I tipped my head enough to see his eyes. "Just like you're planning to cancel yours?"

His brows closed in, but not before I caught the slight wince in his expression.

"Yeah, that's what I thought." Shouldering him aside, I grabbed the catch and yanked the door open, looking back at him one last time. "Never had you down as a hypocrite, Dad."

Ignoring his demands to come back, I cut a direct path for my ride.

10

The address Liv had given me sat on a private road. Not many more than a handful of houses stood at generous intervals either side of the block-paved roadway, each of them with manicured lawns that swept down to equally pristine footpaths and walls higher than my head barricading out their neighbour either side.

Banking into a driveway that cut a dark river all the way to the front of the house, I checked out the other vehicles parked along it. Anything from a personalised Range Rover to a beat up old-style Beetle sat in a long row to the front door, not to mention the extras outside messing up the otherwise too-quiet street. Kind of made me wonder how often the other residents had to put up with rambunctious behaviour. Or maybe humans just had really shit hearing and the house sat out of the others' range—because I could well and truly hear bass vibrating through the walls from my spot.

I parked up next to a rusted Cinquecento and tugged off my helmet. Moody-looking clouds mucked up what should've been a still-light sky for the time of month and prematurely darkened the evening. The chill factor had gotten ridiculous, too, and the breeze snaked around my arms the instant I slipped my jacket off, sending my skin into chicken flesh territory and my nipples prodding at my T. I could've just kept the coat on, but I remembered the parties I used to attend, remembered the way bodies ended up jammed together, remembered the heat. For some reason that made me smile. It also turned me on a little that one of the bodies I could end up jammed against might be Liv's.

That same breeze also carried a faint whiff of weed as I inhaled, and though I knew it'd be coming from the party, habit had me lifting my head toward the source. As I did so, my sights landed on the moon peeking over the housetops. A full moon. One my body had known for the entire day would arrive.

Go in, do my stuff, get my butt home, I reminded myself. *No problem.*

With my jacket rammed through my helmet, I locked them both to my bike and made my way past the cars toward the house. Lights shone out from most of the seven windows I could see, silhouetting bodies in each of the rooms. I climbed the front step and rang the bell. Though I could hear plenty of shouts inside, none of them were to get the door, and over a minute later, I still stood there. Like an idiot. Waiting to get into a house I'd never been to, full of people I didn't know.

For Liv, I reminded myself and ordered myself in search of a new entrance.

From the sounds and scents carrying on the wind, the party wasn't contained indoors, proven when I stepped around the side of the garage and into what we'd have called the happening spot of the party.

Along one stretch of the patio, a table reached around five metres in length, a row of tapped kegs atop it, plastic cups stacked between them, and a bunch of cardboard boxes that seemed to be passing as bins beneath. Between those and me, young people aged anywhere between seventeen and twenty-five sat or stood in cliques, at least half of them puffing on cigarettes, or sucking off reefers, before blowing their tainted breath back out into the evening.

Tamping down the depth of my inhalations, I studied the crowd. Hair flicked about. Hips got jutted out. Shoulder muscles flexed with gestures as small as raising a drink to lips. More prominent, though, was the different levels of laughter, from polite to moronic guffaws to fake twitters.

No Liv, though.

In a swimming pool around twenty yards over, a half dozen females splashed about, as well as a group of males. The fact they all wore only underwear told me the water had to be heated, because my flesh still resembled something from the frozen poultry family.

Again, I scanned the faces in search of Liv, but didn't see her amongst them. Pity. Finding her half-naked in the pool would've been a bonus.

Figuring she had to be inside somewhere, I began navigating my way through the people and smog clogging up the patio.

Smatterings of conversation met me as I went: "... you hear about ..." "All she has to do is ask Daddy and ..." "... so going to get Trevor Benton tonight ..." "Hey!"

I stepped around some guy holding his hands in front of him in an obvious measure of some girl's boobs.

"Hey, you! Super-hot guy!"

I glanced to the side and my gaze landed on a blonde with dripping wet hair. Her elbows balanced her on the side of the pool as her breasts nearly rolled out of the strapless bra she had on. Actually, that was exactly what happened when she flopped an arm about and performed something resembling a wave.

"Yes, you!" She waved again, the action seeming to correct her mishap—not that I'd minded. "Come here!"

Shaking my head, I smiled. "Nah, I don't think so."

"Booooooo!" she shouted after me when I turned away.

Reaching the beer table, I unsheathed a cup and checked out the offerings—from Stella to Strongbow, to some cheap white wine on the end and a few others in between.

At a waft of sweetness, I glanced up.

With shiny chestnut hair slicked back into a tight ponytail and wearing seriously tight jeans with a top that scarcely covered her boobs, a girl stepped from the house carrying a tray filled with chocolate cakes.

My stomach grumbled at a second waft of the sugary scent, and I watched as she weaved through those milling about with her hips flicking side to side, counting down each time a hand grabbed a cake and the pile went down a little more.

She swung around a few guys near the head of the table and her gaze latched on to me, staying there as she went to curve around my rear.

I spun to follow before she could vanish. "These going?" I asked.

She halted, her head tipping to the side. "Depends."

"On ...?"

Her hip hutted out. "On who's asking."

"Me. I'm asking." I snagged two of the chocolate muffins.

"Hey," she said, straightening. "One each only."

I shrugged. "Sorry. I'm hungry." I shoved one of the cakes into my mouth, yanking off half with one bite.

The scowl she sent me was pretty epic before she spun away fast enough to whip my bicep with her hair.

Chuckling through chewing, I turned back to the table, pausing as the doughy-ness of the cake rolled over my tongue—nothing like the muffins Ethan or Beth made. Damn people needed to learn how to bake.

Swallowing my mouthful, I dredged up my rusty talent of filling a cup one-handed. I chugged back a swig to wash down the crumbs crowding my throat, the cider a little dryer than I liked it, and shoved in the second half of cake, demolishing that as fast as the first. As I took a second swig of drink, I realised it'd probably been pretty stupid of me to turn up at a party with nothing in my stomach and shoved in the second muffin before draining my cup.

Something bumped into me from behind, sending me forward a step. "Sorry, man. Sorry."

A hand slapped my shoulder, and I twisted to a kid dressed in what looked like a folded down Spiderman outfit. Not much shorter than me, he rubbed at his bare arms and chest, grinning like an idiot.

"I don't know you," he said, still grinning, grinning, grinning.

I checked my shirt front for stains, rubbed a hand across my mouth for chocolate. "Yeah, well, don't beat yourself up over it."

He grabbed a cup and started filling it. "This is my house." Still grinning, he glanced back to me. "And if I don't know you, what're you doing here?"

I studied him. His bare chest. His smile full of a cockiness that spoke of money and esteem and a whole lot of popularity. Remembering I had a role to play and a promise to uphold, I tipped my empty beaker toward him. "I'm—"

"You're out!" He grabbed the cup out of my hand and filled it from the same keg as his own before shoving it back at me. "Nobody should be fucking walking 'round with an empty. Nobody."

I lifted my beaker and downed another slug, viewing him over the rim as he did the same like we'd become best drinking buddies in a matter of minutes. I couldn't decide whether to like him or loathe him.

Lowering his drink, he shook his head like a wet dog, swaying a little before he steadied himself and his eyes focused back on me. "Yeah ... whod'yousayouwere?"

I just about contained my snort from escaping. "I'm here with Liv."

His mouth popped open, his eyes wobbling about as his head jiggled, before he went back to grinning, grinning, grinning. "You're the d*ate*!" He emphasised the *T*, sending tiny flecks of spit spraying outward.

"I am." I couldn't help smiling that she'd told her friends about me. Smiling, smiling, smiling. If Mr Happy kept it up, he'd have me grinning as stupidly as him by the end of the night. "You seen her?"

He nodded and flicked the tap on the keg again, refilling his drained cup. When he straightened, his cup went right back to his mouth and he downed it with the noisiest fucking gulps I'd ever heard.

"So ..." I said, as he finished. "Where is she?"

Arms flapped around his middle from behind, a high-pitched, "*Johnny*!" screeching out.

Lifting his arms, he peered underneath the left one, grinning, grinning, grinning as a female slid around his body in a tiny piece of red cloth that clung everywhere and left zero to the imagination.

She smiled at me as she settled against his side and his arm flopped around her. "Hi."

My own lips stretched. Smiley fucking smiley. "Hey."

"This is Liv's da*te*!" 'Johnny' said, again emphasising the *T*.

"Ooooh." The girl's lips wrapped around the sound as her gaze skimmed down and then up. "Liv's inside somewhere. Upstairs, I think." She pointed behind her. "Prob be down soon—oh! I know!" She popped apart from Johnny the grinner and waved an arm with enough vigour to do damage. "Maaaaaaaaaand! Maaaaaaaaaaaand!"

I tracked to where she stared—or tried to. My eyes did some weird shit that made the action feel like it went in slow-mo whilst freeze-framing every millimetre of view they took in. I shook my head hard in an effort to clear it, but even the girl who jumped up from some dude's lap and trotted across the garden seemed to be moving in exaggerated jerky movements.

She hopped to a stop in our circle, her mass of nearly white hair swinging around like something fucking insane and her teeth sharp and hungry looking when she smiled.

I had to blink to focus on her.

"This is Liv's da*te*!" Johnny's friend said, again with the emphasis on the *T*. "He's trying to find her," she added.

"Oooh. Okay." The girl with nearly white hair grabbed my hand. "Come on. I'll help you find her."

As she tugged on my hand, the world throbbed—actually throbbed—and I shook my again head, even harder than before, squinting through a vision that seemed suddenly skewed. I seriously fucking needed some sustenance. Like, seriously.

I gripped onto Johnny's arm before the white haired girl could kidnap me. "You have any other food here besides those cakes."

Johnny laughed then grinned, grinned, grinned. "I ain't here to feed you fuckers! I'm here to make sure you have a good time." Pointing at my escort, he yelled, "Get this man a muffin!"

From across the garden, some guy shouted, "Johnny, you fucking twat!" but before I could check on who, the white haired girl trotted toward the house, her fingernails digging into my wrist as she yanked me behind her.

The patio door led through to a dining room, where a long mahogany table held shot glasses and another array of drinks, from alcopops to cheap vodka. The girl swiped up a couple of Breezers as she pushed through a group of lads, before tugging me around an arched doorway into a huge kitchen. The appliance fronts glittered enough to convince me that the place usually held a high shine, but with squashed plastic cups and empty bottles and all sorts of ominous looking substances littering the countertops, not to mention a handful of bums perched on an island and more bodies scattered around, the room just looked a mess.

Not that I cared. I couldn't have given two shits.

On the farthest counter, another tray of muffins had been left, and once we'd dodged our way around the island, I grabbed one up just in time, before the girl manhandled me out another door and into a hallway, where even more people loitered.

I chomped on my muffin as we worked between them, ignoring the bodies pressed up tight and hip bumping going on. The walls they leaned against seemed to pulsate in time to their snogging and gyrations. Throbbing in, out, in, out. Even the hue of the walls seemed to change with the heat, flashing red to white, red to white.

Through double doors on the left, music spilled out, something with a lot of bass that echoed and seemed to send vibrations trickling across on the air.

"Oh—I love this one!"

The girl hauled me smack bang into a pool of bodies that swayed like sunflowers in the wind, their hair sticking out like yellow petals, their arms flapping like leaves weighed down. The distorted sounds pounding out from who knew where seemed to embrace my entire body, like hands of encouragement stroking my senses into wanting to move, wanting to dance, wanting to embrace its fucked up beat right back.

My arm flicked up in the air as the girl's shot upward, dropping again as she wiggled her hips all the way down into a crazy squat. Even as my hips threatened to follow unbidden, I checked the faces of those in the room for Liv.

Lids dripping like melted wax coated the eyes. Mouths sagged open in varying portrayals of abandonment. As arms swept up and through hair, blasts of sweat-drenched odour erupted around me like microscopic pollen.

Spinning, the white haired girl shoved a bottle in my free hand. "You have a name?"

I necked the bottle, downing half its contents to ward off my arid throat, before nodding. "Danny."

Whirling on the spot to face away again, she pressed up against my chest and tipped her head back. "Liiiiiiiiiiiiiiiivvvv! Daaaaaannnnnnyyyyyy's heeeeerrrre!" She peered up at me, her face upside-down. "*Don't worry, she'll come.*"

I blinked at the way her features twisted into some kind of demonic mask, frowning as I tried focusing them back into a sense of order. Her shark teeth grinned at me. Grinned, grinned, grinned, and my own mouth stretched into a smiley fucking smile that made my skin hurt.

Fingers clamped around my hand holding the bottle, and as she tugged me closer, her hips started rolling, and the room and its contents did a freaky fucking carousel dance.

I closed my eyes against the spinning, my pulse banging against my flesh like machine-gunfire, an inhalation sucking up enough scents to make my brain hurt.

Heat hit my back. Hands gripped my hips. What felt like somebody's butt pressed up against mine, while arms snaked around my neck from the front, and the duo mashed me like banana filler in a sandwich to the screechy *do-dum-dum-dum* of the track.

The two bodies began swaying, swaying, swaying until it felt like we were balancing on turbulent waters. The motion churned my stomach, but the weightlessness of my bulk felt really fucking awesome. Realising my hands hung free, I grabbed at something to hold onto, letting my body slip down, my head fall back, my mind empty of some shit I knew should be bothering me but could barely even remember.

As one, we stumbled to the right, but I didn't care.

As one, we jerked back to the left, but I didn't give a damn.

Behind my eyelids, garish white lights flickered and circled, making my eyeballs throb, but I had no issue with that, either.

My head felt loose on my neck on my shoulders. My entire fucking body felt languid as fuck. Languid and liquid and made of silly string and streamers. While just breathing sucked in shampoo and B.O. and mint and beer and something sweet that resembled honeysuckle in a feminine kind of way.

I latched onto that last one. Twisting my head, I weaved through all the scents I wasn't interested in until the flowery sweetness hit right up high in my sinuses and my mouth parted like that would get me a taste of the flavour.

Ignoring the couple of screechy, "Heys!" I broke away from my new friends.

It took only a singular deep sniff for my feet to shoot me forward.

Only three steps for my body to hit another.

For my arms to flap around them.

Only three more beats for us to land against the throbbing wall with all the other entwined bodies and my mouth to smother hers. My groan vibrated through my brain when her lips parted and my tongue slipped through the gap. My growl rumbled through my chest as her tongue rose to meet mine, as warm breaths eked out between us and heated up my aching face.

Teeth closed around my lower lip, biting a little before that tongue licked across there, offering up more of that hot, sweet breath, and I nipped along her jaw, sucked at her pulse, licked my way down her neck to where her collarbone peeked out.

"Taking the pretend boyfriend role a little too seriously, aren't you, Danny?" she murmured near my ear.

My grin returned, and smiley fucking smiling, I lifted my face from her throat until I could see her face.

Eyes not dripping or drooping but smoky smoking fucking hot blue stared back at me from beneath hair that seemed tame too tame tamer than it should've been.

"What'd you do to your hair?"

"What?"

I picked a strand up and, bringing it to my nose, sniffed at it.

She shrugged, somehow making the wall behind her sink back like a flattened marshmallow. "I straightened it."

Placing the hair back against her shoulder, my fingers brushed against the rough, emerald fabric of her dress, and I traced the curve of the neckline down down down and around where it balanced in a line that shouldn't-but-begged-to be crossed over her breasts. Her fricking huge breasts, really huge and swollen and pushing up out of her clothes like they needed me almost as much as my swelling dick suddenly needed them.

"Hey!" A hand wrapped around my chin and jerked my head up. "Up 'ere, tough guy."

I forced my gaze back on her face, skimming over lips that had me licking mine in anticipation of her letting me go there again and landing on those smoky smoking fucking hot blue eyes. Blue eyes that stared back. Directly back. I studied them harder, my eyes squinting with the effort, before it clicked. "I knock your glasses off?"

She frowned. "What?"

I touched a finger to her eyebrow. "Your glasses."

"What—oh, no I switched 'em for contacts. Jesus, Danny, how many have you had?"

"Three."

"Whatever," she said, rolling her eyes.

I grinned. Like a moron who didn't know how not to grin. Bracing my fingertips against the wall either side of her shoulders, I leaned in closer, touched my lips to hers, then pushed away and leaned back in again until she grinned as stupidly as I probably did.

"You're such an idiot."

Laughing, I pressed in, pausing long enough to linger over her lips and taste her. As I shoved back off, a waft of chocolate hit my senses, and my stomach cried at the hours I'd left it wanting. I glanced to the side, searching searching searching for the good stuff, until I caught the tray held aloft and floating a path through the people.

Whipping out an arm, I snagged a handful, snatching my hand back before anyone could argue.

"What are you doing?"

Somehow grinning and muscling a chunk of chocolate gooiness into my mouth at the same time, I spun back to Liv. "I'm starving," I said, while chewing and cramming in more. "So fucking starving."

She grabbed my hand and broke off half of my other cake, and I lurched backward, swinging my arm out of reach before she could get the rest.

"Hey, hey, hey. What're you doing? I said I'm hungry."

"Danny, you can't eat these brownies." When I went to step away some more, she bolted after me. "For God's sake, Danny," she said, stretching after my arm as I raised it. "Don't eat it."

Whirling away, I jolted a step, but almost went flying backward when I collided with a marshmallow wall that'd turned a sordid red. Staggering away from it, I shook my head, my eyes almost flicking loose as they tried to focus.

White to red to white to red, the walls tried folding around me as invisible hands stroked over my throat, down to my chest, pressing pressing pressing until it heaved against the threat of caving in.

The faces of demon dancers turned to watch as I leaned into the wall for support, but the soggy mush of a barrier didn't want to support me and sent me sliding into a pit of muddy marsh water thick enough to crush the bones of my legs.

In my head, the music bump-bumped-bumped. Beneath it, a voice yell-yelled-yelled.

Something wrapped around my arm and yanked, flipping me round so fast I saw only swatches of colours all tangled and wrong just fucking wrong.

I tried to lift a hand to my head to stop whatever kept psycho-waltzing in there but couldn't be sure I succeeded. "Don' feel so fuckin' goo'." My stomach roiled, and I shook my head again like that could quell it, but it only made it a whole heap of worse so much bloody worse. "Relly don' fel so f'ckin' gu—"

The bright lights vanished. Darkness moved in. Cold air wrapped around my body, snaking beneath my clothes and prodding at my flesh with sharp needles that stung like a bitch.

Putting one foot in front of the other felt like climbing a mountain through knee-deep bog-weed while being attacked by a hurricane. I'd no idea how far I got before I collapsed to my knees and just rolled rolled rolled. From somewhere far away I could hear my name being called, but the bog just kept sucking me under under too deep fucking under.

A little voice in the back of my mind that sounded very much like my own told me something was wrong something was very fucking wrong where's Kyle where's Kyle when I need him? *IneedKyleIneedKylemustfuckingringKyle ...*

Navigating my body took effort. Navigating my pocket took Herculean effort.

As my fingers folded around my mobile, I felt like crying. Probably did fucking cry. Like a baby like a big fucking cry baby.

I dragged out my mobile, arm quivering in my lift of it as I brought the phone to my face.

Eyes screwed to slits, I stared at the screen, poking with my thumb and trying to get the key-lock off. Trying to get to my brother's number. Trying to hit dial.

Annoying blaring crawled over me, into my ears, snaking through my mind. Too loud. I shook my head. Needed it gone. Really needed it gone.

It stopped, like a prayer.

I unscrewed my eyes.

Stared out at darkness marred by shadowed splotches.

Turning my head landed my gaze on an orb of light. A massive orb, opened wide like a maw of brightness that held me transfixed until I stared stared stared, unable to look away.

Muted shouting rolled around me. Deep voice. High. Deep. High. Deephighdeephighdeep—

I didn't care.

Just cared about the light as the light became my master.

As prickles raced over my scalp and into my face.

As an ache rampaged through the muscles in my shoulders and calves.

As my fingers flexed into a spasm I knew without knowing why I'd never get out of.

An inferno raged into my shoulder, until I distorted my torso to get away from something I somehow knew but couldn't comprehend that I'd never get away from.

Pain stabbed into the base of my skull, sending my head flying backward.

A cry blasted into my brain. A cry of pain, all twisted and fucked up with a whole load of panic. I didn't know where it came from. I didn't know how to stop it. Maybe I wasn't meant to stop it. Maybe I just couldn't.

The knife slipped an inch into the top of my spine. Another inch, into the second vertebra, pinning and paralysing and somehow numbing and agonising all at the same time—before dragging through skin and bone and nerve and sinew and muscle, in a downward fiery rampage that had my body my entire body bucking upward, my arms splaying outward, my heels kicking downward like I could merely push myself from the moment from the torment such fucking torment.

My body shook. My body rolled. Shadows swamped my vision. Screams insulted my brain.

I didn't seem able to do a damn thing. Not about anything. Not about them. About me. About what the fuck seemed to be slowly and burningly killing me from the inside out.

A voice wriggled across on the damp ground supporting me. A deep voice. One I thought I recognised but couldn't tell from where.

Something solid and rough clamped about my chest. Something rough and solid clamped about my shins. Shackles the lot of them like shackles come to pin me down and force me through the nightmare I seemed to be trapped in.

Until the weightlessness took over.

Not like the weightlessness of before, though, because then I could move, could dance freely, could liberate my soul of all the shit it didn't want to deal with.

As my body flew through air that continued to pierce with its ice-pick fingers, it refused to move. Refused to unlock from whatever prison the orb had put it in. Refused to give me control.

Something soft but unrelenting bashed against my rear.

A draft filled with warmth stroked at my face.

A bang real close too close closer than I liked set my teeth on edge and my brain buzzing for escape, before more bangs rang out, more bangs that echoed and shook my entire body side to side while searing, like I lay on a branch made only of willow buds through a volcanic eruption.

Another assault of cold shrouded my body before there was warmth only warmth and heat and fire and lava and enough thunder in my head to smother the world in raindrops that couldn't be quelled—

Until the earth was gone gone gone and nothing fucking made any kind of sense any more.

11

My soul lay trapped. Trapped in a body that wouldn't move. Trapped beneath blackened fingers of gnarled bark. Trapped by the winds battering my belly and stoning my muscles into a frigid state of convulsion. Trapped by dark and twisted shadows and shapes and splotches of light that haunted my space.

Against my sternum, my heart bang-bang-banged an erratic beat of panic of fear of discomfort, of wishing someone would haul out my insides and fit me with a new set that didn't hurt didn't hurt didn't hurt so fucking much.

Soggy moisture glued my face to whatever ground I lay against. Soggy moisture that stank and reeked and burnt my sinuses until my eyes dripped with acid that smudged everything, the world, anything around me that came into view.

Acrid tar pasted my teeth together in a web of thick drool, strung from tooth to tooth to gum to lips, binding my chin in a perpetual grimace of wanting it out wanting it all out wanting it gone.

Blackness overshadowed me until I could see only black only black, and no light even existed anymore. Maybe I didn't exist anymore. Maybe I'd reached hell reached hell for my sins and I never got the chance to tell Kyle I didn't blame him for his choices. Didn't blame him for wanting what he wanted and having the balls to take it.

As the blackness prodded at me, prodded and poked, my heart hammered even harder.

Heat blasted my face blasted my throat blasted my ear, heat that was possibly the only thing that kept my heart from hitting killing levels.

Because I knew the scent it carried.

A scent so familiar, just detecting it made me want to sob with gratitude that they were there.

So familiar, my heart slowed. Just a little.

My breaths steadied. Just a little.

My grumbles of pain heightened to a whimpered plea. Just a little.

A sucking sound hit my hearing. A blown sound hit my face. A question grunted not asked only grunted but clear so fucking clear to me that I somehow knew they only asked only checked only needed to know I was all right.

I couldn't answer them. How could I answer what I didn't know myself?

I forced out another whimper, but my body instantly recoiled as a surge of lava boiled up in my belly and roared on a direct path for my throat my mouth my nose, liberating itself while binding me. Binding me in suspended death. A suspended death of no breaths no heartbeat no tools to keep going to keep living to keep existing.

The soggy marshland pooled deeper all around me, sucking me down sucking me under—until it fought for residence in my dripping eyes and burned burned burned, and I gave up gave up the fight a fight of futility, of wasted energy, of no results.

With one final shudder of my body, I closed my eyes on the pain and let myself sink.

My body shook, shook, shook, making my stomach churn like crazy.

Blinking, I fought against the stickiness bogging down my lashes, but fast winced at the pale light that bled through, my eyes sore and gritty even opened only to slits.

"Dan." A face blocked my view. A big round moon face surrounded by fire and filled with shadows of concern. "Daniel?"

I grunted, almost retching on the rotten slop still hogging my tongue.

"We need to get you to Nate's." The moon face sounded a whole lot like Dad without attitude, without anger, with only soothing tones. "Can you walk?"

He vanished from in front of me, and steel supports wrapped my torso from behind, pressing down on a stomach so full of tenderness it probably cried tears all of its own.

My body peeled from the pond of gunk and spew that still stung my senses, though plenty still clung onto my hairs, drooling downward like suspension wires on a bridge.

The world tilted sideways. Or maybe I tilted sideways. Greens, browns, blues all splotched together like a too close view of an impressionist painting, and I closed my eyes against the stimuli, too much, too much to even try taking in.

My paws hit something solid. The band about my middle loosened. Legs weak and wobbly, I stood there for a second, two seconds, three seconds, swaying while my muscles wept at the effort of holding me steady.

A vice clamped about my head. "Danny, open your eyes."

I tried to obey, I really did, but too much funk had tucked beneath my lids, my rims, just about every-fucking-where it could find to hide.

"This isn't going so well," a different voice said. Another one I knew, knew so well, but in a tone I hadn't heard in too long. "Danny, try taking a couple steps."

My body jerked just at the prospect, but I lifted a paw, sending myself into a pendulum swing. As the paw slammed back down, my ankle buckled, my chest lurched forward, and my jaw face-planted the ground.

"Jesus Christ. Forget it—just forget it." Arms banded around me again. "I'll just carry him."

"I've got it, Dad. Move over. I've got it."

The bands disappeared. New ones took their place, cinching tight, cinching tighter, tight, tight, tight, until I couldn't breathe. My body seemed to float float float, and flip flip flip. Something solid and tense crushed against my chest and my head hung hung hung.

With the solid ridges pushing against me in a bump-bump-bump of a rhythm, my head swished and swung and my stomach churned and burned as my nose sucked up scents and flavours I'd always loved but currently hated.

I had to rub my eyes before they'd pry open enough to reveal anything. Overhead, a blank canvas of white loomed, whereas to my left a swollen butterfly fuzzed around the edges and buzzed in a small circle like a moth trapped in a jar.

Sour-tasting fur coated my tongue, making it feel too big in my mouth. Just swallowing against the fucked up flavour made my stomach complain, but trying to swallow while inhaling *and* trying to focus on my surroundings sent my gut into an outright revolt.

As my insides performed a hob-nailed somersault, twisting up all my muscles into a knot of cramps, I flung my legs over the side of the bed I lay on and forced myself in the direction of the door.

The landing that'd always only been strides long seemed infinite in my rush for the bathroom, where shrouded sunshine stole through the window like a searchlight in hot pursuit of something to torture. The stench in there reminded me that I'd made previous visits since being brought to Nate's. Many previous visits. As if my aching midsection hadn't already given that away.

Shoulder bumping the wall, I stumbled from the doorframe and folded down onto my knees, just as the acid in my stomach rushed upward. My mouth opened wide on the dry retch, and I gripped onto the seat like I needed it to stay balanced. Probably because I did.

After a few more efforts of dry retching, I folded my arms across the toilet pan and dropped my head to rest there—my aching head that throbbed atop an aching body that throbbed equally as hard.

"What made you think there'd be anything left in there to come out?" Jem said from behind me.

Not ready to lift my head, I shrugged where I slumped.

"Might be about time we got you a bucket, I suppose."

As Jem's footsteps padded from the room, I forced my head from its resting place and, bracing my hands against the toilet, staggered to my feet. The room seemed to whirl as I spun for the door, no matter that I moved at the speed of a slug, and my shoulder scraped the wall all the way out to the landing and across the closed door to Nate's room.

Sunlight I didn't want to embrace smothered every surface in Lia's room when I finally reached it. Shielding my eyes, I waded through the carpet to the bedroom window, with its drapes spread wide and admitting entry to the brightness. One-handed, I fumbled with the tieback, and as I worked it free of its hook, my squinting eyes landed on my bike down below. Flopped onto its side. In the back of Ethan's pickup.

"They didn't exactly have a choice," Jem said, sneaking up beside me. "It was either throw it in there to bring home with you, or leave it parked outside a house full of drunk teens."

I frowned, my brain weaving through what it remembered, but even that hurt too much to endeavour for more than a few seconds. Grunting, I turned away from the window, catching the worry in Jem's eyes, the hurt. The disappointment. Disappointment I couldn't deal with right then. Not when I didn't even know how I'd caused the expression.

As I went to brush past her, she took my hand and wedged something against my palm, folding my fingers around it. I glanced down. A bucket. Right. Dragging myself across carpet that felt like vines clutching at my feet, I made my way back to the bed and, dropping the bucket beside it, sank down and tangled myself back within the covers.

"Can you get the curtains?" My voice grated out, making the request sound like an unappreciative demand. Closing my eyes, I dropped a forearm over them and let out a measured exhale. "Please?"

The curtain rings grazed the pole like an express train over tracks, and my head pounded out a complaint, but at least the penetrating light let off some. I expected Jem to leave then, to give up on my unsociable dick self, but her feet didn't move and her breaths continued their soft rhythm.

She sighed, the sound heavy and pregnant. "Look, Danny …"

Hoping she meant figuratively, I stayed as I was. Looking would take more effort than I had to give.

Another sigh, then, "Whatever it was that drove you to last night … whatever you've got going on in that head of yours … you're going to have to quit being a stubborn pain the arse and start bloody talking to someone. To one of us. Because you're no good on your own."

Eyes still covered, I tracked her movements as she crossed from the window to the foot of the bed.

"On your own—being on your own? It makes you vulnerable. And when you make yourself vulnerable that way, it creates a weakness in the pack. So, you need to quit Danny," she said, an edge creeping into her tone. "You need to quit and you need to get your act together. Because you're not just risking yourself, you're now risking us all."

I finally lowered my arm and ordered my eyes to focus on her, on the frown across her forehead that seemed to hold fear as well as concern and stabbed even more pain into my body on a path to my heart. "Jem, I don't even know what happened last night. I don't have a fucking clue what happened *to me*. I didn't do anything. I swear I didn—"

"Maybe you should save it for Nate," she said, not even giving me a chance to finish. "I'm pretty sure he'll need your explanation a whole lot more than I do. I suggest you start formulating one." She turned for the door, her shoulders sagging way lower than they should have been, and it hurt, really fucking hurt, that I might've been the reason why.

"Jem, wait."

Pausing, she glanced back, her eyes on the verge of glistening. "I don't know what you want me to say to you, Dan. I don't understand you anymore. I don't understand why you'd want to do something like this to yourself, or even how you got to this point ..." Drawing in a slow breath, she shook her head in an almost a defeatist gesture. "Just ... get showered ... or something. Clean yourself up."

She swung from the room, leaving my brain imprinted with the sadness her face had displayed.

I jolted from a freefall, the sensation a weightlessness that felt familiar yet alien all in one lump package. When my lids squeaked open, the butterflies in front of me had given up their vibrating gig to settle onto flowers that were equally as static. Despite my body curled into a foetal ball, a cold shiver rippled through me—probably from the chilled dampness that glued me to the bedsheets. Too weary to bounce up with any kind of vigour, I listened for sounds without bothering to turn my head, but scarcely anything seemed to be moving. Just the soft tones of what sounded like the TV carried through.

I lay there for minutes more. Wondering if Jem sat downstairs, purposely ignoring me lest I somehow disappoint her again. Needing to try and prevent that happening, I flicked back the duvet, ordered my legs out, and swayed to my feet.

The trawl to the bathroom seemed a little less traumatic than the earlier ones, despite the ache in every muscle with each step I took. Thankfully, the sun seemed to have moved over a little, too, lending some shadow where before there had only been light.

I flicked on the shower, not bothering to wait for it to warm before letting myself in. At the first hit of cool water, I grunted, my body planking as my muscles tensed, and I braced my hands against the glass and pushed my back into the spray, staying that way until the water had heated enough for my muscles to loosen and pump back to life.

Some kind of manky crust coated my hair when I shampooed it. Stubbly growth roughened my jaw—as well as more foul-smelling gunk I scrubbed myself clean of. Spatters of the crust dotted my chest and neck, too, and I worked my way southward with the loofah sponge, all the way down to my dirt-clinging toenails. No wonder Jem hadn't been impressed with me. If I felt that shitty to the touch, hell knew what I must've looked like.

After stepping from the shower, I dragged a towel over my shoulders, wrapped a second about my waist, and plodded to the sink. Toothbrushes for all of us got stored in the cabinet, and I grabbed my own, coated it in paste, and wiped a hand over the mirror, almost recoiling at the fucking horrendous mess staring back.

Redness veined my eyes—rimmed them, too. Dirty whiteness gave a dead pallor to my skin and seemed to accentuate the bloomed splotches of muddy grey beneath each eye that made my sockets seem sunk and desolate. The more I stared, the more I frowned, until I rammed my toothbrush into my mush and focused on clearing out the funkiness that lingered in there, instead.

By the time I left the bathroom, I didn't look any better. Enough to make me want to duck around any mirrors in the house. Mooching in Ethan's room, I found an old pair of sweats and a T I knew he wouldn't mind me nicking, and once I'd pulled them on, I took a slow trek down the stairs to let Jem know I was alive.

Just about, anyway.

In the hallway, I glanced toward the open door of the kitchen. No sounds came from that way. No shadows moved about. The living room door stood ajar, through which the TV sounds seeped out, and I nudged it open, pushed my way in there.

On the sofa opposite the screen, Brook sat with one foot tucked up beneath her, an ice cream tub in one hand and a dessertspoon in the other. She glanced over at my entrance, her expression tightening for a beat before smoothing. "Nice to see you up."

Inhaling, I considered my options. "Doesn't feel so good to *be* up," I finally said.

"No wonder." She turned back to the TV, her shoulders hunching slightly. "Beth and Jem went to take lunch for the others—they've taken Lia with them."

"And you got left babysitting me." I tucked my hands into the sweatpants pockets and leaned against the door—mostly because my swirling head needed some kind of support. "What'd you do to deserve that?"

She laughed. The sound was low and throaty—a nice sound, when not aimed at Kyle and filled with promises I didn't want to be privy to. "I'm watching *Mary Poppins*. I always loved this when I was young." She turned back to me, waved her spoon toward the empty seat beside her. "You should join me, seeing as you're up."

Although my muscles had tensed to bolt the second I saw her, I sauntered round and sank down on her other side, my head dropping back against the plush cushions behind it. On the screen, a bunch of excitable chimney sweeps convened on a rooftop, but my gaze cut to the cat.

Still slightly hunched over the ice cream tub she held, she fidgeted atop the leg she had wedged beneath her. Her long dark hair spilled so low down her back, it pooled on the cushion behind her, drawing my gaze to the small waist it covered. The yoga pants she wore fit snug over her hips, hung low on her back, dipping down deep enough to expose a pair of dimples each side of her spine between the tumbling strands. With her sitting there, all slender curves and sleek hair and exotic features, it was easy to see why she attracted Kyle.

So long as I didn't breathe in.

Like she sensed my stare, she twisted, eyes as gold as an Eastern sun seeming to sum me up in a split second. "Ice cream?" she asked, tipping the tub toward me. "It has marshmallow in it."

I breathed out a laugh. "I'm not sure that'd be a wise move."

She smiled, the gesture warming her eyes with a coppery shimmer as she dug the spoon back into the pot. No matter what else I thought of her, I couldn't deny she had the most amazing fucking eyes. "It is probably best I don't offer to fix you something different to eat, either," she said, those eyes lifting back up again. "I wouldn't want to be the one responsible for making you sick again."

"No one would hold you responsible." I glanced back to the TV as Dick Van Dyke raced around the rooftop while singing with his chimney sweep pals, and I heaved out a sigh. "They'd just find a way to pin the blame on me."

"I'm sorry you're sick."

"Why?" I glanced back to her, my frown folding back in. "You didn't make me sick."

She dipped her eyes. "I just meant, I'm sorry that you have to go through this. I'm sorry ... for you."

"Maybe you should just save your pity for someone who actually deserves it," I said. "I already do a decent enough job of feeling sorry for myself." I shuffled deeper into the sofa cushions, but just caught the dullness moving back into her eyes as she turned away. "Shit," I muttered, rubbing at a dull ache that seemed to be plaguing my head. "That came out crappier than I meant it to."

She nodded but didn't turn back. "Apology accepted," she said.

***

When my eyes flickered open yet again, my gaze landed on a gorilla blessedly blocking out the light from the living room window.

"Good. You're awake."

Blinking hard brought Nate into clearer view. Legs wide apart. Arms folded tightly over his chest and only seeming to make him even more imposing than he already could be.

"You can either get to your own feet and follow me into the kitchen. Or I will carry you into the kitchen. How's it going to be, Dan?"

I frowned as the lines of his face finally sank in. The serious pissed off cut of his features. The cool glint to his eyes.

"Move it, Danny. It's time to talk." Like a furious inferno, he stormed from the room, leaving me to stare after him and wonder why the hell everyone seemed so fricking mad with me.

As my brain caught up and accepted his order, I heaved my body upright. Nate had already taken his usual seat at the head of the table when I stepped into the kitchen. The fact nobody else lingered in there told me plenty. The others had to be home, and that they kept the noise levels down to the point I could scarcely hear anything from them warned me they didn't want to be anywhere near what I had coming. I almost wondered how far I'd get if I made a break for it, but sucking it up, I squared my shoulders and stepped toward my spot on the far side of the table. Before I could reach it, though, the seat next to Nate scraped outward and he pointed to that one.

Definitely no escape.

My legs folded as I sank into the designated chair, and through some inner will power, I drew my gaze to his. "What's the problem?"

His cool blue eyes didn't hold as much frostiness as I'd expected when he said, "Talk to me."

"I don't know what you want me to say." I rubbed a palm over my thigh, a distraction he'd likely see right through.

"You're all acting like I've torn the world apart, and I'm wondering what I missed."

"How are you feeling today, Dan?"

"Like hell."

"And you have no idea why?" When I shook my head, he heaved a sigh, bringing his forearm to rest atop the table as he leaned in toward me. "So, what *do* you remember about last night?"

My brow scrunched with the effort of merely thinking, and as I went to shrug my ignorance, a warning in Nate's eyes had me backtracking. "I remember going to a party," I admitted.

"Why?"

I wanted to ask *why what?* but I got the impression I didn't get to ask the questions, and my frown cut so deep it felt like my skin had been stretched like blown gum.

Nate rubbed a finger across his temple like my dumbness caused him a headache. "Why did you go to a party," he said slowly, "when you knew we'd be hunting for the full moon?"

"I'd made a promise." His mouth tightened, so I added, "I promised to help someone out—that's all it was. I knew I'd be home in time for the hunt. I didn't see what the problem was."

"Except, the only reason you were here for the hunt was because Ethan and Kyle dragged your messed up hide home and deposited you in the forest," he said, his voice bordering on a growl. "You shouldn't even have been in the forest last night, with the state you were in, but I wasn't about to let you near the females, so you left us no choice. You," he said, poking a finger toward me, "cancelled out the entire hunt, because you couldn't be left alone."

I swallowed hard. I really wanted to avert my eyes but didn't dare with the way his challenged me against doing so. "I don't remember that," I said.

"So, again, Daniel, what exactly *do* you remember about last night? What happened at that party to change your plans?"

I went back to rubbing my thigh to rid my palm of the dampness gathering there. "I was just popping in to see a friend, and then I was coming straight home," I repeated. "I remember getting there. I remember that." I could remember the other folk in the garden. The pool. The people. People everywhere. But no Liv. I remembered looking for Liv. After that ... "I wasn't there long. Next thing I know, I woke up in the forest and everything really hurt."

Nate's gaze never once wavered, even as he asked, "The friend you went to help out—she the same friend who was with you when your brother got there?"

I went to shake my head, but stopped when I realised I couldn't answer what I had no fucking clue about.

"Who is this girl to you, Daniel?"

"I told you," I said, my skin yanking tight again. "She's a friend."

"A friend you were willing to defer the pack hunt for?"

Confusion twisted my brain into a knotted mess with no ends to unravel. "Nate, I don't understand how any of these questions even add up to each other."

"You did drugs last night."

I knew, from the way his stare intensified, he was watching for my reaction, but my head had already started shaking before he'd finished speaking. As soon as it registered the word *drugs*.

Nate nodded. "The girl who was with you when Kyle and Ethan got there told them. She told them you'd eaten something that had drugs in, and she'd tried to stop you, but you wouldn't listen."

My head shook some more.

"She spoke to Kyle on *your* phone. She spoke to Kyle and told him you were dying. That's what she thought, Daniel. She thought you were going into cardiac arrest.

112

Said something weird was happening to you. Do you know what she was seeing?"

Teeth gritted, I jerked my head side to side some more.

"You were *changing* in front of her."

Shit, shit, shit, shit. My heartbeats unaligned, banging against my sternum in an erratic tune. That couldn't be good. Definitely not for me. Maybe not for her, too, if Nate decided she'd seen something she shouldn't have.

"Luckily for you, Kyle convinced her he knew exactly what was wrong with you and knew how to fix it. Luckily *for you*, because she was on the verge of calling an ambulance." His stare hardened as ire crept in. "An *ambulance*, Danny. Do you understand what I'm saying? What that means?" He didn't bother waiting for my response. "If Kyle hadn't talked her down, hospital is exactly where you'd be now. Tell me. How would you have convinced them not to take your blood when you couldn't even talk?"

My head shook. Maybe it hadn't stopped. Maybe it'd been shaking the entire time he'd been hitting me with shit I didn't remember yet somehow knew to be true.

"Testing your blood would have been the first step they'd have taken, to see what you'd got in your system. They wouldn't have waited for you to wake up—not in that situation. They wouldn't have asked you for permission. They'd have just done it."

I didn't seem able to respond beyond that perpetual shake of my head—a shake my entire body seemed to be joining in on. Because I didn't have any answers. I didn't know what he wanted me to say. I didn't know what the hell I was supposed to do.

Nate curled a hand around my nape and tugged me closer. "Tell me, Danny. What would you have done then?"

I tried swallowing again, but my saliva had taken a hike. "I don't know," I forced out.

"How would you have explained away what they'd have found?"

"I don't know," I mumbled again.

Letting loose a low growl, he slackened his hold. "What the hell am I supposed to do with you?"

"I don't know." I didn't know. I didn't even know what *I* was supposed to do with me. How could I, when I barely even knew what I wanted anymore, beyond a little peace and quiet that seemed way out of reach?

He rubbed at his face, his eyes closing. When his lids lifted, something akin to resignation moved in. "You're under house arrest."

My shoulders tensed. My brow tensed. Every fricking part of me tensed. How could I fix my shit if I couldn't even leave the house? "What about work?" I tried.

"Work can be covered."

"But ..." I didn't want to bring her up in case it led to more questions, but I didn't really have a choice because it couldn't be ignored. "What about Liv?"

"That's her name?" I hadn't meant to share. Not when I didn't know his intentions. As if taking my quiet as assent, he asked, "Who is she to you, Daniel?"

"I told you, Nate. She's just a friend." Tamping down the urge to bolt from his scrutiny, I added, "But she still needs to be spoken to. Still needs things explaining—smoothing over."

He gave a slow nod. "I agree. Do you have a number for her?"

I gave a reluctant nod.

"Good. You can call her, and make this mess of yours all right."

While I'd have preferred free range to get to my arse out of there and deal with my own mess in my own damn way, I'd take the offer, because calling her would be better than letting it hang. Nodding, I pushed to my feet. "I'll find my phone and make the call."

"I have your phone," he said, stalling me. "And you can make the call now." He nodded to my empty chair. "Here."

Great. The offer suddenly didn't seem so generous anymore, but the stubborn set of Nate's jaw practically daring me to argue had me planting my rear back down. I waited as he leaned to the side and worked his fingers into his pocket. They emerged holding my phone, and I took it when he held it out to me, quickly unlocking the screen. A little envelope sat at the top left, a tiny number '12' hovering over it. Twelve messages. In the bottom left? Fifteen missed calls. I glanced up at Nate. "These notifications from you?"

"Not all of them, no."

Liv, then. Had to be. Deciding to save those to view later, *alone*, I swiped through the device in search of her number, and as the ringtone twanged out of the speaker, I sank back in my chair.

It only rang four times before, "*Finally*!" blasted down my ear. "For God's sake, Danny, I've been going frigging *insane* here worrying myself sick over you. Have you never heard of, like, *calling* someone and letting them know you're okay, you bloody idiot?"

Ignoring Nate's drilling gaze, I blew out a breath. "You planning to let me speak at all?" When she didn't argue, I glanced away from Nate like that'd give me more privacy. Somehow. "Listen, I don't have long to talk. I just wanted to call and let you know I'm recovering, before I get shepherded back off to bed."

"Where are you, in the hospital? Do you need me to bring you anything?"

Leaning my head back, I closed my eyes, almost wishing that I *was* in the hospital and could tell her yes. *Yes*, I did need her to bring me something, just so I could … could what?

Not that it'd ever have happened. I'd have to be 'normal' for that.

My chest rose high with the sigh I let slip. "I'm at home." Give or take five miles, anyway. "My family's been watching me. Everything's fine." Swallowing, I added, "Thanks, though." Quiet came through for a few seconds, and I wondered if she expected me to say anything more. I couldn't, though. Not with Nate breathing down my neck like a dragon looking for marshmallows to roast. "Listen, I really have to go."

More quiet, then, "Okay—but you still owe me a decent explanation. In case you were wondering. You can give it to me when you see me next. 'Kay?"

"You got it," I said, hoping I could follow through.

As I hung up from the call, Nate held out his hand, and I dropped the phone in his palm.

"That'll do." His grimness moved back in as he re-pocketed the mobile. "Okay, here's how it's going to be. You're not to leave this house. Not tonight. Not for work tomorrow. Not until you've convinced me you're ready to have your independence back." He pushed to his feet, his hand landing on my shoulder. "And just in case that's not clear, you don't leave here, Daniel, without *my* say-so. Understood?"

With little other choice, I nodded, and as he let go, I tracked his steps to the doorway, along the hall, his steady climb of the stairs.

Letting my head drop back, I shot some curses at the ceiling. *Shit, shit, shit, shit.*

Could my life *get* any more fucked up?

12

An entire evening around a table of staring participants, with a dinner my stomach had no desire to digest, sucked.

An entire night of tossing and turning, while my stomach groaned and gurgled and cramped and cried sucked, too.

So did an entire day of more staring, of overly-friendly inquiring into my wellbeing, of food being served me because *Thank goodness you have your appetite back.* That had to be a sign I was feeling better, right? And food helped. Food always helped. In Beth's book of rules, anyway.

I spent the whole next day yearning for freedom. Just a little freedom. Glancing toward the door and seriously fucking wishing I'd forced my dinner down me the night before, just to convince Nate I didn't feel as shit as we both knew I did.

Because by the time the pickup rumbled onto the driveway that evening, my head had taken a hike from all the mothering and hen pecking and suffocation, and my body had long since decided to climb the walls.

From my slumped spot on the sofa, I quit with speed-scanning the TV channels and tracked the opening and closing of the truck doors, the weighted clump of work boots around to the rear of the house.

Quiet conversation carried through from the kitchen. Nate's deep tones. Beth's only slightly lighter.

Footsteps tramped along the hallway before a dark head swung around the door and Sean's brows arched up. "Jem?"

"She's upstairs. Said it was time for Lia's massage, or something."

He nodded and ducked away, but his head reappeared within a beat. "How're you feeling?"

I half smiled—about all I could be bothered with. "I'm okay."

"Shower's mine," Ethan called as more heavy steps trampled the tiles, and Sean vanished from the doorway, leaving me alone again.

Relaxing back against the cushion I had wedged beneath my head, I waited for Nate's entry. I didn't have to wait long, less than a couple of minutes, before his whole bulk filled the gap at the end of the sofa.

"Feeling any better?" he asked, folding his arms beneath his chest.

Not wanting to appear too enthusiastic—he'd see right through that—I nodded and flicked through the channels some more.

"Good. I need to talk to you."

My gaze cut back to him, looking for signs I'd pissed him off again.

His lips twitched as he nodded toward the door. "Come on. I could use a drink, anyway."

I swung my legs round and bounced to my feet like all my shit was realigned and my life was fine and dandy. As I reached Nate, his hand cinched over my shoulder, and he pushed me forth, leading me ahead of him out to the hallway, left to the kitchen where Beth tinkered about with mugs in the corner, all the way to the same seat he'd made me take the night before.

Great.

Settling his weight into his own seat, he lifted his head, his scrutiny like spines needling into my brain. "You look better this evening," he said, his gaze flittering over my face.

"*Better*-better? Or just better than I looked last night?"

"Is there a difference?" he asked, his lips upping at one corner.

I shrugged before nodding slightly. "I'd say one hell of a difference."

His chuckle eked out, and he glanced up as Beth set a cup down next to him and second one beside me.

"I'll be in the living room," she said, her steps quiet across the tiles as she left us alone.

Nate went back to staring at me, studying me. Like he tried to take a measure for someone he already thought he knew.

"What did I do now?" I asked. Better to dive in and get it over with than wait to see what he wanted to pin on me next.

He slid a hand around his mug but didn't lift it. "Your dad plans to tell Kyle and Josh about Maghon over dinner tonight."

My brow tightened. "What about Maghon?"

"That they're back in touch and he's been meeting with her." His gaze skimmed side to side, like he needed to double check both my eyes for any signs of inner disturbance.

"He plan to tell them that I'm the reason they got back in touch?" I asked, frowning.

"Actually, I believe he's planning to keep that bit of information to himself." He finally lifted his cup and took a sip before setting it back down. "He thinks you've already got enough on your plate, without your brothers questioning your silence to them on this."

Resting my elbows on my knees, I nodded, studying my fingers as I linked them together. "More lies, then."

There were a few beats of quiet before Nate spoke again. "You know, your dad blames himself for what happened to you—for what you did. The mess you got into. He told me the two of you argued night before last, right before you stormed out to meet your friend. He said you'd argued over his involvement with Maghon."

"And what exactly is that involvement, Nate?" I picked at a rough bit of nail on my thumb. "What's even their deal?"

"I don't know."

My frown deepened. "Don't know because you're misunderstanding? Or don't know because he hasn't been telling you shit, either?"

He heaved in a long breath and let it out slowly. "I don't know because I don't think even Connor, himself, knows."

I jerked my gaze up to meet his, and Nate's all-knowing smile snuck in, despite him claiming to be clueless.

"I can tell you what I think, if that will help," he said, and I nodded. "I think Connor and May have finally found an opportunity to do right by your mother and sort out their issues. And that it's an opportunity they're both now in a place, mentally and emotionally, to take. That's what I think."

I let his words settle into my mind, let myself mull them over. Had Dad been carrying guilt all the years since he lost Mum? Was that it? Why the hell wouldn't he have shared that?

"Whether or not that's all there is," Nate continued, "I don't know, and I guess I won't know unless your Dad enlightens me. However, I'm solid in my self-assurance that, once Connor's figured things out for himself, he'll come and talk to me. He'll let me know."

I frowned. "And us? Me, Josh? Kyle? Do we get to know?" Would Dad come talk to us? He'd definitely flunked in that department so far.

He gave a slow nod. "Your dad's never lied to you before. Not really. I doubt he'll start now."

I wished I could be so sure.

Beth had rustled up a fast dinner of steak and chips with battered onion rings and a spicy pepper sauce. Thanks to the massage Jem'd given her, Lia seemed to be snoozing, leaving the adults to eat undisturbed—a trial ritual she and Sean had started a few days before. Seemed weird, though, seeing the two of them digging into their meals without the little one getting passed back and forth.

Finishing up chewing on a chunk of sauce-coated steak, I glanced past Ethan beside me, shovelling in food like he hadn't eaten in months, and nodded to Beth. "This is great. Thanks, Beth."

"You're welcome," she said, and though her smile was subtle, I knew she loved the praise.

Digging my fork into meat, I began sawing again, stalling when buzzing carried across from the sideboard. My gaze sliced over to the culprit—my mobile.

The others continued eating like they hadn't even noticed, except the slight stiffening of their shoulders told me they had.

Playing along, I turned back to my plate and shoved in another mouthful once I'd broke some steak free.

Five minutes later, the phone buzzed again.

I glanced around at the others. Just like before, they all seemed pretty intent on their meals.

I didn't buy it—not for a minute. Even so, I ran my fork across my plate in search of missed morsels before bringing it up to my lips and sucking it clean.

As though satisfied everyone had finished, Beth pushed away from the table and began collecting up plates. I relaxed back in my seat, my belly feeling swollen after downing my first complete meal in a couple of days.

The chair beside me screeched over the tiles, and Ethan headed across to where Beth rinsed the dishes in the sink and kissed her cheek. "Thanks for dinner. I'm heading out to Shelley's,"

He turned for the hallway without awaiting permission, and I couldn't help but envy his lack of opposition.

"Shower time," Sean said, climbing to his feet, also, and as he headed out, Jem followed in his shadow, her hand wrapped around the base of his shirt.

Smiling almost to herself, Beth poured a dose of liquid into the sink. Smiling like she held the best position in the world. Maybe she did, in her eyes. Who was I to judge that?

Over on the sideboard, my mobile buzzed again.

That time, Nate's head twisted toward it, his eyes narrowing as his frown moved in.

"It been doing that much?" I asked him.

"On and off all damned day," he said.

"Is it Liv?"

On a heavy sigh, he nodded and reached for the mobile. Surprising me, he tossed it my way. "She's still worried about you."

Swiping my thumb over the screen showed the multiple notifications blocking up the taskbar. I didn't bother going through those, but clicked straight through to my messages and opened the feed of the ones I knew had to be from Liv.

HOW ARE U DOING TODAY?

FYI, U SOUNDED LIKE POO ON THE PHONE LAST NIGHT. CAN U AT LEAST CALL & LET ME KNOW U'RE FEELING A LITTLE BETTER.

DON'T BE A DICK, DANNY!!!! QUIT IGNORING MY TEXTS!!!!!

Scrolling through showed even more.

I turned to Nate, trying to gauge his mood and hoping it didn't fall in the bracket of shitty. "She's not going to give," I told him. "Not until she's seen for herself."

As his gaze sliced to the side, he muttered something beneath his breath that resembled a curse. After seconds of my watching, waiting, hoping, he finally glanced back. "I'll have to think on this."

It took me a whole seventy-two minutes, and even a little pleading, to get Nate to waver.

I even followed him into the living room and disturbed his evening news, leaning forward to block the TV as I tried, "At least let me try and set this straight so we can all move forward."

Nate sighed and rubbed a hand down his face. When he glanced back at me, his eyes held a warning despite the dip of his chin. "Okay, you can go." I went to nod my thanks, but he cut in with, "But I want you back in an hour."

Shoulders stiffening, I flung a hand out. "Come on, Nate. It's a thirty minute ride *each way*."

"Ninety minutes, then," he said after seconds of drilling me with his stare, and my tension uncoiled a little. "And if she brings up last night, you better convince her she didn't see what she did."

"So, what *do* I tell her?"

Setting his paper aside, he gave me his full focus. "You tell her it was a seizure. You didn't know what you were taking—"

"I *didn't know* I was taking *anything*."

"You didn't know what you were *doing*, then. And you had an allergic reaction that resulted in a seizure. And you're fine now." He studied me for a half-beat. "Do you think you can manage that, Danny? Or do I have to send an escort to make sure you play your part?

I nodded. "I can manage that."

"Good." He glanced toward the clock. "Be home by ten." That gave me almost two hours. "Don't let me down."

13

I didn't care that rain slashed down and pelted my visor. I didn't care that wind snuck through my jeans and froze my thighs. Because it felt like an eternity since I'd had the vibrations of liberation buzzing up my body.

After hauling my bike down from the pickup and checking it over, I'd only found a couple of dinks where it'd rested and bumped against the truck bed's sides. Nothing that couldn't be polished over. Nothing that couldn't be fixed. So, after a quick assurance that it'd start just fine, I'd climbed aboard and got my arse on the road.

My adrenaline raced from the rush of parting air as it granted access en route to The Hang & Hide. The scenery whizzed by so fast there could've been a five-headed octopus plodding along for all I gave a shit. If not for my gritting my teeth in concentration at each dip, each curve, I might've let loose a big, fat *Yahoo!*.

The car park seemed to be heaving way more than usual when I arrived. Cars filled up over half of the slots—though, even that didn't label the place as kicking. After parking up farther over than my regular spot, I slid off my helmet and headed for the entrance.

The din of inside hit me before I'd even opened the door. Within, a mass of college-aged lads clogged up the pool table. Amidst them there seemed to be a doubles match going on.

Per what'd become my usual routine, I scanned the bar, where Joe poured drinks with his acquired enthusiasm, not bothering to make eye contact with the five or so guys hanging over the counter and chatting away. My gaze cut to the bathroom corridor, back over the pool playing fiasco, to the booths on the right. Some of those who had interest in the pool match took up the first couple, where they kneeled on the benches and watched over the divider.

In one of those booths, Blondie sat like she'd been demoted from her favoured barstool. Unusually, though, she didn't sit alone, but with a guy whose thigh pressed against hers, whose arm hugged her shoulders and held her snug at his side as he leaned in, his lips moving close to her ear.

Scanning over them, I swung my gaze even farther right. To the first booth aside the entrance, and the head of red brush partially concealed by something I didn't want, nor expected, to see there.

Sitting next to Liv, some guy built like a rugby tackler relaxed back against the booth's rear, his right foot propped up on his knee and a paper in his hand—a paper I instinctively knew belonged to Liv. His head tipped in Liv's direction, and his lips formed sounds that my ears didn't seem able to detect, thanks to a bunch of static fuzzing up my hearing.

In response, Liv smiled. He probably thought she liked him, liked that he'd disturbed her, liked that he'd shown an interest. With the tiny scrunches of tension at the side of each eye revealing her true feelings, though, I didn't believe that smile for a second.

Not bothering to do the bar run first, I nudged stools aside with my toes and waded through to the bench seat opposite them.

Liv spotted me first, something akin to relief lightening her features as her shoulders dropped by a fraction of an inch.

Only when I bumped a stool against the guy's knee did he glance up. Irritation flashed in his eyes despite the smile he gave, but I ignored him. Just kept my gaze on Liv as I set my helmet down in my claimed seat. "Everything okay?"

She nodded. A little too hard. "Sure."

"You need a drink?" I asked.

She shook her head. Again, a little too hard.

Shunning my jacket, I draped it over my helmet, and dropping my butt onto the bench opposite the dude, I leaned forward, propped my elbows on my knees, and gave him my best *get the fuck out of here* stare.

The guy stared right back. Did a decent job of it, too, but it only took a few beats for the harsh lines of his forehead to ease up, like some kind of understanding had drawn in, and he glanced to Liv, back to me, his one eyebrow arching in an unasked question.

With a single dip of my head, I answered him. *No, she isn't as available as you thought. Yes, I really fucking want you to fuck off.*

Like he'd planned to do so all along, the guy slid the paper he held back onto the table and, without saying another word, pushed up and left us alone.

I tracked him all the way over to those playing pool before I turned to Liv. "What was that all about? He being a dick?"

"Not really." She shrugged. "I think he just wanted to get into my knickers and he thought showing an interest in my Uni work might help him achieve that."

"Did I just ruin that chance for you?" I asked, my scowl practically folding my forehead.

Her laugh burst from her. "No, Danny."

I watched her a moment, as she took the paper he'd deserted and shuffled it back in line with the others on the table, as she positioned her pencil alongside them like she needed the order despite the chaos around her. "If I ask about your Uni work and what you're studying ..." I waited until her gaze rose again. "... will you assume I'm trying to get into your knickers, too?"

"You're asking now? After six weeks?" At my unwavering stare, she rolled her eyes. "Fine. I'm studying teaching."

"To become a teacher?"

"No. To become an oilrig driller," she said, staring right at me.

My lips quivered before I stemmed the smile. "You like teaching?"

"Yes."

I grunted. Didn't seem much else to say on the matter.

"Your grunt speaks volumes," she muttered.

I leaned forward a little. "Liv, it doesn't matter to me what you're studying. Could be flame throwing, or scuba diving, for all I care. You don't need a degree for me to like you. You had my attention the moment you let me take a seat by you and then proceeded to act like I wasn't there."

She dipped her face, but not before I caught the light flush to her cheeks. Giving a small shake of her head, she dunked a hand into her bag and emerged with an eraser, which she rubbed over the top sheet of her work. She seemed to do it for longer than necessary before she finally lifted her gaze back to me. "Are we even going to talk about Tuesday, or do you plan to ignore it?"

Yeah, that. I swallowed. "Is ignoring it an option?"

"No," she said, her stare unwavering.

Just as I'd figured. "Do you want a drink now?"

"Avoiding the subject isn't an option, either."

"I'm not avoiding it," I said, pushing to my feet. "I just need a drink."

The rush at the bar had died down to a couple, and I wormed my shoulders past them and leaned on the top. Joe skulked over and stood in front of me, looking pissed off that I'd come to hound him, and though my mouth opened to order the usual, I paused. Nate might've let me out, but if I went back smelling of booze, it'd likely be my last external or un-shadowed trip of the year. With my gaze glued to what I really wanted to order, I asked for two cokes, paid, and carried them back to the table under the scrutiny of Liv.

Handing her a glass, I took a sip from my own, but instead of sinking back down on the far side of the booth, I nudged her bag aside and took the spot next to Liv.

From the next section over, Blondie sent me a smile. She could send me as many as she liked. I didn't know how else to let her know I wasn't interested.

Resting my elbow atop the booth's rear blocked her out some, and I twisted to face Liv more and gripped hold of her thigh, ignoring her, "Hey!" as I swung her butt round until she faced me, too.

"I'm sorry about the party." I went to duck closer to Liv, but stopped when she looked about to recoil. "I'm sorry I fucked up."

Her gaze dropped to my lips as I spoke, rising back up to my eyes as she asked, "Why did you?"

My lips curved a little. "Because fucking up's my speciality lately."

She puffed out a breath heavy with exasperation. "Why'd you eat the cakes, Danny?"

"Ah, that." I paused a sec, studying the way her lenses enlarged already stunning eyes, the way the hint of my reflection wrecked my view—until the impatient jerk of her head snapped me back. "Because I'm an idiot who didn't know what the cakes were."

She let out a snort filled with a whole lot of *Yeah, right*.

I gripped her chin and held her steady as I lowered my gaze to hers. "I'm being serious, Liv. I didn't know."

Her tongue snaked out and wetted her lips—about the only part of her that seemed to be moving. "Okay," she said quietly.

"I'm sorry I did a shit job of acting at boyfriend material," I said, still holding onto her, mostly because I liked the softness of her skin against the rough pads of my fingers. "I know you wanted to convince your friends and that dickhead of an ex—"

"He didn't even show up," she said.

A small laugh left me before I could stop it. "So, it was all for nothing, then?"

"Not exactly." A smile played on her lips. "You actually did a great job of convincing anyone who *was* at the party. And by nine the next morning …. Trust me, he'd heard."

My eyes narrowed. "Heard what, exactly?"

She tugged her chin from my hold and lowered her eyes a little, though her smile remained. "About my big, tough boyfriend who's crazy mad about me."

My brow folded beneath the lost effort to stay in the loop. "Guess I *must* have done a good job playing the part, then." I really wanted her to lift her face again, because I couldn't get a handle on her shifting mood, and something told me I was missing out on something important.

Like she'd read my mind, her gaze peered up until it met mine. "You don't remember?"

Remember what? Whatever it was, the blush creeping back over her cheeks told me it was something my brain really should've held onto. I shook my head, wishing that could swirl what I couldn't recall back into there. "I really don't."

Her gaze dropped again as she muttered, "Typical." I got the impression she hadn't meant for me to hear, but enhanced hearing, and all, left little chance of that. "I think we'll leave it like that." A smile creased the corners of her lips when she looked back. "For now."

I reached out a finger to trace those creases, but she caught hold of my hand before I could touch.

"So, what did the doctors say?"

The switch in convo threw me for a beat, but I recovered before my brain could send the order to ask *what?*. "That I'm good and healthy," I told her.

"Didn't look that way to me at the party."

I peered down at where she'd placed my hand on the small spot of bench between our legs, her finger still wrapped around it like she didn't trust it to stay put. "I'm sorry I put you through that." I curved my fingers until they folded over hers. "I'm sorry I worried you."

"Worried is an understatement."

Something in her tone had me looking back up at her, at the darkening concern shifting the hue of her eyes. "It scared me, too," I admitted for the first time. "If I'd have known what was in the cakes, if I'd have known how my body would react to them, I'd never have eaten them. Trust me on that."

"Your brother said it was a seizure."

I nodded.

"Danny, it was *horrible*."

Horrible. Right. I knew changing wasn't exactly a pretty activity, and certainly nothing for spectators to eat popcorn over, but hearing it so bluntly put definitely stung some.

"I was scared to death for you." The shaky breath she let out slammed my own feelings to the kerb.

"I'm sorry. Truly. Sorry about every fucking bit of it. But I'm okay now. Look." Gripping her hand, I brought it up to my face and patted it against there. "I'm fine." I tapped her palm over my shoulders, my chest. "Just fine."

She tugged her hand free, but she laughed. "You're such an idiot."

I shrugged. "Another speciality of mine."

She nodded like she agreed. She'd be right to. The smile slipped from her a little as she twisted away and reached for her papers.

"Something I said?" I asked.

"I just have an early start tomorrow." She scooped her papers up and slipped them into her bag, her gaze full of sincerity as it sought mine. "Honestly. I have some tests on in the morning. I always need an early night before those."

I probably should've gone back to my own bench, given her the room she needed to pack up. Selfish shit I could be, though, I just stayed there in her way, more than happy to stall her, even if only for a minute or two.

"You coming in again this week?" she asked.

130

I shrugged. I couldn't exactly tell her that my pass to come out and play lay in the hands of my dad and my Alpha. That'd just make me sound like an even weirder dick than she probably already labelled me as. "I hope to," I said instead.

Gripping her jacket in one hand, she took the handle of her bag with the other and stared at me like she wanted me to shift.

I flipped my knee aside, helping her out. Her knuckles still skimmed the inside of my thigh, though. Her shin still bumped up against mine. I turned away, like not watching her would take away the sudden urge to have more of her touching me, and my gaze connected with Blondie's. Tearing it away, I scanned farther round the room, and my eyes narrowed on the kid who'd been sat with Liv when I arrived.

Mostly on the way he seemed to be setting the pool cue aside as his sights zoned in on where I knew Liv readied to leave next to me.

Swinging back, I snapped my fingers around Liv's wrist, waiting for her to glance down before I told her, "I'm walking you home."

A slight crease marred her brow. "You don't have to do that."

"I'm not doing it because I have to." I pushed to my feet and reached for my gear off the far bench. "I'm doing it because it's what I want."

"What about what I want?" she asked, but she smiled as she said it.

"So long as it's the same as what I want, we're all good." I nudged her toward the door. Luckily, she didn't argue, and after sending a warning glare over my shoulder at the interested dude to back the fuck off, I followed her out into the cool, damp air.

"This way," I said, taking her arm and guiding her toward my bike.

"Um ... I thought you said *walk* me home. I am *not* going on that thing."

"Calm down, Red. I just need to lock my helmet up so I don't have to lug it around with me."

It took only a minute to secure it, but the rain still found me in that time and soaked into the shoulders of my T. I slid my leather over the damp patches, glad Liv'd already pulled her lightweight jacket on when I turned to her and held out my arm. "Ready?"

"Jerk." She pushed my arm away and started walking.

"I was being serious," I said, my long strides taking me to her side in less than a blink.

She sighed, the sound cutting through the dull evening, but a moment later, her hand slipped over the crook of my arm. "Happy now?" she muttered.

I nodded, resisting the urge to grin. "Getting there."

For minutes, we walked without speaking. Rain spattered a quiet beat against the pavement and the shoulders of my coat. Our feet pounded out a wet timpani, neither of our steps matching but somehow still managing to create a rhythm all the same. Beneath those, our breaths came shallow and steady, creating small clouds before our faces and leading the way.

"It's not far," she said, breaking into the quiet. "About fifteen minutes."

"Fifteen minutes can pass like a blink when you're content."

"Or it can drag like a decade when you'd rather be somewhere else."

I barked out a laugh and glanced down to her. "Which one applies to you?"

Her lips squidged to the side before she smiled like she couldn't contain it any longer. "I'll have to let you know."

"I wonder if it'll ever change between us," I said, following the line of the pavement into the next road as she led us around it. "If you'll ever reach a point where you no longer call me names and hit me with insults."

A few beats of splashed footsteps passed before she peered up at me. "I hope not," she said.

Around fifteen minutes later, we turned into a cul-de-sac lined with blond brick houses and small kempt gardens that met the pavement.

Liv's steps slowed as we neared the arc of properties at the far end. "This is me," she said, her shoulders bunching up.

I studied the house behind her. The light shining behind the curtains in the downstairs window, the glass polished to a high shine in the porch sheltering the front door. An equally gleaming silver Audi sat on the driveway in front of the garage, lit up by a security light our approach triggered. "Nice house," I said, turning back to her.

She nodded, but with little substance to the action, and reaching out a hand, she grabbed the cuff of my sleeve. "Thanks for walking me."

"Anytime," I said.

When she didn't say anything else, I mentally ordered myself to leave. To make the first move. Take the first step away.

Except my body didn't obey, and she didn't move, and my eyes didn't look away from the way hers peered through lenses affected by the lamp's glow. I could've stood there for hours, just staring, just appreciating, just wondering *what if*—if I didn't have a stupid curfew I'd promised to adhere to.

"I need to get going," I said, and before I could change my mind, I ducked in close and planted a light kiss on her cheek.

She froze beneath my lips. I froze, too, though mostly because the scent seeping from her pores smelled like sweet honeysuckle and suddenly seemed so familiar and right, my brain scrambled to remember why.

"Danny, are you sniffing me?" she said, her voice barely more than a whisper.

I considered lying, but instead said, "Maybe."

133

"Why?" she asked, equally as quiet.

My nostrils brushed her jaw, and my lids lowered at the sweet, sweet body odour clinging there, too. "Because you smell fucking amazing," I murmured.

Risking pissing her off, I nestled in closer until I found the dip below her ear. Encouraged when she didn't move, I drifted a little higher along her hairline, where the clinging raindrops seemed to enhance her scent, smiling to myself when her head tipped to the side. "Makes me want to—"

"Olivia?"

My entire body stiffened at the intruding female voice. "Do you know this person?" I asked, my lips brushing her skin.

"It's my mum." Her tone held a smile.

Bringing my lips a little higher, I whispered, "Is her timing always this bad?"

"It's a practiced art form of hers," she said against my ear, sending heat on a bullet-dive for my crotch.

I chuckled and pulled away until I caught a fresh glimpse of those smoky blues of hers. "See you tomorrow?" I only hoped I could get out. Because I really wanted to find out if she'd let me continue where I'd just left off.

She nodded with her chin dipped, an almost shy response.

I took a couple of steps backward, barely able to tear my gaze from her, but, for some reason, catching on her mother when I finally did.

A little like Liv, but with way less hair, the female stood backlit in her doorway like something exiting an alien spacecraft, but I could still see the twisted expression of disapproval in her features.

I probably should've said hello. Or maybe even something to reassure her—though, of what, I didn't know. *Hey, no worries, Mrs F. I'd have taken good care of your daughter. Probably have shown her the time of her life.*

Clamping my big mouth shut before I could ruin the situation, I dug my hands deep into my pockets and headed off back the way I'd come.

14

By the time I neared The Hang & Hide, moisture trickled over my jacket and dripped from my hair. With the scenery switching from homes, to wild brush and timber used as dumping grounds, I only had two more streets to reach the bar.

Trees created long shadows across the pavements, despite the moon hiding behind clouds. Face lowered against the weather, I traced their outlines with my eyes, my own shadow abstracting them one after another. Headlights cut through the deepening dark, and I lifted my gaze long enough to follow as the car swept past me, its tyres sending up a spray of soiled moisture from the road to hit my jeans.

Any other day, I'd have grumbled out a promise of unintended retribution, but I could only think about Liv. About Liv under the lamplight. Liv just standing there when I kissed her cheek. Not objecting when I'd moved closer. Not even muttering a complaint.

I smiled at the memory. She hadn't minded. Gave me hope that I could try it again.

Raised voices drifted out on the air, and my head tilted to catch the sounds. As I rounded the final corner, The Double-H came into view, as well as two figures in the shadows of the car park who seemed to be in some kind of personal tussle.

Not my fight, I told myself, heading for my bike. I didn't know the time, but I knew I didn't have any spare for sorting out other people's issues if I wanted to be back by the hour Nate had ordered.

Though, at a high pitched, "*No!*" my head snapped up and round, and I realised who half of the argument was.

Blondie tugged back a hand the guy she'd been sat with yanked toward him. "Let me go!"

"You don't get to lead me on and then tell me to get lost afterward." Spinning away, he hauled her with him, her heels buckling under her tripping feet.

My own feet started moving before I could stop them. "Hey!"

Blondie twisted round, her eyes wide as they found me. "Help me."

The guy jerked her away another step, and her head seemed to jar on her shoulders.

I picked up my stride. "Hey, you should let her go." Reaching them, I grabbed hold of her arm he tugged, and gripping his shoulder, I spun him round until he had me in his sights.

"Maybe you should stay out of it," he barked, shoving me back a step.

Bracing my foot against the tarmac, I pushed back against him, and as my chest bumped his, his hold loosened on the female. Good. I had his full attention.

"This is not your problem, buddy." His dark eyes levelled with mine, placing him in pretty much the same height bracket as myself. His size didn't worry me, though. Despite the strength I'd felt in his shove, I knew I'd still outmatch him with fucking bells on. "Why don't you turn your pretty boy face around and walk the hell away?"

I glanced to the side. Blondie stood with her arms wrapped around herself, her hands brushing up to her shoulders like she needed to fight off the cold. "You want me to leave?"

She jerked her head side to side, backing off a few steps as though scared of the backlash from the admittance.

I turned back to the dickhead. "Sorry, but the lady wants me to stay. Seems the only person not welcome here is you."

His entire face twisted, his eyes darkening until they resembled pitch. "Fuck you!"

His breath hit my face, a combination of lager and the kind of staleness that came from not brushing enough, but I ignored it and smiled. "It's a good offer. But I like my females a little shorter."

A growl tore from him as he stepped back, and his fist swung toward me, but I ducked before he could hit. Thrusting back up, I knocked his arm aside and dug my fingers into his throat. Not giving him chance to try again, I marched him in the direction of the building, taking his weight when his feet stumbled beneath him. As his back slammed against the structure, I pushed my face in close until he could see only me.

"You're lucky I don't have time for this shit, tonight, because I'd like nothing more than to fuck you up right now. That could change, though. Piss me off anymore, and I might change my mind." Shifting back a little, I opened my hand, thriving on twisted satisfaction when he rubbed at the spot I'd gripped. "Walk away," I told him. "Walk away without another word and we'll call this done."

His lip started to curl as his body tensed, but like he thought better of whatever action he almost took, he pushed past me. "Fuck you," he muttered. "And fuck you, too, bitch!" he shot at Blondie as he strode past her toward the road. "Fucking prick tease."

Twisting to track him, I sucked in a deep breath, unfolded my curled fists. His feet met the pavement, his shoulders high as he rammed his hands into the pockets of his jacket, and exhaling, and I turned to the female. "You okay?" I asked.

Her whole body seemed to be shaking as she nodded. In the next breath, she shook her head.

Shit. Drawing in another deep breath, I asked, "You live around here? You have far to go?"

"I have a room just up the road." Not looking at me as she spoke, she swung her torso toward where her head led. "I … I should probably go. There."

Her entire body seemed folded in on itself as she walked away in the opposite direction the guy had gone. I watched her for seconds, her slow steps, the tremors rippling through her, and felt like a bastard for just standing there. I felt like even more of a bastard when she paused on the pavement and, instead of carrying on up the way she was, turned toward where the dickhead had stormed off, like she needed to check he'd really gone. I kind of hated that the cocky self-assuredness I'd always seen from her in the bar had taken a hike.

Closing my eyes, I heaved a sigh. *Nate will understand*, I told myself. He'd probably be more pissed if I went home and told him I'd just left her there.

When I lifted my lids, the female still hadn't moved more than a couple feet. "Hey," I called and waited for her to turn. "If you want, I could walk you to your room?" Holding my hands up, I tried on a smile. "No strings attached, I swear."

Her lips parted, and she looked about to tell me to get real, but after another glance back along the pavement the guy had walked, she sent me a small nod.

Tucking my hands in my pockets and hoping that made me appear less menacing, I strode over to her. She spun forward as I reached her, and we fell into an easy step along the path.

"You said you have a room?" I asked.

She nodded, her arms still hugging her upper body. "At the truck stop."

My brows bounced up. "You drive a truck?"

She laughed, the sound high and clangy like a couple of bells. While it set my teeth on edge, I mostly just felt relieved that she'd relaxed some. "No, I don't drive a truck. But the rooms there are decent and cheaper than in the city. Quieter, too."

I nodded. "I like quiet."

"I've noticed that about you," she said.

She'd probably noticed a whole heap about me with the amount of times she'd checked me out over the past weeks, but I didn't say as such, just sliced my gaze her way, found her facing forward. Facing forward, in my estimate, made the comment non-flirty. Though, who'd want to flirt after the fight she'd just had?

The road we trod led straighter than the route to Liv's. Whereas Liv resided off in a fairly secluded estate, the truck stop sat on the main stretch of road. Almost twenty minutes of walking coated us in rain that'd begun soaking through to my skin, so I breathed out a sigh when the forecourt for the fuel station came into view.

The overnight accommodation stood at the rear of the property, with a live-in tender's house behind the petrol pay booth, and a row of smaller chalet-type huts in a row against a backdrop of pines. Other than the nightlights illuminating the closed fuel station, the place sat shrouded in shadows of grey.

Rounding the pay kiosk took us to a deeper darkness, and beside me, Blondie's steps faltered, her heel scraping against the tarmac. "Would you mind walking me to my room?" she asked, concern lacing her tone.

"Sure," I said, blocking the urge to pull out my mobile and check the time.

As we crossed the remaining tarmac toward the chalets, no curtains twitched, no shadows stirred, even though the tap-tapping of her shoes sounded like a round of echoing gunfire and drowned out the purr of the crickets over in the bushes and the manic buzz of night-biters under the overhanging shelter of the kiosk.

She led the way to the second of the six chalets and drew out a key from a bag she had crossed over her chest. Staying back, I stood guard as she inserted it in the lock, as she twisted her hand and pushed open the door. Rather than take a step inside, though, she glanced back to me, her brows creased with whatever worried her.

"Would you mind stepping inside with me? Just for a minute, while I check the windows are all secure. Please?"

I stemmed the urge to roll my eyes, because I really didn't want to get more involved than I already had, and I really, really didn't want her to get the wrong fucking idea about why I'd helped her out. The plea in her stare, though, had my shoulders sagging in defeat, and I covered the remaining steps along the short pathway until I stood behind her. "After you," I muttered.

She stepped inside, and after a brief pause to give her some space, I followed after her, the pair of us immediately blanketed by the blackness within. I tracked her muted silhouette and muffled footsteps across the room, and a lamp flicked on, offering up a soft light that placed her beside a double bed.

As she crossed to the window overlooking the front of the buildings, I scanned the small space. The taupe comforter matched the shade of the curtains she drew back, as well as the cord carpet over the floor—like they expected anyone who visited to be crusted in dirt and figured it to be as good a shade as any to help cover that up. A bedside table sat at each side of the headboard, a lamp on both. A narrow wardrobe took up space in one of the corners, and in the spot opposite, a lipped shelf held facilities for making hot drinks. Only two doors led off the small room. As I'd already entered through one of them, I had to assume the second hid a bathroom.

"Done," she said, drawing my gaze back to her. "I'll just check the bathroom." She began heading for the far door, her hands wringing. "Can't be too careful."

I couldn't help but feel sorry for her, the way her nerves kept showing. Being afraid of others stronger than me hadn't been something I had to worry about too often.

The light blinked on as she went in, and a couple of scrapes and bangs carried through.

A tiny prick stabbed the back of my neck, and I slapped a hand there, but checking my palm showed I'd missed whatever bit me.

"All done," she said, stepping back into the room, and I lifted my gaze back to her. "Thanks, you know, for doing this."

"No problem." I turned for the door.

"I don't suppose you'd want to stay for a drink?" she said, stalling me.

"Uh …" I rubbed a hand over my jaw, but frowned at the way it sent tiny tingles dancing over my skin. I glanced down at my hand, blinking at the way my fingers smudged around the edges.

Just tiredness, I told myself. Just tiredness and hunger and after-effects of the drugs from the other night.

"I lef my bike a the bar," I said, the words sounding distorted in my suddenly hollow hearing. "I relly shou go grab it."

"Oh. Okay," she said

I'd already spun away, though, and the room fricking spun with me.

With my pulse kicking up a storm, I lurched toward the open door in an effort to throw my body through the opening, but somehow only managed to bash into the jamb.

Grunting, I shoved off it, but instead of pushing outside, I pin-balled into the opposite lip of the frame.

"Shid," I muttered. "Sunfin wron wid dis door."

I tried turning back to the room. For some reason, it seemed important to tell the female I wasn't having her on. I wasn't mucking about. I really couldn't get through the fucking door.

Except, just the twist of my body landed me hard on my butt, with the sharp edge of the doorframe scraping my spine, and when she stepped into my line of sight, a heavy fog clouded my view.

"Oh, dear." Her high pitch rang in my ears. "Is something wrong, darling?"

I shook my head, but the damn thing nearly flew off my neck and a bunch of bones clattered around inside there like an alert reverberated tenfold, while my body slumped even closer to the floor.

"Do you need help?" she asked. "Is there anyone I can call for you?"

I squeezed my eyes shut. When they reopened, her face loomed closer like a big fat ball blotted with blurry blobs, and my heart hammered against my sternum like it needed an out.

My brother, I wanted to scream. *Call my brother*.

My lips wouldn't meet, though, and something growly and indecipherable to even my own ears blurted out.

"That'd be Kyle, yes?" she asked, but I couldn't have heard her right.

No fucking way could I have heard her right.

Need. To get. The hell. Out of here.

Fists clenched, I tried to regain use of my drooping limbs, but received only burning through my shoulders for my efforts.

Teeth gritted, I tried to kick myself up, cursing when a sharp pain stabbed through my shin.

Help me, I wanted to yell at her. *Fucking get my phone out and get me help! Stop just fucking standing there and staring and fricking* do *something!*

Only, my tongue flopped when I tried to roll it. My lips fattened to sausage size when I tried to form sounds.

Refusing to give up, refusing to accept that my body was somehow zoning the hell out on me again, I opened my mouth to roar out the order.

Drew in the needed breath.

Before I could eke any sounds out, my spine skidded over the doorjamb, my face butted the floor, and an explosion of agony splintered my skull.

Fuck! was my last thought before my brain shut down.

15

Banging stirred me, and I wanted to yell at whoever thought hammering so early was a good idea to wizen the hell up, until I realised the noise came from inside my own head. A groan bubbled against the assault, its passage denied by a throat dry and course and swollen.

I opened my eyes, but it took effort and made the noise in my head hit dangerous levels. Grinding my teeth, I blinked a few times, the action seeming to make my eyeballs throb, like the time Karl Jameson had stabbed my cornea with a pencil over some dragged out argument we'd been having. I'd been ten at the time. Once I'd finished teaching him what I'd thought of his hit, Jameson couldn't even grip the pencil, let alone hurt anyone with it.

Not that that had anything to do with where the hell I was, how the hell I got there, and why the hell I felt like a steaming pile of shit.

Vision slowly focusing, I checked out a stained off-whiteness above me. I twisted my head to the side, ignoring the fact that my entire body seemed to tremor when I did. Despite shadows licking every surface, I could make out dull-painted walls, a wardrobe, a shelf. I forced my head up from the softness supporting it and took in heavy curtains closed over a window, a couple of doors leading off. Some kind of bedroom. Or bedsit.

I patted what supported me. My fingers brushed over a satin-like texture. A bed, making my first estimation correct.

Swinging my legs over the edge of the mattress set my head on a tilt-a-whirl spin. Elbows propped on my knees, I gripped the sides of my skull, closed my eyes on the skewed room, and concentrated.

First, on inhaling. More smells than my brain wanted to decipher got sucked up—from perfume to spunk, to piss and B.O., as well as a faint essence of cheap coffee and caramel.

I switched to listening. No immediate sounds. I seemed to be alone. Beyond my four walls, though, engines grumbled, footsteps clumped, low chatter called out or conversed.

Ordering my lids up again, I reassessed the space from my new angle. Scanned over the walls. Over the furniture. Over the doors. While some hint of familiarity needled my mind, the fuzziness up in there halted the pieces from falling together.

Thinking some light on the situation might help, I reached for the bedside table, but paused when my gaze landed on my bike keys there. Sitting right next to my wallet. My mobile, too. All three of them laid out like I'd placed them there myself before settling in for the night.

What the fuck I'd gotten up to the night before, I had no bloody clue.

"Must've been one hell of a party," I mumbled, my voice so deep and gravelly I scarcely recognised it myself.

Scooping up my phone, I pressed and swiped to unlock the screen.

Nothing.

I tried again with the same result. Stupid battery must've been dead. Meaning I had no idea what the time was, no way of calling home, no way of arranging for someone to come get me.

I glanced back to the table. At my bike keys. Maybe I didn't need anyone to come get me. I could just drive myself. All I had to do was lift my arse off the bed, drag my hide outside, and find my wheels. Assuming I could even manage the beast with my head all a-funky.

My knees wobbled when I pushed to a stand, the room going all swirly like I'd fell into a kaleidoscope filled with shit instead of sparkles. Taking a sec to figure out which

145

way was up, I made a slow stretch for my wallet and keys, slipped them into my jeans.

Around seven feet separated me from the door that stood beside the window. I took the first step, then the second, the third one a little easier than both of those, even if my stomach did feel on the verge on a full-out revolt. A duet of knobs barred the way out—one that accompanied the Yale lock and one that required tugging down. I took hold of both, twisting and yanking and tugging until a barrage of light and sounds and smells and dampness blasted me in the face.

My eyes instantly squinted, my hand automatically flying up to hide me from the assault. As I blinked my way through the daylight, faded grey asphalt came into view, a few blocky buildings, a trickle of cars coming in from the right and zipping off to the left. Fuel station, judging by the stench.

I stepped out the door, greeted by clusters of clouds overhead and rain on my face, and slowly lowering my hand, I attempted to get my bearings. Something at the back of my brain niggled, niggled, niggled, until a memory snuck forth, of crossing the petrol forecourt, of walking toward the shack I'd just stepped from.

Of Blondie.

What the hell did I do?

Hoping to God it hadn't been anything to sully my conscience, I drew the door shut at my rear and set out on a precarious stagger toward the road.

The noises of the vehicles seemed to roar through my head, while the stenches carrying on the air tugged at my stomach walls until shallow breathing became my only option. Even once out on the main stretch of A-road, vehicles growled past, the speed of each colour whizzing by sending my brain into a spin that had me closing my eyes to halt the sideways veer my body kept trying to do.

Although my subconscious didn't seem keen on sharing my destination, I caught up as soon as The Double-H popped up on my right and blew out my relief. I'd no idea how many steps, how many stumbles, or how many minutes it took for the familiar sight to come into view, but I knew it was way too many in every category.

My bike sat toward the right-hand corner of the building. *Right where I left it*, my head offered, like I'd known all along. Maybe I had. Through the rain streaking the air, I made a beeline for it, already reaching into my pocket and pulling out my keys. My helmet hung from the bike's right side, and I unlocked it, tugged it on. A small, irritating part of my brain questioned the sanity of even starting the engine in my state. I ignored it. I had no choice. Something told me I'd already be in trouble enough, without missing work, too.

As I swung my leg over the seat and heaved the bike upright, my gaze swung round to assess the car park, landing on a spot a little over to the left. Blondie had been stood in that spot the night before. With a guy. A guy I'd chased off before offering to walk Blondie home—to the truck stop.

What'd happened to Blondie, though? She hadn't been there when I woke. Hadn't left any signs of ever being there.

More to the point, what'd happened *with* Blondie? Especially after I almost kissed Liv.

I stalled out on that thought.

I'd almost kissed Liv.

Please, I silently begged. Please let nothing have happened between me and the blonde. I fucked up enough in my life, without adding what I'd gained with Liv, too.

I should've crashed. And burned. Possibly even died. If I judged by the number of wonky swerves I'd made and wobbly corners I'd taken on the way home.

The fact the house stood quiet told me the others had already left for work. They'd probably given up on me. Figured if I couldn't be bothered to keep them updated, why should they be showing concern in return? I couldn't help but wonder how many shots I had before they'd wash their hands of me altogether.

Only one vehicle was missing from the driveway, though, so just to check, I called out as I entered the house.

Nothing but the slight ring of an echo bounced back at me, the kind that only came from an unclaimed space.

Wrapping an arm around my hairline to narrow my skewed vision some, I cut through the kitchen, into the hallway, and borrowed the wall for support on my way up the stairs. In my bedroom, I plugged my mobile in to charge, stripped off my clothes, and headed for a shower to wash off the stench clinging to my sweaty 'pits and spine.

By the time I returned to my room, my phone'd been on charge for almost ten minutes, so I switched it on, left it to boot up and tugged some work clothes out of my dresser. Boxers, cargos, wool socks, shirt, followed by boots. Once I'd slid them all on, almost flipping over in the process of lifting one leg after the other, I checked my phone.

YOUR BATTERY IS LOW, sat on the screen.

"I fucking know," I muttered, swiping the warning aside to reveal a hoard of alerts across the taskbar. I slid it down to read them.

Eight missed calls. From Dad. From Nate. One from Liv that let a half smile slip in amongst my frown.

Five text messages. Most of them were from Liv, which I decided to save for later, when my head didn't feel like a cesspit and my mood would've had a chance to pick up.

One of them, though, was from Dad:

DANNY, YOU HAD BETTER HAVE A DAMNED GOOD REASON FOR DISOBEYING NATE AND YOUR PHONE BEING SWITCHED OFF. CALL ME.

And one from Nate:

CALL ME.

I probably should've done exactly as they asked—demanded, more like—and made the call to at least one of them there and then, but I'd be in work soon and knew I'd get jumped on the second I arrived, whatever my decision. Figured I might as well only get yelled at once than twice.

Speaking of … I lifted my eyes toward the time. Eleven forty.

Eleven fucking forty.

Over twelve bloody hours late.

I rubbed a hand over my face, stretching the skin. "Jesus Christ."

Yeah, definitely waiting until I got to work would be best. If I had more than one bollocking coming, at least being in public might mean an attempt at restraint on Nate's and Dad's behalves.

Snatching up my soiled jeans, I dug out my bike keys and wallet, and after transferring them into my work clothes, I scooped up my jacket and headed out to the arse kicking I knew I had coming.

The ride to work took my weary head through rain and sun then ice pellets before I broke through to another dry patch. At least my dizziness seemed to be abating, even if my senses hadn't returned to full par.

Like they'd all been awaiting my arrival, the heads of all those within eyeshot lifted as I rounded my bike through the gates and parked up behind Dad's truck. I'd scarcely deadened the engine and swung myself off, when Nate began a storming stride toward me like the human equivalent of a bulldozer.

I tugged my helmet off fast, setting it down on my seat as I lifted a hand to stall his barrage. "Nate, wait—"

He rolled a hand around the back of my neck a fraction shy of bashing into me, and before I could say another word, his iron grip clamped over my nape. The yank of his arm practically lifted me from the floor as he shoved me in the direction of the cabin. One step after another, I stumbled forward under his command, his hold almost paralysing me from any alternative.

149

At the couple of steps up to the hut's door, he gave another nudge, leaving me little choice but to pull down the handle and step inside. Even once in there, Nate's grasp didn't let up. He marched me across the creaky flooring. Marched me around the desk he and Jem used for doing their paperwork. Hooking his foot around the wheeled base of the office chair, he pressed down against my neck, until my head bowed, and forced me to sit.

Only then did he let go.

Without lifting my face, I tracked his heavy stomps to the far side of the desk. Flinched at the weighted slap of his palms against the table top.

"You'd better start talking, Daniel, and it better be good." Damn, even his voice sounded like a solid punch to the gut.

"I'm sorry," I uttered.

"Look at me, Daniel. *Look* at me!"

I slowly raised my gaze, bringing myself face to face with an orb of fury that looked too hot to touch.

"Sorry just does *not* cut it this time, boy. Do you understand me?" Not waiting for my answer, he growled on, "You gave me your word. Your *word* that you would be home by ten last night. This is *not* a game. Not to anyone besides your bloody self, anyway. How many times do you think we should accept this kind of *selfish, inconsiderate* behaviour from you?"

I swallowed. The sound seemed to blast through the quiet his ended tirade left behind. "I don't know what happened last night, Nate."

In my periphery, his hand fisted against the wood of the desk, but I didn't dare remove my gaze from his, despite the storm I could see brewing in there. "You don't get to use that excuse for a second time. This time, I want answers. Proper answers—and they better be full of reasons I should forgive your disobedience."

As his face pushed nearer, I had to double blink to keep him in focus. "I was coming right back last night. Just like a said."

"Except you didn't. Which meant I had your dad on the phone worrying about you. Again. And I ended up falling asleep at the kitchen table, after trying to wait up for you. So, again, Danny, give me a good reason I shouldn't be railing on you right now."

"I'm sorry. But, like I said, I was all set on getting back on time. I'd spoke to Liv and sorted everything out with her, and I walked her home, and then I was coming straight home, but—"

The door to the cabin brushed over the flooring and Ethan stamped inside. "Dad ..."

Drawing in a long, heavy breath, Nate pushed up off the desk and turned toward his son. "Can't this wait?"

"Not really." A weighted frown dragged down Ethan's forehead. "We've got company."

"Who is it?" Nate stepped closer, his broad frame stiffening when he reached the doorway. "What are *they* doing here?"

"Only one way to find out," Ethan said, and he marched from the cabin, his feet heavy on the steps and the dirt they crunched.

Before I could ask what was going on, Nate followed him. I pushed to my feet, but like he'd heard me, Nate barked out a command of, "Stay there, Daniel!"

He hadn't specified where 'there' actually was, though, so I moved for the door, frowning as hard as Ethan had when I saw the police car parked behind my bike.

Two uniformed officers had already exited the vehicle. I leaned into the doorframe, hoping to catch at least some of the conversation as Ethan reached them.

The officer on the right spoke too low for me to hear the words he directed at my pack brother, but when Ethan turned to Nate instead of answering, I definitely caught those.

"They're looking for Daniel."

"Daniel?" Nate sounded as concerned as the hit of it that jolted through me. I didn't need to hear any more for my feet to be hopping me outside and carrying me across the site to the small gathering.

Ignoring the turn of Nate's head and the warning glare he sent me, I asked, "What's going on?"

The chatty officer turned to me, his dark, tiny eyes like a couple of bullets looking for a target. "Daniel Larsen?"

Coming to a stop in front of him, I nodded. "Yeah, that's me. What of it?"

The slight glance he sent his partner seemed to hold some kind of message and had my body tensed to spin and my feet braced to run.

Nodding, he held out a badge I barely paid attention to. "PC Corben. This is Police Constable Davis." He nodded toward the other guy before looking back to me. "Mr Larsen, we're investigating an incident we believe you may be able to help us with. Would you mind coming down to the station to answer a few questions?"

My heart clattered in my chest but I kept my face as placid as hell. "What is it you think I've done?"

"We're not suggesting you've done anything. We'd merely like your input on an incident that's occurred."

"Maybe if you told him what this incident is …" Nate said, stepping to my side.

Unperturbed, PC Corben smiled. "I think this is something best discussed down at the station."

I glanced to Nate, found an interrogation in his eyes. I tried to convey without speaking that I didn't know—not what was going on, why they'd come to me, how they thought I could help them. *Or* what'd happened. Mostly, though, I hoped he'd get that I really hadn't done anything wrong.

The way his shoulders eased up a smidgen told me he had. "When did you want him to come?" Nate asked, looking back to them. "I'll bring him myself."

"Now." The PC's stare could've rivalled Nate's for intensity. "And that won't be necessary."

"He's working," Nate said.

The tiny half smile tugged at one side of the guy's already wonky mouth. "Are you his boss?"

Nate nodded. "I am."

"Then, I can inform you directly. Daniel will be out of work for a few hours while he's answering some questions down at the station."

The growl Nate gave wouldn't have been heard by the outsiders, but it told me everything I needed to know. He couldn't do a damn thing to stop the issue.

Booted feet clomped up behind us, and I turned to see Kyle. He glanced from me to the officers and back, the black swarm in his eyes threatening to prod at his irises' borders—it only happened when he got real passionate about something.

Before he could cause himself—or me—any trouble, I stepped around the officers toward the car. "Let's get this over with, then."

PC Davis had the back door of their vehicle open as soon as I reached it.

"What the hell are you doing with my son?"

I twisted round to find Dad raging across the site like a fucking tornado.

"Let him go this instant!"

At the sight of him, my back tensed with the urge to break free again, to let him sort it out for me, like he always sorted everything out. I didn't, though. I couldn't. Not after my behaviour of late, not after our waning relationship. I didn't deserve it.

"It's okay, Dad," I said, but Ethan had already stepped into his path, his hands reaching for Dad's mammoth shoulders

"Don't," Ethan said, his voice low.

"You better have a good reason for this," Dad said, stalled but obviously not done.

Behind him, Josh approached, his steps slow and cautious, a frowning Sean shadowing behind. "What's going on?" Sean asked.

Paused in the doorway of a vehicle I didn't want to get into, I studied them. The uncertain glances they sent all over the fucking place. The disbelief in their voices. Though, I couldn't work out quite where that disbelief was aimed. At me?

Despite the shaking that crept through my legs and had my entire body trembling, I rubbed a hand down my face and braced my arm on the door top like I had no fucking troubles in the world. "Guys, it's okay. I haven't done anything. I'm just going to answer some questions and clear up whatever's going on. I'll be back at work in no time."

"When you're ready," Davis said, nodding for me to get in.

"Wait." Nate strode over and wrapped his fingers over the door the constable seemed intent on closing. Turning to the younger of the two officers, he said, "Do you mind?"

"Not at all," he said, but he didn't move away.

Nate turned back to me. His jaw twitched. His eyes flickered left to right, as though he was trying to figure something the heck out. When they finally settled on me, he said, "You won't be at the station alone. I'll send someone to support you." He stared harder, like he'd hidden a message in those words and he wanted me to understand.

I did understand. Don't tell them a fucking thing. I'll send help.

"Okay?" he asked.

I nodded. "Okay."

"Take a seat, son," Davis said, gesturing for me to do exactly that.

As Nate stepped away, he didn't once take his eyes off me, and I sank into the rear seat of the car. "I am *not* your fucking son," I muttered to myself—like twisting the panic bubbling within me into a darkness I could aim elsewhere would help it go away.

Because I had a thousand and one scenarios playing out inside my head.

Something had happened to Liv—though, why would they bother coming to let me know of that? Not like I'd be on her list of immediate contacts.

Or I'd broke some law on the roads—though, why take me in for questioning when they could just send a fine?

Or—the one bugging me most—something had happened last night. Something I had no fucking idea about. Because I could scarcely remember a damned thing after reaching that truck stop.

Through every one of the farfetched and downright alarming notions running through my head, I kept my gaze on Nate, while concentrating on keeping my blood flow slow and steady, my pulse a regular beat. Kept my eyes on Nate because I couldn't bring myself to look at Dad. I couldn't handle seeing his disappointment in me. Not right then.

The door slammed shut on my view, the slightly smeared glass marring the outside a little.

The front doors opened, and a couple dark shapes filled the front of the car beyond the gridded partition.

The engine started, a low growl that seemed like an intruder on the quiet my acquiescence had created.

With a slight grind of gear alignment, the car began its bumpy backward roll toward the exit, taking from me the six outlines of those I'd just left behind.

16

Vomit coloured walls—four of them. Shitty coloured door—one. One table. Four chairs. All of them hard as hell. Surrounded by a billion particles on the air carrying an assault of scents.

Welcome to the interview room, where you can't wait to leave but you ain't going nowhere 'til they let you out.

Didn't help that the two officers who'd come picked me up had dumped my hide in there, and then informed me that 'someone will be along shortly'—which, translated, probably meant: we're leaving you to stew awhile before the interrogation begins.

In case they watched me from some hidden room, I sank as casually as possible into my chair. My fingers itched to fiddle. My hands itched to drum my knees. My knees itched to jig. I held myself rigid to stall any of those from happening. The shit I had going on inside my head—the doubts? Those, they didn't need to know—whoever *they* might end up being.

My butt balanced on the tip of my seat while my shoulders scarcely fit against the backrest. Tipping my head back hooked my nape over the lip, the hard plastic digging into the skin there. Above me, stains left the ceiling a patchy mess—hell knew what they spent their budget on, but it wasn't the décor.

Closing my eyes, I let my mind sink back. Back to the night before. Back to Liv. To Blondie. To the guy who'd been harassing her.

My lids flipped open.

No fucking way. No way he'd have tried pressing charges over a bit of grappling.

Would he?

I heard the footsteps before the door handle depressed, and as I lifted my head, two new guys stepped into the tiny room. Neither of them wore uniform—which couldn't be a good sign, if any of the shows on TV were any reflection. Out of uniform often meant a higher rank.

The one who led the way looked like a TV-stereotype. Creased khaki trousers that didn't really fall into any category of style. Creased white shirt that couldn't really classify as white anymore. Nodding my way, he made a slow walk to the opposite side of the table, like he was trying to get my measure on the way.

Behind him, the other guy smiled at me as he closed the door. The first guy's polar opposite, his pinstriped suit and coordinated shirt and tie made him look like he'd just stepped from a business meeting. He crossed to the table at a brisker pace, a couple of A4 envelopes in one hand, his other outstretched. "Thank you for coming in, Daniel."

I frowned at his hand for a moment before straightening in my seat and reluctantly shaking it.

As the scruffy dude scraped a chair out and sat, Pinstripe said, "My name's Detective Constable Bletchley." He drew out a seat for himself. "This is my partner, DI Tanner."

'DI Tanner' leaned back and folded his arms. "From CID."

I stared at him like he'd just tapped his feet in a Fred A-fucking-staire dance-off. "CID?" The Criminal Investigation Department didn't deal with slap-and-tickle's.

"That's right," Bletchley said.

Back and forth. Like a tag team. *Noted.* I glanced to Tanner and waited for him to speak, but Bletchley continued instead.

"You're probably wondering what you're doing here."

I didn't answer. Just stretched open my palms on the table top and shrugged.

"There was an incident late last night, which we're investigating, and we have reason to believe you may be able to help us with that."

I seriously fucking doubted it. "Okay," I said.

157

Neither of them said anything. Not for almost a full minute, according to the ticking seconds on the wall clock.

DI Tanner shifted in his seat, making the metal legs grind against the floor. "Where were you last night, Daniel?"

I knew I probably shouldn't tell them anything, knew I should keep my mouth shut, but as the question was one I could answer with certainty, I found myself saying, "At The Hang & Hide."

Bletchley pulled some papers out of one of his envelopes and studied them. "And where is that?"

"On the main stretch into Derby."

He nodded like I'd confirmed what he already knew.

"Until what time?" Tanner asked, his gruff voice terse and abrupt.

I shrugged. "About nine."

"Then what?" Tanner again.

"Then what …?"

"What did you do?" Bletchley asked. "After you left The Hang & Hide."

I drew my arms back, letting my wrists rest against my thighs, took my time collating the wording of my answer. I might've had to adhere to what they wanted from me. Didn't mean I couldn't make them wait. I drew in a deep breath and held it before its release. "I walked a friend home."

"Does your friend have a name?" Bletchley asked.

"Liv."

"Just Liv?"

I closed my eyes on the permanent scowl Tanner seemed to have going on and inhaled. Exhaled. Thought back to the papers Liv always had spread out on the table. "Olivia Fanella," I said, opening my eyes.

"And where was that?" Bletchley peered down at his papers again. "Where did you walk her to?"

"I don't know the name of the road—it was the first time I've walked her back. It wasn't far, though." Remembering

Liv's words, I added, "About fifteen minutes away from the bar."

"So …" Bletchley glanced up at me, all politeness, his features an open book of understanding I didn't believe for a second. "Around thirty minutes there and back?"

I shrugged again. "I guess so."

"And what did you do then?" Tanner barked.

"I went back to The Hang & Hide."

"And then?"

I swallowed, my throat closing over the rest of the night's events. Because none of their questions sounded like an innocent 'helping with their enquiries', no matter how much they tried to bullshit that they were. Their questions sounded more like they were tracking *my* movements.

"Are you even going to tell me what this is about?" I asked. "It's all well and good you dragging me out of work like this, but at least give me a reason."

Bletchley glanced at Tanner. Tanner glanced at Bletchley, his wispy, greying eyebrows resembling a couple of antenna. At Tanner's nod, Bletchley drew something from a second envelope.

"You know her?" Tanner asked, jerking his chin toward the sheet Bletchley set on the table.

I lowered my gaze to it. As soon as it registered what they were showing me, the blood running through my veins froze up into a solid mass of ice.

Splayed hair took up most of the photograph. Blonde. Lots of blonde. Darkened in patches by a red rustiness. The skin that'd been pale already had paled even further, dark only where smudged by a greyness that must've been bruising, amidst which dark eyes stared straight out at nothing—eyes that'd reminded me of liquorice jelly beans.

Trying not to lose my shit, I fisted my hands under the table, studied the picture harder. Lower. To where a sheet had been drawn over her chest—probably to maintain some of her dignity—and to what the sheet couldn't hide.

Blood had seeped through the cotton. As if that wasn't enough of an indication of the injuries hiding beneath there, scratch marks peeked upward toward her collarbone. Deep scratch marks. Like those made by claws.

Jesus fucking Christ.

I could feel my jaw locking up. My shoulders locking up. My entire fucking body locking up, as the room started to swim.

Working my teeth open, I managed, "What happened?"

"Do you know her?" Tanner asked again.

Yeah, I knew her. Yeah, I'd seen her the night before. Yeah, I'd *been* with her the night before. Last time I'd seen her, though, she'd been inviting me in for drinks and ... I couldn't remember a fucking thing after that.

Slowly lifting my gaze, I focused on Bletchley. "Do I need a solicitor?"

"I don't know," Tanner said, tugging my attention to him. "Do you?"

17

I sucked in a deep breath, doing my damnedest to control the tics trying to outbreak across my face. On the exhale, I considered my options.

Keep talking. Hell, if lucky, I could probably dig myself one hell of a hole I'd never climb back out of.

Or shut the fuck up. Worst that could do was convince the two detectives I had plenty to hide and have them labelling me as guilty as Bundy.

What a fucking choice.

I'd no idea what the duo opposite saw in my face, but they seemed to be taking it all in. Tanner with his hard-edged stare and grim-set mouth, once more leaning back in his seat with his arms folded over his chest—a usually defeatist gesture making him appear even tougher to crack. Next to him, Bletchley rested his elbows on the table, hands folded, his composed face offering a soft politeness, like he didn't mind how long it took me to answer him— dude had all the time in the fucking world.

I think I preferred Tanner's approach. At least he let his attitude show. Bletchley reminded me of a silent predator, hiding his true nature and just waiting to rear back and strike.

After minutes of their scrutiny, Bletchley said, "Daniel, a legal representative can be appointed to you, if you don't have one."

The door swung open, like someone'd barged into it from the other side, and a female forced herself inside. "That won't be necessary." She nodded toward the two detectives. "Gentlemen, I'd appreciate a moment with my client."

I stared at the missile of hard femininity, vaguely aware of the stiffening shoulders on the other side of the table, the exchanged glances. Apparently, they had no argument for the request, because both chairs scratched backward over the floor, and both bodies hulked upward and made slow progress toward the door.

"Good to see you, Andrea," Bletchley said.

Stepping to the side, the female held the door wide, not even twitching toward a smile at the greeting. "I'll let you know when we're ready."

As soon as they'd gone, she closed the exit with a definitive click and turned to me.

"You okay?"

Was I? I'd no fricking idea, but I nodded anyway.

"Good." She marched over, her heels tapping a quiet beat against the toughened lino, and took the seat beside mine. "Niceties first. My name is Andrea Hastings." She set her briefcase on the floor next to her chair and twisted toward me. "And I agreed to be here because I was a friend of your mother's."

The air left my lungs like she'd sucker-punched my solar plexus, my head a swarming mess for a few breathless beats of my heart before I rearranged the muddled pieces upstairs. "Nate sent you," I said on a breath.

She nodded, even that action brisk and efficient looking. "He did," she said, and I wanted to kiss her. Wanted to kiss Nate, too, when I got the hell out. "Though, if you want me to do my job," she continued, "you're going to have to talk to me a heck of a lot more than you've been talking to him or your dad."

"How did you know my mum?" I asked, studying her.

Blonde streaks broke up hair the colour of bran, which she wore tied back in a seriously tight bun. Added to that was the crisp navy skirt suit she wore—a suit that screamed *fuck with me and I'll snap off your testicles and make you watch while I feed them to my gerbil*, or some shit. For some reason, the attitude I saw in her made me relax some, though the pale green eyes she looked through softened a little when she answered, "We played sports together in school. Nadine was one of the best track runners we had.

But now isn't the time for reminiscing." She pulled her briefcase onto the table. "We don't have much time, so you'd better tell me what you know."

"What if I don't know anything?"

Shrewdness had booted her empathy aside when she glanced back to me. "Do you know why they brought you in?"

I inhaled. Exhaled. "I think they think I killed someone."

"Did you?" she asked, and I hesitated, mostly because I didn't know. Not for sure. Like she'd noticed my pause, she added, "Client confidentiality. I'm not going to tell them anything detrimental to your case. Talk to me, Daniel. Did you kill the victim?"

"If I did," I said slowly, "I don't know about it."

"Not really an answer, but we'll get there. Tell me exactly what happened last night. Start to finish. If you leave anything out, I'll know, so keep your lies for whoever you're hiding them from. There's no place for them here between us. Understood?"

I nodded. "Sure."

It took a while to recap the previous night, from arriving at the bar sans the reason for visiting, to walking to Liv's and back, the tussle between Blondie and the dickhead, escorting Blondie ... and the fact I couldn't really remember anything after that.

Andrea'd taken notes through it all, prodded at any holes, accepted when I told her I'd filled them as much as I could.

Thirty minutes later, she clicked the depressor on her pen once, before setting it down and clipping her way over to the door. Fingers wrapped around the handle, she glanced back to me. "Ready?"

I nodded, though it was a lie. No matter her presence, or the strong determination visible in every nuance of hers, no matter the outcome, something told me I wouldn't be walking away from the interview unscathed.

She tugged the door open and stuck her head out. "Okay, we're ready."

Like they'd been standing right outside the door the whole time, Bletchley and Tanner waded back in like a couple of kids who'd been sent to the corner of the room for a misdemeanour.

They settled back in their seats, Andrea in hers beside me, and Bletchley replaced his envelopes on the table. "Let's start back at the beginning, shall we?" He glanced at me, gave an encouraging smile.

I waited for the nod from Andrea and retold what I'd already gone through with them before they left. Yes, I'd been at The Double-H; yes, I'd walked Liv home; yes, it'd been at around nine, so it must've been around nine thirty when I returned to the bar.

"And what then?" Tanner asked. "Did you go back into the bar?"

Andrea gave another tiny nod, so I told them, "No."

"So, did you go home, then?" Bletchley asked.

I told them the truth. "No."

"Why not?" Tanner asked.

Be honest about where you went, I'd been counselled. Be honest, because if they'd called me in, they must know something, and it wasn't worth the risk of the one lie I told being the very thing to contradict their info. Fingers twisting together beneath the table, I released a quiet breath. "There was an argument."

Bletchley frowned. "What kind of argument?"

"Between a guy and a woman," I said. "He seemed to want her to go somewhere with him. She didn't want to go. But he was being pretty forceful about it, and it bothered me."

"Why?" Bletchley asked?

"Because it sounded like he thought she'd led him on and owed him something sex-wise. She was telling him no, but he didn't want to hear."

"So, what did you do?" Tanner asked, his resident scowl deepening the set of his eyes.

"I approached them, and she asked for my help, so told him to back off." I shrugged. "When he didn't listen, I made him back off."

"How?" Bletchley rubbed his thumb and forefinger over a corner of paper he held between them. "Were you violent toward him?"

I paused, considering for a moment, before shaking my head. "Not violent. Aggressive, yes, but not violent."

"Is there a difference?" Tanner growled.

"I didn't hurt him," I said, meeting his hard stare. "That's the difference."

"Could you have—if you'd wanted to?"

"Yes," I said simply.

A few beats of quiet passed, them staring at me, me contemplating what I'd just admitted to. Bletchley dropped his gaze to his papers. "What happened then?"

I shrugged again. "The guy cursed at the both of us and left."

"Leaving you and the woman alone?"

Swallowing, I nodded.

"Did you know the man or woman?" he asked.

I cleared my throat, leaned back in my seat. "The guy was in the bar with the woman last night, before I left to walk Liv home. I hadn't seen him before then."

He lifted his face, eyebrows arched. "And the woman?"

My nostrils flared with my inhale. "Only by sight. She's in the bar pretty regularly. *Was* in the bar pretty regularly," I corrected.

"What did she look like?"

I narrowed my eyes—because something told me they already knew. "She looked a hell of a lot like the woman in the photo you showed me before Andrea arrived."

"This photo?" Bletchley pulled it out from his small stack and placed it on top.

I let my gaze drop for a beat before lifting it back to his. "Yes."

"Can you give us a description of the man who was harassing the woman on the car park?"

I shifted in my seat, readjusting my butt cheeks as they threatened to deaden. "Dark hair. Dark eyes. Around my height, maybe. Perhaps an inch shorter."

"Clothes?"

I closed my eyes and dug backward through my brain. Shaking my head, I lifted my lids. "Nothing, really, except that he wasn't scruffy, but he wasn't overly smart either. Just ... somewhere in between."

"What happened after that?" Tanner leaned forward until I had the pair of them propped on the table and bearing their gazes down on me. "What happened after the other guy left?"

"The woman was scared."

"Did she tell you this?"

I opened my mouth to tell them yes, but closed it as I shook my head.

"So, what made you believe she was scared?" Tanner said, keeping me on him.

I shrugged. "Her behaviour." He opened his mouth, but before he could nudge me, I told him, "She seemed to be checking to make sure he'd gone. And she *looked* scared. She was shaking."

The scowl deepened when Tanner's eyes narrowed. Beside him, Bletchley seemed to be studying every inch of my face. "And what happened then?" Bletchley asked with their favourite question.

I glanced to Andrea, but she just gave a small nod, told me, "Go on," so I turned back, took a deep breath.

"I felt sorry for her, so I asked if she wanted me to walk her home."

"Did she accept?" Bletchley asked.

I nodded.

"And where was home for her?"

166

"She was staying at the truck stop a mile down from The Hang & Hide. I walked her to there."

Their stares made it clear I hadn't finished. That they wanted to know more. Know what'd happened after that. So, I told them. I'd walked her to the door of the chalet. The second one along. Yes, I'd gone in with her—but only because she asked me to.

"And what then?" Tanner asked, leaning farther forward over the table.

That's what I'd like to know, I wanted to tell him, but I doubted admitting I had no memory of the night before would exactly work in my favour. "She checked her windows," I said instead, carefully measuring each word. "She wanted to make sure they were locked."

"In case the guy who'd harassed her came back?" Bletchley asked.

I gave a half shrug. "That's what I figured."

"What did you think about her being scared of him?"

"She was a woman who'd almost been dragged off against her will." I frowned at the detective's idiocy. "She had every right to be scared."

"Did *you* think he was a threat to her?"

"Well, I guess that depended on whether or not he knew where she was staying."

Bletchley pressed his lips together and peered down at his papers. "And what happened then—once she'd made sure her windows were secure?" He glanced back up, a non-smile thinning his lips even further.

Beneath the table, I picked at the seam of my cargos with my thumbnail. Inhaled. Exhaled. "She asked me to stay. For coffee. She asked me to stay for coffee."

"And did you?" Tanner asked.

A big part of me just wanted to tell the truth. To tell them I hadn't a fucking clue. That I thought I hadn't. Could've sworn I'd bloody declined. Yet, every bit of evidence since waking that morning screamed of a story to the contrary.

My head went to shake *no*, but I quickly smothered it with something that just about passed as a nod. "I stayed, yes."

Tanner's left eye twitched like he had a tic. "For how long?"

I picked harder at my trouser seam. "All night."

Bletchley's brows winged up. "You stayed all night in the truck stop room of the woman who you offered to walk back?"

My nod was a jerky mess.

"Did you have sex with her?"

I shook my head, a harsh jolt of my chin to the side.

"But you stayed the night?"

"Yes," I said against the grind of my teeth.

"Did she ask you to?"

In my lower periphery, the boom of my heart set my chest bumping beneath my shirt, and I prayed they couldn't see it. Couldn't see my fear. Couldn't see I'd reached a point where the lies might begin. "Not really. It just happened," I said, forcing my voice steady. "I must've just fallen asleep."

"So, you spent the entire night in the truck stop room of the woman you aided?" Bletchley asked again.

I nodded, keeping my breaths shallow in an effort to control my pulse.

He flipped through his papers and drew one out. Flashing it beneath Tanner's nose first, he twisted it around and set it down on the table in front of me. "Do you know what those numbers represent, Daniel?"

I studied what had been written on the sheet: 0215 – 0445.

"Those numbers are the estimated time of death of the victim," Bletchley went on. "Sometime between two fifteen and four forty-five this morning."

I lifted my gaze back to the two detectives, but my jaw clamped too tightly together for me to respond.

"So, maybe you could explain to me how you could have spent an *entire night* in a room, with a woman who was killed during the early hours of this morning?"

My hands fisted tight at the implication of his words. That they thought they'd caught me out on a lie. Except they hadn't. Not on that detail. "Because I didn't say *she* was there all night," I told them. "I didn't say I'd spent the whole night there *with her*."

Bletchley stared hard at me before straightening back from the table. "You're going to need to give me more explanation than that, Daniel."

"I must've fell asleep, like I told you." I went back to picking at the seam of my cargos, ignoring how the skin at my thumb tip had started to grow sore. "When I woke up this morning, I was alone. She'd gone."

"And you didn't think that unusual?"

I levelled my stare at him. "Haven't you ever woken up in a strange bed, alone, Detective? It's not like *I* wouldn't have up and offed if I'd woken and she was still there. I had work to go to. I just assumed she had other commitments, too."

"What time was that?" Tanner said, piping up after minutes of being quiet.

"I, ah … I'm not sure." I counted back from when I'd reached home, checked the time after my shower. "Maybe somewhere close to ten."

"Can anybody vouch for that?"

"Most fuel stations have cameras," I said drily. "Why don't you try those?"

"We will. Where did you go once you left the truck stop?"

"I walked back to The Hang & Hidefor my bike," I said, relieved to be back on details I knew with clarity. "From there I went home, got showered and changed, and went to work." I risked a small smile. "You already know what happened after that."

Neither of them smiled, not even Bletchley as he hit me with, "And what time did the woman leave the room?"

My fingers stiffened against my thigh at the backward step. I'd figured going full circle up to their appearance would've been enough. Stupid of me, I realised. "I don't know," I said.

"You spent the night in the room with her, and the woman you slept wi—"

"I never said I slept with her."

Bletchley gave a small dip of his chin. "The woman you shared the room with up and left at some point during the night, and yet you have no idea what time that was?"

"I didn't hear her leave. I must've slept through it."

"Are you usually a heavy sleeper, Mr Larsen?"

"Detective Constable Bletchley, my client has already told you everything he knows. Is there really any reason to keep rehashing the details you've been given?"

"A woman was found dead, Ms Hastings—murdered. And we will ask as many questions as it takes to find out what happened to her and who was involved."

"And do you have any other questions for my client?"

A glance passed between Bletchley and Tanner, Tanner's scowl deepening until his whole face seemed to be folding.

"Need I remind you both that Mr Larsen came here today voluntarily?" Andrea's tone held a no-nonsense sharpness. "He has answered all of your questions, as you've asked them. Unless you've got something to charge him with, I believe that makes this interview completed."

Bletchley's chest rose high with the sigh he released and he pushed back from the table to his feet. After sending a dark glare toward Andrea, he turned his gaze on me. "Please wait here, Daniel. We won't be long."

I watched as he twisted away and headed for the door. Watched when Tanner scraped his chair over the floor with enough of a screech to set my teeth on edge. As the two of them vanished through the exit.

As soon as the door made its return swing and clicked closed, I let out my pent up frustration on a gush of breath and turned to Andrea. "How did I do?"

18

The clock on the wall ticked like a build up to something monu-fucking-mental. With my shoulder blades pressed back hard enough for the seat to dig into them, I tapped my foot against the floor with every second counted off, tapped my fingernail against the underside of the table.

It'd been twenty-three minutes and sixteen seconds since the two detectives had walked out of the interview room. After assuring me I'd done okay, Andrea had left, too—to make some calls, she'd said—but I could hear the quiet murmur of her voice just outside the door, could follow the non-pattern of her clicking heels.

Left to my own devices, my head had tried going wild again. Wild with trying to remember. Trying to figure shit out.

Wild with accusation of what I couldn't dispute.

The handle shoved down from the outside, and Andrea marched back in.

"What's taking so long?" I asked before the door had even swung shut.

She clipped over to the table and sank one of her butt cheeks on the edge. "They're most probably just corroborating your story wherever they can."

"How?"

"Well, you gave them places you can be traced to, along with times you were there. They'll look for evidence that you've told them the truth about those. So, they'll make sure you really did walk Olivia home by talking to her …"

The insides of my chest dropped to somewhere below my sorry hide. "What do you mean, they'll talk to Liv?"

"Exactly that." She stared like she worried I hadn't been honest. "Is there a reason they shouldn't?"

Apart from the point that I really didn't want Liv to know I'd been picked up by the police, didn't want her to even contemplate the idea that I'd been involved in a murder … no. My teeth ground as I shook my head.

"Good. They'll probably check that you were in the bar before then, and see if there's any way to prove your bike was parked there all night. They'll also check out the chalet you said you stayed in last night."

"I told them—they just need to ask for cameras."

"Daniel, they'll probably also check for any signs of a struggle. For DNA. It's going to take some time."

"And if they find anything that implicates me?" I asked through my gritted teeth.

She released a sigh, sympathy I didn't want to see leaking into her eyes. "Then, they probably won't be letting you go home today."

I let my head fall back. "Shit."

"That's worst case scenario," she said. "You need to be prepared for it. However …" She sucked in a deep breath. "If what you've told them is true, and they don't find anything to contradict it, there's a good chance the CPS will tell them to let you go."

"What's the CPS?" I asked, not even bothering to lift my head and look at her.

"Crown Prosecution Service. They're pretty much who'll decide whether you walk out of here or get detained."

"Great," I muttered. "Can't wait."

***

"Did you speak to Nate when you went outside?" My arms, resting atop the table to support my dropped head, muffled my voice as my face squished into them. A further forty-three minutes had passed since Andrea's return, and the ticking of the clock had really started to piss me off. Whatever had happened the night before, I still felt like a pile of crap, and I'd probably be asleep before the detectives came back.

"I did," she said, the scratch of her pen pausing. "But only to tell him we were waiting on the detectives to do their job, now."

I rolled my head to the side and peered across at where she'd repositioned herself in one of the chairs opposite. "That all?"

"He's not my client," she said, meeting my eyes. "You are."

I almost told her to go call him again, tell him to let Dad know everything was going to be fine, but I couldn't do that to him. Couldn't lie. Not about something as unpredictable as the situation I'd landed myself in.

Tucking my face back in again, I thought about that. About how it was my fault, and only my fault, and there wasn't a single damned other person I could even try pinning some of the blame on. Jem had been right. I shouldn't have cut myself off. I should've listened to her before it'd gotten to such an unreturnable point. Though, how the hell could I have seen something like a stupid wrongful arrest coming?

You don't know it's wrongful, whispered through my head, and I buried my face deeper. Screwed my eyes tight like that could somehow block out my doubts. And I prayed that the whole fucking fiasco had been one big, fat mistake because I really, really needed it to be.

***

I'd counted through another two-thousand eight-hundred and forty-two seconds of ticking and my eyelids had started to feel like a couple of lead shutters, when the door to the interview room swung open again.

Forcing my head and my lids upward, I focused on the blurry figure, until Tanner's face rounded into a pissed off sharpness, and I wished I hadn't bothered and just left him looking like a blob. Pushing up from the table, I rubbed hard at my face, while Tanner stalked to the corner of the room and propped himself in the corner, folded his arms over his chest.

"Don't get up on my account," he grumble-growled at Andrea, as she started gathering her things.

174

Ignoring him, she pushed everything across the table and rounded to sit by me, and a couple of beats later, Bletchley filled the doorway Tanner had left ajar.

"Andrea. Daniel." He nodded to each of us on his way to his earlier seat.

Tanner didn't move from the corner when his partner sat, just continued staring. Or glaring. Like he thought the added height helped his intimidation efforts.

"Did you check everything out?" Andrea asked before Bletchley could even speak.

He shot his gaze toward her, an edgy uncertainty in his expression, but he nodded. "We did. It all tallies up."

"So, we can go?"

"Actually, I just have one more question for your client." As he turned to me, his eyes seemed to be searching. Searching my face. My soul. Like he knew exactly what he was looking for and a whole lot balanced on whether or not he found it. "Daniel, do you know where a body is taken after it's been removed from a crime scene?"

I think my whole face might've screwed up with the frown that moved in. What the hell kind of question was that? I glanced at Andrea, but only seriousness lined her features, and she gave me a tight nod like I should answer. My frown didn't move, though, when I turned back to Bletchley. "I dunno—the morgue? The coroner's office? How the hell should I know?"

He stared harder still. Moments seemed to pass before he nodded. "Okay, you can go."

I had no fucking idea what the hell had just happened. It must've shown in my face, because the detective dipped his chin until closer.

"Daniel, you're free to leave," he said.

Like my body had got with the programme ahead of me, my legs pushed me upright. "Thanks," I said, offering him my hand like I owed him something for the release. Maybe I did.

He shook the offering. "Thanks for coming in. We'll be in touch if we need to ask you anything else."

The exit led to a narrow corridor that felt almost as constricting as the interview room, and I breathed a low sigh of relief once the space opened up. Under Andrea's instruction, I went through the process of retrieving my belongings I'd relinquished before heading in to be interviewed. Knowing I'd be in need of a lift, I tried my mobile. Flat again. Hardly surprising for all the charge it'd managed to get.

Tucking it into my pocket, along with my bike keys and wallet, I pushed through a door that took me out to the main foyer, the space bright and imposing despite the heavy rain I could see falling beyond the doors.

"Danny, can you wait here for me a minute?" Andrea said behind me, and I turned to see her paused in the doorway. "Take a seat. I just need to speak to DC Bletchley. I'll be out as soon as I can."

Though the gateway to freedom sang like a siren at my back, I nodded. "Sure." Wasn't like I had anywhere else to race off to. I didn't even have a way to get home.

As she vanished back the way we'd come, I sank into one of the faded-yellow, plastic chairs lining the walls. Across to my left, beside the door that'd closed behind Andrea, a female in uniform sat behind the high reception counter. She'd scarcely looked up when I'd exited, and she didn't look at me then. Behind her, shelves and files lined mint green walls—the same colour that spanned across to the double-fronted glass doors to outside.

In a chair opposite, some guy in tracksuit bottoms that looked a few sizes too big for him jigged his leg up and down, the movement wobbling his hands where they rested in his lap. The peak of the baseball cap atop his head hid his downturned face, and every few seconds, he sniffed real hard and lifted his hand to wipe beneath his nose.

I sliced my gaze away, toward the exit. Toward where the rain hit the glazed doors in a beat that couldn't be heard on the inside. Not even by me. Somewhere behind the counter, a clock ticked. Ticked. Fucking ticked. When I found myself counting along with each click of the hands again, I knew I had to get out of there. Away from the stifling atmosphere, the ticking of the clock, the clicking of fingers over keys that seemed to be drumming out from all corners of the building, away from the buzzing static that seemed to overhang every other sound.

With a single shove upward and three long strides, I was pushing through the glass doorway and into cool air full of freshness compared to that inside.

The rain found me as soon as I left the sheltered overhang and clomped down the few steps to the front car park, but I didn't care because it felt fucking glorious after hours of being cooped up. Beyond a single strip of parked vehicles, cars splashed left and right on the road, like rush hour had hit, and it occurred to me that for all the seconds I'd counted, I didn't have a bloody clue of the time.

On the other side of the road, a small strip of businesses still had their interiors lit, telling me it couldn't be too late. My gaze flitted over them, landing on a small coffee house with checked curtains and the promise of something hot to drink. If I hadn't agreed to stay put, I'd have been over there like a shot, but I had agreed, so instead I just stood there. Hands tucked in pockets. Head tipped slightly back as I took slow breaths in, let slow breaths back out.

Too antsy to stay still with open roads in my sights, I started toeing at the tarmac, then stomping at the tarmac. Within minutes, I'd started pacing. Past the front entrance. Back and forth. Each about-turn taking my path a little wider. Each extra few steps taking me a little closer to the corners of the building.

Across the car park at the side of the building, a door opened and shut before footsteps beat the tarmac. "Danny!"

My head whipped up as my steps stalled, and through the rain, Kyle strode toward me so fast he was almost at a jog.

Like an idiot, I just stood and stared as he neared. Just stood and stared as he reached me. Still like an idiot, I just stood staring when he flung his arms wide and flipped them about my shoulders, the strength in him so fucking apparent with the way he yanked me close against his chest.

His fingers dug into my scalp as he crammed my head in close to his. "Thank fucking God," he whispered. "I thought for a minute there you weren't ever coming out."

"It's okay," I told him, slowing bringing my hands up to grip him back. "I'm okay."

I'd never wanted those words to be truer.

19

Sitting in Kyle's truck kept me dry from the rain, while I updated him on my ace of a day. It also kept me dry for the whole bunch of *What the fuck*'s I received in return.

When Andrea stepped from the building, some twenty minutes later, a frown pinched her brow as she paused on the car park and her gaze darted from car to car.

"That's my cue," I told Kyle, and saving her the trouble of finding me, I pushed open the pickup's door and slid from the vehicle.

The rain hit my already damp shoulders as I strode toward her, sending a chill seeping through my skin. Like she'd heard my approach, she turned and started over, her heels scraping the tarmac while Kyle's boots clomped behind me.

"Anything I need to know?" I asked, meeting her halfway.

She smiled, but the expression held little amusement. "Seems you were their number one suspect due to a witness calling it in."

"Who?" Kyle asked over my shoulder, drawing her gaze toward him.

"My brother," I said. "He's cool."

Nodding, she continued, "That, they wouldn't tell me. However, I did get it out of Bletchley that said witness has gone to the wind."

"Meaning?" Kyle asked before I had chance.

"Meaning the contact number they left when they made the call is already disconnected. They can't locate whoever it was."

Kyle's low growl told of his irritation, but I could only frown. Could only wonder who the hell would want to do something like that to me. Sure, I might've pissed off the guy Blondie had been with in the bar. At a push, I could even go so far as to place the kid who'd hit on Liv onto the list of folk I'd jousted. Even so … neither interaction could be considered bad enough they'd want to try framing me for murder. Surely.

"Bloody convenient," Kyle muttered, breaking into my thoughts.

"Yes, it is," Andrea said. "But unfortunately, it's more common than people realise."

"Did you ask what was with the weird question before they let me go?" I asked, forcing my mind back to the moment.

"Something else they wouldn't divulge." Andrea shrugged. "Whatever it was about, it seemed to be the deciding factor in them letting you go. However, just in case they decide they haven't finished with you—which they may well do until the case is closed …" She slid a small card out of the front pocket of her bag and handed it over. "Here's my number. Use it if you need to."

I tugged out my wallet and tucked the business card in there. "Aren't I supposed to pay you, or something, for today?"

"Connor's already taken care of it." She hooked her bag over her shoulder. "Now you need to take better care of yourself."

I gave a half-hearted smile and shook her hand. "Thanks for everything."

She nodded. "You can thank your dad."

I watched for a few beats as she headed off toward the front of the building.

"She seems …" Kyle trailed off like he couldn't find the right word.

"Tough," I finished. "She is." I turned toward the truck. "Now, for God's sake, get me the hell out of here."

Despite the dull streets passing by beyond the windows, the inside of the truck felt confining. I couldn't help but wonder how vast a space I'd need for that feeling to go away.

"Dad wanted to be at the station," Kyle said beside me. "But Andrea told us all to stay put and let her deal with it."

The truck jolted a little as we stopped for a pedestrian crossing. A woman with a pushchair crossed the road in front of us, a second child walking along with his hand gripped around the pushchair's bar, his head scarcely as high as the female's hip. They looked so organised— pristine clothes, behaviour not often seen in young kids, delicate steps that almost glided them over the tarmac—the complete opposite of the noise happening inside my head.

"Still, Dad didn't want you there alone." Kyle slid the gearstick into first and pulled away again as the lights flashed yellow. "Said you'd need one of us there for when you came out. So I volunteered."

I tossed a sideways glance at my brother, wondering why the hell he'd be the one to volunteer over anyone else. Especially as we hadn't been getting on for months.

Like he hadn't noticed the look, he continued, "Dad's worried sick about you. He's been worried sick about you, anyway—for weeks now …"

A guilt trip. Great. Like I didn't already have enough shit to deal with. Blanking him, I let my thoughts drift back to my bigger problem: who did it; who might've done it; who'd have good reason to do what'd been done to me. Why me, even?

"… you need to do now is keep your head down …" Kyle waffled on.

I switched to replaying the interview over on a loop. Their questions, my answers. Liv. *Fucking hell, Liv.* "I need to ask a favour," I said, before he could go on some more.

His eyes pinched at the corners. "You really think you have any of those in reserve right now?"

I glanced away, out of the side window lined with stretched raindrops. A whole row of Tyrolean'd houses flickered by before I turned back. "Probably not, but I need it anyway."

He adjusted his hands over the steering wheel, his expression unreadable while he swung us around a curve in the road and slowed for an upcoming intersection. Once he'd passed the crossroad, he said, "So, talk to me."

I drew in a deep breath—because I knew he wouldn't like the request, not one fucking bit. "I need to borrow the truck."

Kyle's barked out laugh detonated through the small cab. "You're fucking insane."

"Forget it," I muttered, returning to staring out my window. The windscreen wipers squeaked over the glass in the corner of my eye, the constant swish reminding me of the irritating ticking of the clocks I'd had to listen to all day. "Just drop me off somewhere, and I'll make do on foot."

"Again … you're insane. And *I'd* be the insane one if I turned up at home without you attached to my hip. No. No, you can't have the bloody truck." We reached an island, and Kyle didn't even brake to make the turns.

Body swaying with the truck's momentum, my hands clenched again in my lap. Then unclenched. Fists. Not fists.

In my periphery, Kyle sent a few glances my way. "What d'you need the truck for, anyway?"

"I need to go see someone," I said, resting my hands and letting my knee jiggle instead.

"Who?"

"Just someone."

During the long pause that followed, the houses started to split up until standing farther apart, their lawns expanding in size, as well as the garages.

"I'll take you," he said, after a while.

I heaved a deep sigh, the sound of it loud as the air sucked through my nostrils.

"Okay, tell me why you need to go see this *someone*," Kyle said, sending me a sharp glance.

The houses gave way to fields. Fields of corn and yellow rapeseed. "I need to set things straight." I shifted in my seat until I faced him a little more. "About today."

"This is the girl you said you walked home last night?"

I'd told him about Liv when I'd recounted the police interview to him. I nodded.

"Who is she, really?" he asked. "Your girlfriend?"

I shook my head. "She's just a friend."

"How long have you been seeing her?"

"I haven't been *seeing* her. I go to the bar, and she's there. What is this—an inquisition?"

"She's in the bar as much as you?" He lips curled. "Sounds like a lush."

"Fuck you. She's a student and goes there to study because she finds it easier to concentrate there."

"You seem to know her pretty well, considering she's just a friend."

I swiped my palms over my thighs. No idea why being questioned about Liv made me edgy, but it did. Every damn time. "We just sit together. Sometimes we talk. That's it. She's not interested in anything more." Damn, I'd almost sounded sulky as I said that.

"And you?" he asked, like the bastard'd caught my tone.

"And *me* nothing." I twisted away. "I keep telling you, she's just a friend."

"Who the hell are you trying to kid—me, or yourself? I know how we guys sound when talking about *just a friend.* I know how we sound when talking about *just a hook-up.*" His nostrils flared with his inhale. "Doesn't sound to me like you class her as either of those—especially with you giving so much of a shit what she thinks of you—and what I think of *her.*"

My knee quit jigging as my hand re-clenched. "I haven't hooked up with her. I'm not you."

183

"Fuck off, Danny. I still rest my case." He sent me a quick glance, a frown firmly in place over his eyebrows. "Might as well just come clean about it."

My lips twisted into a sneer before I could stop them. "You're a hypocrite, Kyle."

His hands tightened around the wheel. "Yeah, well," he said, his voice measured like he held himself in check, "in hindsight, maybe I would've took it a different path than the one I did."

"With Brook?"

"No." He pulled into the oncoming lane, overtaking a snail-paced Punto in front of us. "With you guys," he said, once he'd switched back into our lane.

"Except you didn't. You just waded her right in there and caused a big old ruckus." My lips twisted into an attempted smile, which I knew without seeing it I hadn't pulled off. "Puts you in no position to criticise me."

"It's not the same. Nowhere near the same. You have no reason not to talk to us about this girl." His eyes glowered when he set his gaze on me. "Unless there's something you're not telling me."

"Why?" I snapped. "Because she's not a *cat* I need to be ashamed of introducing?"

He opened his mouth, but only for a second before he clamped it shut. The steering wheel groaned beneath his white-knuckling fists, and he turned his darkening gaze back toward the rain-obscured windscreen, his jaw locked tight, like he was scared of saying whatever he'd been about to.

Part of me wished he'd just fucking say it, get it off his chest. I'd long grown sick of beating around the issue with him. Long grown sick of him just pretending there was no great divide between us.

With no warning, he slammed a foot down on the brake pedal, sending me flipping forward against my belt, and jerked the wheel to the left into a layby. Around ten metres in, he stamped the brake again, bringing the truck to a neck-jarring halt. Before I could even think *what the fuck*, let alone ask it, he'd thrown himself from his seat and smacked the door back in place.

Rubbing my neck, I watched his vicious storm around the front of the truck, his eyes full of a creeping blackness he aimed at me. Reaching my side, he almost hauled the door off its braces, before shoving his hands through the gap, jabbing off my seatbelt, and yanking me out with a hand wrapped around my jaw.

The side of the truck bashed my rear when he rammed me against it and pushed his face into mine. "I am not fucking ashamed of Brook. I was never ashamed of Brook." The first threads of black began a slow spiral outward from his pupils. "What I am ashamed of is the cock-sucking way in which you've behaved like a spoiled little turd ever since you've known about her." He practically snarled the words at me, the black of his eyes dancing like onyx tentacles over the whites. "You want to know why I kept her a secret? Because I feared a reaction exactly like the one I got from you. Take a look in the mirror, if you want to know why I kept quiet on my feelings for Brook, you little prick."

I tried shoving his head away from mine. "Get the hell out of my face."

Letting out a growl, Kyle just pressed against me harder, the darkness spreading like spilled tar. "I'm so sick of your low kicks and fucking judgemental attitude, like you know even the slightest bit of shit about us."

Meaty scents wafted over on the breeze, warning that we'd landed in an active food spot, at same tht time movement at the edge of my vision told me we'd caught ourselves some attention from other layby users I hadn't had chance to spot when we'd pulled in. Seemed not even cool rain could stall rubber-neckers from the chance of watching a potential brawl.

I ducked my gaze to his "You need to calm yourself down."

"Take a look at your own life, little brother." His lips twisted, like my words hadn't even registered. "Try sorting your own shit out, instead of worrying about mine."

More movement caught my focus over to the right, a few shuffles of feet, low muttering. They all probably thought I was in trouble. That I needed help. I doubted we had more than a few seconds before someone came to investigate, and with the state of Kyle, an intervention was the last thing we needed.

I gripped his shirt front, twisting my hands around the fabric. "Your eyes are about an inkblot shy of being full-on black, and people are staring. Calm. The hell. Down."

"Screw you," he said, his voice a low rumble.

I ground my teeth, my irritation beginning a slow devolution into temper. "This kind of outburst from you, just over someone saying something about Brook you don't like, is exactly what's caused stiffness between us to begin. I don't get it. What makes her so much more important than your family that you're willing to turn on us for her?"

"You really don't get it, do you? Brook is my mate. My *mate*, Dan. As much as Jem is to Sean, or Shelley to Ethan."

"It's just a bullshit excuse, and you know it," I shot back at him. "Sean never behaves this way. Nor does Ethan, over Shelley. Just you who's the fucking nut-job about it all."

"When have they had to deal with the opposition Brook and I have?" His face pressed in closer again, but only for a half beat before he drew back, his jaw working like he fought to regain some composure. "Brook's not going anywhere, Danny. Where I stay, she stays." His fingers loosened around my jaw a little. "When are you going to grow the hell up and deal with that?"

I shoved his hand away completely and rubbed at my chin. "I am dealing with that."

"That's the biggest pile of bullshit you've ever tried feeding me."

"I bloody am. I even sat with her the other day."

His gaze snapped to mine. "Only because you had no choice."

So, she'd told him about it. Made me wonder what kind of version he'd been fed. "I had a choice. I always have a choice. I could've chose to turn my hide around and walked back out of the room. But I didn't. I stayed. I stayed because I wanted to make the effort."

He frowned. "Why? You haven't bothered making an effort before, so why bother now?"

My heavy sigh lifted my chest as I pushed past him. Covering the few strides over the verge, I sank down onto the lip of a grassy mound, letting my feet hang down the mossy slope on the other side. "Because I'm tired. I'm tired of fighting. Tired of being out of sorts with my family." I dragged my fingers through the tangles on my head, glancing at Kyle when he set his butt down beside mine. "I'm tired of my life full stop right now."

"So, sort it out."

"I'm trying. That's why I need your help."

He ripped up a chunk of grass, shredding the wet blades and dropping them back to the ground. As he sat there, the black of his eyes made a slow retreat inward. After a few minutes of neither of us talking, our breaths slowly evening back out, my fingers no longer itching to clench and fight back against his force or words, Kyle pushed to his feet. "Wait here."

I twisted to track him as he strode off, and spotted a food van, just as I suspected. Kyle stopped at the serving window, giving some verbal order I couldn't quite catch with the rain muffling the air, and the cook turned away and set about sticking something pink and raw-looking on his frying slab.

Like we no longer held enough interest for them, our spectators seemed to have given up on us for the shelter of their vehicles again. I'd no idea when that'd happened. Some of the cars had even left.

Slouching forward and propping my arms on my knees, I stared out toward the scenery instead, where a field of some kind of veg stretched outward, a second field farther out almost meeting the nearest perimeter of the forest. *Our* forest. Home. Exactly where I should've been headed—if only to show everyone I was okay and everything was peachy and I wasn't really a murderer despite some bastard's efforts to paint me as one.

Except, my head revolted at the idea. Same as it refused to let go of the vivid image of Liv bouncing around in there. Or the look of horror it'd created for her face at the police's intrusion into her life.

The thought of her taking their inquiries seriously made my gut twist and roil—because why wouldn't she believe them?

Footsteps I recognised as Kyle's approached, and inhaling, I smelled the food he carried before he reached me.

"Figured you'd be hungry." A double cheeseburger with added egg waved beneath my nose. "And probably in serious need of caffeine, judging by how shitty you look."

A Styrofoam cup slid in next to the bun, and I all but snatched the offering from him, wedging the burger between my teeth before I'd even set my drink down on the grass next to my thigh. "Thanks," I mumbled as grease slid over my tongue. Who'd have known a shitty roadside burger could taste so fricking good? Not even the rain hitting the bun and sending it soggy could've put me off.

Beside me, Kyle chowed through his own burger equally as fast—making him blessedly quiet for a few beats. Added to the forest sitting in sight and the freshness of air surrounding us, it was the closest I'd come to any kind of peace in days. I didn't even care how wet my arse had grown by the time I swallowed down the last chunk and wiped my mouth with the complementary greasy napkin.

"So, this *friend* …" Kyle brushed crumbs from his jeans legs. "You want her?"

I didn't even have to think about the answer. I'd pretty much wanted Liv since the first night I'd met her. Even so, I surprised myself with my honest, "Yeah."

"Does she want you?"

I un-lidded my cup and tasted the mediocre coffee. "No idea. We get on. She gives me shit." I shrugged. "I kinda like that she gives me shit—it's amusing, you know?"

"Yeah, I get you." He scrunched up his tissue and wadded it inside his emptied cup. "You made a move yet?"

I shook my head. "Not really." She'd have probably have ran a mile if I'd pushed.

"Does she know you like her?"

"She'd have to be pretty slow not to figure it out." I glanced at him, and his expression seemed sad for a beat, like he felt sorry for me. "Her last boyfriend was a dick. I think she's playing it safe."

"Then, it's up to you to convince her you're not a dick—even if you act like one sometimes."

I scoffed out a laugh, but it held no humour. "After today? Yeah, that's going to happen."

"And yet, you're still determined to go see her." He smiled, his smug attitude filing in before he hung his head and seemed to be thinking.

I watched in my periphery. Waited for more questioning. Wondered if I could make a break for it and beat him on foot. The answer to that was pretty much: no fucking way. Kyle'd gotten too fast for his own good over the past few months. Wouldn't necessarily stop me trying, though, if no other option showed its head.

Before I could make any rash decisions, his head nodded. "Okay, I'm going to help you."

I tipped my head to the side far enough to meet his eyes.

"But I'm not giving you the truck, Danny. You want my help, it's going to have be accepted how I'm willing to give it."

My shoulders tensed. "Which is?" I already suspected I wouldn't want to agree.

189

He inhaled. "I'll call Nate—"

I shook my head, but he snapped out a hand and gripped my nape.

"You owe it to the pack to know you're okay and what you're up to. You've vanished on them and fucked yourself up enough already. Don't add to it, Dan. They don't deserve it."

I tugged my head free of his grip, my muttered, "Shit," floating off on the breeze.

"These are my conditions," he said quietly beside me. "You hear me out and accept I'm only trying to help you do what you need to do." He rubbed his hands down the legs of his cargos. "Or I'm taking you home, whether you like it, or not."

My fingers clenched between my thighs. My teeth gritted against the urge to tell him to fuck off. Forcing the words out past my tight jaw, I asked, "So, what's your amazing plan, beyond calling Nate and dropping me in shit?"

"With me and Brook?" he said. "I didn't think I had any support. I didn't think I had any choice but to go everything alone and figure my own shit out. Turned out I was wrong." He leaned forward until his elbows rested on his knees, his head facing forward in my periphery. "I talked to the pack. I talked to Nate. All I had to do was get him to understand how important she was to me, and I earned his backing."

"Your point?" I asked.

"My point is, you don't have to make the same mistakes I did." He ripped up some more grass. "All we've got to do is convince him this is important to you, and he'll let you go."

A harsh breath scoffed out from the back of my throat. "Nate is no fucking way going to let me go anywhere on my own."

"I told you, I'll drive you."

"Yeah, because turning up with a shadow, like I can't be trusted out alone, is really going to convince her I haven't done anything wrong." My lip curled as I turned to him. "What fucking planet are you on?"

"The same one as you, unfortunately." He glanced away, his eyes narrowing on some spot in the distance. "How about if I just tail you." He held his hand up when I opened my mouth to protest. "Hear me out."

I nodded for him to continue.

"I'll stay out of your way."

"I'll still know you're there."

"She won't. That way, you can say what you need to say to her without me hovering over your shoulder like a creep, and nobody'll be pissed that you did one again."

"There's a flaw in your plan."

"No there fucking isn't."

"Yes, there fucking is." I jerked a glance toward the truck. "How can you trail me when there's only one vehicle?"

He just grinned like a smug bastard. "Another good reason to call this in." Before I could argue further, he hopped to his feet, his hand already wriggling his phone from his pocket as he strode across to the truck. Twisting back, he leaned his butt against the pickup's bed, his gaze on me as he lifted the mobile to his ear like he didn't dare look away for too long.

"I want your word, though," he said, staring down at me.

"On what?"

"That you won't try buggering off the second you think you can lose me."

"I didn't agree to your idea. Didn't you catch that?"

"Figure it out, Dan," he said. "You don't have a choice."

20

The bulky black pickup slid in behind Kyle's truck, and a crop of dark hair emerged, followed by a set of broad shoulders. Ethan. Figured. Only someone with a death wish would pit themselves against him and my brother together. Probably the reason Nate had chosen him to send.

"You have got to be the jammiest bastard on earth," he said, as he rounded the truck toward us.

I grinned. "Not jammy. I just had a decent defence."

I'd ended up speaking to Nate myself on the phone. While he hadn't been too convinced that I should get my own way, he couldn't argue the case I'd thrown at him. That damage control needed to be applied. The police had been to the bar to check out that piece of my story. Chances were, they'd talked to more than just the staff, and that'd bring a whole lot more attention than we liked. So, after I'd assured him that getting one person to believe I was innocent would start the ball of doubt rolling through the lot of them, he'd reluctantly given in and told me I could go. Though, not before he'd warned me to keep Kyle in my sights at all times. Or else.

"Still jammy," Ethan said. "You need me to run through the rules?"

"No, I don't need you to run through any *rules*." My fingertips dug into my hips, where my hands rested. "I know I'm not allowed to lose you. I know I'm not allowed to run off and disappear. I *know*."

"Good." He jerked his chin up. "Your phone switched on?"

I winced. "About that … my phone's flat."

They both just stared at me. Then at each other, before Ethan held out his hand.

"Switch with me."

"What'll you use?"

He prodded over his shoulder with his thumb. "There's a charger in the truck, so I'll just charge yours up. You can call Kyle, if need be, while it's charging."

I handed over the dead mobile, waiting as he worked out his own.

"Try not to fall over and land with your mouth wrapped around any drugs," he said, slapping it into my palm. "And don't get yourself arrested."

"I wasn't arrested. Just questioned. It's not the same thing."

"Semantics." He poked a finger into my chest. "Do not fuck this up, Danny. You go off the rails again and make me or your brother look like a dick, I'm going to beat the shit out of you."

"And I'll clap while he's doing it," Kyle said.

I believed them. "I won't fuck up," I said.

Ethan smiled. I hated that smile. It only showed up when he knew his threat had been well and truly received. "Good."

Two minutes later, they'd climbed into Ethan's truck, and I'd shut myself inside Kyle's. Their beady eyes narrowed on me when I checked the rear-view mirror. Like they knew a part of me really wanted to slam the pickup into gear and spin away as fast as I could. Instead, I made a big show of slowly fastening my seatbelt, getting myself comfortable, before lowering my gaze to the time on the dashboard clock.

Seven sixteen. Where the hell had the day gone? At least it diminished the chances of my having to be faced with her mother's stern expression when I knocked on Liv's door, because Liv would likely already either be at The Hang & Hide, making her way to The Hang & Hide, or thinking about going to The Hang & Hide.

With that destination in mind, I slipped into first and pulled away from the verge-side.

***

Weekends always brought a slightly thicker crowd to The Double-H than on the weekdays, especially in the early evening when folks grabbed a few beers before their treks into town for the nightclubs there. Despite that, the car park seemed no fuller, and I pulled up in my regular slot, waving Ethan and Kyle toward the far side of the tarmac. As far away from me as I could make them go.

The rain'd let up somewhere between the layby and the bar, but my already dampened clothes still clung to my back, my thighs, my butt. I probably looked a state—I definitely smelled rank—but I just told myself Liv had seen me rolling around trashed and I must've looked a whole lot worse that night. Maybe.

Opening my door, I went to follow its out-swing with my body, but paused at a buzzing ring. 'Kyle' blinked from the screen of Ethan's mobile, and answering, I placed it to my ear.

"Remember what I said, Dan," Ethan growled. "Don't be a dick."

I cut him off and jumped out, making an exaggerated show of wiggling the phone their way and sticking it in my pocket, before slamming the door closed on the truck.

Chatter spilled from within the bar as soon as I pushed my way inside. As the door *swooshed* closed behind me, I stood in the entrance, inhaling a whole wash of scents that told me all I needed to know.

My eyes scanned over a small gathering of guys around the pool table. Only guys. No females. No Liv. I let my gaze skip to the right, over the first booth. A few girls, their outfits little bigger than bikinis—definitely some of the nightclub crowd. One of them, a brunette, glanced my way. Flipping her hair over her shoulder, she leaned into a mass of red hair next to her, her lips moving with words I couldn't hear.

Jaw tight, I watched the redhead, waited for her to lift her face. It took six long seconds, and when she finally did, her eyes linked with mine from across the room. Pale, hazel eyes, with nowhere near enough depth and smokiness to belong to the ones I'd hoped for. Though, I should've known from the outfit that it wouldn't be Liv.

A group of older teens took up the next couple of booths, from girls sipping their drinks, their expressions serious like they had a game plan they intended sticking with, to guys jerking around, ribbing each other, trying to cop a feel from a girl wearing a dress that exposed all of her thighs and then some. One guy had a girl sat sideways on his lap, both of his arms wrapped possessively around her. The way her body curled into his suggested she didn't mind one bit.

I studied them all. Their carefree attitudes. Their freedom. In truth, I should've already been searching the booth nearest the door. It should've been the first place I'd looked. Because I knew Liv was there somewhere. I'd caught her scent when I first stepped in. Something held me back, though—like my subconscious thought it'd be good for Liv to have time to spot me before I headed over and pleaded my case.

Mentally counting backward from three, I swung my focus a little more to the right. To our booth. To my bench. To Liv's usual table. Liv's empty table.

Frowning, I spun and made for the bar, shouldering through a couple of guys hogging up the stools. "Joe!"

He didn't speak. Not verbally, anyway. Mid-pull of someone's pint, he let his eyes slice toward me, his expression dark as he studied me from beneath lowered brows. Releasing the pump, he turned back to his task and set the drink on the counter.

I waited as he held out his hand in his customary way, as money got slapped into his palm, and as he pivoted for the register. Once he'd rang up the sale, he tilted his head my way, his eyes doing that dark studying of his again, except his brows seemed to dip even lower.

That glance alone told me the police had been in, spoken to him. And that Joe probably didn't know what to make of me anymore.

His steps to me were slow, and he placed his palms atop the bar, their broad size like a threat of their own as he leaned in toward me. "Why are you in my bar?" It was the first time I'd heard Joe speak. His tone was like rocks bashing about in a cement mixer, almost disguising a Cornish accent I could just about detect.

"I need to see Liv. Is she here?"

His eyes seemed to dare me to keep looking as they narrowed. "The police came into my bar."

I swallowed. While Joe on his own didn't scare me, the inkling I had about baseball bats beneath the counter, and the fact he could probably turn his entire patronage against me with a nod, did.

"*You* ... brought police into my bar."

"It wasn't my doing," I said.

His jaw shifted. "Certainly wasn't anyone else's doing. Why were they looking for you?"

"Because they think I did something I didn't."

His stare hardened, like a couple of chunks of granite probing my brain. Without saying a word, Joe pushed himself back from the bar and strolled along to some guy waving a note over the counter.

"Is she here, or not?" I called after Joe.

He just took the guy's money and proceeded to pour drinks like I hadn't spoken. Even though the slight twitch of his cheek told me he'd heard me just fine.

"Shit." I pushed away from the bar myself, but froze as my sights landed on a pair of battered Converse.

Above those, pale blue denim clung to shins I'd memorised the shape of, and higher, a T-shirt hugged her hips, a cluster of mini yellow pill-shaped characters stretched wide over her chest. I let my gaze lift higher, to her face.

Her lips pressed thin in a weird non-expression. Her eyes stared out at me through her lenses, wide and unsure, like she really wanted to bolt but her body didn't hear her.

I took a step forward, lifted my hand. "Liv—"

She spun and dashed away.

Ignoring the stares our exchange had earned, I strode after Liv and rounded into the corridor to the toilets, just as the fire exit door banged shut.

The regular stench seeped around the door of the Men's on my jog past, and reaching the aisle's end, I pressed down on the bar and pushed my way outside.

Ethan and Kyle stared at me through the windscreen of the truck, before their gazes cut to the right, toward the front lip of the car park. Letting the door swing shut behind me, I marched that way and, rounding the corner of the building, caught her hastened step onto the pavement.

"Liv!"

Stumbling a little, she glanced back over her shoulder. Her body seemed to sway on the spot, like she couldn't decide whether to carry on running, or turn back and see what excuses I had. Her lips even parted a little, as if she had something to say.

Not waiting to hear, I half jogged over the tarmac until I'd claimed the pavement in front of her feet. Peering down at her, I held up my palms. "Please, Liv, I need to speak to you."

She took a step backward, and I lowered my hands.

"Why are you running from me?"

"Why did the police question me about you?" Her tone came out casual. I might've bought it, if not for the tight knot making grooves between her brows and her eyes flashing out a world of hurt.

"Because they think I did something bad."

She took another step backward and might as well have stabbed me in the chest with the nervous tension rolling off her. "Did you?"

I shook my head. "No."

"Everyone knows."

I frowned. "Knows what? And who's everyone?"

She nodded toward the bar. "Everyone knows the police have been asking about you." Her eyes slid back toward me. "You don't get to cause speculation in a place like that without everyone finding out within the hour."

"They don't even know me," I said, my jaw tightening around the words.

She shrugged and took another step away, but the action seemed almost unconscious like she didn't realise she was doing it. "Doesn't matter. People love gossip. You gave them some."

I glanced toward the bar before turning back to her. "They're talking about you, too." I'd meant it to be a question, but realised midway through that I spoke the truth. "Because I sit with you."

"Doesn't matter," she said again.

My frown deepened. "Is that why you weren't out in the bar when I got there?"

She didn't answer, just lowered her gaze from mine and begun picking at the cuff of her shirt.

I reached out and cupped her chin, lifted her face. "Do you want to get out of here?"

Her entire body stiffened when I touched her, but her shoulders quickly relaxed, her features softening despite the scrunch of her brow. "I don't like what they're saying about you, Danny."

"Whatever it is, I can guarantee it won't be true." I brushed my thumb over her jaw, unable to help myself. "Will you come with me—let me explain?"

Her chin lifted free of my grip, and I slipped my hand to the nape of her neck and held her steady again as I dipped my gaze to hers.

"Whatever they're saying about me is bullshit, and I'm still exactly the same person you trusted to go the party with you and trusted to walk you home last night." I drew in a soft breath, letting it out as I studied her eyes and the slipping uncertainty there. "Do you still trust me, Liv?"

She took a few beats to answer, but she finally nodded.

I chanced a small smile. "Then, will you please let me take you somewhere away from here, so I can explain why everyone suddenly thinks I'm some kind of criminal mastermind? I even brought four wheels so you wouldn't get wet."

She breathed out a laugh, but the sound and her expression were so gentle, anyone else mightn't have caught them. "Okay," she said quietly.

"Okay," I said, my sigh gushing out.

Taking her hand, I sent Kyle a rapid nod and led her toward the truck.

21

"Here, turn off here," Liv said, pointing toward a track on the left.

Following her directive, I indicated and slowed for the turn, spinning us onto the rough gravel once close enough.

The place seemed to be some kind of tree-enshrouded car park, a rural picnic stop, with public footpath signs pointing off into the trees. The retreat even had public toilets, and probably because of those, a handful of jazzed up cars sat in a semicircle deeper in, young males and a few females lounging over the bonnets beneath the shelter of the leafy canopy, scattered cans on the cracked tarmac. Likely the locals' idea of a cheap night out with friends.

Swerving away from them, I headed for the farthest and quietest corner, away from them, away from where I could see Ethan and Kyle parking up in my rear-view mirror. Sliding into an empty space, I didn't brake, but continued on past it until I'd bumped us over lumpy grass and broken branches and we had trunks hiding us on three sides.

"Interesting choice of parking space," Liv said from beside me

When I turned to her, she had a hand braced on her door handle, the other poised over her seatbelt. Like she planned on making a leap for freedom.

"I thought we deserved some privacy," I said, keeping my voice calm. Matter of fact.

Her eyebrows quirked up as she glanced out toward the army of bark spread out before us. "For what?"

"For talking." My own shoulders unstiffened as she relaxed back into her seat a little. I unclipped my seatbelt, then hers, too. "I owe you some answers."

The tree coverage placed her semi-profile in shadow, but I could still see the tightening around her eyes. "Yes, you do—no." Her hand fluttered upward before dropping back down. "Actually, you don't owe me a thing." Her head twisted against the seat back until she faced me. "It would be nice to know what the heck is going on with you, though."

I nodded, a small gesture she might not even have caught through the waning light in the cab. "I'm sorry I sent the police to your door."

"They said they were investigating a homicide." Her gaze didn't back down as she said it. "Tell me you weren't involved in that."

"I wasn't." Unable to help myself, I reached out a hand, curled a finger around a wave of red brushing her shoulder. "It was a misunderstanding."

Folding her fingers around my wrist, she lowered my hand. "Then, why did you need an alibi?"

Blowing out a heavy sigh, I retracted my hand and slouched against my seat's back. "Because after I left you last night, I walked the victim home to where she was staying."

"You make a real habit of that, huh? Walking girls home from the bar." Though said casual, it didn't quite mask the tightness of hurt in her tone.

"It wasn't like that." Even as I said it, I realised how pathetic and too close to most guy's excuses it sounded.

"So, explain to me, then."

I did. About getting back to the bar and finding Blondie there in a scuffle. About getting into it with the guy giving her grief. About walking her to the truck stop, seeing her inside. Her eyes stayed aimed at me the whole time, carrying a hint of suspicion mingled with a heavier dose of sadness, as well as something that looked a lot like I'd confirmed something she'd already been told.

Needing a distraction from relaying the non-ending—the only ending I had for the night—I said, "You know who they found. Before I even told you."

She nodded. "The police asked me about her. And you. About whether you'd shown any interest in her." She

201

smiled, but it was weak. "Don't worry, I told them the truth."

"Do I want to know what that was?"

Her smile widened, just a little. "That you never really paid her any attention at all."

"That's because my attention was already claimed." I knew she'd gotten my implication by the slight flush tinting her cheeks. As I studied her, though, a troubled wariness crept into her eyes, kicking aside her smile as a frown moved in.

"And now *you* are the attention of everyone." Letting out a heavy sigh, she flopped her head back against the seat, her lids lowering over her eyes. "God, the rumours are ugly." Her eyes opened and she sliced them toward me, her voice low as she said, "They all think you murdered someone, Danny. They think you're guilty as hell."

"I don't give a damn what they think." I unclamped my grinding teeth. "I didn't do shit. They've probably only jumped on the chance to stir up crap because I'm an outsider and not one of them."

"And you thought barrelling into the place on the busiest night of the week would help dull their speculations? *I* still don't even know the truth of them. I still don't know why—or how—any of this led to you being arrested."

"I don't care about their bloody speculations, either. They're bullshit. And I wasn't arrested. Just questioned." At her raised eyebrows, I told her, "Because some unknown idiot said they'd witnessed me with Blondie—before they vanished off the radar."

"What does that even mean?"

"It means, they dropped me in shit for no fucking reason that I can see, and they've done so good a job of disappearing, the police can no longer get hold of them. Like I said: they vanished off the radar."

"Who the hell would want to do something like that to another person?"

I shrugged. "No fucking idea."

"Did you piss someone off?"

I shrugged again, mostly to avoid having to go into any details. Because, no doubt, I'd probably pissed at least one person off lately, though nothing to the level that'd warrant stitching me up.

Her eyes tightened as she worried at her lower lip with her teeth. "Whoever gave them your name might have been in the bar tonight, Danny. Last night, too." Her gaze cut back to me. "Someone must have started the rumours—because everyone in there seems to know. Everyone seems to have heard you were arrested."

"I don't care that they *think* they know." Though, she could definitely be right about whoever caused my shit having been present and the catalyst for the gossip.

"They've done nothing but talk about it today, and talk crap to me about their bloody accusations—"

I grabbed her wrist, tugging her toward me as I leaned in. "How many times, Liv? I don't give a rat's shit what any of them in there think of me. Not one of them. I only fucking care what you think." I took a moment to focus fully on her face. On the way her eyes had widened slightly behind her glasses. The way her lips had parted and vibrated beneath her passing breaths. Unable to help myself, I tucked aside a strand of hair that hugged her jawline. "I only care about you."

Her gaze dipped, toward my mouth, causing a tightening in my stomach muscles. When she glanced back up, her eyes locking onto mine, the cloudy blue of her irises had enhanced to a stormy grey.

I brushed my thumb across her cheek, combed my fingers into the hairs at the nape of her neck. "Jesus, Liv."

"What?" she murmured.

"You can't look at me that way and expect me not to act on it."

She seemed to pause for a beat, her body stilling as her tongue stroked over her upper lip, its tip pink and glistening with moisture that I really, really wanted to taste.

After far too long, her left eyebrow quirked up a fraction. "Maybe I don't expect that."

A groan rumbled through my throat as I dipped in and kissed her. The second I pressed my mouth to hers, she yielded, her lips parting slightly as she slanted her head.

Her tongue slipped out, grazing my teeth, and I wanted to remove the barrier of her glasses, climb over the seats, and make the sighs she let loose build into whimpers and cries. Wanted to do something about the way my body heated. Like get naked. With her.

Inhaling fired up my synapses with a heavy dose of feminine arousal, softened only by the faint honeysuckle slicing though, and brought with it a whole heap of familiarity I couldn't quite place. As did the pliability of her lips beneath mine. The curving of her body into the hard lines of my own.

I pulled away, leaving her staring up at me all glossy-eyed and swollen-lipped.

"What's wrong?" she whispered.

A frown tightened my brow. "This isn't the first time we've done this," I said, like the reason for the familiarity of kissing her had been clear in my mind all along.

Her lips popped open, imparting a small puff of breath, and she shook her head. "No, it isn't."

"When—" I cut off before I even finished. Because there was only one time it *could* have happened without me remembering. "The night of the party."

She nodded.

"Did it feel this good then?"

Her eyes skimmed away, but only for a moment, and when she looked back, she gave a small nod.

My frown deepened. "Then, I'm really fucking sorry I didn't hold onto that memory."

"That's the beauty of memories," she said, her voice quiet but steady as an anchor in calm waters. "There are always new ones to be made."

So I kissed her again. Fell into her again. Invaded her mouth again. Until the heat brewing in my groin threatened to spontaneously combust and every bit of clothing between us felt like way too fucking much.

Fingers digging through her clothing in search of her hips, I tugged her butt toward me, revelling in her whimper as I hoisted her leg over mine. Even that didn't bring us close enough, though. Nowhere near close enough. Not when it felt like I'd been waiting a frigging eon to hold her, to kiss her.

Kicking a foot against my door, I shoved toward her, pressing her against her seat as I leaned over her side of the truck and braced a hand against the window's ledge.

She didn't protest, and I sent up a silent thanks for that. She also didn't protest when I tugged her thigh higher and dropped my hips. She merely groaned as my groin met hers and I risked grinding against her.

Fingers weaving through my hair, she dug their tips into my scalp and drew me closer, as her other hand pulled her glasses up and off, and she sucked at my prodding tongue like she'd never tasted anything so damned good.

At a bang against the rear of the pickup, Liv jolted beneath me, her lips snapping from mine and leaving me instantly cold. Thunder-grey eyes stared upward, wide and sullied by alarm.

"Get it on!" The yell came from outside, full of a deep gruffness and a whole lot of humour, but in the next breath, the tone changed with the almost whined, "Wha' th' fuck?"

I lifted my eyes above the bottom of the window, to see a couple of the teens from the car park. They swayed as they walked backward, bottles in their hands, giving it the big *I am* with their arms spread wide.

Following the line of where they aimed their scowls, I spotted Ethan and Kyle planted near the rear end of the truck, their wide-legged, crossed-arm stances brooking little space for argument to anyone stupid enough to go against them.

As if well aware that the hulks standing guard were almost double their size, and definitely double their bodyweight, the complaints of the two teens lessened to mumbles as they spun and loped away.

I lowered my gaze back to the brightness of Liv's below me. "Sorry."

"It's okay."

"No, Liv, it's not." It really fucking wasn't. Being interrupted by my family? I could deal with that—we all lived in the same house, shared the same spaces. Being interrupted by strangers, though? No fucking way. And it wouldn't have happened if I hadn't let my hormones get the better of me. "Come on, let's go."

Pushing up from her, I wrapped my fingers around her arm and lifted her up to sit. She instantly bent over and patted at the floor, but I scooped her lost glasses up for her and tucked her hair aside as I guided them back into her face. After one more kiss that seemed way too inadequate compared to what I'd just had, I wedged my butt back in own seat and reached for the keys in the ignition.

Muted hurt dulled her eyes when I glanced back over. I hated seeing it there. Hated that I might've caused it— somehow. As I started the engine, I slipped my free hand along Liv's palm and linked my fingers with hers, taking her with me as I put the truck in gear. Grabbing the wheel with my other hand, I twisted to see out back as I reversed us out of the huddling trees and swung the vehicle around to face forwards.

Kyle and Ethan had gone—probably already back in their vehicle and ready to chase on our tail. Not worrying about them catching up, I rolled the pickup back down the gravelly track.

As soon as we'd pulled out into the road, Liv asked, "Where are we going exactly?"

"Somewhere else we can talk." I checked the rear-view, not quite knowing whether to tense up or relax at Ethan's truck slipping out into the traffic behind me.

Her eyes narrowed slightly. "What was wrong with where we were?"

"It was too isolated. And less than twenty yards away from all the local drunks." I glanced across at her, gave a half-smile. "Unless you want me to get the urge to pounce on you again, you might want to choose somewhere a little more crowded this time." I turned back to the road. "Because you deserve better than how I just treated you back there."

You deserve better than me, I should've said, but damn if I could bring myself to voice the words. As much as I suspected they might be, I really didn't fucking want them to be true.

"Take a left up here," she said, pointing.

I obeyed the command and took us onto a quieter road, lined both sides with houses that boasted double-floored bay windows and stained glass doors.

"Then take the third on the right."

She pointed again, and I liked that she used her free hand, that she never once tried removing her fingers from where I held them. Though I really wanted to tug her hand into my lap anytime I wasn't shifting gear, I settled for brushing my thumb over her wrist, because I really liked how her rapid pulse fluttered against my skin each time I did.

It only took a handful more turns for my senses to click in and my bearings to make an appearance, and with both of those, a deep suspicion that had my mood on a slow downward plummet.

Around three minutes later, I followed her instruction and turned into the familiar cul-de-sac, my frown squishing up the skin on my forehead. In my wing mirror, I caught my shadows taking the turn but pulling to a stop on the outer corner. The pair of them had their heads ducked forward, like they studied the street for possible escape routes I could slip out through.

"You can pull onto the driveway," Liv said as I slowed near the kerb, and I let the truck roll on, swinging the wheel to the left and stopping in front of the white garage door.

Just like the last time I'd gone there, the security light flared out over the driveway, despite it being just a little after nine and only on the cusp of dusk. Unlike last time, though, the Audi didn't claim the spot I'd just taken, and lights didn't spill from the windows of the house. No disapproving frowns being thrown at me from the porch, either.

I lifted our joined hands, dropped them back down onto the ridge of her seat. "I thought we were going somewhere to talk again."

"As far as I'm concerned, there's nothing left to talk about."

I let my head drop back against my chair and closed my eyes, clamping my lips over the *Shit!* I wanted to let out.

Me and my stupid urges. I couldn't just hold back. Couldn't make myself wait a little longer. I'd had to go and push, and I'd known, I'd bloody known, that pushing her would only push her away.

"You've explained everything to me," she continued.

I frowned, waiting for the blow. Waiting for the 'It's probably best we stay away from each other' speech.

"You told me you didn't do anything to that girl."

I opened just one eye and risked peeking out at her, but Liv didn't look my way. Staring outward toward the garage door, she sat rigid, her free hand balled into a fist in her lap.

"And I believe you."

She turned to me then, and I let my other eye open, rolling my head against the seat until I faced her.

"I *believe* you, Danny," she said, like she needed to hear the words again herself more than she needed me to hear them. Like she hadn't quite believed she'd meant them the first time. "So, there's nothing left to talk about. Not where

208

the police and whatever they're investigating are concerned, anyway."

I hadn't realised how much I'd needed some kind of validation from her before I'd heard it, and the relief of catching the conviction in her voice hit hard enough to cause pain as it shot through my muscles and straight to my heart. I swallowed, trying to focus on her words around my own emotions. "What *is* left to talk about, then?"

Her features seemed to twitch, like she wasn't quite sure which expression fit her feelings. "Sometimes, words aren't the right tools to communicate." She said the words quietly, almost as though afraid of them, before her gaze cut a path toward her front door. "My parents are away this weekend, Danny." More words spoken quietly as though feared.

I kind of felt that fear myself. Fear of what, exactly, she was saying. Of what that could mean. For me. For *us*. Barely daring to breathe, I asked, "Why are you telling me this, Liv?" I needed to be sure. I didn't see any room for uncertainty between us.

She didn't answer. Just worked her fingers free of mine and reached for her door. Swung her legs out. Hopped to the floor.

Before she walked away, she spun back and leaned in, her eyes meeting mine without a single ounce of indecision misting their clarity. "I told you because I wanted you to know."

She backed away and the click of the closing door clashed loudly against the noise in my head.

I watched as she walked the length of the driveway. As she tugged keys from her pocket and unlocked her way into the porch and then the house. I also watched how she left both of those doors open. Like an unspoken invitation. Like she wanted me to follow.

I'd never wanted anything more in my fucking life.

Vibrations buzzed through my pocket, exciting my already interested dick, despite my brain knowing who it'd be and what they likely wanted.

I wriggled it out and answered with a grunt.

"What are you waiting for, Danny?" Kyle said into my ear.

"I think she just invited me in," I said quietly.

"No." A one-word response I had no intention of heeding.

"She told me her parents are away and left the doors open. She left them open for me."

"Shit." The mutter came through as a deep growl. "You're going in, aren't you?"

I shrugged though he couldn't see the action. "I have to. Sorry, bro."

Cutting off the call, I reached across and shut down the engine.

A final glance toward the house showed the doors still open. Just the affirmation I needed to shove open the truck's door, throw myself out onto the driveway, and stride my arse toward the house and the female I'd been wanting to explore for weeks.

I couldn't help but smile as I pushed inside the porch.

22

The porch interior was as clean as the outside of the house, bleached laminate on the floor, white stone along the low walls that supported the windows. Poking out my index finger, I nudged the main front door until it opened wide enough to reveal what I'd gone in search of.

Perched on the third step up, on the stairs straight ahead, Liv stared back at me, hands tucked behind her up-drawn knees, the inside edges of her socked feet pressed as tightly together as her calves. A low breath eased past her lips, and she smiled, though what seemed to be nerves made the expression crooked. "I thought you weren't coming in for a minute there, and that would've been embarrassing."

"Why?"

She shrugged. "Just because."

Pushing the door in the rest of the way, I stepped onto a grass-woven doormat with 'Welcome' sprawled across it in big black letters.

"Wait!" Liv shot to her feet, and I paused, my right foot hovering halfway over the threshold. "You can't wear those boots in the house." She gave a jerk of her chin. "You should leave them in the porch."

Retracting backward, I scooped down and loosened my laces, using my heels to work off the boots. Feeling it mattered to her, I took a moment to straighten them, next to the few pairs of shoes already lined up on a spotless shoe rack, wincing at the difference between those and mine.

"Sorry, but my mum doesn't let us wear shoes in the house," she said.

As I stepped back onto the welcome mat, the dried grass dug through my socks into the soles of my feet. I wondered if I'd be expected to wipe even those in case of unnecessary soiling—because the natural-white carpet didn't look like it'd ever been touched, and certainly not by feet that'd been in the same socks and shoes for the entire day. "I can see why," I muttered, letting my gaze wander round.

The same nearly-white carpet stretched off to both the left and right, through doorways on either side of the front entrance. To the right, a faux marble mantelpiece surrounded an equally faux log fire, beneath a gilt-framed mirror that reflected white. Lots of white. On the walls, on the sofa. The clear coffee table did little to counteract the lack of colour, neither did the central rug that matched the carpet in shade.

The room on the left at least had a little more character, with pale stone walls and a bleached wood dining table. Little more colour than that graced the room, though.

I turned back to Liv, my gaze catching on a white cupboard unit along the small bit of wall between the dining room and the stairs, but mostly on the white picture frame sitting atop it and the mass of red hair it surrounded. Stepping forward, I picked up the photograph, my lips curving at the coy smile Liv aimed at the camera.

After setting it back exactly in place, I looked across to the female herself, standing there like a splash of vibrant colour over the blank canvass. "Nice place you have here."

Her lips twitched. "Is that why you came in—to nose around at where I live?"

Taking a step closer to her, I shook my head.

"Then, why did you?" she asked, her swallow visible within her unadorned neck.

I dipped my face. Until right in front of her. Until my eyes could see only her greys and the reaction of her pupils. "For you," I said and pressed my lips to hers in a small kiss that tested the waters. Tested that I hadn't misinterpreted her intention when she'd invited me inside.

Though I half expected her to pull away and ask me what the hell I played at, she didn't. She just stood there. Lips trembling against mine. Chest rising with each breath to skim mine. Eyes one hundred percent focused on me.

Surprising me, she lifted her hand to my side, her fingers imprinting through my T-shirt onto the flesh beneath, and I took that as the nod. The okay. The *yes, you may kiss me, what the hell are you waiting for?*

I tipped my head to the side, kissed her again, using my tongue to part her lips. As she let me inside, her eyes shuttered closed, and I slipped a hand over her hip and around to her lower back, drew her closer. Like a couple of opposites, we seemed wrong against each other but so fucking right at the same time. Her soft, complying lips to my demanding ones. Her soft curves to the hardness of mine.

Letting a groan rumble free, I pressed in closer. Stroked my tongue along the roof of her mouth, feeling the ridges there, before encountering the soft moistness of her tongue sweeping past. I loved how she licked and tasted me right back the second my tongue retracted. Loved how she moved her hands to grip my biceps, as if to hold me still while she explored.

My nose nudged against the side of hers as I kissed her harder, her glasses frame rubbing at my cheekbone when I sucked in her lower lip, before I released it and tasted her again. I dug my fingers into the hair at her nape and tugged her closer. As close as I could get her. It still didn't feel anywhere near close enough. I wanted to steady her swaying body and climb on top of her. Climb inside her. I wanted to swallow her whole just to see how she tasted.

Yanking her hips to mine, I leant into her, loving how she gasped into my mouth, how her fingers tightened around my arms, how she didn't give one fucking ounce of complaint at the move. Still, with every emotion our kiss in the truck had stirred surging back to the forefront, I wanted her closer. Needed her closer. Something no amount of tucking and leaning seemed to be achieving.

I pushed into her harder, and her mouth popped from mine at the same time her heart hit a rapid rhythm. Blinking, I just registered the tilting of the room and the bash of the step against my shin in time to throw a hand out to catch the fall, sweeping my other upward just fast enough to cradle her head before it could hit.

I opened my mouth to apologise, but staring down at her, her eyes all glassy and lust-filled, and inhaling the beginnings of arousal already emanating from her, I realised I wasn't sorry at all. Not one fucking bit. Because I was exactly where I wanted to be, and she exactly where I wanted her, and damn, I really needed to just kiss her some more.

As I ducked my mouth back to hers, I recognised the low thunder of a growl brewing deep within my chest, but I supressed it. Lowered my body over hers.

Her chest pushed against mine as mine bunched over hers. One of her legs had got trapped between mine when we fell. One of mine had gotten trapped between hers. Even then, with not a sliver of air separating us, it still didn't feel close enough. Not close enough for her, either, judging by the roll of her hips lifting her pelvis.

Sliding a hand down, skirting her breast, I reached for her thigh and tucked it over my hip, skimming my lips over her jaw as I lowered my groin a notch further. She tipped her head back against the step when I nibbled at her throat. Arched her back as I tasted the skin that led downwards. Gripped at my shirt front when I dared brush my lips over the covered mound of her chest.

A tug of her hand drew my mouth back up, and eyes closing, she slanted her lips over mine, her tongue swiping over them and leaving them moist. Dropping her spine back to the steps, she gave another roll of her hips, a gasp bursting into my mouth when her crotch brushed the top of my intruding thigh. She pushed up again, her fingers fisting my shirt as if in some desperate attempt to keep me where she wanted me, until another sweep against my thigh had a whimper chasing on the tail of her gasp, and I couldn't take it any longer. I needed more. More of what she kept doing. Of whatever she wanted to do. More of her.

Wriggling an arm beneath her back, I scooped her up, my other hand folding over her thigh and tugging her leg high as I pushed to my feet. With her pinned against my body, I staggered us up a step, not even bothering to ask permission, just taking the move as accepted when she curled her other leg around the back of mine and clung on like she had no bloody intention of letting go.

One hand still wrung the front of my shirt, screwing up the fabric into a tight a knot, but she cupped her other around the back of my neck, forcing my mouth back to hers. My tongue back to hers.

Her moan vibrated against the roof of my mouth in a way that had me stumbling up the next three steps as fast as I fucking well could. I hoisted her higher, and as she tightened her legs around me, I slid my hand to her butt, squeezing the rounded flesh there, grinding her crotch against me, my groan matching hers as a scent as intoxicating as the devil's aphrodisiac itself pulsed upward from her core and set sparks buzzing through my brain. My dick could've happily exploded from that intake alone, never mind the demands my entire body seemed to be making—to toss Liv back to the carpeted stairs and tear every ounce of clothing from her there and fucking then.

The wall stalled a sideways wobble and bounced me right, and as I managed to gain another step upward, the view in my periphery showed space off to both the left and right. Doors both sides. Before I had to figure out which way to go, Liv's hand flicked out, her fingers folded around the wall on the right, and she tugged us that way.

Despite the way her core blasted out heat that penetrated my clothing, the way her chest bumped and hugged mine, the way her lips fed from me in an evident and unabashed hunger I'd never have expected from her in any of my wildest dreams, she seemed to know exactly what she was doing. Because with another outward reach of her hand, she snapped down the handle of a door on her left, and with a shove on that door, we were in.

215

In wherever she'd guided us to.

In where I planned to taste every damn inch of her, as many times as I could, for however long I could get away with.

As I practically threw us into the room, her leg slipped from over my hip, her foot hitting the floor and grounding us from going too far in. Releasing my hold on her butt, I took advantage of the pause and grabbed the hem of her T, yanked it over her head, tossed it aside.

Stepping back, I let myself absorb her. Her softly rounded stomach cinched in by her jeans. The paleness of her skin. Moving higher, the dips and mounds of her shoulders, her collarbone. Finally, letting my gaze settle where it really wanted to. On the black lace of her bra, and above that, the exposed swells of her breasts. Firmer than I'd expected. Even bigger than her clothes had ever revealed. Absolutely one hundred percent better than how I'd imagined them in my head, night after night, sometimes even as I'd stroked myself blind.

I took each and every one of those nights and replaced them with the reality standing before me, and the growl bubbling away inside of me pushed at my barricade a little harder.

As though uncomfortable with the weight of my attention, she raised her arms, a flicker of uncertainty passing over her features as she went to cross them over her chest.

I reached out for her wrists before she could conceal herself completely, gently pried them away and tucked her hands against my chest. Ducking in, I placed a kiss to where the downy hairs fluttered over the pulse below her ear. "You don't have to hide from me, Liv."

"You're probably used to girls who're skinny and pretty," she said quietly.

I stilled, the frown heavy on my forehead. "If that was all I wanted, I wouldn't be here now." I drew back until I could see her eyes, hating that the emotion clouding their brightness might've been caused by some kind of pain. Cupping her face, I held her steady, hoping she'd see enough in *my* eyes to know I meant every bloody word as I told her, "I don't want a girl who's skinny and pretty. I want a girl who's full of life and sexy as hell, with hair of fire and eyes of thunder, who makes me feel like I'll go up in smoke with a single fucking taste of her lips."

The smile she let through seemed a little watery, until a short laugh, filled with a shyness she didn't usually show, burst from her. "God, Danny, that was almost poetic."

"But true," I said, my own smile pushing out. "Every word of it."

Drawing her in slowly, I brought her lips back to mine, keeping the kiss soft. Convincing. Because I had meant it, and I needed her to believe that.

It took a few seconds, but her lashes made a slow flutter back down as her eyes shuttered. Her face made a slow tilt upward as she let me back in. Her sigh gradually eked out as she relaxed.

Letting my hands glide downward, I gripped her shoulders, bringing her to me even closer as I deepened the kiss once more, encouraged her lips to part once more. As our breaths merged again, her fingers fisted back into my shirt, and I let my own glide lower still, over her shoulder blades, the ridges either side of her spine, exploring the small dimples peeking out over her waistband. Until her clothing once again stalled me. Clothing that I wanted to shred into a hundred pieces just to make sure she could never use it again to cover herself up.

I settled for tugging her snug against me, worked my lips over her cheek to her jaw. Pausing to nibble at the juncture of her neck, I inwardly smiled when her muscles relaxed against mine and her shuddery breath heated my throat. Skimming lower took me to where her pulse beat out, like a trapped moth pleading freedom, and I parted my lips, closed them over the fluttering. As I scraped my teeth over her skin, her arm enclosed my neck, a low moan vibrating my ear as her fingertips dug through my hair and into my scalp as if to hold me there.

Opening my mouth wide, I latched onto the same spot and sucked, my tongue flicking upward against what had to be a sensitive spot for her, confirmed when her body arched into mine and she swayed against me. Her deep moan that rumbled out seemed to un-restrain my trapped growl, and her skin vibrated beneath my lips as the sound rippled along my tongue. As if in response, her breath caught, turning that erection-inducing sound of hers into a sharp gasp.

"You're fucking killing me, Liv," I murmured against her skin.

"Ditto—" She gasped when I scraped my teeth lower to the corner of her shoulder, cutting the word short.

"Sorry ..." I sucked another ounce of flesh in, massaging the tiny goose bumps of her skin with my tongue. "But these fucking—" I slid a hand around to the front of her jeans and grabbed the stud fastening. "—clothes have got to go."

A small tug and push with my thumb and forefinger had her waistband popping loose, and a second tug had the zipper buzzing downward. Slipping my hand beneath the denim, I found the edge of a course lacy ruffle. I followed its line over her hip, working the jeans down as I went, until I ran out of fabric for guidance and my palm landed on the soft and supple flesh of Liv's bare arse. A thong, then? *Nice.*

Shoving the denim down farther, I freed the other cheek and cupped both in my hands, pinning her to me as my mouth continued its caressing assault. "Lose the jeans, Liv," I ordered against her shoulder, pausing for only a beat before suckling my way up her neck, smiling at the way she tipped her head to let me in deeper. Smiling even wider when she wedged her free hand between us and wiggled her hips as she shoved the jeans down.

A flash of coolness rushed between us when she pushed away just far enough to kick them off her feet, and the second her body returned, I moved my hands down enough to get a decent grip and hoisted her up to my waist. As her arms wrapped about my shoulders, her legs over my hips, I brought my face back to hers, taking in the darkening hue of her eyes enlarged by her lenses, the flush that'd already begun a slow creep over her cheeks.

"You are fucking beautiful, 'Livia Fanella," I whispered, "and don't ever let anyone tell you any different."

She seemed unsure how to accept the compliment for a moment, and I half expected her to just kiss it away, pretend like I hadn't said anything, act like no one had ever told her that before, but her lips twitched at the corners. "I'd say the same about you, except I seem to be the only one half naked around here."

An order not given as an order. Either way, it sent my blood surging south.

I marched us to the wall aside the netted window. Holding her there with my hips, I leaned my torso back and grabbed enough of my shirt to tug it upward and over my head. As soon as I'd dropped it, my hands went back to Liv's hips as I looked to her, smiling at the appreciative way her attention flickered over my chest. "Better?"

Her gaze cut to mine. "God, yes."

I grinned—couldn't help it. I'd known what she'd see before I'd even removed the shirt—because I'd never had any doubts about the fact I had the body of a fucking superhero. I'd even been scouted once for sports modelling at the age of nineteen. Like posing to order amid makeup brushes waiting to attack would be the kind of deal I'd go for. Yeah, thanks but no thanks.

My smile wavered when I spotted the doubt creeping back into Liv's eyes. Before it could take over completely, I leaned in until my lips met her ear. "I'm really glad you like what you see. Because I really, *really* want you to touch me, Liv." I could've said need—probably should've said it, because the yearning for her hands on my body cut way closer to a need than a want. When she didn't move, I reached up and untangled one of her arms from around my neck and brought it between us. Skimming along her arm, I found and unfolded her fingers. As soon as I placed her palm over my chest, heat seeped into me, right through my skin to my bones, the sensation spreading outward as though laying claim to my soul. Closing my eyes, I lowered my forehead to hers and let out a sigh. "Just keep touching me like that. Exactly like that," I whispered.

Her head moved a little, a nod against mine. "Okay," she whispered back, and her fingers curled against my chest. The arm she had draped around me slid a little lower, until her forearm brushed my shoulder, her hand creating a trail of warmth over its blade.

My head tilted a touch to the side, and my lips reached for hers, her own head tilting, her own lips reaching, as if neither of us had to think about what to do because our bodies already had it covered. Letting my hand slip back down to her hip, I hoisted her closer again until her crotch hit my waist and sent all kinds of sparks shooting outward. She made a small sound, all feminine arousal that made the blood burn like lava through my veins, and as I swallowed the noise like I could somehow consume it, I inhaled deep, almost swaying at the scent she gave out. A scent that screamed of desperation and want and *fuck me now*, and if I could've bottled the stuff, I'd never fucking need the porn channel again.

My dick definitely liked her flavour, too, because it reared its head against the underside of my cargos, until she had to have known what she was doing to me. Had to have felt how my body tried its best to climb inside her despite the barrier of clothing still blocking its way.

Except the moment only seemed to be about Liv, not me. Like pleasing her was paramount. Something I had to do. Something I had no choice in. If only she'd let me.

Hooking an arm beneath her butt held her to me, and I brought my free hand up to her face, sliding my fingers around her neck and tipping her head back as I drew her lips between mine. Licked my tongue across hers. Moulded my mouth against hers as I smoothed that same hand downward. Over her shoulder. Her collarbone. Testing the waters with slow feathering over the top swell of her breast.

She didn't protest, but merely folded her fingers tighter over my chest. Found a chunk of flesh to cling onto beneath my shoulder blade.

Kissing her still, I dared moved my hand a little lower, over the lace of her bra until I cupped below her breast with the palm of my hand. I snuck my thumb beneath the fabric in search of her nipple, and as it brushed the hardened nub, she gasped and arched into me. Her fingers dug into my chest, forcing my growl out on a quiet rumble.

Pinning her once more with my hips, I reached around to her back, made fast work of the clasp holding her bra in place. As soon as I had it loose, I tugged the straps down her arms, freeing it over one hand before untangling from the other.

My gaze dropped to what I'd unleashed. Firm, impressively plump mounds of beautiful flesh just begging to be touched, and definitely tasted. I didn't even look away as I chucked the bra over my shoulder and totally out of reach of going back on. Damn, I doubted I could've looked away if I'd tried.

Not even bothering with a lead in, I hooked an arm back beneath Liv's butt and pressed the heat between her thighs tight against my strangled erection as I cupped her left breast with my free hand. Not only bigger than I'd imagined, but fuller, heavier, too. One hundred percent fucking perfection of pale skinned beauty.

With a fresh growl brewing within my chest, I dipped my face, feathered a kiss across the top swell, and bringing the rosy tip to my lips, I covered her nipple with my mouth, flicked my tongue across its tightness. Letting my growl send vibrations over it at the arch of her back and the clutch of her fingers against my skin.

"Danny," she whispered, her voice a little shaky.

Wrapping my lips around the peak of skin again, I suckled the nub deep into my mouth, and I had to force down the urge to fuck her against the wall, when she whimpered and her fingers twisted in my hair like she needed to make sure I didn't stop.

I closed my teeth around the hard nipple, my hips jutting forward against her as I scraped over the nub, gently tugging its tip outward. The whimper she gave skirted both pleasure and pain, and I lathered where I'd nibbled, using my tongue to cool there before warming with a small blow of breath. As I clamped down and sucked once more, the slight tilt of her hips urged her body into mine, and I gripped her hip, held her still as I ground my erection against her, almost dizzy with the scent pulsing from her, the high-pitched gasp she gave.

Drawing back just enough to free my mouth, I lifted my gaze to where she rested her head back against the wall behind her. Her lips slightly parted. Her eyes softly closed. Cheeks heightened by a rosy blush. Studying her, I really wanted to explore just how much more expressive I could get her to be, and I was moving before I even had to think the bloody order, my backward strides as long as I could make them in the direction of the bed.

Her eyes flipped open as her arms tightened around my shoulders.

"I need to touch you, Liv," I told her. "And I really need you to fucking be okay with that."

The backs of my knees bumped the divan, and I sank my butt down, a hand wrapping around each of Liv's thighs and splitting them across my own as I took her down with me. Staring at her through the lenses of her glasses, I saw no uncertainty. Only the sheen of lust-fuelled haziness peeked from beneath half-lowered lids.

"Tell me it's okay," I urged. I didn't know why I needed to hear the words, I just did.

"It's okay," she said, her voice low and heavy with arousal.

"*Tell* me," I ordered, and I held my breath, awaiting her answer.

Tugging me forward by the hair at my crown, she rested her forehead to mine, swept just her lower lip across mine. "It's okay for you to touch me."

It's okay for you to touch me. Such a simple sentence, but spoken with such soft assurance, it had me wanting to go in search of somewhere vulnerable, some spot easy to penetrate, easy to fucking bite through.

Instead, I drew only her offered lip between my teeth as I spread my legs wider, widening the span of hers right along with them, and brushed my hand over her leg to her inner thigh.

Watching her as she trembled, I took my fingertips higher, until they met the hem of her underwear. The fabric covering her crotch—soaking wet fabric, telling me what I already knew. Yet, somehow, the confirmation had me lowering my lids and groaning in a way the assumption hadn't.

"I need to touch you some more," I murmured without opening my eyes.

"Then, touch me some more," she whispered, not an ounce of hesitation in her response. Like she really needed me to hurry up and touch her as much as I wanted to.

Tucking a finger beneath her underwear, I pushed them aside, my knuckles brushing her moist spot, instantly soaked in her juices. Her body shivered against mine, though I doubted cold had anything to do with it. My own body was only a fraction shy of shivering itself.

As I ran a single fingertip over her opening, coating it some more, I inhaled. Deep. Long. The headiness of her scent stirring both my brain and body up into a world of fucking insanity until my dick all but knocked against the

223

inside of my pants with a plea to be let out. I couldn't let that happen, yet, though. Because I knew the second I released it, I'd quit giving a shit about pleasing Liv and be all about getting inside her as fast as I damned well could.

Drawing in a deep breath to steady myself, I chased the seam leading to her opening, let my finger dip inside. Just a little. Just enough to induce her gasp and have her hips twitching toward me.

Pushing in another inch, I braced the ball of my hand against her sensitive mound, where the tiny nub rubbed against my skin as though begging for attention. Her breaths hastened against my throat, and I slid in a little more. Drew back out. Slipped in a second finger to join the first. Pressed back against her with the ball of my hand.

A whimper burst from her. Loud and unrestrained. Her hands shifted to grip my shoulders, fingertips digging into the skin, sharp despite her trimmed nails.

With my eyes closed, every detail seemed enhanced. The way her breaths fanned my skin. The tiny sounds she made, alternating between a gasp, a moan, a whimper. The silky smoothness of her skin as I squeezed her butt and held her against my explorations. Even the pooling of her arousal in the palm of my hand, the tightening of her walls around my fingers with each probe, each withdrawal, her heels pushing at my calves as her hips shimmied up a tiny dance, stroking herself against where I pressed.

Opening my eyes offered a whole new dimension. The visual reaction. The high colour in her cheeks and the brightness of her irises where they peeked out beneath lids almost fully closed. Hair just beginning to cling to her brow with the first hint of sweat there. Her lips held open, folding around every sound that eked out. Her breasts swaying with her movements, nipples proud, teasing over my skin each time I shifted closer.

Dipping my head, I drew one of those stiff peaks into my mouth and tugged her in tighter as I pumped my fingers in and out, flexed then relaxed my hand against her stem of pleasure. So much evidence of her arousal poured into my palm, it spilled into the creases, dripped itself free. As the air, the whole fucking room, filled with the essence of Liv, pain fired outward in my groin and stabbed at the head of my dick.

"Shit." I snapped a hand round to my waistband, grabbed for the button there.

"What's wrong?" Liv asked.

"Suffocating," I said, yanking the button free.

Small fingers wrapped around my thumb and pulled my hand away before placing it on her hip. Those same fingers worked my zipper down, parted the opened waistband of my cargos, took hold of the elastic of my suddenly too-tight boxers. I didn't seem able to take my eyes off her movements, as she pulled the fabric away from my skin, letting my dick spring loose.

Everything seemed to move in slow motion from there. My heartbeat seemed to slow. Hers seemed to slow. The way her fingers slipped within the stretched cotton seemed to be slowed down.

The second she wrapped a hand around my erection, the spell broke, and I let out a groan, closed my eyes again. Inhaled long and hard as she adjusted her grip, firm despite the delicate slimness of her fingers. Despite her hand scarcely spanning my length.

The fingers of her other hand wove into my hair, and as her gentle tug lifted my face, my eyes opened to hers. Glossy, even through the ever growing dimness of the room. Free of lenses, too—and I wondered when the hell she'd removed her glasses without me even knowing.

She melded her lips to mine, her tongue forcing past until it swept my own tongue, her head slanting as her lips caressed, as her fingers stroked my dick. Pulling back a little, she met my gaze once more, nudged against my buried fingers. "Please don't stop, Danny. I need this."

Wrapping my fingers around the thin thong over her hip, I gave a sharp enough yank to snap it, and with the restriction dropped, I curled my fingers deeper inside her. Stroked her front inner wall where, experience had shown me, females loved to be stroked. My other hand brushed over her arse, in search of the central dip, and with the tips of my fingers skirting as close to her anus as I suspected she'd allow, I forced her forward against my hand once more.

"Oh, God," she whispered. Her hand squeezed my dick, making me jerk.

Gritting my teeth, I thrust my fingers into her harder, rubbed over her swollen mound harder, adding a third finger on the retraction, before sliding into her again.

Her fingers twitched around my shaft, and I had to close my eyes for a second as every one of the muscles in my body locked up.

When I pulled out of her again, drove my fingers into her again, she thrust against my hand, her whole body undulating into the move, yanking my dick along for the ride.

Breath hissed through my teeth as I tried holding my shit together, but when her thumb swiped through the leaked fluid at the tip of my head, I nearly unravelled alto-fucking-gether. My next breath barely escaped past my clamped jaw. "Liv, if you don't quit tossing me about, you're gonna end up sprayed."

She let loose a breathy laugh, but as she took my mouth with hers again, her grip relaxed some. She didn't release me, though—and I didn't want her to.

Letting her mouth take control, my muscles still coiled tight from her touch alone, I worked with the nudges of her body, pressing against her as she pushed forward, sliding out as her hips tipped back. Her tongue licked along mine, and I thrust into her harder, deeper, grinding my hand against her labia, slipping it up to her clit and grinding there as I withdrew, until we'd built up a pattern of slipping in and out, clenching and releasing, kissing and tonguing, and Liv's muscles began coiling in preparation for what was to come. Her whole body rigidly tight. Her mouth fervently clinging to mine. Fingers ignoring my request to quit crushing my dick, the tugging and squeezing slowly kicking back in like she had no control of the situation. Just as my own control was starting to take a hike.

The next gasp she gave blasted the inside of my mouth, an echo of ecstasy that stirred up my taste buds, and just as I thought I'd do exactly as threatened and shoot my fucking load all over her, Liv's body locked up, her whimpers silenced. The fingertips digging into my shoulder stilled. Hell, even those clutching at my shaft quit moving, as her lips poised over mine and only blindness stared back at me from her thundercloud eyes.

Scarcely daring to move lest I miss the mark, I held steady myself, waited for the nod, for the slight nudge of her pelvis that would tell me when. The instant it came, I brushed the ball of my hand against her.

A deep groan rolled past her lips.

I slipped my fingers into her as deep as they'd go.

Her face tipped upward. Her back arched. Her knees started to rise, scraping the soles of her pointed feet along the backs of my legs.

Drawing my fingers out of her, rolling my hand against her had her groan deepening further still, and smiling to myself, I drove those fingers right back in. Then out. A rapid fire pumping that set her entire body twitching. Had her hand freeing my dick and grabbing at my shoulder like she needed something a little more stable to hold onto. As her final groan flew from her, I pressed my face to her throat to catch the vibrations, inhaling the sweet fucking nectar overflowing my palm and soaking my trousers, until a growl rolled out of me and I knew if I didn't do something fast I'd explode without even knowing how she felt stretched around me.

Letting my dick lead the way, I shoved us up off the bed, ignoring the widening of Liv's eyes as I swung us round. As soon as I'd lowered her to the mattress, I rammed my cargos over my hips, not even bothering to kick them fully off before I climbed on with her, my thighs nudging hers aside, and I wedged myself deep into the V of her groin.

"You should probably tell me to stop," I mumbled, positioning the head of my shaft at her entrance. "Like, right now, Liv, if you're not okay with this."

She didn't speak. Just stared up at me. Eyes wide and full of acceptance, her fingers making a reach toward my chest.

Good enough for me.

I thrust forward, and her slick passage sucked me right the fuck in, her walls still contracting from her orgasm around me like a clenching fist. So much so that the second I'd hit home, my release shot from me with a violence that had my whole body shuddering and my arms struggling to hold me as up my chest collapsed down to meet hers. Teeth gritted, I tried to restrain the cry barking its way up my throat but stood no fucking chance. As my lips parted, it rushed out, along with another wave of seed pulsing out of me, out of me and into her, my body shaking in blessed relief like that'd been my goal all along. Like I'd needed it without fully knowing as such. Without fully knowing why.

Arms braced either side of her, head hung low, I loosened my jaw and tried regaining my breaths. "Shit," I muttered. I felt like I'd run a fucking marathon.

"Danny, did you finish already?" Liv's quiet voice brought me back to awareness. To the way her legs fitted around mine, her fingers spanned over my waist just above my hips, the way her breasts cushioned my own chest from crushing her completely.

Tipping my head to the side brought me close to where she turned her own face toward me, her seeking eyes asking the same question she'd just voiced. "I came," I told her. "I didn't finish."

Her chest pushed up as she inhaled. Dipped as she exhaled.

"It's your fault," I said, nipping at her jaw. "I bloody told you to stop messing with my dick, but you didn't listen." She smiled, and I lowered my face to the dip of her neck, nipped along the tendon there. "I just need a couple of minutes."

"Couple of minutes for what?" she asked, her fingers feathering across my hip, skimming my butt.

"To be ready again."

A small laugh escaped her, bumping her chest upward and sending vibrations to mingle with the ripples still buzzing through me.

"Probably less than that," I said, nuzzling my way downward and scraping my teeth along the line of her collarbone.

Her hand had moved up, and she massaged at the muscle just below my shoulder blade. "Anyone who's ready again that fast isn't normal," she said, sweeping her hand back down again and prickling my skin, in a really good fricking way.

I gave a short laugh, the sound a deep chuckle that shook my shoulders. "Who the hell told you I was normal?" I could already feel my dick swelling again, pressing against her inner walls. Testing my resolve. Hell, if I hadn't needed to push through the aftershock of coming, I'd have been ready to pound into her again before I'd even fully emptied out.

A laugh rumbled her flesh again, and as I placed soft kisses over her breastbone, her fingers tangled into my hair. Her pelvis nudged upward, the move seeming to flex her body around mine and make my reinterested erection even harder. I didn't know if she'd done it consciously, but I didn't care. Liv could touch me wherever the hell she liked and however the hell she liked, and I'd probably be happy about it.

I drew out of her a little, taking her nipple between my lips and sucking as I slid back into her and ground against her mound, still swollen from her own orgasm.

Her breath caught above my head, and she seemed to hold it for a beat before exhaling. "God, Danny, you take Viagra before you left the truck, or something?"

My lips curved around her breast, and I withdrew again, pushed back into her again, loving how her body trembled and her fingers tightened in my hair. "I don't need any drugs. I've got you." Blowing over her stiffened peak, I folded my mouth around it again and sucked, before lifting my face until I could see her eyes peering back at me. "And I really need you to drive me crazy all over again. Only this time ..." I wriggled an arm beneath her back, the other around her butt, and, rolling, I pulled her over me until she straddled my thighs. "Only this time, you won't be using your hands."

Her cheeks blushed a deep red, and she rested her head against my shoulder like she could hide from me.

Gripping her hips, I lifted her a couple of inches, pushing up to meet her as I lowered her back down. I tucked my face against hers, planted a gentle kiss to her jaw. "You okay?"

She nodded, but didn't raise her head. Hands grabbing onto my biceps, she lifted up a little, just like I'd done with her, giving a tiny sigh when she dropped back down.

I smoothed my hands around to her spine, resting them against her lower back. "Again," I told her.

Finally raising her head, she met my steady gaze with that of her own, and again using my arms as support, lifted and lowered, her passage clenching around me as she put her muscles to work.

"Keep going." Letting my hands slide back to her hips, I kicked off my clinging clothing the rest of the way and lowered my back to the bed, denying myself the urge to drop my focus to where I could see her breasts swaying.

Her hands moved to my chest, pressing down as she slid along my shaft again. Fingers curling over as she slipped back down. Her lips parting on an expelled breath. She held eye contact for only a minute before her lids drifted shut, and with her head tipping back a touch, she tilted her hips up, her arse pushing out, before she rocked forward again, her crotch rubbing over my groin, and a heavy breath rushed from her.

Letting my gaze go where it wanted, I watched as the next backward swing of her hips brought her arms tight around her breasts, urging them together in a way that had my mouth watering. Watched as her arms opened a little and set them jiggling, their dark tips poking at the surrounding air.

I pushed up just high enough to catch one of those tips with my mouth, and as her clit brushed over my skin again, I suckled it deep between my lips, letting my tongue flick over it. Her fingers clenched against my chest as she trembled, and I shifted to the other breast, took that one into my mouth, again waiting for her to trail her juices across my pelvis before sucking and licking. Loving how her body reacted to something so simple.

With my hands tightening over her hips, I urged her to rock over me again. Urged her to slide back. Took her nipple into my mouth in search of another round of trembles. Feeling like I'd scored when she gave a whimper and gripped at me harder.

Lathering my mouth higher, I kissed over her breast, over her collarbone. Urging her to keep going, I reached her throat, suckled there. Nipped my way toward her shoulder. Her neck. Her ear.

"This," I murmured. "This is exactly what I've been dreaming of you doing to me for weeks."

Her shuddering breath hit my shoulder, and she shoved her hips back higher, harder. Sweeping her hands up to my shoulders and grasping there, she slammed back down, flicking her hips forward, that time giving a gasp that coated my skin with heat.

With the next swing back of her hips, I reached a hand behind and, bracing against the bed, I shoved my dick up to meet the downward plunge of her body, a growl rumbling free when she gave a high-pitched cry. Letting my other arm reach round to hook her waist, I pulled her body against mine, buried my face into the hair waving around her neck. Once more, surging up off the bed, I rammed up to meet her forward thrust. Holding her even tighter when her face nuzzled into my neck and her arms hooked around my shoulders, her fingers knotting themselves back into my hair.

Like she no longer needed telling, her body seemed to know exactly what it needed to do without instruction. With her holding me close, with me clinging to her like I needed the anchor, I gave her control. Just sank into her and let her body work its magic. Let my hips thrust forth to merge us even deeper as I tasted her flesh.

Letting my mouth skim over her throat, I drove my dick up, weightlessness buzzing through my chest as a spasm tugged at my toes.

Massaging her pulse with my tongue, I thrust up again, tension creeping along my calves as an almost painful tightness cinched my hardening balls with the rapidly-growing need to come again.

Scraping my teeth along her shoulder, another upward urge of my hips had every muscle in my thighs coiling tight as though ready to spring. To attack. To push us both over the edge in a mutual release of pleasure.

With her inner passage twisting and tightening and crushing my dick, my mouth practically flooded with the need to taste her. To feed from her. In every fucking way possible. In a way that I seemed to have very little control over. As her whimpers and cries echoed through my mind, my lips moulded around her skin, my teeth skirting so close to biting down I should have been fucking terrified, yet I didn't seem capable of fearing something that felt so bloody right. My lips travelled her throat, her neck, her breasts—fuck, those breasts of hers tasted divine. If only she'd let me, I'd happily have feasted on those alone for the rest of my sorry life.

Lips clamped back around one of her nipples, I fought against the rising tide of tension pulsing through me. Not yet. Couldn't come yet. Because I knew Liv to be close. Knew in the frenzied and jerky movements her hips had devolved to. Knew in the way her cries had become drowned by the erratic mood of her breaths. The way she wrenched at my head with her fisted fingers, and the pooling of her juices spreading over my stomach.

After almost a whole agonising minute of holding my body locked tight, Liv's cries quietened. Even her breathing quietened. For a moment, the thrusting of her body seemed more controlled. More precise. Like she knew exactly what she wanted, and exactly how to earn it, and hell if she'd let anything stop her from reaching her goal.

A careful sweep across my groin had her trembling all over, her mouth opening with sound not yet ready to depart. She brushed backward, rocked forward, and as she slammed against my stomach, her whole body seemed to spasm. "Oh, God," she almost gasped as her face lifted from my shoulder and looked to the ceiling. Her fingertips sliced into the flesh of my shoulder. She didn't push back again, just gave a tiny wiggle of her hips, and as her lips stretched open, a sharp breath gusted out, and chasing on its tail, a wailing cry of fucking ecstasy that I knew I'd take to bed with me for the rest of my life.

Grabbing her hips quick, I forced her groin up and down. Up and down. Working her over my dick in the final strokes needed to finish me off. With her walls clenching around me like a fist pumping me to completion, I let the contortions take my muscles hostage. Let the heat soar through me.

A loud grunt erupted past my lips as I shot seed, and my entire, juddering body planked, my eyes screwing themselves shut. Jerking against the bedsheets, I let the ripples wash through me. My rigid toes reaching upward. My unyielding arms holding her exactly where I needed her, to ride out the release. Body still twitching, I unleashed a held breath. Sucked in air. Blew it back out. Going through the same routine for seconds before even an ounce of blood and oxygen began making its way to my stalling brain instead of my dick.

As my heartbeat made its first steps toward normal, I opened my eyes, and my lips instantly curved at the sight of Liv.

Head hung slightly forward, hair sticking to her glistening brow, she sat atop me, eyes tightly shut. Her palms lazily rested against my chest, and her lips parted as her breasts made a slow rise and fall in a way that drew my gaze down.

My smile vanished as soon as I took in her chest. The marks there. Marks that blemished her otherwise perfect skin, in a half moon pattern that stretched from one shoulder, down over her breasts, and up to the other shoulder.

As I recognised those marks for exactly what they were, my pulse bounced around like a raging timpani.

Shoving up to sit, I placed my fingers over the damage. The raised ridges of the outline. An outline of teeth. My teeth. Fucking, all over her like some kind of branding.

Shit. Shit, shit, shit.

One set of teeth marks was bad e-fucking-nough. A whole spray of them? Jesus, I was fucked. And I was in so much fucking trouble.

Ducking down, I studied Liv's face.

She hadn't moved. Hadn't spoken. Hadn't opened her eyes.

What if I'd done what every single one of us was forbidden to do? Only Sean had broken the rules, a couple of years earlier, and he'd lived with the guilt of that every day since.

Taking her shoulders, I gave her a gentle shake. "Liv?"

Her lips parted on a heavy sigh.

"Liv, talk to me."

Her eyes slowly opened. Eyes holding not a single ounce of pain, like I'd expected, but only the glassy laziness of post-sex satisfaction.

Bringing my hands up, I cupped her face, angling it up until she had little choice but to look at me. "Liv, you okay?"

She smiled. A slow-spreading smile that wrinkled her cheeks and made her eyes seem even droopier. "I'm great," she whispered.

The breath gushed from me so fast, it left an ache in my chest, and as every muscle in my body seemed to go lax, I flopped back down to the bed, scrubbed my hands over my face.

"*That* was great," Liv said above me, and I found myself laughing, the sound deep and broken and, possibly, a little bit deranged.

No fucking way could any of those bites have broken the surface—because no fucking way would Liv not be burning up and screaming about it right then if they had. The relief rushing through me was like a physical force, sending the blood scorching through my veins and pounding against my insides.

"How long this time?"

Shifting my arms aside, I let them drop to the mattress and stared up at her still-smiling face. "For what?"

"Until you recover," she asked, but her fingers fluttered up and pressed to her lips like she couldn't believe she'd asked.

My dick twitched, definitely liking that she had. "I already told you earlier. Two minutes max."

She frowned, but her smile still lingered. "Are you *sure* you didn't take Viagra before coming in here."

"I already told you, no." Grasping her hips, I pushed her to the left, forcing her onto her back as I rolled over top of her. "It's all you." I palmed her breast, rubbed my thumb over its tip. "And the fact that you have *the* best tits in the history of tits. It helps, you know?"

235

She laughed, but she sounded as much embarrassed as happy about the compliment.

Lowering my face, I circled my tongue around her nipple, halting when my gaze landed back on the marks I'd made. I pushed up over her until my mouth reached hers. Hooking a hand around her thigh, I wrapped it around me, leaning to the side to do the same with the other leg. A small wriggle of my hips had me nestling back deep inside her, before I began an easy pattern of tiny movements, stirring a little more stiffness into my erection with each one.

"Okay, I'm ready." I propped my elbows beside her arms, slipping my hands around her shoulders, spanning my fingers around the red blotches I'd made. Laying a gentle kiss over her lips, I brought my gaze to hers. "This time, though, we're gonna take it a lot slower." Because no way in hell could I risk losing so much control again. "Okay?"

"Okay," she whispered, and I pushed into her again.

23

I blinked open my eyes. Textured ceiling hovered above me, darkened by dullness. Unfamiliar padding supported my back. A quiet drumming created an unfollowable rhythm as rain hit the window, situated to my left, just like in my own room but nothing like it at all.

I inhaled. The action forced lax muscles to work, muscles that felt wasted yet content, like they'd done everything they could to gain everything they'd needed. It also sucked in just about every scent in the room, all of them telling tales of Liv's life, ending with the latest: the best fucking night of sex I'd ever had. Hopefully, the best night of sex for Liv, too.

I'd no idea what time we finally admitted the defeat of exhaustion and sank into oblivion atop the bed. I just knew we'd spent a whole lot of hours creating and recreating orgasms, and that I'd done exactly as I'd done in my head for weeks—sank to my knees before Liv in the shower and drank in all that she tasted of. All sweetness and tanginess in the perfect blend of female, running into my mouth like an offering of nectar that'd had me palming my dick and stroking myself to completion, because no way could I have waited for some kind of release.

The memory of the taste, her cries that should've shattered the tiles, the slickness of her body as the water had polished it to a glistening sculpture all had my dick twitching and wishing we'd never left the shower at all. That we'd stayed there all night, Liv feeding me perfection, my taste buds, my throat lapping it up.

Wrapping my fingers around my throbbing morning erection, I let my head flop to the side, trying to work enough energy into my muscles to take my body with it, but I didn't make the roll. Because no red hair lay scattered over the pillow beside mine. No body depressed the mattress or moulded the sheets. No Liv.

I lifted my head, like maybe she was there but I just couldn't see her. Stupid, really. Even the smallest female wouldn't have hidden that well.

Kicking the covers aside allowed cool air to swamp my body, and releasing my dick, I shuffled to the edge of the bed and forced my body up enough to swing my legs over and sit. Head twisting a little toward the door, I listened out for sounds. Chased the tick of the clock, the creaks of a house with little activity, all the way to quiet movements somewhere on the ground floor, near the back of the house.

I stretched for my boxers off the floor and fed them over my legs, not even bothering to stand and pull them up before doing the same with my cargos. As I slid the trousers over my thighs, something solid knocked against my leg, and I slipped a hand into the pocket, pulled out Ethan's mobile he'd given me before I'd gone in search of Liv.

Temptation and my pulsating dick almost had me ignoring obligation, but I couldn't be a total bastard and leave him and my brother hanging. God knew, coming in to see Liv had been a shitty enough thing to do to them already. A promise of flesh and pleasure always had the ability to make a male forget responsibility, though.

Lighting up the phone screen showed the time: five twelve. Not even trying to calculate how long that made my visit with Liv, I headed into Ethan's contacts, found Kyle's number near the top of the logs, set the call into motion. It connected after less than two rings.

"'Bout time," Ethan answered, his voice holding an echo like they had me on speakerphone.

"You better have got what you went in there for, Danny, because my arse is killing me and I have a crick in my neck that'll probably take a week to get rid of," Kyle said.

I smiled. "You're still here?" I'd known they would be.

"Where the hell else do you think we'd be?" Kyle asked.

I pushed up and stalked to the window, tugging up my clothes as I went, and nudging aside the net curtain, I peered outside. The front end of Ethan's pickup peeked around a cluster of high bushes a few houses down. "I see you."

They both leaned forward in their seats, peered upward through the rain-dashed windscreen toward where I looked out. "And we should have been seeing you. Hours ago," Kyle answered. "It better've been worth it."

I grinned down at them. "It was worth it."

"Good. Now get out of there," Ethan said. "And pull up around the corner and grab Kyle, so I can go straight home. My bed is calling to me."

"Give me ten minutes."

"Five. And by the way," Ethan added. "When Shelley's over later, I'll let you explain to her why I had to cancel on her last night."

The phone blanked out, and as I lowered it from my ear, 'Call ended' blinked on the screen. I could always have called him back, just to piss him off a little more, but the tinkles and shuffles coming from downstairs reminded me whose house I was in. Whose bed I'd slept in. Whose body I'd came in.

My mood didn't feel like plummeting just yet.

I grabbed up my shirt from the bedroom carpet, and found my discarded socks en route to the ajar door. Not even bothering to pause to clean myself up, I jogged down the stairs, hovered in the hall while I tugged my T over my head. The noises were clearer from there and seemed to be coming from both sides, like the downstairs was either open plan or a full circle of rooms.

Chucking my socks down by the front door, I ducked left into the living room, its bright whiteness shadowed despite the open curtains. I made the error of glancing in the mantelpiece mirror as I passed and winced at the dark circles my lack of sleep had created, not to mention the way my hair stuck up in knotted dirty-blond clumps.

Tugging on my shirt, I followed the waft of coffee on the air.

As I rounded a doorframe near the rear of the room that led to a kitchen, I paused over the threshold at the sight of Liv.

Staring out through the window, she stood with her back to me. She didn't even seem aware that I'd come downstairs, let alone that I watched her, and using the oblivion, I took a moment to drink her all in.

Thick, knitted socks covered her feet, the fibres a deep raspberry that stood out against the sandstone tiles across the floor. Above those, the pale skin of her legs led up to where her tailed shirt skirted her thighs, its cotton an emerald green that put the beech-wood units to shame. And above all of those, that hair of hers. That damned hair that poked out like rebellious flames licking the air.

Just as she had the evening before, Liv resembled an exotic piece of art amid the lacking canvass of her family home. I could've stood watching her all day. Hell, I could've hoisted her up, there and then, and taken her on the worktop.

If I didn't have Ethan's abruptness ticking away the minutes in my head.

"Hey," I said.

Her shoulders jerked, but only a little before she turned to me. Her lips stretched, slowly at first as if unsure, and then she smiled. A great smile. One that had my own mouth responding. One I wished I could see every morning when I woke up. "Hey yourself," she said. "I thought you'd sleep later than this."

"How long was I out?"

Her nose scrunched up, and she glanced toward a sandstone clock on the wall. "Less than an hour."

That explained why my body still felt exhausted but raring to get back at it with Liv all at the same time. It didn't, however, explain Liv's early rising. The sun had scarcely even begun climbing the sky.

I tucked my hands into my pockets, leaned into the doorframe. "I was surprised to find you up when I woke."

"I couldn't sleep," she said, moving across the kitchen and flicking the switch on the kettle.

I frowned. "Because of last night?"

Her head wobbled, like she didn't know whether to nod or negate. "Not necessarily in a bad way." She went to glance away but turned straight back as though changing her mind. "You want to stay for breakfast with me? I could cook …"

"I would, except …" I pushed up and went to step into the room, but at a sharp hissing, I halted, my gaze dropping to a ball of spikey white fur blocking the doorway to what I presumed was the dining room. Great. "You never mentioned you had a cat."

"You don't like cats?"

I kept my gaze glued to the sharp pointed teeth, as the runt gave another hiss full of spit and promises I didn't want to explore. "I, uh—I kind of have a shitty history when it comes to them. And yours looks like she wants to rip out my throat." Not that it'd get that far. I could've broken the ratty thing with my little finger.

She laughed. "She's a *he*. And Mr Tiddlywink wouldn't hurt a fly."

"Yeah, well, I'm not a fly, and Mr fucking Tiddlywink definitely doesn't look opposed to using to those claws where I'm concerned."

"Okay, okay, I'll save you," she said, only just keeping more laughter in check. Stepping toward the cat, she swung her arms toward it, flicked her hands. "Shoo, Mr T!" The stupid cat ran off hissing and spitting, but Liv still tagged on an extra insult of, "Leave poor, little Danny alone."

I scowled. "I was doing your cat a favour. He wouldn't have won if he tried taking me on."

"Bravado," she said, stepping close enough to reach out and tug on the hem of my shirt. "Spoken like a true guy."

Further protests sat on the tip of my tongue, but they needed saving for another time. Another time when I *had* more time. Wrapping my fingers around hers, I drew her nearer still and heaved in a heavy breath. "Listen—"

"You're leaving," she cut in. "Aren't you?"

"It's not because of you—hell, I'd stay here the whole day and then some, if I had the freedom to do so."

She stared up at me, her brow creased up by any number of emotions. "But?"

"But you were the first person I came to see when I left the station yesterday."

Her frown lifted a little. "I was?"

I nodded, and unable to stop myself, I rubbed my thumb over the softness of her jaw, settling my palm against her pulse as I continued to stroke. Like I felt the need to soothe her as I told her goodbye. "My dad ... he's probably been sitting up waiting on me to get home." I could already picture him—I just didn't know how the greeting would go. "I owe it to him to go back and talk to him about what happened."

"You do," she said, giving a small nod.

I let my hand fall from her face, regretting the distance it brought as soon as I had. "Walk me out?"

"What will the neighbours think?" she said, but, smiling, she stepped back and tightened her fingers around mine as she wove around me and into the living room.

"Do you care?" I let her lead me past the sofa, my focus entirely on the way her body moved.

"If I cared, Danny ..." She spun and backed herself through the second doorway into the hall. "You wouldn't have been invited in, in the first place."

"Good." Stalling her from moving away any farther, I tugged her into me and wrapped my arms around her body as I ducked my face and inhaled the scent that'd kept me company all night. That'd probably keep me company every night for the rest of my life, whether in memory or reality. Dragging my nose from its burrowing, I pulled away from her, reaching for the front door before I could change my mind and say screw my family. "I've really got to go."

She nodded, and I could sense how closely she watched me as I stood in the porch and worked each foot into my waiting socks and boots, could see the unrest of her fidgeting hands in my periphery. Once booted up, I reached for the porch door, almost stepping through it before ordering my arse back around. Not exactly a wise move, when I saw the way she stared at me with disappointment and yearning I felt within myself, and possibly a little hurt in her eyes, too. Not trusting myself to do anything more, I stepped back to her and pressed a lingering kiss to her forehead before moving away. "I'll see you soon," I told her and pushed outside into the rain and gloom.

"That kiss felt a lot more like a goodbye than a see you later," she said, before I'd even hit the driveway.

Halting, I turned. I hadn't intended it to come across like she said, but the way she leaned into the doorframe of the porch and peered up at me through her tumbling red hair told me it had, anyway. Needing to wipe the doubt from her eyes, I made the few strides back toward her and, not even bothering with small talk, dug my fingers into the hair at her nape and closed my mouth over hers.

Her body instantly sank into mine, and I loved that. Her throat instantly offered up a groan, and I loved that even more.

I also loved how she still smelled of her and me and everything we'd become overnight. Like our hours of passion had created a new scent for us both and we'd never smell quite the same ever again.

Curving an arm under her butt, I lifted her enough to align her chest to mine and kissed her like I had no fucking intention of stopping any time soon.

Except, I did have to stop. I could fully imagine the unwanted attention we'd be getting from the pickup down the street.

Groaning, I forced my lips from hers, leaned in against her forehead, and closed my eyes. "Shit. You are a *really* bad influence, you know that?"

"I kinda like that I'm a bad influence on you," she said, her breath heating up my face.

Though my lips curved at her words, regret washed through me as I set her back on her feet and pressed the tamest kiss my brain would allow against her lips. "Like I said, I'll see you soon. Okay?"

"Okay," she whispered, but that time when I pried my body from hers and urged myself away, I had the memory of her smile to take with me.

24

"She's cute," Kyle said, as soon as he'd settled into his seat.

I pulled away from the kerb, following the taillights of Ethan's truck.

"Like a miniature Marilyn Monroe," he continued. "Except with glasses. And much cooler hair."

I glanced his way as we hit a junction, my gaze skimming over his hair, only a shade or two darker than Liv's.

I'd been right. He and Ethan had totally seen my goodbye to Liv. And they'd definitely mentioned it, when I'd pulled up alongside Ethan's pickup for Kyle to jump in with me.

Turning back to the road, I manoeuvred us out onto the B-road, watching how the lights on Ethan's ride lit the wet tarmac up with a red glow.

"Now I've seen her for myself, I get why you were in there all night."

I ignored him. Bastard was only goading me, anyway.

"Leaving us outside in the cold and the wet."

I took a sharp left bend at thirty before speeding us up again. Best thing about early morning driving was lack of traffic. We'd probably be home in less than half an hour.

"Aching," he continued, his voice beginning to drone. "At risk of getting questioned for our loitering behaviour." He shifted in his seat, his foot kicking against the bottom dip of the dash. "At least tell me you were careful," he said, his tone more serious.

I frowned across at him, but fast glanced back to the road when he tried probing me with his eyes.

"Danny?"

I shrugged. "Well, I didn't bite through her skin, and she's still human," I told him.

"Not exactly what I meant," he muttered. "Wait, though. You *wanted* to bite her?"

I snuck a peek out the corner of my eye, at his suddenly curious tone. I didn't like that tone. It always meant he was thinking too hard about something.

Offering up another shrug, I told him, "I never said that."

I expected him to argue some more, but all he said was, "Interesting," in a way that suggested he really did find it so.

I did glance at him that time. I didn't like the way his frown seemed perfectly natural alongside the pleasure his weird smile gave out. "What's interesting?"

"Nothing." He nodded toward the windscreen. "Watch the road."

I turned back in time to slow my speed for another sharp bend. "If you've got something to say, just bloody say it, Kyle."

"Nothing to say," he said, the irritating fuck, even though his tone told me he had plenty going on inside his head. After a small pause, he added, "Some things are just better figured out for ourselves."

I twisted toward him again, but he merely jerked his chin to the side.

"Watch the damn road, Danny." And, like he'd decided the conversation was definitely over, he sank down farther into his seat and closed his fucking eyes.

Bastard.

We entered the house via the back door. Not unusual. Though, it did seem unusual walking into an empty kitchen when I knew everyone bar us was home. I guessed it'd been a while since I'd crawled home at the larks' rising.

My boots stomped the tiled floor on my way through to the hallway, but as I went to make the turn for the stairs, Kyle tugged me round and thumbed toward the living room door.

"You owe it to him," he said, before he squeezed past me and jogged up the stairs himself.

I glanced toward the door he'd indicated, a twitch of my ears picking up the breaths from within.

"Are you coming in, or not?" Dad said from beyond the ajar door.

"I'm coming," I said, and pushed my way inside.

On the seat nearest the window, Dad sat balanced on the edge of the cushion, his arms overhanging his knees. His hair coiled outward in probably his most dramatic style to date, and I swore a hundred more lines creased his face than had been there the morning before, when the police had taken me from him.

I paused a few feet into the room. "You okay?"

He nodded, but even that action held such weariness that guilt pulsed inside my chest. "I would ask you the same thing, but I can smell you from here, so I'm going to assume you're just good and fine."

"It was something I needed to do, Dad."

"*Sex* … was something you needed to do?"

I could understand him being pissed at me. He had every right. But if he didn't get it, he never would. "Not sex. *Liv.* I needed to see her."

"To tie up loose ends, you told Nate."

"I did that." At least, I thought I had.

"Okay," he said simply.

"I needed to see her," I said again, like I needed him to get the importance of that, even if I didn't fully understand it myself.

"Okay," he said. "I believe you." He pushed to his feet and bridged the couple of strides until he stood right in front of me. Not giving me a chance to argue, he gripped the back of my neck and tugged me in close, leaving me little choice beyond staring into the green eyes he'd passed onto me and Josh. "You don't ever scare the shit out of me like that again, Daniel. Do you hear me?"

"I hear you."

247

He drew me in harder and enveloped me with the mass of his body, until Liv's scent factored out and Dad's scent factored in, and everything about the moment reminded me of childhood and parents who'd always, one hundred percent, given a shit.

"I'm sorry," I muttered. "I'm sorry I brought whatever this is on the pack, and I'm even sorrier I brought it on you."

"I know." His words rumbled through his chest and into mine. "You really should've gone straight to Nate's this morning, though. I'm not the only one who's been sitting up, waiting on you to come home."

"Maybe I thought you deserved my apology more," I told him.

His nod brushed the side of my head before he drew back, and his eyes seemed to study my face. "I appreciate that, Son. Now get yourself to bed, okay? I'll settle things with Nate. And we can discuss whatever this situation is that you've gotten yourself into at a more reasonable hour."

I accepted the extra tightening of his arms around me that came, and I even accepted the kiss Dad slopped against my temple. Feeling like some open wound had been at least partially healed, I trudged my hide from the room and climbed my arse to bed.

Three hours I'd managed to get. Three hours shouldn't have been enough, but after the night of being with Liv, my body felt all kinds of rejuvenated and raring to go. Problem with that, though, was my dick seemed to be leading the way in the enthusiasm rankings.

Letting the water splash over my body, the steam swirling Liv's scent clinging to my skin through the shower stall, I pumped my fist around my shaft. My muscles twitched with release so fucking near, and I leaned into my braced hand, pressed my forehead to the cool tiles. Worked my hand a little faster as my rapid breaths turned to grunts.

The first spray left me fast and hard, almost buckling my knees, my muttered, "Shit," a strangled sound of relief. Another tug urged another shot from me, before I slowed my hand and stroked the next few rounds out. My body jerked with every damn one of them, until my dick quit demanding, my muscles quit spasming, and only my heaving breaths refused to calm.

Someone banged on the bathroom door, but I didn't move. Couldn't be arsed to move.

"What the hell are you doing in there?" Josh said through the door.

"Enjoying myself," I muttered.

"Too bloody much, by the sounds of it. Get a move on. You're not the only one needs to shower."

"You're just jealous," I called out, as I pushed off from the wall and reached for the soap.

"Of your hand?" Some kind of snorted grunt seeped through the door, but his footsteps carried him away, and I spent the next few minutes rinsing myself of the remnants of Liv.

Meaty scents carried upward by the time I descended the stairs, as well as a voice I recognised but definitely didn't expect to hear.

I jogged down the last few steps, strode the length of the hallway to the open kitchen door, and stopped short at the weirdly domesticated scene I walked in on.

Over at the counter, Dad stood shoulder to shoulder with Aunt Maghon, of all people, dishing up a bunch of readymade breakfast baps that dripped grease everywhere.

He glanced over his shoulder at me. "Maghon stopped by with breakfast for everyone," he said.

"Danny-Boy," she said, twisting far enough to send me a smile.

"Can you call the others?" Dad asked.

Wondering when the hell their meetings had progressed to her *stopping by for breakfast*, I padded to the bottom of the stairs and yelled, "Breakfast," up to the others.

Back in the kitchen, Dad carried the plates over to the table, while Maghon pushed them in front of seats, setting napkins beside them. By the time Kyle and Brook came into the room and took their seats, and Josh rushed in still soaked from his shower, I'd gone from frowning to myself, to studying the anomaly of a scene across the table. Though, the way the others just accepted it told me I'd been the only one unaware of the morning's plans.

Yeah, thanks for the warning, guys.

"Perfect," Kyle mumbled, as he shovelled in a bap the size of my head into his mouth. "Should deffo come for breakfast more often, Aunt May."

Although his head was lowered, I caught the sideways smile Dad sent toward Maghon. Caught the smile she gave back, too, and my eyes narrowed on the body language of the pair of them. Body language that had no resemblance to that of two people who'd simply aired out their fucking differences.

Tucking aside my assumptions—for then, anyway—I gripped hold of my food and tore off a chunk of bread filled with an entire English breakfast, sans the baked beans. I'd barely had time to lick the grease from my lips when my phone rang in my pocket, and, pausing to clear off my hands on a napkin, I worked it out.

As soon as I looked at the screen, though, I frowned.

ANSWER ME DANNY glowed above the flashing 'answer' motif.

I swiped over the screen and held the phone to my ear. "Hello."

"Danny," a female said. "How're you doing, darling?"

My entire body locked up into a rigid knot of muscles at the voice I recognised instantly. Swallowing hard, I lifted my gaze and found Dad's astute attention wholly on me, despite the way he tried to pretend it wasn't. His eyes scrunched slightly, questioning, but I sliced my gaze across to Maghon and pushed back from the table.

"I'm gonna take this in the other room," I told them, not looking at anyone else as I rounded the table.

"You should take your food with you," Maghon said. "Eat it before it gets cold."

How could I tell her I'd just lost my appetite? "I'll eat it after," I said absently, ducking into the hallway.

My heart thumped as I climbed the stairs. As soon as I'd shut myself in my room, I placed the phone to my ear and growled out the words clanging around inside my head:

"You're dead."

25

"It's not nice to start a conversation with a threat," the female said down the line.

I gripped the phone harder, paced the room, my pulse prancing about like a fricking show pony. "No, I mean *you* are dead. I saw the photos. You fucking died."

"Ah, those." A perverse-sounding giggle tinkled down the line. "We did do a good job of convincing everyone, didn't we?"

"Who the hell are you, and if you're not dead, why the hell did you try framing me for a murder that didn't happen?"

"I need to speak to Ethan," was all she said.

I paused, mouth open, wondering how the hell Ethan had gotten thrown into the mix. "Why?"

"If you want to know who I am, you'll take the phone to Ethan. You have twenty minutes. If Ethan is not on the end of the phone when I call back, I shall come to you and show you exactly how much that displeases me. You can rest assured, your morning visitor won't like me very much."

Ice soared through my veins and plummeted my temperature, and as the line went dead, I strode to my bedroom window and stared out like I'd find whoever the hell the female was standing at the end of the driveway and watching the house. Because she had to be watching. Had to be. How the hell else could she have known we had a visitor?

Nobody stood there. Nobody peered through the gates from the road outside.

I had no fucking idea what I'd done to the woman, but I'd obviously done something, and that something had pissed her off. A real fucking lot.

What the hell Ethan had to do with it all, though, I'd no bloody idea.

You have twenty minutes. The words vibrated through my skull, and I shot for the door to the landing, but halted at the wall of muscle blocking my way out.

"Who was on the phone?" Kyle asked, his arms crossed as if to make himself even more of a barrier.

"I don't have time for this. I need to get to Nate's."

He levelled his eyes with mine. "Who was on the phone, Danny?"

Instinct urged me to knock him aside and tell him to go hump himself, but I couldn't risk the fight. Couldn't risk Aunt Maghon witnessing the tussle. Definitely couldn't risk the female from the phone call—who should've been fucking dead—carrying out her threat.

"I don't know who was on the phone," I told him, only a partial lie, because I didn't actually know who Blondie was. Or what she wanted. "And this isn't the place to discuss it." I nodded my head toward the stairs as Maghon's voice carried up from the kitchen, where I suspected Dad only gave her minimal attention and tried listening in on us instead.

Nodding, Kyle stepped back. "I'll drive you, then, and you can tell me on the way."

Again, I could've argued, but I had bigger meals to dish, so when he jogged down the stairs, yelling out to Dad that we just had to pop to Nate's to tend to an SOS, and pulled open the front door, I kept my mouth shut and followed.

Ethan stared at me, all kinds of *what the fuck* pumping from his every pore. "How the fu—" He glanced toward where his dad sat in his usual seat at the head of the kitchen table and back to me. "How the *hell* can anyone get themselves into this kind of messed up situation, Danny?"

"I didn't get myself into anything. It—whatever *it* is—got *me* into *it*." I looked toward Nate. "I need your help, okay? I'm asking for it."

253

Nodding, Nate leaned back in his chair, crossed his arms across his broad chest. "Run through the phone call one more time."

"There isn't time. She's callin—"

"It wasn't a request, Daniel."

Resisting the urge to roll my eyes and pace the room, I recalled the conversation I'd had. The female's admission of setting me up. Her twisted attitude, like the whole stunt she'd pulled was a game. Finishing with her threat to show up at the house, I shrugged. "We came here right away."

"That's it?" Nate asked, and I nodded. He looked to Ethan. "Who'd you piss off?"

Ethan breathed out a laugh, but it held no humour. "Just about everyone I ever met."

"You need to think harder than that. And fast. Because this is definitely somebody who's mad at you, and he"— Nate uncrossed his arms and pointed at me—"is the one getting kicked for it."

"He's not getting kicked for it," Ethan argued. "He's just a fucking pawn." At his dad's glare across the table, he sighed. "Sorry. Pawn—he's just a pawn."

Nate turned to Kyle. "Do you have any ideas who this might be?"

Running a hand through his hair, Kyle said, "Only female I know who could be this mad at him should be running in the other bloody direction, not toward him."

"Who?" Sean said as he strode into the room and headed for the kettle.

My phone rang before Kyle could answer.

For a couple of long seconds, we all just stared toward where the device vibrated in my hand, before I held it up, showed them the ANSWER ME DANNY flashing on the screen.

Pressing to connect, I lifted it to my ear. "You have any answers for me yet?"

"Is Ethan with you?" she said.

"Yes."

"Ah, so you *are* capable of doing as you're told. Maybe I should give that Alpha of yours some tips on how to control his wayward pup."

"Maybe you should just go fu—"

Ethan tugged the phone from my hand and pressed it to his own ear. "Who the hell is this, and why should I give a shit about what you want?"

The high-pitched giggle I'd heard from her myself blasted out of the earpiece, and Ethan's gaze slowly rose up toward Kyle. The way he stared, the darkening of his brown eyes, the tightening of his jaw all told me that Ethan knew from that sound alone who held the other end of the line. He quirked his eyebrow up in question, and at Kyle's nod, he turned to his Dad.

'Catherine,' he mouthed.

The worst fucking name any of us could've hoped for.

As Nate's hands fisted atop the table, Sean quit with grabbing for coffee and came closer.

"Okay," Ethan said into the phone. "I know who you are. So, how about you just answer my second question."

"Did you miss me, darling?"

His jaw ticced. "Just tell me what this is about. I don't have time for your games."

"You're going to make time," she said, her tone sharpening. "Because you owe me, Ethan."

His lip curled as his scowl moved in. "I don't owe you shit."

"You screwed up my plans. You ruined everything I worked hard to achieve. So, *yes*, you owe me."

Ethan growled. "Sorry, but I don't pay back debts I've had no fucking say in."

A huff of breath blew down the line. "While I'd love to back and forth with you all day, we're wasting time. You *will* pay me back for sabotaging my last enterprise, so just agree and make it easier on yourself."

"And if I don't?" Ethan asked.

"If you don't …" she said, suddenly sounding brighter again. "The police just might find another body. And not only will *she* be found in Wild Woodington, *on Holloway land*, but the *redhead* I've already picked out for the role definitely won't be getting back up afterward and walking away."

My pulse picked up speed even as Ethan asked, "Redhead?"

"Correct. And after the night Danny's spent with her, the police will find plenty of evidence linking him to the victim."

The snarl tore from my throat before I could stop it, and I lunged across the table for the phone. Before my feet even left the floor, arms banded about my chest and a hand slapped over my rippling lips, as Ethan jerked the mobile out of my reach.

Giggles rolled out of the earpiece, and I fought against the restraint, thrust back my elbow, but the arms only tightened, pinning me in place.

"Do not give her the satisfaction," Kyle whispered near my ear. "She's not fucking worth it, Danny."

"Okay, so I have your attention," Catherine said.

The vibrations running through my chest buzzed even louder as I held my body rigidly still in Kyle's grip and tried to shake off his hand pressed over my lips.

"Shall we discuss business now?" she continued, pausing only a moment before adding, "Good. This is the arrangement. It's non-negotiable, and you will comply."

With the next shrug of my shoulders, Kyle's hands loosened, and every one of us seemed poised to strike in Ethan's direction, like we could somehow vicariously attack through to the other end of the call.

"At exactly midnight, you, Ethan, will come alone to a pick-up spot. To ensure you obey the *alone* part of that order, I will call you thirty minutes prior to midnight with the location of a place of my choosing. If you deviate from this directive, or if you're stupid enough to not turn up—

256

which I'm sure you're not—my colleague will deliver the pre-mentioned redhead to the pre-mentioned location. Comprendre?"

The phone clicked dead.

"Shit," Kyle muttered.

26

I twisted farther away from Kyle and held out my hand. "Give me the truck keys."

His eye twitched. "I'm not giving you the keys."

"Give me the fucking keys," I said again, and when he didn't budge, I spun for the wall beside the door to the hallway, where the keys to all the Holloway vehicles hung in a row.

"Do not take another step," Nate said. Though his tone was quiet, it held enough pull to halt me in my tracks.

"I need some wheels, Nate."

"For what?" he asked.

"What do you mean, *for what*?" Throwing my arms up, I fully faced him. "Didn't you hear what that psycho just said? I need to go check on Liv. I need to go now. Right fucking now!"

He shook his head, his stare unwavering.

"'The hell, Nate?"

"It might be a trap," Ethan said, nudging himself ever so slightly toward the key rack, like he thought I wouldn't bloody notice.

"I don't care if it's a trap. Liv is in danger—"

"Call her." Nate jerked his chin toward my phone in Ethan's hand. I opened my mouth to object, but he shook his head again. "Just call her, Danny. It's faster than you driving hell bent over there, and once you've spoken to her, we'll decide the next step from there."

"And if she doesn't answer?" Something splintered in my chest at that possibility.

"Only one way to know." At Nate's nod, Ethan passed me the phone.

I flicked through into my phonebook, scrolling down until I found Liv's number, and swiped to call. Nobody spoke when it started ringing, not even Jem as she pushed past behind Ethan into the kitchen and went to stand beside Sean.

After four rings, it went quiet, then, "Hey," came down the line.

My exhale gusted from me, and I had to clear my throat to manage a returned, "Hey. How you doing?"

"I'm okay," she said, sounding a little shy and really happy to hear from me all at the same time. It was enough to ease the ache in my chest, and I dropped my butt down into the nearest chair, like just standing up seemed suddenly overwhelming. "You?" she asked after a second or two's silence.

I rubbed a hand over my face and around the back of my neck. "Yeah, I'm good. I'm real good. I, um—I just wanted to see how you were."

She laughed, and the blackness cinched within me unfurled itself a little more. "I think we just covered that, Danny."

I smiled, despite the shitty situation poking its way in from the offside. "Sorry. Conversation isn't—"

"Really your strong suit," she cut in, and another of her quiet laughs met my ear. "Listen … I'm not really doing anything this afternoon …. Did you want to …"

I glanced up at Nate, caught the tiny shake of his head. Curling my fists, I turned away. "I'd love to," I said to Liv, totally meaning it, even though I knew from the way he shifted in his seat, Nate'd slam my hide if I made any promises. "But …"

"But you can't," Liv finished for me.

"Sorry. I just—I have family stuff going on this afternoon. I think I might be needed for that, but we should definitely do something once that's sorted."

"Okay," she said simply.

I found myself smiling. "Okay. I mostly just wanted to check you were okay."

"Damn, that's twice round the full circle now. Yes, Danny, I'm okay. I swear."

"Okay," I said again.

"You call me," she said, her tone light like she smiled. "When you're free, or whatever."

"I will," I told her, but by the time I ended the call, my smile had slipped and the lightness that'd claimed me while I talked to Liv had lifted. I twisted back to Nate. "She's okay."

"Good." He rested his arms atop the table and looked round at us all. "Now we plan."

Within thirty minutes, the entire pack sat around the table, including Brook, and Nate had made me and Ethan fill them in on the situation. Even Gabe had driven over to join in the discussion, and his face dropped like he'd just been castrated, at the mention of Catherine.

Gabe had been the whole reason Ethan and Kyle had ended up taken by vampires for a twisted scheme the year before, placing the then-seventeen-year-old in the seriously bad thick of it all. After the pack had managed to clear up the whole fuckup, we'd let ourselves relax and believe it to be all over. Stupid really, considering the one vampire to have slipped through the pack's fingers just happened to be the mastermind behind it all.

Catherine.

"Shit," Gabe muttered, for about the tenth time.

"Okay." Nate leaned back in his seat. "Best way to play this?"

"There's not really much of an option," I said before anyone else could suggest something stupid. "Either Ethan plays by her set rules, or Liv gets hurt." Though, in my mind, I was already working out how I could get my arse to where Catherine would be, just to let her know what I thought of her threats and games.

"I can cover your friend."

The quiet suggestion drew me from my plotting, and I turned toward the cat. Brook stared back at me and seemed to be offering more than just words in those amber eyes of hers. "It should be me who goes," I told her.

"And walk right into Catherine's expectations of you?" She turned to Nate. "I'm happy to shadow and make sure she's okay."

"What makes you think you'll be any safer doing this than me?" I asked, needing the argument even though I suspected Nate wouldn't budge on letting me go. Three times he'd told me to sit my arse down and wait on the plan, while we'd paused for the others to arrive. The fourth time had been a direct order, with enough grit and growl behind it to stall my arguments—for a little while, anyway.

"Because you're a werewolf, and werewolves are deadly allergic to vampire venom, should anything go wrong." She met my gaze. "I'm not."

"That's hardly a compelling argument when I'm already biting my tongue over here at your offer, Brook," Kyle said.

She turned to him, her lips curved into a slight smile that didn't warm her eyes. "Do you plan to somehow be involved in ending this with Catherine?"

He let out a low growl like he knew her argument already. "Yes."

"Despite what she did to you the last time?" As his eyes narrowed, hers darkened to a rich shade of burnt caramel. "You are not the only one who would like to see this vampire ended. I wonder how you would react if I insist on accompanying whatever happens tonight?"

His teeth ground. "That's never going to happen."

"You do not own me, Kyle. However, I do not wish to fight with you over this despicable female, so I will compromise on this. You should, too. Let me do this much, at least." She glanced toward me, her jaw a rigid line of determination. "I will watch her for you. Yes?"

My gaze immediately cut to Nate, and I opened my mouth, the argument balanced and ready for spewing, but at the small shake of his head, I clamped it shut again and gave a reluctant nod Brook's way. "You need to call me if there's even a sign of trouble, though."

What I didn't voice was, if that happened, my compliance would be off the table.

"I will." Sliding from her seat, she leaned in to kiss Kyle, murmured some promises about playing it safe as she took his truck keys from him. "You need to tell me where I'll find her," she told me as she made for the door.

I followed her out to the hall, pausing at the front door to quickly gave her the address and directions, before adding, "If she's not there, try the divey-looking Hang & Hide on the main road. You can't miss her red hair, so she'll be easy to spot."

"Like a little redheaded Marilyn Monroe with glasses," Kyle called from the kitchen.

"Noted," Brook said, giving her focus back to me. "I'll call you once I have her in my sights." With a reassuring smile, she turned for the front door, but before she could open it, I pulled back on her arm.

Those heated eyes of her spun toward me, and I swallowed. "Thanks," I said, the wording seeming the wrong size for my mouth. "For doing this. I appreciate it."

With a murmured, "My pleasure," in that exotic tone of hers, she pulled open the door and headed outside.

"Okay?" Nate said, when I ducked back into the kitchen, and I nodded. "Good, so onto the next issue. Catherine wants Ethan to come alone so she can do whatever the hell she has planned for him. That can't happen, so I have an idea." His gaze skimmed us all until it landed on his son. "But first we need to figure out just how much we want to finish this ourselves."

"You want to bring outsiders into this?" Ethan asked.

His dad nodded. "I think it's time to call in on a favour that's owed us."

27

Nate's grand idea? Fight vampires with vampires.

During the stint where the others had landed themselves in Hotel De Catherine the year before, there'd also been vampires and shifters and other beings locked up in those cells, just waiting on their turn to be pitted in the cage against another. Given that Ethan and Kyle's first encounters with vampires consisted of Ethan getting his arse kicked, followed by imprisonment, degradation, exposure to the human world, and threats of being chowed on, the pack hadn't been too keen on opening those cages containing the fanged bastards themselves.

While snuffing the lot of them and having done with it seemed like the better option, Nate figured the repercussions just wouldn't be worth the hassle, so Ethan had got in touch with a vampire he'd 'met' during his investigations, handed over the job of releasing the caged vampires to him, and the pack's consideration had earned us a modicum of respect and a returned favour to cash in on.

"They might not want to give up their kind to us," Nate said, "but that doesn't mean they wouldn't be prepared to handle this new issue themselves. Especially as Catherine's last enterprise risked exposure for them, as well as us."

Ethan nodded. "It's worth a try," he said, before turning and staring at Jem.

Letting out a sigh, she pushed back from the table. "I'll go call Jess."

The vampires we needed to get in touch with lived in a different county. Witchurch. Jem's sister also lived in Witchurch, and while she didn't exactly endorse the local bloodsuckers, she definitely had a knack for getting in touch with them.

"Okay, so, what if they won't help?" Dad asked, as Jem stepped from the room. "What then?"

"They will," Ethan said. "If their word is worth anything, they'll come good."

Jem slipped back in a few minutes later, her phone still in her hand. "She's contacting them now—said she'll call back once she has."

Sean wrapped his hands around her hips as soon as she drew near, tugged her down onto his lap. "You know this is all the involvement you're getting, don't you?"

She stared hard at him before glancing away, the, "We'll see," muttered under her breath barely on the audible scale.

At a loud vibrating, Ethan stood and worked his phone out of his pocket. He glanced at the screen before answering. "Jess."

"One of these days, you'll actually ask me yourself when you need a favour." Even through the phone, her voice held a heavy dose of pissed off.

"You miss me. It's only natural," Ethan said into the mouthpiece.

"Hadn't better let Mum hear this shit," Gabe muttered from opposite him.

"It was a joke." Ethan seemed to be addressing the lack of response coming down the phone line, as much as his mate's son. "What do you have for me, Jess?"

"I contacted the locals for you," she said. "And they've reluctantly agreed to meet."

"Today?"

"When I stressed the urgency of the situation, yes. It's okay, it's something else you can thank me for."

"We're grateful. Trust me, we're grateful. Where and when?"

"There's a tiny coffee shop on the very edge of Witchurch, called The Witching Hour …"

"Sounds charming," he muttered.

"It's an all-nighter," she said, like that explained everything. "Be there at six p.m. prompt, or be square."

"I'll be there."

"Once again, my work here is done."

"Thanks, Jess. I appreciate it."

"Finally, recognition. Bye, tough guy. And don't forget that bedroom of—"

"Bye, Jess," he cut in, and hung up the phone. Only a blind dude would've missed the way his eyes shifted toward Gabe, but all he said was, "And now, we wait."

The next couple of hours were spent with us all throwing in reason-tenders for why we should be the one to go meet the vamps. Mine came in the form of: it's mostly my damn fault we're in this mess, and: it'll help take my mind of Liv for a while.

At least Brook had rang an hour earlier, letting me know she'd eventually located Liv when she showed up at The Double-H. She'd also managed to position herself about as close to her as she could get, by asking to share a table away from the tracking eyes of the males in the bar. Obviously, Liv hadn't had a problem with that—and I most definitely didn't. Still didn't stop me from feeling edgy. Edgy as fuck and in desperate need of distraction.

Four thirty rolled around before Nate called us all back to the table. "Okay," he rumbled, once he had our attention. "Ethan and Kyle, you'll go and meet the vampires in Witchurch, because they already know your faces, and I doubt they will be happy doing business with someone unfamiliar. However, given previous encounters with them, when there were only the two of you—" He, no doubt, meant the first time Ethan and Kyle met the Witchurch vampires, when Ethan'd ended up battered and bruised after one of them had decided to show him who was boss of their town. "—you should take Danny."

I let out a pent up breath.

"Gabe should come, too," Ethan said. "At least for this. He has as much right as us two to see this through as far as he can."

Nate's lips pressed into a thin line, but he nodded toward the young wolf. "Just for this, and nothing else. No arguments—it's not up for debate. Same goes for those of you staying here." He pushed up from the table into a towering block of intimidation. "You should get going. Find the place. Scope it out. And damned well call me before you enter."

"Witchurch, how I've missed you," Kyle muttered beneath his breath.

After parking outside a Job Centre—Jess's workplace, according to Ethan—we'd trekked the descent of a winding narrow-pathed road. Not many folks beside us graced the streets. Just a few shoppers yet to make it home from the last minute dashes before the shops had closed. One or two employers heading for their release after shutting shop for the day. Whereas they all seemed able to weave across the pavement with little notice being taken of them, the four of us pretty much lifted the chin of every person we passed. Like they'd never seen a group of guys all out for an early evening stroll through what seemed to turn into a ghost town at the locking of doors and tugging down of shutters. The whole place was eerily quiet and bizarrely conspicuous in equal measures.

"That's where we met them the last time." Ethan thumbed to an alleyway on our left, halting as he frowned across the road.

A male stood beneath the darkened curve of the alley's archway. Arms rigid and ready at his sides, he sneered as he jerked his chin to the left. "Keep on walking, dogs."

"Good to see we're worthy of a welcome committee." Turning away from the sentry, Ethan continued along the path, taking a sharp right curve a few strides later.

In keeping with the first street, the second sloped upward in a similar winding way, the shop fronts and overtop residencies seeming to lean in partial canopy across the too narrow and lumpy, tarmacked road. The lower floors of them all sat in solitary silence, no shadowy movement or lights splashed across the wares. All except for one, on which the door hung partially open, releasing the strong, rich odour of decent coffee into the street.

Black paint covered the entire façade, around windows that allowed little view of the inside, thanks to the emerald green satin and brocade curtains hanging across all but their top third. Even without lifting my gaze to the white chalk-effect scrawl over the coffee shop's banner, I knew we'd found The Witching Hour.

As our group stepped into the road to cross, a body just inside the doorway came into view. Dark hair, lean and lanky body. Dark, dark eyes that labelled him as someone we'd come here to meet.

The same kind of eyes I should've paid attention to on Catherine, but didn't. Could've saved myself a whole heap of shit.

A few steps from the entrance, Ethan waved us to a halt, and the tall vampire stepped forward enough to block the way in.

"Ethan Holloway?" he asked like he already knew the answer.

Ethan nodded. "That's me."

"An agreement was made for a meeting with you, not these," he said, nodding toward us.

"Funny, because I didn't request to speak to you, yet here you are." Folding his arms, Ethan leaned in a little and lowered his voice. "How about you just let us the fuck in, because I don't have time for games, and I'm definitely low on patience right now."

"Let the pup in, Lo," a voice called from inside

Scowling, the male stepped back a little, and as Ethan pushed past him, he paused on the threshold and turned to his left, his eyes twitching all over the damn place—telling me there was definitely more than just the speaker hiding in there.

"We really going to willingly walk into a room full of vampires?" I muttered.

"Yeah, we are," Kyle said, and he followed Ethan inside.

28

Despite the dreary fronting of the coffee shop, the interior of The Witching Hour seemed light and airy, with yellow gingham cloths covering the scattering of round tables, and electric sconces offering up surprising brightness from their spots on the walls.

Though, all that brightness did was better highlight a vampire built like a bulldozer standing at the far corner of the floor, his charcoal eyes staring out from beneath a mop of chestnut hair, and a vampire with arms like spaghetti watching us from a seat beside the counter, his lips unsettled like he struggled to keep the threat of his fangs hidden. And it definitely exposed the vampire relaxed in a seat beneath the window, his pale blond hair seeming to make his eyes look even blacker. With the guy at the door, that made four vampires in all.

The blond's gaze skimmed over the four of us before returning to Ethan, and he smiled in a way that didn't really resemble anything genuine, as he said, "Pup. You better have good reason for returning to my town."

"Why else would I be here?" Ethan rumbled.

The vampire jerked his chin toward the empty chair opposite himself. "Sit."

As Ethan dragged the wooden feet across the tiled floor, Kyle twisted until he faced the threat hovering over by the exit, and Gabe nudged his way closer to the tank in the corner. Leaving me the noodle to cover Ethan's back from.

"Talk," the vampire ordered, once Ethan had sank his butt down.

With little other way to put it, Ethan told him, "Catherine's back."

Anyone unaware of the situation might've missed the slight narrowing of eyes in the room, but none of us could've missed the stiffening of blondie's shoulders and the way he straightened in his chair.

"You know this, how?" he asked.

"Because I've spoken to her, when she contacted me by telephone a couple hours ago."

A few quiet seconds passed before he asked, "What did she want?"

"Me," Ethan said.

The vampire nodded. "Of course. Payback. She would most certainly come calling for that." He relaxed back in his seat again. "So, what do you think I can do about this?"

"Clean up what will likely end up being another mess caused by one of your own kind. Because she's bound to create one." Ethan rested his forearms atop the table and leaned in. "Or, at the very least, tell us what you know."

The vampire smiled that non-smile of his. "I do not feed information on my own kind to werewolves. Did you not learn that already?"

"Then, you didn't owe me a favour," Ethan said. "Now, you do."

"The favour I handed out in return for your consideration was neither unconditional, nor beyond subject to my own terms."

"I'm beginning to think nothing ever is where your kind are concerned. Should've known not to trust a vampire at his word." Letting out a low growl, Ethan shoved his chair back and tensed to stand. "This meeting has been a waste of my time."

"Tell me," the blond said, pausing him. "What demands did Catherine make of you?"

"I'm through answering your questions," Ethan muttered, already twisting away.

Before he'd taken more than a step, the tower in the corner lunged forward and grabbed his arm. I tensed to dart in, but as the vampire barked out a command for Ethan to answer the question, both Gabe and Kyle swung around with growls rippling from their throats.

The vampire holding Ethan hissed their way, his head flipping left and right like he didn't know where to aim the fangs gliding downward from his gums.

In the corner, spaghetti limbs pushed off his stool, his own flashy gnashers coming out to play, while the doorman kicked the door shut and slammed a hand against it.

Me? I pretty much stood like a spaz, trying to figure out whether to join Kyle and Gabe in their posturing, or throw a fist at one of the two uncovered vamps.

Only one in the café not strutting and stressing was blondie. He hadn't even moved, except for his eyes—which flashed toward Kyle and went through a whole range of expressions, before narrowing like he'd found a new puzzle to unfold.

Still staring at Kyle, he said, "A hybrid." He cut his gaze to Gabe. "Two hybrids."

Like he'd only just noticed the weirdness about the two wolves threatening him, the chunk of muscle twitched his attention in their direction, his entire body seeming to go real still when he took them in.

"Not hybrids," Kyle ground out. "We tend to just use the term *fucked up*." He turned to the one holding Ethan, who stared at Kyle like he'd visited the freak show tent of a carnival. "Had your fill?"

The vampire glanced toward the blond at the table. "The rumours are true," was all he said like Kyle hadn't even disputed the hybrid label.

"It would appear so." Blondie nodded, no trace of his earlier smile on his face. "You can let the pup go now."

Not waiting for the vampire's fingers to relax, Ethan jerked his arm free and turned toward the blond with a glare that'd been known to make most males wither. "You either have something else to say, or you don't. Either way, you better decide fast because I don't have time for fucking about and second guessing."

"Is Catherine responsible?" He didn't specify what he referred to, but he didn't have to. Both Kyle's and Gabe's eyes looked like black ink had been spilled across the whites.

Ethan jerked a sharp nod.

The blond leaned back in his seat, his gaze cutting toward the window. To anyone not paying attention, he looked like just another daydreamer, but the tightness of his jaw and the tension in his fingers gave away what brewed beneath the façade.

After almost a full minute of quiet, he said, "I will not clean up your mess for you. Playing housekeeper to dogs is not something my reputation will allow."

Ethan let out a growl too low for human ears, but it reached the vamp's hearing, because he finally glanced back.

"I did not say I wouldn't assist in some other way." He nodded toward the chair again. When Ethan didn't rush to sit, he let out something that resembled a sigh, seeming almost pained as he added, "Sit down. Please."

Taking his time, Ethan reclaimed the seat, and the vampire turned to his pal in the corner and beckoned him over.

The tower of muscle stepped forward and leaned in close, but despite the blond's lips moving, I didn't catch any sound. A few seconds later, the big vamp pushed away and strode for the door, bypassing the one on guard there and swinging himself free into the street outside.

"He won't be long," the blond said, drawing my gaze back.

"Long for what?" Ethan asked, starting to sound pissed off with the whole deal.

"For him to bring something that will help you," the vampire said with one of his non-smiles. "Perhaps you will answer me while we wait. What does Catherine want *from* you, exactly?"

"I don't know what she wants, except that she wants me to go alone, so I'd imagine she has some retarded notion that involves fucking me up." Ethan's teeth ground. "Probably another shitty scheme of hers to place the entire supernatural population in danger. Whatever she wants, it won't be good, and I'm not going to like it. And whatever she has planned, it needs to be stopped before it starts."

The spaghetti vamp had returned to his stool as they spoke and sat tapping his fingertips against the countertop in an irregular rhythm, while the one by the door bumped his back against the wall and stayed there, as if he wanted to prove that none of us gave him cause for concern. Even Gabe's and Kyle's posture relaxed a little, though their eyes still stayed alert. Alert enough to slice toward the entrance at approaching footsteps.

The big vampire slid back in through the door and closed it behind himself, before striding to the table and placing something small down in front of Ethan.

Ethan picked up what resembled a jelly bean. "Thanks, but I'd have preferred a Snickers."

"It's a tracker," the blond said, ignoring his humour. "Once you are with Catherine, your pack will be able to locate you."

Ethan stared at the bean for a few beats before lifting his gaze back to the vamp. "Are you really naïve enough to believe Catherine won't frisk me?"

"Actually, I'm certain she will, but I very much doubt she has it in her power to frisk the contents of your stomach."

He wrapped a fist around the tiny object. "No offense, but a tracker isn't going to withstand a visit to my gut."

"The tracker wouldn't, no. But the protective casing surrounding it will." The blond pointed to Ethan's hand. "There is a tiny bump. Find it. Press it."

Releasing his grip on it, Ethan ran his thumb over the small surface, before pausing and squeezing. The bean popped open.

Forgetting who we hung with, I stepped forward for a closer look at the tiny chip within the small capsule.

"How is this activated?" Ethan asked. "How is it tracked?"

The blond glanced up at his pal, and he pulled out a tablet mobile, tapped at his screen some. A minimal bleep came from the chip in Ethan's hand, and the vampire nodded. "It is activated." He slid his phone back into his jacket pocket and withdrew a square of card, which he dropped to the table. Pointing at a website address across the top, he said, "This is where your pack will track it. And this" —he tapped a series of digits beneath that— "is the serial number for the tracker, to ensure they follow the correct one."

"Even in its casing, this thing is still going to be surrounded by stomach acid," Ethan said. "It's not going to last indefinitely."

"They last long enough for your location to be detected," the blond said. "Your ridiculous bodily needs will likely dispose of it before the casing can be eroded."

In other words, if Ethan wanted to be found, he couldn't take a dump.

"So, that is that," the vampire said, his expression hardening. "We have assisted you in your situation. You will take the tracker and consider our debt paid."

It wasn't a question. More a: *this conversation is over; now get the hell out of my town.*

Clicking the capsule closed, Ethan nodded. "Yeah, you can consider it paid."

29

"We're changing location," Brook's voice said through my mobile. She'd gone into the bathroom of The Hang & Hide to make the call.

Trees and houses flashed past the rear window of where I sat in Ethan's pickup, dotted with what colour remained of flower borders ruined by too much rain and too little sun. "Why, and where to?" I asked, catching Kyle's eye as he twisted in his seat at the front.

"I'm not comfortable here. It feels too vulnerable, knowing they are already familiar with the place. And I am not yet sure. I asked your friend for recommendations. She suggested a place a short walk away on the edge of town, and when I told her I wasn't sure of the way, she offered to show me, as she has finished what she came here to do."

"Don't let her walk away after she has." My pulse jumped at the idea of Liv being exposed again. "Invite her to come with."

"I already have," Brook said, her tone smooth and unaffected by my barked order. "And she already said yes. We are leaving in just a few minutes."

"Well, I'm just headed home to grab my bike so I can do a drive by. Text me as soon as you reach where you're headed. I'll come find you."

"Olivia is okay, Daniel," Brook said quietly.

"I know. I just …" I plucked at the bridge of my nose.

"Need to see for yourself," she finished.

I nodded, though she wouldn't see. "Just text me," I said, ending the call as Ethan pulled up in front of home.

He lifted his gaze to the review mirror, his hard stare meeting my reflection. "Don't fuck up," was all he said. "Don't make us have to come bring you back."

"Try having some faith," I muttered, shoving open my door and sliding out. "I'm not a complete moron."

"Good," he said, rolling away as I slammed the door shut, and I turned toward the home.

Mostly, the house being empty and quiet meant we were all at Nate's. Together. Coming home to still shadows and silence in our current circumstances was enough to put me on edge, as I let myself in and strode along the hallway.

Pausing on the kitchen threshold, I scanned the four corners, checked the security of the back door, before spinning back and doing the same for the living room and Dad's office.

Satisfied, I made the trudge upstairs, headed for the bathroom. Took care of personal needs. Switched out sweatpants and trainers for jeans and boots. Checked my mobile a few dozen times.

Twenty minutes later, the text came through from Brook: FEAST OF EDEN. MACKLEBURY LANE.

It took only a few swipes and taps of my thumb on my phone to figure out the way to the restaurant they'd chosen, and I grabbed up my leather, shrugging it on as I descended the stairs. Both my helmet and keys sat on the hall table, and I scooped them both up and headed back outside, working my helmet over my head as I rounded the house to the carport.

Thankfully, the overhang protected my bike, meaning my arse stayed dry as I swung a leg over and planted myself down. A twist of the keys, a press of a button, and I was rolling, but only a few yards down the driveway, my mobile buzzed and vibrated through my groin.

Planting my feet, I balanced my bike as I worked it out. *Nate*. I blew out a sigh. He was probably calling to tell me he'd changed his mind. I couldn't go. Or he'd come up with something much more important than checking Liv was okay for me to do—like it'd be more important to me. While I wanted to stick it back in my pocket and pretend I hadn't heard it while on the road, something had me tugging off my helmet and hitting connect.

"What's up?"

"Where are you?" he asked.

"Just about to head off and check on Liv and Brook."

"Come straight here instead." A demand.

I just about held my growl in as I asked, "Do I get to know why?"

"Because you're being watched. And we've just received a call from Catherine telling us that if you're going where she thinks you're going, Liv will be gone before you can even reach her."

White filled my vision, and I felt myself falling into that same blankness, as my fist tightened around my phone and dropped to my thigh. Gritting my teeth in a jaw-lock, I held back the roar of frustration, held back the spew of *Motherfucker* I wanted to toss out, my nostrils flaring and retreating with each breath I tried to control.

"Danny?"

I blinked past the whiteness until the blurred green of field and forest across the road filled my vision.

"Danny, did you hear me?"

I lifted the phone back to my ear. "I hear you. I'm coming back." Ending the call, I just sat there. Eyes scouring the landscape for the snitch who'd screwed with my plans—my needs—while the grinding of my teeth Z'd through my brain. I glanced down at my phone again, and before it even registered what I was doing, I flicked through my history to the number labelled 'Answer Me Danny' and hit call.

It rang too many times, but just as I thought she wouldn't answer, the line clicked.

"Danny, I presume," she said. "I wondered how long it would take one of you to try the number I'd used. Not a smart move."

I unclenched my jaw. "Just so you know, first chance I get, I'm coming for you."

Not waiting for a response, I hung up. Just sitting there, face twitching, eyes twitching, fingers twitching with the urge the smash something, I took a few beats to steady my mood before lifting the phone again and calling Brook.

"Hello?" she answered.

"There's been a change of plan," I told her, my jaw beginning to ache from holding it so rigid. "I can't come. I'm being watched."

After a quiet pause, she said, "It's my boyfriend—bailing on me," her voice muffled like she spoke away from the phone.

"I kinda know that feeling." Liv's quiet reply hit me with a combo of pain and elation, and I had to swallow the need to talk to her before I could demand Brook hand her the phone.

"You are lucky I met a new friend today," Brook said, her focus returning to me. "And that I am currently enjoying myself. Otherwise, I might be mad at you."

My lips twitched at her play acting, despite how hard I still gripped the phone.

Away from the mouthpiece again, she said, "Do you have plans for after dinner?"

"No … no plans," Liv said in the background.

"Did you want to do something?"

"Uh … sure. Works for me."

Back to full volume, Brook said, "You hear that? You are off the hook. I made new plans."

I rubbed a hand over my head, let out a deep breath. "You're amazing, you know that?"

A long pause ensued, before she said, "Thank you."

"I'll call you later," I said. "Okay?"

"Okay."

With the call ended, I stared down at my phone. Stared down at it like I could see through it to the way Brook had become exactly what *I* needed her to be. To do exactly what *I* needed her to do. As if it could somehow explain why she'd even consider that after the way things had been between us.

Maybe she wasn't who I thought she was. Maybe she hadn't deserved the attitude I'd given her for the past handful of months.

One thing I did know for certain: I owed the cat an apology as much as I owed that fucking vampire a beating.

30

I'd been at Nate's a good couple of hours before a phone call came in from Brook.

"She thinks I'm drunk," she said when I asked how things were.

"Are you?" I asked, leaning back against the pillows on the bed in Lia's room.

"Of course I'm not."

"She totally is," came a voice in the background. Liv's voice.

"Is Liv drunk?" I asked.

"She's definitely tipsy," Brook said.

Liv's giggle carried down the phone. Not high pitched like a girly giggle, but deeper and seriously fucking hot. It really made me hope to someday see her tipsy for myself just so I could hear it first-hand.

"So, I won't be home tonight, you're all alone," Brook said in a semi-playful tone.

I pushed up onto my elbow. "What do you mean?"

"My new friend won't let me drive."

"She's *not* driving," Liv said in echo.

"She said I'm not allowed when I'm drunk. Even though I'm not."

"You are so drunk," Liv chimed in.

Brook hiccupped down the phone.

I frowned. "*Are* you drunk?"

"What do you think?" she whispered.

"Don't leave her," I said, frowning harder. "She has no one home with her this weekend."

"She said I have to stay with her," Brook said, slipping back into her role.

"She *is* staying with me," Liv barked.

My eyes squinted at the ease with which she'd invite a stranger back to her place. Just how convincing a role had Brook played? "You sure she's only tipsy?" I asked.

Brook laughed like I'd just told her the funniest joke of the year. "No, you may not come and join us. You can stay right where you are."

Damn convo was getting hard to follow. "So, you're staying with Liv?" I asked. "At her house? All night?"

"Yes," Brook said, her tone light as if she grinned while saying it. "And I shall see you … whenever I decide to come home."

"Whenever I *let* her come home," Liv said, that giggle of hers working its way back under my skin.

"Ring me when you get to Liv's," I said. "Okay?"

After Brook saying she would, and after they'd sang a duet of 'bye', she hung up the phone. Leaving me staring at the walls and wishing like fuck I could be the one there, the one protecting Liv from everything and everyone. Wishing like fuck I didn't have the restrictions placed on me I did, because without them, I'd one hundred percent be spending a second night with her.

Fuck Catherine and her fucked up notions.

Fuck her and her schemes and her twisted revenge plotting.

Fuck every damn thing about her.

My hand wrapped the phone in a death grip as I lay in the shadows of the room, thinking of all the ways I wanted to hurt the vampire. Thinking of my hands around her throat. The rough shake of her body.

Fuck that—I'd clamp my canine teeth around her spine and rip the fucking thing out, until nothing but a ragdoll lay broken on the ground. Even then, staring into eyes even more lifeless than they already were would do shit to appease. So I'd sink my teeth in again. And again. Until nothing but blood and matter and splinters soiled the floor with a slippery mess.

I could almost taste the saliva that'd pool around my tongue. Could almost hear the screams she'd make—ones that'd spur me on into a frenzy until I attacked and attacked, with little care for anything beyond ending a life.

I broke from my thoughts, realising how deeply my chest rose and fell, how tautly my muscles had coiled through my body. Realising just how much I really did want to fuck up the vampire for all the shit she'd caused me. The stalking and luring me to her chalet. Getting me arrested by the police. Making me fucking doubt myself over a false murder. Question what, exactly, I was capable of.

Though, lying there, vaguely tracking the movements and mumbles of the rest of the pack downstairs while my thoughts threatened to darken again, I knew exactly what I was capable of. Even worse was the fact that it didn't scare me anywhere near as much as it should've, and the fact that I resolutely wanted to carry out every single fantasy I'd had.

The roiling night sky inked up the expanse I could see through the bedroom window, while fat splats of rain drummed the glass like a tribal death toll. Maybe upstairs in the dark wasn't the best place for me to be right then. Or maybe I just shouldn't have been alone with only my own head for company.

I checked the time on my mobile. Little over an hour to go before we could expect Catherine's phone call. I decided to allow myself a few more minutes for stewing—after all, I'd earned them. Then, I told myself, I'd head down, seek out some lighter company than I, alone, could provide.

Plans had already been made by the time I sauntered my arse down to the others. Ethan would take the call, get the address for the meet and head out, and after giving him a big enough head start to avoid suspicion, those Nate selected would slip off in pursuit, while Jem sat at home, manned the tracking info, and let them know exactly where to go.

Simple.

I left the living room, where everyone looked about ready to twang from the tension, and ducked into the kitchen, where only Beth busied herself making drinks and cleaning stuff that was already clean.

"You okay, flower?" she asked, pausing in brushing imaginary crumbs from the countertop.

I nodded, tried on a smile. Must have been convincing, because she went right back to her task.

Leaning against the doorframe, I tucked my hands into my pockets, glanced around the room. Nate's laptop had been set ready on the table, with the tracking page already loaded. The website already showing a throbbing red dot.

Narrowing my eyes, I zoomed in on the dot's location and, taking a step forward, brought the tracker itself into view, in a small wooden bowl tucked behind the lid of the laptop. All Ethan had to do was pop it into his mouth and swallow it down, then the rest of us would find him without even having to look, swoop in, and end the sick game Catherine seemed so hell bent on playing.

Standing there, part of me wanted to steal the damn laptop—make me the only one who'd know Ethan's location so Nate would have no choice but to let me go. Because I had every intention of being there. I had every intention of being first in line to give Catherine exactly what she deserved.

Before I could do something stupid, I forced my gaze up to the wall clock.

Eleven twenty-three. Seven minutes to go.

Refusing to let either of the two devices out of my sight, I dragged out a chair and slumped my butt down.

Three minutes later, my phone buzzed. I worked it out of my pocket, checked the screen.

YOU HAVE 1 NEW TEXT MESSAGE.

I swiped in and, seeing Liv's name, tapped to view what she had to say.

HEY

Nothing else. Just 'Hey'.

Lips twitching, I responded: HEY. YOU OKAY?

I'M DRUNK, she texted back, followed by another that read: MY CEILING IS DANCING, with a crazy-eyed emoji after it.

My smile threatened to spread, until the reality of the evening kicked it aside. I could *want* to sit and goofy-text back and forth for hours however much I liked, but the fact was, I had about three minutes of calm left before the storm.

Not giving me chance to respond, my phone buzzed again, with the text: SEE? DRUNK.

From below the words, an image stared up at me.

A really distracting and totally tempting image.

Eyes a moody blue and lens-free turned inward in an obvious attempt to look far-gone. Dishevelled red hair curled all over the shop, around softly glowing features and over a pillow I'd shared less than twenty hours earlier. Above the lip of a duvet I recognised, the top swells of breasts I already missed peeked out.

Liv.

In bed.

Most probably naked.

All soft and pliable and floaty and free.

Saliva pooled on my tongue before I could stop it, and as my jeans tightened, I shifted in my seat, hoping Beth wouldn't notice.

Fuck.

Phone held in a grip born of need, I stared down at the screen, almost surprised by the edgy yearning doing gambols through my chest. Because I seriously, *seriously* wanted to bypass a text response and just turn up on Liv's doorstep. Get her to let me in. Lie her down on that springy mattress of hers. Make some noise with slow and lazy sex.

Taste her some. Make her scream my name while I tasted her some. Taste her some more.

Hell, maybe she'd taste me some.

And not a single one of those thoughts helped with the rapid swelling happening down below.

I closed my eyes against her picture before it took me beyond damage control. "You're killing me, Liv," I whispered beneath my breath.

I jerked at vibrations hitting my palm, and, as the mobile started ringing, I lifted my lids.

ANSWER ME DANNY filled the screen.

I pushed up from the table, marched along the hall, just as Ethan rounded the living room doorframe.

"Is it her?" he asked.

Nodding, I tossed him the phone. She'd only ask to speak to him, anyway—might as well cut out the middleman. As he backed into the living room with the others, I followed him partway and leaned against the wall alongside the doorway.

"It's me," he answered.

Nate already stood, his seat unusually occupied during such a meeting as he focused on his son. Dad sat rigid in the other armchair, one hundred percent paying attention despite his lowered head suggesting otherwise. Along the sofa, Josh and Kyle sat beside Jem and Sean, while Gabe stood stiff and ready next to where Shelley perched on the footstool, her fingers giving each other a workout in her lap.

"Good," Catherine said down the phone. "You're learning."

Shelley's lip all but curled as her eyes narrowed on the device in Ethan's hand.

Feet planted apart and shoulders set in a bulldozer stance, Ethan looked totally ready to take Catherine down. I knew exactly how he felt. "Just give me the instructions," he said.

285

"I know your buddies are probably listening, so I'll make this very clear," she said. "Come alone. I only need one wolf. Not an entire pack. So, if any of your little friends turn up here and try to sabotage my plans, my promise will be carried out. Do not think we won't get to the little redhead. Do not think her parents being there will deter us …"

Frowning, I pushed up from the wall, my head tilting as I listened in closer. Like I didn't think I'd heard what I heard. Like it didn't mean what I thought it did.

"You know me better, Ethan, than to believe I wouldn't order them killed, too, if it got me what I wanted."

Fuck me sat on the tip of my tongue but I bit it back. Because as much as I wanted to blurt out the obvious, I didn't want to draw attention to what Catherine had just given away.

That she didn't have a single fucking pair of eyes *on Liv*. Didn't know her parents were away. Obviously didn't know of Brook's sleepover. She'd been fucking blagging the whole time.

I slipped from the room into the hallway, reached backward for my helmet off the stand and hooked it over my arm as I zoned in on the directions spilling from the phone.

The old abandoned air hangar near the disused airstrip on the county's edge. I knew it. I'd even tested my bike out there for speed, back when I first bought it and needed someplace to think.

"And remember," Catherine said into the room. "Leave your little friends at home, Ethan. I only need one wolf."

Grabbing up my jacket from the newel post, I strode along the hall.

In the kitchen, Beth rummaged around in the larder cupboard, her back blessedly turned my way. I pushed through like I belonged there, scanning over the laptop, the glowing spot on the screen. Rounding the table, I dipped my fingers into the wooden bowl, palmed the small bean-

286

shaped tracker, and as I shoved my way out through the conservatory, I slipped it into my mouth and swallowed it down without a second thought for anything beyond my own personal goal.

If Catherine only needed one wolf, she was in luck. Because I had every intention of damned well giving her what she asked for.

31

The damned wind tore at my sides as I turned into Noblewood Reservoir. Only those familiar with the area would know the shortcut. Whether or not Ethan had ever used it, I didn't know, but I'd hoped it would buy me some time. With the rain giving me a bug-eyed view as it splatted against my visor, I made a swerve to the right, onto the generous footpath that circled the water.

The one time I'd visited the airstrip, I'd made the mistake of doing so in the afternoon. The path had been so full of dogs being walked and pushchairs being pushed, I'd had to abandon the route. Total opposite of its emptiness as I rounded a bend onto the stretch leading to the visitor centre. Not a single pair of eyes glowed in my headlight, nor a single bush rustled with creatures racing from my approach. I could smell them, though. Critters I'd usually be happy to hunt often gave off a tangible essence of fear, and the wind carried a strong dose of it, so, even if not me tearing through the joint, something had them spooked.

A car park fronted the visitor centre, and I followed the arrows to the exit, wove out onto the road that led in. Rather than turn left toward the regular bypassing route, though, I took a right onto a narrow road hugged by thistles and thorns and opened up the throttle.

Less than a mile later, I slowed for a sharp twist to the left before picking up speed once more over an overrun track that led to what resembled a ramshackle barn in the darkness. No streetlights had edged the road out from the reservoir, and none shone from the hangar ahead. Not that I'd expected them to. If I'd ordered someone to meet me, my intentions not of the friendly nature, I wouldn't have lit myself up like a firefly, either.

The closer I got, the clearer the hangar became, and the way it's doors had been left ajar, plus the van that hadn't been hidden quite well enough around to the side. So, they were in there. Which meant they had to know who approached, considering none of the others in the pack rode a bike and I'd made no attempt at stealth.

Pulling right up to where the hangar's roof overhung the building, I kicked down the stand and shut off the engine. With that quieted, the rain hitting the corrugated roof above sounded like a marching army. Smart way to mask any movements within.

For a moment, I contemplated keeping my helmet on for protection—my jacket, too. But deciding the restricted view and stiffness of my wet jacket hindering my movements were too much of a negative, I worked both of them off. After hooking them both over my handlebars, I swung a leg off and stepped toward the entrance.

Outside had held darkness. Inside held blackness, when I poked my head around one of the doors. Letting my body follow, I pushed into the hangar, blinking real fast in an effort to adjust my vision to the lack of light, and paused a few feet in. When nothing jumped out at me, I went in a couple more paces, paused again.

"I know you're in here," I said. "And I know you know I'm in here. So, why don't you quit hiding and—"

Tightness cinched my throat. I brought my hands up, grabbed at whatever was there, and my fingers slid over a couple of loops of thin wire. Twisting my head to the left scored pain over the skin of my neck, but it also revealed a figure dressed in black. Working my fingers beneath the wire, I jerked my body forward. Just as fast, it got yanked right back, and the scuffle of feet to my right rear told me I most likely had two of them at my back. Two of them holding me tight with whatever contraption the wire around my throat was attached to.

"You really don't know how to behave yourself, do you?" Catherine's voice drifted from the far corner, and a second later, she stepped forward, her blonde hair half hidden by something dark.

"Sounds a bit hypocritical, coming from you," I grated out.

"Maybe. But when a dog misbehaves, we all know what happens." She waved toward either side of me. "They get put on a *leash*." Her steps seemed to barely graze the concreted floor as she came closer. "Rather fitting, don't you think … that I found these at an old animal control centre. They're especially useful for picking up strays."

I tugged forward again, but soon stopped when the wires tightened—not only around my throat but over my fingers as well. "Why don't you go fuck yourself?"

"I tried that once," she said, and as she came within a foot of me, she opened her mouth, exposing fangs that even the shadows couldn't disguise. "But I find it's always tastier with two."

Everything within me wanted to snap out a hand and shake the arrogant bitch to death, but the whole fingers stuck beneath their trap thing caused an issue. "Just get on with it, Catherine. You've got what you wanted. Now take me and go."

"What I wanted was Ethan. Instead, you gave me … *you*." She said the word like I'd bought her a poisonous plant for a birthday present.

"So, you didn't get *who* you wanted. But what you need is one wolf." I smiled, though it probably came out a bit demented. "What the hell do you think I am?"

"Maybe … but what can be done with a wayward pup who can't be controlled." She leaned in close. Close enough that I could've clamped my teeth over her jaw and ripped out a good chunk of flesh—if not for the scratch of those fucking fangs just below my ear making me reassess the danger of that. "Or maybe," she whispered, "I *have* a way to control you."

My jaw clenched as I swallowed. "Then, I fail to see what the fucking problem is."

Quiet vibrations buzzed the air. I'd have expected it to be Nate, if Catherine's call to Ethan on it hadn't forced me to leave it behind.

Catherine took a step back and worked a phone free from a pocket. The screen set a glow across her features as she brought it up and answered. "Yes?"

"Incoming vehicle. Four-by-four this time."

"Passengers?"

"Just the driver."

She sucked in a long breath through her nostrils, then let it back out again. "Let it come." She hung up from the phone, tucking it away again before lifting her dark eyes back to me. "Seems you're not the only one eager to give me what I want."

Ethan. Had to be. "Two for the price of one is usually considered a good deal," I told her.

"Funny," she muttered, and through the dimness, her eyes narrowed and studied, like she really didn't have a clue what to do about the baggage she hadn't planned on.

Watching her right back, I tried working my fingers free of the wire. It was a stupid move, because the more I twisted or turned, the tighter the damn noose cinched itself. Or maybe that was the doing of the two shitheads behind me.

As the rumbling of an engine came close enough for detection through the overhead drumming of the rain, Catherine turned toward the rear of the building.

The engine shut off a little way from the hangar. Three beats later, a door clicked, followed by a wet-sounding thud, all punctuated by the muted slam of a truck door. Focusing on the slopped footsteps, I tracked them across the ground outside. They paused just beyond the metal sheltering us, and a painful creak snaked through the space as a sliver of dull light crept in.

A heavy silhouette filled the gap ahead. Unmoving. As if studying where it had to go.

None of us moved. The others seemed to be waiting to see what'd happen, but one inhalation told me the shadowed outline belonged to Ethan.

Which meant I was either about to be the recipient of a rescue attempt, or I'd be getting ripped a new one pretty soon.

Or both.

Before anyone inside the hangar could decide on whether to make the first move, a sharp streak of light beamed through the space. Squinting against its brightness, I watched as it swung over to the left corner, along the far wall, before scanning across the middle space and landing on us. It was a good tactic. Meant he could see us a whole lot better than we could see him. I twisted away from the glare, gritting my teeth against the grating at my throat.

"You okay, Danny?" he asked.

"If I ignore that I'll likely need to wear a scarf for a while—"

"He's fine," Catherine cut in.

The beam jerked her way. She didn't even flinch. "You mind letting my brother go?" Ethan asked.

"Yes, actually, I do," she said.

"You want me to step in there and give myself over, you're going to have to give a little, too, Catherine."

"What makes you think I don't already have more of my men trained on you, right now, just waiting to take you down, darling?" She made a tutting sound. "Surely, you know me better than to make demands, *or* assumptions."

"I can't say I understand what the problem is," Ethan said. Anyone who didn't know him might've missed the hint of desperation hiding in his tone. I didn't. "It's not like you need him—so, why not let him go?"

She released a dose of that annoying giggle. "Because I don't want to."

I stepped forward, growling as the wire cut a new track through my neck.

"Stay out of this, Danny," Ethan barked, slicing the torchlight across to me.

I couldn't have done much of anything else, anyway—not with 'it' and 'that' at my back

The rain danced a heavier tune overhead while both Ethan and Catherine seemed to be considering their options.

"So, what exactly are your plans?" Ethan asked after a few beats. "You must have some. I mean, only an idiot wouldn't have prepared for an eventuality like this."

Catherine stepped to the right a couple of paces, out of the light, before pivoting on the spot and making a slow glide back. "Well," she said, drawing out the word, "Best case scenario: I permit him to come with us. Worst case?" She tapped at her chin. "His family might never recover his body."

Ethan gave a low growl. "Fuck you, Catherine."

Pausing to my left, she waved a hand in dismissal. "Maybe later, darling. I'm thinking." As if said thinking involved me, she made a slow turn my way, her eyes filled with a speculation I wasn't sure I wanted in on. "Okay, we're wasting time. I've made up my mind. Load them both up." Clapping her hands together, she began marching toward the door I'd entered through. "I'll decide what to do with the fool later."

The two loops around my neck tugged me to the right, before nudging me after Catherine. A second later, a voice behind me prompted, "You, too," telling me she definitely had other helpers besides the two on me, and another couple of footsteps beat around ours.

Outside, rain still dripped everywhere, dampening me as soon as I was herded around to the side of the hangar—the side where I'd spotted the van on my way in.

Judging by the darkness of his eyes, another vampire waited beside the vehicle. He opened the rear doors of what looked like an old security van, and after he'd patted me down and coming up empty, the nooses guided me

293

toward the opening, as Catherine carried right on past, toward a Land Rover parked in the shade of the building. Once my knees hit the sill of the truck, I received another shove from behind, and not bothering to argue, I lifted a foot up, ducking my head as I climbed inside the van.

They hadn't bothered to fit any lighting in there, and the space didn't have any windows, but I could still see the benches lining either side. Partly bent over, I shuffled another step forward, but the wire trap tugged me down and sideways, until the backs of my knees bumped one of those benches and my butt sank down. As soon as I'd sat, the wires fidgeted around my neck, slicing their way back out of skin they'd cut into, and scraped over my head. I let my hands drop from my throat, but couldn't quite un-flex my fingers, and turned to look at the bastards responsible.

"Move up," the one on the left said, poking the air with his broomstick leash. Dirty-blond hair flicked in a kiss curl across his forehead, from a too-high hairline. While not quite as tall as my six-two, he made up for it with broad shoulders and boulder-block arms.

Obeying, I slid myself farther inside while checking out the other one—dark hair, slim, tall, rangy-looking muscles. Rangy-looking muscles that'd held me steady just fine.

The two of them stepped aside, and Ethan filled the gap, a real pissed off expression lowering his brows. Aiming a hard stare into the back of the truck, he made the climb inside and sat on the opposite bench, a foot, or so, in from the door.

"Move along," said the same vampire who'd ordered me.

Gaze fixed on the panel straight ahead of him, Ethan let out a growl. "Just shut the fucking doors."

The vampire seemed to hesitate, like he considered arguing, but must have decided the fight unworthy because he closed the doors on us. Leaving the two of us alone, in the back of a van, heading for fuck knew where, with a tension palpable enough to steal all of our oxygen away.

Ethan glared through the darkness like he wanted to murder me himself and save the vampires the job, and I shifted in my seat, even went so far as to open my mouth.

"I'm so fucking mad at you right now, I can't even look at you," Ethan said before I could speak. "So, you can save your *sorry*, or whatever the hell else you think you need say. Because I'm about as far from being in the mood for conversation as I've ever been. Understand?"

Yeah, I understood. Loud and clear. Not even bothering with a verbal response, I dropped my head back against the cold metal of the vehicle and let myself fully contemplate what the hell I'd gotten myself into.

32

I'd started the journey off counting through the passed seconds, but had grown bored at around seventeen minutes. Since then, we must have travelled at least double my count and then some.

The quiet in the back of the van only seemed to make the journey longer. Ethan still hadn't spoken a word. Hell, he hadn't even moved beyond the rocking of his body caused by turns and braking or pulling away.

The security truck slowed and made a turn, but didn't speed back up again. No further swerves told me we drove along a straight stretch—for one minute-twenty, by my count. A sway to the left, then another to the right bumped me against the side of the truck, before the vehicle righted itself again and finally stopped.

I held my breath for a few seconds, listening for other traffic—any signs that we might be at a junction—but when the engine quieted, I figured we had to have arrived at Casa Catherine.

The front doors of the van opened, and after some movement that jerked the van about, the doors banged closed and footsteps sounded out.

"Coming, ready or not," I muttered.

"Don't kid yourself," Ethan said, glancing at me for the first time since we'd left. "There's no fucking way on earth you'll ever be ready for whatever this psycho has planned. Because it *will* be bad." His head dropped back against the van panel. "I only hope you did what we think you did before you left. Otherwise, we are in some serious shit, here."

"I did," I confirmed, assuming he referred to the tracker being ready for detection.

The rear doors swung open, exposing the same two vampires who'd secured me back at the hangar. Though, unlike at the hangar, light shone out from somewhere, hitting their eyes and making them look like polished obsidian.

"Do we need to restrain you again?" asked the stocky one. "Or are you going to behave?"

"Daniel doesn't know how to behave," came Catherine's voice, right before she appeared next to the two males, holding those fucking dog leashes again. "I'm pretty sure Ethan can confirm that much."

Ethan didn't so much as look at her, let alone reply, not that Catherine seemed to care. She just stretched right into the van with one of the wire loops on its pole and aimed it for me.

"Be a good boy, now, and slip this over your head." She smiled, tipping her face toward the Ethan's glare. "See? I can play nice, darling."

"Do what she says," Ethan muttered, and he turned his gaze on me, the darkness rolling out from his eyes all but saying, *You've only got yourself to blame.*

I guessed he had a point. Reaching for the loop of metal, I ducked my head and fed it through.

"You should move those lovely fingers of yours, this time," Catherine said. "You never know what use I might find for them."

My lips curled. "Only in your dreams, *darling.*"

Giving a small giggle, she tugged on the leash. "Okay, out. Both of you."

Stepping aside, she let Ethan climb down and nodded at the rangy vampire, who gripped both his biceps from behind. Surprisingly, Ethan didn't try to shrug him off, didn't argue. Almost like he'd already decided that they'd all get what they wanted so he might as well give it to them. Or like he figured he might as well play along until the rest of the pack came to visit.

At another small yank of my chain from Catherine, I rose from the seat toward the door, letting her think she guided me as I hopped down and scanned the area.

A circular flowerbed explained the last couple of turns the van had made, and beyond them, a long tarmacked driveway stretched off between rows of trees, probably toward the entrance. The broader of the two vamps pushed the rear doors of the van closed, and as soon as he did, the premises we'd been brought to came into view.

Some kind of mansion loomed over us, wide as shit and all gothic-like, and so fucking predictable after the castle she'd kept the others in the last time.

"Nah-ah, no looking," Catherine said, jerking me toward her. "From this point forward, you'll both be wearing these."

She chucked something black and fabric to the stocky vampire, and he stepped forward, lifted one toward my head. I recognised it for the hood it was about a half second before he blacked my vision.

"Is this fucking necessary?" Ethan asked.

"I'm afraid so, darling. Can't have the two of you knowing your way around, now, can I?"

I caught a shuffle of a foot, before Ethan barked out, "You want this on me, I'll do it myself," in a tone that betrayed just how much he hated the whole situation.

I had to confess, I wasn't exactly sold on it myself. Even less so, when a hard pull on the wire once more hacking at my throat dragged me away from the van. And toward God knew what.

We'd climbed stairs and took twists and turns that'd disorientated the heck out of me by the time Catherine called us to a stop.

"Okay, remove their hoods," she said.

A hand gripped the top of my head, yanking a chunk of hair up with the hood, and I swung toward the thickset vampire with a low snarl of warning as soon as my vision was freed.

He returned the gesture with a half-cocked smirk. Bastard.

"Your quarters," Catherine said, taking a step forward and nudging me along with her.

The room they'd taken us to resembled something from a historical drama, except for the colour of the walls. Pink walls. Dotted with cornices in gold, and rounded naked women pouring water from vases. Weirdness. Absolute fucking weirdness.

"I had the room specially made up in anticipation of your arrival," Catherine continued. "Your favourite kind of bars at the window. A steel-reinforced door. However, I plan on you sticking around a lot longer this time, darling, so I figured I'd make it more comfortable for you."

"You'll need a lot more than a bed to convince me any of this is a good idea," Ethan muttered.

"Not just a bed." Catherine smiled. I decided I really fricking hated it when she smiled. "I gave you bathroom facilities, too." She handed my leash over to one of the others and, taking his hand, led Ethan to a corner of the room hidden behind a gold and pink ornate screen. Ethan just plodded along with her like he had no objections, and the two of them vanished around the screen. "Toilet," came Catherine's voice, "sink … a bath big enough for two." She gave a screechy giggle.

"Like visiting The Ritz," Ethan said, his voice saturated in sarcasm.

"There he is," Catherine said in return. "That's the Ethan I know so well."

"You don't know shit about me."

"I know more than you realise." She reappeared around the side of the screen, her gaze landing on me as she poked at the air. "This. This is not for you. Let's just be clear on that."

Ethan popped out behind her. "What the hell does that mean?"

"It means, darling," she said, spinning back and facing him, "this isn't Danny's room."

"You want my cooperation, then you'd better change your mind on that," Ethan almost growled. "Danny stays in here. With me."

She shook her head, let out a tutting sound. "I learned from the last time. Give you some friends, and you all start thinking too much for yourselves. You're staying in this room … and you're staying in here alone."

"Let Danny stay," Ethan said, his voice low.

"Can't," she said. "It's his own fault for turning up unannounced."

Ethan spat a low curse out toward the far wall, lifting his gaze back to Catherine. Through clenched jaw, he said, "Please."

With every muscle in my body locked tight, I waited on her answer. I probably wanted to leave that room even less than Ethan wanted it to happen, and I couldn't seem to take my eyes off the female as I willed her to say yes.

"As much as I love seeing you beg, the answer's still no." She twisted back and nodded toward the vampire holding me. "Move him out."

Ethan bolted forward a foot, as I dug the toes of my boots into the carpet, but the wire around my throat tightened, and before I knew it, my knees had hit the floor and I could scarcely draw breath.

"Take one more step, and Daniel will get hurt." The hard tone of Catherine's voice warned how much she meant the threat. Half-turned toward Ethan, she waved a hand my way again.

An upward yank had my hands flying toward the restriction over my windpipe, while my feet shoved me upward in the hope of lessening the pressure.

"Where are you taking him?" Ethan asked.

"To a room that has been specially prepared."

"For what?" I managed to grate out past the wire.

"For the good use I can put you to," she said, smiling.

300

"What *good use*, Catherine?" Every muscle seemed to bulge beneath Ethan's sweater, like he had trouble holding himself back. "What the fuck did you want me here for?"

"That's an easy question." She shifted back a few steps, sank down into the bed's end. "You're here to help me with my new business—seeing as you broke up my last one, that is."

"I am not fighting for you," he ground out.

She laughed. "Don't worry. It's much more civilised than that. This time you get to feed your hunger on paying customers. Humans are such idiots."

"What the hell are you talking about?"

"Humans," she repeated. "They're idiots. You have no idea how much they'll pay to get bitten."

Fear entered his eyes, masking any bravado he might have tried to show. "What. The fuck. Are you saying?" he asked slowly.

"Humans want to …" She pushed to her feet and moved to in front of him, rested a fingertip against his chest. "… be … like … us."

A wave of dread forced its way through my body. What the ever loving fuck. Surely, she couldn't mean that. It had to be the craziest idea on the fucking planet.

The way his lips parted and his brows dropped told me that Ethan didn't quite believe he'd heard her right, either. He gave a single, hard shake of his head. "No."

She nodded. "Actually, yes."

"I'm not fucking doing it."

She turned away from him, came toward me. "Yes, you will."

"I won't be a part of this insanity, Catherine," he said, the first hint of fury beginning to kick his fear aside.

She shoved me toward the door, the smile she sent me enough to freeze my veins. "You will, for Danny's sake."

Ethan's entire body seemed to still. "He's not to be a part of this. Do you understand me? This payback has got nothing to with him."

"Oh, don't worry. Danny's not going to be biting anyone." One final push from Catherine sent me backward into a long hallway, before she leaned against the doorframe and peered back into the room. "What I have planned for him is going to be far more fun."

As the growl finally tore from my pack mate, Catherine slammed the door closed and turned to me with a glint in her eyes that scared the fuck out of me. "I hope you're ready, young pup. Because you're about to have the time of your   life."

33

Once more staring at the inside of a cloth sack, I put one foot in front of the other as the leash tugged me forward. "Don't the humans understand the risks of being bitten by one of us?" My voice came out amazingly normal, seeing as my insides churned like they were twisting to get away.

"They know there are risks," Catherine answered from in front of me.

"Do they know they can die? It's rare for someone to survive—you know that, right?"

"I am aware."

"But are they?" She tugged me to the left, around a corner, judging by the angle. When she didn't answer, I asked, "What the hell are they even hoping to achieve from it, anyway?"

Sure, the whole being wolf side of things came with its benefits, but aside from the hunt and being stronger, we mostly lived hidden amongst humans—like humans.

"Let me think …" Catherine said. "No disease … rapid healing … extended youth …" She halted me and lifted the hood from over my head. "Immortality."

I frowned. "We're not immortal."

"No. But we are," she said.

"Yeah," I said. "Until someone severs that annoying head of yours." I ignored, for then, that werewolves weren't the only deal on the table

She smiled. "Wouldn't you just love to be the one to do it."

My eyes narrowed. "You have no fucking idea."

She nodded toward something behind me, and the skinnier vampire rounded us, a set of keys in his hand.

"So, tell me," I said, while he unlocked the door we'd stopped by. "You have everything you need right here, already. Why even bring our kind into it, at all?"

"Because," she said, stepping backward as the doorway swung open behind her, "not everyone wants to live forever. For some, just living their lives free of sickness and aches and pains—*without weakness*—is enough." She tugged me inside the new room after her. "We can offer them that. With mentoring. Round-the-clock care. And the reassurance they won't be unleashed back into the world until they have full control of their new abilities and needs."

For some …. Made me wonder how many 'clients' she had lined up. Shelving that thought, I asked, "So, bringing Ethan here—it isn't just about revenge?"

"Not *just* about revenge, no." She smiled. "Okay, hold him."

A couple of sets of hands gripped both of my arms. Stocky and Rangy—one on each side.

Reaching forward, Catherine fiddled about with some kind of clasp on the handle of her contraption. The movement sawed at my neck some, and I gritted my teeth against complaint, until the wire surrounding my skin finally sprang loose.

"Duck," she ordered, and I complied as she lifted the loop upward and off.

Resisting the urge to rub at the soreness, I glanced around the room they'd brought me to. Pale grey walls with a faint floral pattern running over it in upward rows. A bed the size of England in the middle of the room, draped in a silver throw of crushed velvet. In the opposite corner to in Ethan's room, another screen, but bigger in size.

"Fancy," I said.

"More fancy than you're worth," she said, "but I had to go with what I had."

I brought my stare down to meet her dark one. "You have no idea what I'm worth."

"Oh, I'm going to find out. You can trust me on that one." She sashayed backward, farther into the room, and the two vice grips either side of me shoved me right along with her, until she stopped a few feet from the bed and held up a hand. As I got yanked to a halt, she tapped her fingertip against my sternum, leaving it there as she leaned in closer. "When the police showed up and arrested you, how did you feel, Daniel?"

My lip curled as I tried to shrug myself free of the two vampires, but they just tightened their hold and jolted me toward the deadly blonde. "What do you think?" I asked her, my voice barely more than a growl.

She stepped closer until her toes butted mine, a glint of madness polishing the blackness of her eyes. "I think you thought you were fucked."

Grinding my teeth together, I caged in the retaliation balancing on my tongue. Damned if I'd give her the satisfaction of a reaction twice.

Her hand trailed downwards, over my ribs, my stomach, coming to a stop at the waistband of my jeans. "You weren't," she said, curling her fingers over the denim. "Not until you tried messing up my plans." She gave a small tug, setting the stud of my jeans free, and it took every ounce of will power not to buck like crazy. "Now ..." She drew down my zipper, and my body revolted on impulse, shooting my arse backward, only to be stalled by a solid wall of muscle. "*Now*," she repeated, "by the time I've finished with you, you're going to understand the true meaning of the word *fucked*."

Before I could do a damn thing about it, she grabbed the waist of my jeans and yanked them down until my boots blocked their route. I kicked away, but the two vampires at my rear shoved me forward again, as she dropped like a missile and reached for my foot.

"The fuck are you doing?" Jerking against the vampires holding me, I tried to kick my legs out of her reach, but the denim bound my fucking legs together, so all I managed to do was swing my body half round and my foot straight into her waiting hand.

"Get the hell off me," I warned, but with a swift pull, she had the boot free and chucked aside.

My growl pushed out when she grabbed for the other boot, and I yanked my knee up and kicked out, on a direct route for her head.

Like she knew the move well, though, she knocked the blow aside, flipped an arm around my shin, and gripped me hard. It took less than a heartbeat for the second boot to go flying—which was about the time that my brain and body spazzed out.

Forcing myself away from her, I actually managed to move the two males by a couple of feet. I twisted to the left, hard enough to send an ache shooting along my side. A snarl of frustration bombed up my throat when I was thrust back around and a deep laugh hit my ear.

Blinking past the panic, I focused on Catherine, the way she studied me with a small smile curving her lips. "The fuck do you want with me?"

"Haven't you figured it out yet, darling? I want your seeds." She jerked her chin up. "Get him on the bed."

My body was swung to the right, and I scrabbled at the carpet with my toes, like I could somehow cling to the fibres and hold myself still. They merely scratched over the rough wool, no matter how much I contorted my body to try and get a good grip.

"Let me go." I yanked my left arm forward and heard a hollow *pop*, but blanked it enough to keep fighting. "Let me the fuck go."

"Will you stop being silly before you hurt yourself," Catherine said like she didn't really give a shit how much self-damage I caused.

As if her words were some kind of trigger, heat blossomed from my shoulder and sent an inferno soaring to my biceps and neck, until my knees sagged beneath the agony. I might've cursed, but I couldn't really be sure how many of the shouts and curses clouding up my brain made it past my lips. Only clarity I had of the moment was knowing I was being moved whether I fucking liked it, or not. Knowing I didn't seem strong enough to do jack shit about any of it.

I scarcely had chance to argue further before my body went horizontal and the ceiling stared down at me.

The cry definitely left my throat as my limp arm got yanked above my head, along with the right one, and after a couple of clicks, the two vampires stepped away, leaving me panting like I'd just gone a few rounds with Ethan and had been raging twenty times as bad.

"I won't do it," I ground out between breaths.

"Oh, you will," Catherine said, that sick smile still in place.

I spat a glob of phlegm in her direction—about the only weapon I had in the moment. "I'm not doing shit for you."

"Yes. You are."

I booted out a leg toward her. "Fucking make me."

"Sweetheart, I thought you'd never ask." She pushed my leg back onto the bed like it was an easy task, no matter how tightly my muscles strained, and made her way around the bed toward the far side of the room. Toward where the screen blocked off the corner.

Once she'd vanished behind it, only a couple of knocks and clinks carried through, giving no indication of her actions, and a minute later, her footsteps re-hit the carpet and she reappeared around the screen.

The smile she wore earlier had nothing on the sadistic glint lighting her eyes as she waved what she held. A big fuck-off syringe filled with what-the-fuck fluid.

"Be careful what you ask for," she said, stopping beside the bed. "Because I always deliver."

The two bastard vamps strode to the foot of the bed. The second they reached out, I hauled my legs up and drove my feet out toward them both. Stocky just caught my foot like the blow was nothing, but I managed to send Rangy staggering back a few steps. Not that it bothered him. Jaw set, he came right back at me and snatched up my foot before I could draw it back again.

With my butt writhing on the bed to get me the hell away from them, and a string of grunts swelling up my throat, I set my glare on Catherine. "Do not fucking touch me," I forced out past my rapid breaths.

"Sorry, darling." She grabbed my dick and pulled it upright, the clenching of her fist debilitating enough to quit any idea of bucking away. "Bit hard to do without using my hands."

My breaths snorted through my nostrils. "There's a fucking word for what you're doing—you know that, right?"

"Yes," she said, sending a quick smile my way. "It's called enterprising."

She stabbed the needle into the end of my dick.

My body planked with the pain, and my mouth stretched wide as a low scream tore from me. Like needles spiking through my shaft, the liquid invaded me, until I couldn't fucking move. Could only lie there. Fingers flexed in their contorted pose. Head tipped back far enough to bring dizziness. Breaths completely and utterly fucking vacated.

When she withdrew the needle, it didn't hurt any less, and I sucked in a sharp breath that had me coughing and heaving for the next shot of air.

She appeared in front of me, the face of a fucking sociopath, smiling like she hadn't just done what she had. "You, my darling, are now worth a fortune."

I managed only a retarded noise that might've been as much a plea as an insult.

She patted my face. "I know. But it won't hurt for long." She turned away and paced across the bedroom, pausing when she reached the door. "You never know, Danny, once you've seen the treats I've got lined up for you, you might even thank me."

With another of those fucking smiles, she let herself out of the room, taking her fucking monkeys with her, before she shut me inside.

Inside and cuffed to a bed.

Feeling like a pile of shit the size of Kilimanjaro.

With the beginnings of the most painful hard-on I'd ever experienced in my life.

34

Around five minutes after Catherine had stabbed me with what the hell ever, the pain had begun to slowly move out, like a poison-sucking sniper crawling backward through my veins, until all that remained was a burning numbness.

And the swollen agony of a dick in need of service.

I'd rather have fucked myself before I'd ever ask for help with that, though.

Catherine could go fuck herself, too.

Using the time alone, I studied the room more closely. If I could get free of the shackles, which I'd been testing the resistance of since the others had gone, I was pretty sure I could master an escape. Hell, I'd have been prepared to squeeze my arse inside a sooty heating shaft, if it would've gotten me out of there.

I glanced toward the bathroom. Maybe that'd have windows without bars. Or a mirror I could smash for a blade.

At the very least, I could've locked myself in and hand-fucked the tension out of myself—because I didn't fancy using my solid dick as a beating baton in a fight against the vamps, even if it could've done some damage in its current condition.

I barely heard the breezy-soft footsteps prior to the door handle tugging down, and I slumped back against the covers as the door swung open again.

"Feeling a little better?" Catherine asked as she waltzed into the room.

I didn't answer. Mostly because I couldn't think up a retort that wouldn't make Catherine more amused than she already was.

"Do you have any idea how magnificent and delicious you look right now?" She reached the side of the bed, and I gritted my teeth against flinching when she glided her palm over my hip. "The clients are going to very happy." Her gaze dropped to my crotch. "*Very* happy."

"Fuck you," forced its way past my lips.

"Not me, no. Though, looking at you now, I have to admit that I'm sorely tempted to test the goods."

"You'd better kill me first if you do, because that's the only way you'll ever achieve that fucked up notion."

She smiled. I tried to tell myself that my veins didn't ice at the way she studied me, but they did—enough so that my entire body froze when she lifted a knee onto the mattress and swung her other leg over my hips. Letting her groin drop until she'd seated herself over the length of my shaft, she pressed her hands against my chest as her eyes closed, and shifting her hips left and right just a little, she let out a sigh.

Jaw clenching, I swallowed. Swallowed down the repulsion threatening to spew from my throat, because as much I really fucking hated the contact, as much as I'd rather it be any face on earth staring down at me other than Catherine's, I could feel my fooled dick swelling even harder and hoping for more. "Get the fuck off me," I managed, despite my body saying otherwise. "Or—"

Her fingers pressed over my mouth as she reopened her eyes. "Why bother with empty threats, Daniel?" She twitched her hips forward then back again, her lids half-lowering again. "You and I both know, I could do this all day, if I chose to, and you wouldn't be able to do a thing about it, darling."

"Doesn't mean I wouldn't try," I growled.

"But why bother when you could just lie back and enjoy it? And from what I can feel ..." She slid her hand over my stomach, twisting it at the wrist as her fingers skated my pubis. "... you're enjoying it very—"

I lurched upward, a snarl rippling free. Jaws opened, I aimed for her throat, but she jerked aside, leaving my teeth to skim her shoulder before she vanished from reach and my shoulders screaming in protest as the cuffs stalled my efforts.

Frowning down at me from over my thighs, she tutted. "That wasn't nice, Daniel. I hope you're going to treat my guests better than this."

Breathing hard through the agony blazing through both my shoulders, I let my lips twist into a cold smile as hatred fired my blood. "I will kill anyone you send in here with the promise of my body. And I will succeed, Catherine, even if I have to rip my limbs from their sockets. You'll end up with a bloodbath."

She climbed from over me and dropped to the carpet.

"You'll end up with nothing but blood and guts and human remains to clean up." My gaze followed her, as she crossed the room and rounded the screen. "How fucking appealing do you think I'll be then, when you send your clients in and I look like the cause of a fucking massacre? How much money do you think they'll pay you then, you fucking sick fuck?"

"I really didn't want to have to go this far with you," she said from the adjoining room, "but you've left me no choice."

A breath later, she reappeared carrying another fucking syringe.

I shook my head. "No! No fucking way!"

"Darling, you brought it on yourself."

As she approached the bed, I wrangled the hell out of my shoulders as I tried throwing my legs over the far edge of the bed. Hooking an ankle over the mattress lip, I tugged myself away from her, grunting out a deep growl of desperation when the muscles in my arms reached the point of tearing and the cuffs gave no indication of letting me go.

As soon as she got close, I gave up with the restraints and instead gripped hold of where they tethered me, and I rolled toward her, gunning my right leg toward her face.

She ducked before I could hit and shoved my foot away like it was nothing more than a minor irritation. "You're acting like a brat," she said, her voice heavy with disapproval.

"And you're acting like a psycho rapist."

Gripping tight to the bedframe once more, I tried another kick, but she just shoved me away again. Shoved me away and moved in closer, that bastard syringe snug within her palm as she positioned her thumb over the plunger.

My body instinctively shied away from her. My butt shooting across the mattress. My legs booting me away. My breaths panted from me as I tried rolling my torso and the pain in my left shoulder screeched a path along my biceps.

Catherine just tutted like she was dealing with a child in a tantrum, but those eyes of hers never once stopped watching, watching, watching.

When she struck, she moved so fucking fast my eyes couldn't track it, and as the needle plunged into my right arm and back out again, a growl tore through my throat and blasted toward her.

She didn't so much as blink, but just stood there, studying, her eyes holding a shrewdness fucked up by a dose of intense insanity.

Glaring right back at her, I did a mental check of my body. Tried to figure out what the hell she'd given me. Its effects.

No liquid pain pumped through my veins like the last shot. Not even a prickle of discomfort.

Instead, my right arm relaxed above my head, the muscles softening until the elbow sank against my skull. My ragged breaths lengthened. Lengthened and regulated like some fucker had placed an oxygen mask over my face to help me breath.

"'The hell you gi me?" I snarled, but the words came out wonky even to my ears.

"Just a little something to help you relax." She leaned in, propping her hands against the bed beside me until her face was way closer than I wanted it to be. "Is it working?"

313

"Go fuh ursef," I slurred, as my leg muscles uncoiled and it felt as though my entire body was sinking into the mattress. Though, even that sensation felt like a fluffy cloud of nothing folding its wings around my frame, welcoming me into its depths. Depths I wanted to hide inside of until all the shit was over and I could go home again. Even my heartbeat seemed to get in on the act, slowing and slowing until it tapped a gentle rhythm against the inside of my sternum.

Not for one second, though, did I cease with my urge to kill Catherine. Despite wanting to let go, wanting to succumb to the weightlessness that lent a sense of freedom to my body, my mind stayed one hundred percent willing to tear that bitch apart—especially when she brought her face to within a couple inches of mine and smiled.

"Bite me now, darling," she whispered.

I tried to. Ignoring that I was doing exactly as she'd suggested, I really fucking tried. Tried lifting my head. Tried drawing my lips back to expose my maws. Tried thrusting my head forth toward the chunk of her throat my eyes had fixated on.

About all I managed, though, was a throaty grumble—and that lack of ability drove the nail home.

I was absolutely, seriously fucked.

35

I spent the next few minutes stewing over how much I wanted Catherine to pay. *How* I wanted her to pay. I'd never actually wanted to kill anyone before, but I definitely wanted to kill her. Because I hated that she'd not only humiliated me and stolen my dignity, but that she'd made me totally fucking helpless to do a damned thing about it at the same time.

She'd also ripped my shirt from me, taking the last scrap of clothing I'd had left.

I didn't think I'd ever hate another being as much as I hated her right then. Didn't think it possible to hate so much. The sensation built a solid ball of nausea in my gut and burned a hole of fury through my brain—both of which seemed to be growing with each passing minute, while I lay there with no other outlet for my feelings. Hell, I didn't even seem capable of clenching my fists or grinding my teeth.

The bitch needed to hurt for that. More so, she needed to hurt for the underlying emotion that prevented those feelings from creating a super nova explosion inside me.

Fear.

No matter how much I tried to tell myself to calm, to quit stressing, I knew, deep down, that if my limbs were taking any kind of notice of the signals my brain kept shooting at them, they'd have been trembling the fuck all over the place.

Where the hell were the pack?

Sure, they'd have hold ups preventing them arriving within a similar timeframe as we had. It wasn't like they'd have been able to move until we'd left with the vampires. Wasn't like they could follow on our heels and hope nobody would notice, because then everything would've been over before we'd even begun.

Didn't stop me really needing them to turn up right that fucking second.

At the tiny squeak of the door handle, my entire body went into imaginary lockdown. Like I could've done otherwise, I held myself as still as I could, rigid and ready against whatever was coming.

"Oh, my ..."

The voice was quiet and soft and female, and my mind battled against the invisible binds as my treacherous body showed interest.

"Does he need to be ..." The same voice.

"Werewolves have a tendency to *bite* when they get frisky," Catherine said from across the room, and I swallowed down what'd likely come out a garbled mess of *fuck you*. "As you didn't sign up for that, we considered it necessary to offer some level of protection against it happening."

"He doesn't mind?" the quiet female asked.

"Darling, you're not the only one here who had to complete and sign pages of paperwork."

A growl bubbled in the back of my throat, falling acres short of intent as it puffed past my lips in a pathetic whimper.

Like the explanation had sufficed, light footsteps crossed the carpet until a female came into view. Dressed in only a short slip and matching satiny robe, she folded her arms over a small chest as she eyed my body, from the glare of my eyes, all the way down, pausing at my crotch for a second, to my feet.

Her gaze flickered back up toward my face. "He looks ... intense."

"He's a werewolf," Catherine said from her spot, like that explained everything.

The female nodded absently before coming a step closer to the bed. Reaching out a hand, she stretched out her fingers toward my hip until their tips made contact. She

316

stroked downward, over my thigh, and let out a breath as though relieved that I hadn't attacked her already.

I would've if I'd been able.

"Happy?" Catherine asked.

Again, the female nodded, her oak-coloured hair bobbing around her face as she seemed to check me over more thoroughly. Her fingers twitched against my skin, too close to where I knew my erection sat waiting, and she tilted her face toward the doorway. "Do we get privacy for this?"

"Is that what you want?" Catherine asked.

The female glanced back over my groin, my chest. "Yes."

More footsteps preceded movement in my left periphery, and, catching the lifting of the screen, my gaze tracked it, and Catherine's gofers, to the foot of the bed, where they set it down.

"Rick here will be right beside the door, should you need him at all," Catherine said, still coming no closer.

"You're not staying?" the female asked, glancing over her shoulder.

"I'm afraid I have other clients' needs to attend to for a little while. If you let Rick know when you've finished, he'll escort you back to your room. Do you need anything else, before I go?"

She shook her head, the dark strands of hair wisping around her eyes as she went back to her staring. At me. At all of me. Until footsteps had crossed the room, and orders for keeping me in line had been whispered, and the door clicked shut, leaving us with no sound other than the breathing of the only two people in the room in need of breaths.

Finally breaking contact, she took a few steps back. She probably considered it some kind of sexy shimmy, but I mostly just wanted to gut her and mess up that porcelain skin of hers until she changed her mind about what she was about to do.

Her shoulders shrugged up, and as they dropped back down, the robe she wore slid downward, over her arms, drifting to the floor.

She came back to the bed, lifted a knee to rest beside my thigh as her fingertips grazed the skin there. "I'm told your name is Daniel," she said, her voice real quiet. "My name is Clary."

Like I fucking cared.

Her fingers brushed inward, toward my inner thigh, hitting the sensitive spot right below my nut sack, and I watched her. Just fucking watched her—while cursing my stupid razzed-up body for responding. Because I had no other choice.

"We're going to have a lot of fun," she whispered, her gaze lifting to my face as she swept her palm over my balls. "I promise you."

A tight grip cinched my dick—my body would've jolted had it been able—and without letting go, she brought her other knee up onto the mattress until she knelt beside me.

Her hand stroked its way up my shaft. Back down again. I wanted to shut my eyes against the intensity in hers, against the lust I could already see brewing there, but even those bastards wouldn't obey my commands.

Her next upward rub was harsher, faster, leaving a groan full of pain and want and repulsion clogging my throat. I half wished she'd just do some serious tossing, get me some relief already—as well as rid my body of the seeds she coveted.

She didn't, though. Releasing her hold, she placed her hands on my hips as she pushed up onto her knees and swung a leg over my thighs. As soon as she settled against my legs, I knew she'd come prepared with no underwear.

"You don't like to talk much, do you?" she said.

I wanted to tell her that I could talk plenty, if I needed to, but she wouldn't have liked a damn thing of what I wanted to say to her twisted hide.

"That's okay." She gripped the hem of her skimpy nightdress and yanked it up and over her head, leaving herself naked. A small flush covered her throat as she tossed the garment aside. "It probably just means you're a man of action instead. I like that in a guy."

Her hands came down to press against my stomach, like she wanted to make sure I got a good look at the small breasts she was trying to enhance.

I couldn't have given a shit about her tits. I'd seen better. I'd seen the best. Kissed the best. Been caressed by the fucking best.

I just wanted her to get the hell off me.

As soon as she pushed back up on her knees again, I knew it wouldn't happen. Shit just wasn't going to go the way I wanted.

Wriggling her way over me, she broadened her stance to fit over my thighs, her hand tickling over my stomach until she'd got me in another death grip.

The taste of vomit hit the back of my throat as she tugged my dick toward where heat practically pumped out of her and stenched up the room.

Her juices spread across my tip as she rubbed her folds over the end of my dick, and her breaths hastened. "You see how wet you have me?"

How fucking wet *I* had her? I hadn't done shit, and the fact she considered molesting a male who hadn't even moved yet to be okay spoke volumes about her sanity levels. I wanted to open my mouth and scream out my frustrations. Tell her, if she touched me one more time, I'd shred her crotch to pieces so she'd never be able to fuck again.

Why the hell couldn't she see that in me? Why the hell couldn't she tell?

I'd never been one to beg, nor to grovel, but as I stared up at the woman, her eyes bright with the promises she'd made to herself, the first hint of a tremble affecting her thighs and hands, I begged in that moment. Begged and prayed for the pack to show up, like right that fucking second, and save me from the depraved humiliation.

Giving no warning, the female shoved my dick against her entrance and impaled herself on me.

Her loud gasp arrived first, followed by a deep moan as her eyes shuttered, and I lay there, mad as I'd ever been at my body for feeling relieved without permission, and at the groan that begged for release.

For the first time in my life, I hated my dick. Loathed the bastard. I wanted to reach down and punch it—pummel it until it was sorry for going along with the game. For being disloyal. Unfaithful.

For being fucking *wrong*.

Nausea roiled in my stomach and sent another scorching burn upward to my throat.

"Yes," she whispered, her lids reopening as she gazed down at me with a smile. "*God*, yes."

I ordered my eyes to move, and when they seemed to obey, I sent up a silent thanks that at least some part of my body still bent to my will, as I shoved her from my sights and focused on the rim of the ceiling above the headboard.

I hadn't wanted her to touch me.

She had.

I hadn't wanted her to have my body.

She totally fucking blew that denial out of the water.

I might not have been able to do anything about her wants, but I'd be damned if I'd give her my emotions, too.

She hadn't earned them.

Not like Liv had.

At the thought of her, a flash of wild red hair and the rosy cheeked smile of a satisfied female roamed my head, and a stab of pain cut through my chest.

How the hell could I look at her again?

My back nudged against the blanket beneath it. A second time. A third.

Skin rubbed against skin with every jolt of my body.

Wetness soaked over me with every ram of hers.

I'd never be able to speak to Liv again—not knowing how my body had betrayed her.

Palms shoved against my chest.

Fingertips spiked around my nipples, threatening to draw me back.

I mentally shook myself, forced my awareness to collapse back into my mind, to remain on the female I should've been laying with.

Not the one who'd stolen the liberty.

Liv. *Just think of Liv.*

Except, thinking of her had me swamped by the descending guilt.

Guilt of my actions. My inactions. My *lies*.

Because I had lied to her.

At a high-pitched moan, my balls tightened, and I swallowed back the sick feeling trying to spew its way out of my throat.

Liv. *Focus on Liv.*

I'd lied to her since the moment I'd met her. Since I'd sat with her in the pub like I was just a normal guy. A normal, *human* guy. One who came without dangers and a fucked up life.

Because life didn't get any more fucked up than the current moment.

My balls cinched tighter.

The moaning grew louder.

The answer was simple.

I would never be able to look at Liv again.

I wasn't fucking worthy of such an honour.

It was clear from the start, and I'd ignored it.

I wasn't worthy of her.

A grating cry whined out from above me, and body blazing like a fist had gripped me to jack me off, every muscle in me rushed in and forced the release from my dick.

If I'd have been able, I'd have shuddered the hell all over the place. I'd have been panting like I'd just been on a hunt.

321

I'd have groaned, probably cursed. Basked in the ride of successive ejaculations.

If I'd been able.

Even a reaction to the act had been stolen from me.

It felt like a little piece of me had been stolen, too.

Gasped breaths seesawed in and out of the female, but she didn't let up with those stabby fucking fingers of hers even with her thrusting done. "That was amaz—"

A crash sounded like it'd taken the door off its hinges, and she yelped as the noise of it bounced off the walls.

What sounded like some kind of fight broke out behind the screen, scuffling, dull thumps, grunts, and the female dug her fingers into my skin even deeper as she half twisted and stared beyond.

Another smash reverberated around the room as the screen flew sideways, and in the next second, a snarled blasted through the room.

I didn't even have time to blink before the female snapped sideways with a scream and a tornado of fury barrelled past on her tail.

36

Kyle stood staring downward in my periphery, his body gently swaying in tune with his breaths. Even with my restricted view, I could see the crimson spatters coating his upper body—blood that both concealed his scent and told me not a drop of it belonged to him.

With my gaze locked to the side, I watched as he twisted away from where the female had landed and turned toward me—bringing the full force of his emotions into view.

Blackness had claimed his hazel irises. Blackness that splintered outward, the dark tones resembling the missing shards of a broken window. Another result of one of Catherine's fucked up fiascos.

Just another reason she needed to be eliminated.

The kaleidoscopic effect continued to change as he loomed near the bed, his muscles corded as hell, his gaze flickering all over the fucking place. My body. The cuffs.

My dick.

His eye art seemed to go a little haywire at that point.

"You okay, Danny?" he asked, his focus finally coming to my face.

I wanted to tell him, No, I'm not okay.

I'm about as far from okay as I've ever fucking been.

Where the hell were you?

Where the fucking hell were you?

Where the hell were you when I trusted you to come?

I never said a word. I couldn't.

My silence just seemed to send his eyes crazier, and his frown cut slices into his brow as he moved forward. "I'm going to get you out of here, okay?"

I still didn't answer. All I could do was watch, while his knee squashed the pillow beside my head, and he reached for the cuff around my left wrist. The muscles strained through his biceps, and a long, low growl rumbled past his lips, before he snapped backward enough to yank my arm and send heat blazing through the numbness in my shoulder. Nausea lurched through me again, but like he hadn't noticed the pain he'd just caused, Kyle pushed up and rounded the bed, where he did the same for my other arm.

"Do you think you can walk?" he asked, glancing down at my face.

I stared back at him. Just fucking stared. If I could've walked, I would've been the hell out of there already.

He frowned again, the grooves cutting even deeper, and reached for where my wrists lay limp above my head. As he tugged my arms down to my sides, agony tore a path along my muscles, forcing a whimper free that I knew, from the way he paused, he'd understood.

"What the hell have they done to you?" His gaze scanned over me before landing on my damaged shoulder, his mumbled, "Motherfucker," barely there as he hooked an arm around my torso and hauled me into a sitting position.

Climbing over my legs, he tugged my head against his collarbone and, pinning me there, grasped hold of my left bicep. "This is gonna hurt. Just so you know."

The rolling shove he gave to my shoulder smashed all the other aches to pieces and set sparks shooting around inside my brain. When Kyle pulled back, his features had blurred until they resembled an impressionist painting. I cursed my stupid eyes for leaking when they were the only useful working thing I had left right then.

"I want you to wait here a second," he said. "I'm going to grab someone to cover us while I help you out of here."

The bed bounced, Kyle's outline vanished from in front of me, and my body slumped to the side. As my face mashed the mattress, the reality of his words sank in.

That he was getting someone else.

Someone else who'd come in there.

Someone else who'd see me laying on the bed, all helpless and hard and violated as fuck.

The held breath swelled my lungs, and as I forced it upward and out, I threw as much sound into as I could.

Kyle's footsteps ceased. Came back.

"Jesus Christ," he mumbled. "I thought you were mad at me, but you can't even fucking talk."

His body blurred even further and his footsteps kicked up again, a loud bang smashing somewhere to my right.

He reappeared beside me, his body low. "Catherine's going to die for this." He could've been talking to himself as much as me, as the blanket I lay on came around my side and he tucked it in front of me. "I promise you that, Danny."

The blanket wrapped around from my other side, and once he'd cinched it tight, he pulled me back into a sitting position and tucked his shoulder against my chest. "I'm sorry in advance," he told me. "Because this is probably going to hurt, too."

He swung me up and over his shoulder, and my arms seemed to scream on my behalf when they flopped down to hang low. With only a smudged view of Kyle's rear, I was on the move, my body jolting and swinging with each stride he took. He paused, but only for a beat before he took off again, his steps picking up to a light jog.

Coloured walls passed by my periphery. I wanted to ask where the others were, but muted thuds and shouts told me they were probably at least in the building. Probably dealing with other fucked up vampires who really needed to die.

Kyle's steps slowed again, and the angle of his body shifted. A small brushing sound followed, and then we were mobile again, the whoosh of a door sending a draft over my head.

Voices travelled through from somewhere, growing louder with each step Kyle covered, like he headed us toward those.

Cutting through another door took us right to them and into a space flooded with light. Kyle seemed to lose his flow for a half beat, before his steps increased in speed. The talking ceased as he bounced my body down some stairs, and before I'd even got over the ache in my gut, he swung my feet down and straightened me up.

I sensed the body behind me before Kyle dragged an arm around my middle.

"Hold him here." He cinched a second arm around my chest and shoulders—Gabe's judging by the scent. "And here. Don't let him go."

He turned and jogged down a few more steps toward a scene my brain had trouble fathoming. "What the hell's going on, and what the fuck are they doing here?"

37

Kyle came to a stop beside Ethan, the two of them only a few steps from the bottom of a broad staircase that'd been gilded in gold. I didn't need to do a full sweep to spot the high ceiling, the chandelier hanging down as though to trick the mind that it'd entered a civilised place. Down in the carpeted hallway, a red wolf stood growling on the left. Dad. Matching his posturing on the opposite site, Josh leaned forward with his curling lips barely under control.

None of those stood out as much as the ornate double-wide-door out of there, set amidst a wall of windows.

Or the fifteen wide group of vampires blocking the way.

The vampires from Witchurch.

All of them surrounding the female standing dead centre in front of them.

Catherine—with the blond we met the night before right at her side.

"These double-crossing bastards said we can't have her," Ethan said, his voice barely more than a growl. "They fucking tricked us into this so they could track her themselves."

Kyle's hands curled into fists. "No!" He took another step down, but every one of the vampires seemed to curl toward his movement, like they'd all fucking strike at the same time, and he paused again. "*That* … is coming with us." He crossed to the right of the staircase in front of them. "You have no fucking idea what she's done to us." He paced to the left, like a caged animal looking for weakness to get at its prey. "You have no fucking idea what she's done to my family." He stabbed his arm outward, and though it pointed at nothing, I knew from the heat in his voice he meant me. Coming to a stop in front of the blond, he let out a low growl. "She's ours to take."

"Catherine is no one's but mine to deal with," the blond said.

"You used us. You fucking used us."

"Yes," the vampire said simply.

Kyle's entire body tensed with the snarl he released. The vampires barely even stirred, except for the rapid eye blink from Catherine. Jogging down the last two steps took Kyle face to face with the male blond. "Why?"

"Because she's my sister."

I'd have frowned if I could've. Hell, I'd have probably lost my shit if I could've. The bastards must've been playing us from the beginning, and we'd done everything according to their plans.

"Say ... that ... again," Kyle grated out.

"Catherine is my sister," he repeated.

"Sorry, darling," Catherine said beside him. "You're not the only one with family."

Another growl blasting from him, Kyle shot out an arm and grabbed Catherine around the throat, but as soon as he made contact, the blond thrust out and grabbed Kyle in a mirrored move.

On the steps behind them, Ethan's knees dropped, like he prepped to jump in, and to the sides the hackles rose along Dad's and Josh's spines.

"Let her go," the vampire ordered.

"Fuck you," Kyle rasped out.

"Let her go, or I will send your pack home with one less member."

I wanted to latch on to his words, but I couldn't take my eyes off Kyle.

"You've no right asking us to walk away," Ethan said. "She's a danger to us—a danger to every-fucking-one. She needs dealing with."

The blond's gaze cut toward Ethan. "I agree. But she is not yours. She is ours."

"Really? Because she's spent the past year like she belongs to nobody but herself. You had your chance to deal with her, and you didn't."

"My sister is very good at hiding in plain sight. When you stepped into my café, you were the first to have had any kind of contact with her since last year. I was not about to miss an opportunity like that."

After a short hesitation, Ethan asked, "Why do you want her back? She's nothing but fucking trouble. You'll never be able to control her."

The vampire offered up a small smile. "I did not say we wished for her to return to us."

Gabe stiffened behind me, his arms like a couple of steel bands crushing my chest.

"We came here tonight," the blond continued, "to put an end to this. To put an end to Catherine's … *behaviour*." He said the word like he found it distasteful. "You are not the only ones she is putting at risk." He looked back to Kyle. "Now, please, let go of my sister, and you have my word that I will release you unharmed."

Kyle's shoulders seemed to undulate with his breaths. The muscles pulled taught along the arm connecting him to Catherine.

"Kyle, do as he says," Ethan said quietly.

My brother's face twisted to the side against the grip on his neck, and he glanced at his friend, exposing eyes blackened to all corners and as polished as those belonging to the fifteen vampires he opposed.

"*Kyle*," Ethan urged.

Turning back until his face was less than an inch away from the blond, Kyle unclenched his fingers from around Catherine's throat. "Consider this a debt you *re*-owe us," he said, his voice far from under control.

The vampire released his grip, and Kyle backed away up the steps until he'd retaken his place beside Ethan.

"You are correct." The blond gave a slight nod, and faster than my eyes had a chance of following, he whipped a hand out to his left.

With a rapid grip and sharp yank, Catherine's body jerked left as her head jolted right. The blond's fingers uncurled with a flourish, and Catherine plummeted, hitting the floor with a quiet thud.

As her heaped body lay beside him, her head tipped way over like something deformed, he ran his fingers through his hair, his eyes squinted like the act had caused him some pain. "*You* will consider that repayment in full."

It wasn't a question. I doubted any of the pack would've questioned it anyway. Both Kyle and Ethan stared at the vampire like their brains hadn't caught up to what he'd just done. Kyle looked like he wanted to murder the blond for stealing a job he'd delegated to himself.

The vampire waved a hand toward the male who'd stood to Catherine's other side—the bulldozer from the café, I realised. "Burn her." He half turned to his other pals. "Burn all the bodies. Leave none. Clear the place out."

"We clean up after *ourselves*," Ethan told him, stepping forward.

The vampire glanced back. "You want to clean up. We want to clean up. There is only one obvious solution to that, pup."

Twisting away, he stepped over where Catherine's arm lay extended across the floor and filed through the other vampires toward the doors. Cool air rushed inside when he pulled them open, and he stepped out into the beginning of a sunrise like he hadn't just pissed us off, like he hadn't just killed his sister, and like none of the tasks he'd just assigned were in any way his.

38

Cloud. Tower block. Lamppost. Cloud, cloud, cloud. Every one of them seemed to whoosh past the rear window of Kyle's truck. Lying across the rear bench on my back, I watched them all come and go. Anything to steal my focus from where I'd just left. Anything to help me ignore Kyle's constant backward glances that sang of pity.

Only the two of us had left the mansion. It'd taken Kyle less than five minutes to convince Ethan they hadn't needed us, with whatever he whispered in his ear, and he'd somehow managed to carry me out of there with no further question from any of them.

I knew when he glanced back at me again by the brushing of his shirt against the seat. "You doing okay back there?"

Yeah, I was doing just peachy fine.

A flock of swallows flew above, in a silhouetted formation that seemed to have little purpose. I tracked them as they vanished behind office blocks before reappearing, while focusing on my fingers and choosing not to reveal that they'd finally begun to move.

The longer we drove, the more pins and needles bled through me. First in my extremities, spreading through my limbs—the sensation like taking an ice bath then being stuck in front of a raging fire. Holding my jaw tight, revelling in my deepening breaths, I blanked every stab and prickle. Mostly because if Kyle knew I could move, he'd probably ask me to talk. Expect me to talk.

I didn't want to talk to my brother. I could scarcely bring myself to even look his way.

I managed to keep that up for most of the journey.

Twisting around to me again, he said, "We're nearly at Nate's."

"Don't you fucking dare," I forced out, my voice sounding like it'd gone through a cheese grater.

I sensed him eyeing me for a second before he turned back to face the front. "You need checking over."

"Take me home," I demanded, barely above a whisper.

"Sorry, Nate's ord—"

My entire body burned as I threw myself up and grabbed hold of his arm.

The truck swerved, almost hitting the kerb, before he righted it and glanced at me.

"Fuck Nate," I told him. "I want to go home."

His gaze flicked left to right, from me to the road, back again. God knew what he saw in my expression, probably a heavy dose of desperation, but he slowly nodded. "Okay. I'll take you home."

A wheeze whistled past my lips as I rolled my body back down to the seat and went back to staring up at a sky that couldn't seem to decide what mood to take.

I knew how it felt. Sickness, disgust, and a hatred that twisted up my insides all battled with the relief washing through me at having left that place, at the knowledge that it was over. All of them churned up my body and left me feeling exhausted. I couldn't even find the energy to be pissed that the vampires had killed Catherine so fucking un-dramatically. Though, there was no denying, the part of me that'd hungered for revenge and retribution felt like an unnourished pit that gnawed at my soul.

"It's good to hear your voice again, Danny," Kyle said from the front.

"Screw you," I mumbled, and the quiet laugh he gave felt like the closest thing to normal we'd had between us in months.

The house was blessedly quiet when I dragged my hide into the kitchen like a cripple in need of pain relief.

Kyle had tried lifting me from the truck.

I'd told him to try it.

He'd tried chucking his shoulder into my armpit.

I'd told him I might've been useless, but I could still walk, dammit.

Leaving him no choice but to watch my stubborn performance, while I'd hauled one leg forward after another.

Pausing for breath beside the kitchen table, I let the familiar scents sink into my system, trying to shake off those that'd insisted on accompanying me home.

"You gonna let me help you upstairs?" Kyle asked from behind me.

"I can get myself upstairs," I told him.

"Are you going to let me do anything to help?"

My shoulders heaved with the breath I took, and on the exhale, I shrugged the blanket from around my shoulders and chucked it back at him. "You can burn this," I said, forcing my body forward again. I never wanted to smell that fucking thing again.

The stairs seemed miles ahead, and by the time I reached them, my breaths came fast and my grunts came hard. Dropping my knees to the first step, I let my elbows catch my upper body and stayed there a moment, seeking composure and whatever ounce of dignity I might've had left. Kind of hard when my dick still swung around and throbbed like it wanted to play some more.

Drawing in a deep breath, I brought my foot up and pushed off the step in the right direction, but before I could go farther, something wedged up beneath my butt.

Growling, I twisted far enough to see Kyle with his shoulder tucked under there. "Get the fuck off me," I warned.

"Make me."

Shoving down behind me, I tried doing exactly that, but he just nudged upward again, leaving me no choice but to step up, and up again, pushing me the hell up, through every one of my grumbled curses, until I stood swaying on the top landing.

"You can quit with the heroics now," I mumbled.

Weaving around my body, he headed past me and along the length of the landing. The door at the end opened with his nudge, and he went inside, tugged open the shower cubicle in the corner, set the water running.

I'd taken less than three steps when he turned back around.

"Don't even think about it," I warned him.

I wanted to tell him to go the hell away. Leave me be. Quit staring at me and mollycoddling like he expected me to break at any moment. He might've been right, but not for one second would I do it in front of him.

Reaching the bathroom felt like some monumental achievement. Ignoring Kyle's scrutiny, I headed straight for the stall.

"Once you've showered, we need to go check in with Nate," he said at my back.

I paused with my hand on the shower door. "You go check in with Nate."

"He's expecting both of us."

"I don't care." Stepping inside the enclosure, I shut the door on him. "Go, Kyle. I don't need you here."

"Danny—"

"*Go*," I told him. "I can take care of myself."

I waited for him to argue further, but he didn't, just plodded right on out. As soon as the door clicked behind him, I let the water swallow me up and twisted until my back hit the tiled wall.

Slumped there, I breathed. Breathed like it was the first time I'd breathed in hours. Like it was the first time I *could* breathe.

Except that fucking scent I didn't want to be smelling still clung to me everywhere.

Reaching for the shower gel, I uncapped it and upended the bottle above my head. The cool of the liquid soap merged with the heat of the water, and I squeezed. Squeezed until my head was smothered and the bottle wouldn't squeeze anymore. Then, shutting my eyes tight, I scrubbed. My face. My ears. My neck. Shoulders and chest, stomach.

I paused at my groin. My hard-on still taunted. I didn't need my eyes open to know that—it ached like a bastard begging for a wet hole. Like any wet hole would do.

I washed around it, over my pelvis and hips, down between my thighs, where I scrubbed the underside of my balls. Even they were hard as rocks and in need of some sympathy.

Sliding my palm upward had my dick dancing in glee. I swept up over my shaft before tugging downward and washing beneath the surface. A low growl bubbled out from me at how much it liked that. It didn't deserve to like it. Fucker didn't even deserve to be touched.

Still didn't stop me circling a hand around its stiffness, though. Didn't stop the knot of heat uncurling through my body at the idea of some relief. Even squeezing hard enough to have me drawing in a sharp breath didn't seem to deter how much it wanted me to continue.

I made a slow tug upward, and the groan I gave swamped me in repulsion that left me nauseous. I didn't stop, though. I couldn't stop. I needed to offload as much as I hated the idea of it, so I yanked downward, letting my fist slam against the flesh at its base, digging my fingernails in a little on the upward draw. Gritting my teeth, I pulled harder, then harder, a growl trying to fight its way past my lips as my arm worked like a mofo to get the fucking deed done and over.

It didn't take long. Less than a minute later, my nuts cinched into tight knots, and my dick fought back against my piercing grip.

Body shuddering, my release poured from me, and opening my mouth, I let my frustration roar free, until my cries vibrated the glass around me and my throat stung.

As my knees finally gave out and my butt dropped to the shallow pool, I gave myself permission let go, to let the weight of the fucking lot of it spill from my eyes, until my chest ached with a hollowness I doubted would ever be filled again.

39

Chest squashed against my duvet, face burrowed into my pillow, I traced the movement around the house. One set of footsteps. One arrival. Not Kyle's return, judging by the weight of each tread.

The footsteps moved from the kitchen, through the hall. They paused near the front door, then made a steady clip up the stairs. As they reached my door, the soft sound of breathing took over, and a quiet rap sounded against the wood.

"Who is it?" I asked, not bothering to lift my face.

The door swung open. "It's me," Brook said. "Can I come in?"

"Sounds like you already have." The way my arms stretched the span of the mattress had my shoulders aching as I twisted my head to the side. "Liv okay?" Just the mention of her made my heart pound a little harder.

"She's fine," she said, hovering near the door.

I took a breath. "Thanks," I said on the exhale. "For staying with her. I appreciate it."

"I know." She quieted, and for a moment I thought I might've missed her leaving, but then she breathed again. "Actually, we had a lot of fun last night."

If I hadn't been such a fuck-up, it could've been me having lots of fun with Liv the night before—a thought that sucker punched my gut like a battling ram.

"She's a really nice girl," Brook added.

Yeah, I knew that. I'd known that within days of meeting her—which should've been the point I'd made myself stay clear.

"Maybe you could invite her to meet your brothers sometime."

My eyes tightened along with my jaw. I'd already made my decisions regarding Liv. Decisions that had nothing to do with anyone but me, and my reasoning even less so.

Feeling the need to be alone again, I merely told her, "Maybe."

It didn't take long before more footsteps joined Brook's downstairs. A heavy plod weighted each step up to the landing and into the bathroom, where the shower switched on. I still hadn't moved from my prone position when the same feet re-emerged and paused outside my door.

A heavier knock than Brook's hit the outside. I closed my eyes. Evened my breaths. Uncurled fingers that didn't want to relax.

Like they'd taken my quiet for acquiescence, the door opened and Dad's scent swirled through.

I sensed him standing there. Sensed him filling up the doorway and staring.

His feet brushed the carpet, and I followed his movements in my mind, until his shadow hit my face and the heat of his body warmed my hand.

"Danny?" His voice came out quiet.

I ignored him. Pretended I hadn't woken, hadn't heard.

His heavy sigh blew out next, and his hand cupped my head as his breaths coated my face. Pressing his forehead to my temple, he stayed there a moment, his fingers curling around my hair.

"I love you, son," he whispered, before his body vanished from against mine and a cool draft moved in to claim the space.

I had around a couple of hours of extra hiding before new activity created noise. A truck out on the driveway. Scuffling and grunting outside somewhere. The shove of the back door and low voices downstairs.

Boots clomped along the hall and marched up the stairs. No pause outside my room. No knock to enter. Just a shove

338

against my door and, once they'd entered, the bang of it closing again.

I'd feigned sleep for all of ten seconds before Kyle said, "I know you're not asleep, so you can quit with the theatrics."

I opened my eyes. "Maybe I just didn't want to be disturbed—everyone else took the hint."

"Yeah, well, I thought you might like these."

I rolled to my side, peered from under my armpit. My leather and bike helmet hung from his hands.

"We fetched your bike back, too."

With a sigh, I swung my legs over the bed and pushed up until I sat facing the wall, grateful that my hard-on had finally reduced to a semi. "Thanks."

He just stood there for a moment, before my gear dropped to the carpet and he rounded the bed. Sinking his butt down, he took a spot a couple of feet away, rested his elbows on his knees. "Nate wanted to know how you are."

My jaw tightened as I mirrored his pose, my fingers itching to clench where they hung between my thighs. "What did you tell him?"

"That I didn't know. Because I don't."

Unclenching my teeth, I swallowed. "How much *does* he know?"

A couple of seconds' quiet passed, before he answered, "Not as much as he should."

Meaning that Kyle hadn't told him how he'd found me. At least, not yet. Head nodding, I glanced away from him, like I could hide how much it meant to me that he'd kept his mouth shut.

"Why can't you look at me?" he asked quietly.

Because you saw, I wanted to tell him. *Because you fucking saw shit that nobody should know about me. Stuff that I didn't want to have bared witness to, myself.*

I sniffed in, hard, let it back out past my lips. "How did the clean-up go?"

His stare hit the side of my head like a heat gun, but I blanked it. "It went," he finally said. "Everything's done."

"I'm sorry I didn't help out."

"You had other shit to tend to."

He could try all he liked to steer the subject back, but he wasn't the only one holding the wheel. "Did you find many affected?"

"By what?" he asked, his voice deepening.

My hands finally fisted. "Did you find many *bitten*? Fucked up? I dunno."

"Yeah," he said. "A handful mid-phasing from vampire bites. The bastards from Witchurch took those—wouldn't let us touch them."

"What about werewolf bites?" I asked, not sure I really wanted to know the answer.

His blown breath filled the air with his scent. "Just one."

My shoulders stiffened. "Ethan?" I glanced his way enough to catch his nod and frowned. "They got him to agree?"

"They had a strong bargaining chip," he said simply. "One that would've convinced me to behave, too."

Me. He meant me. "Fuck." I rubbed my hands over my face before letting them drop back down. "What did they tell him?"

"That if he didn't do exactly as Catherine ordered, you'd be bound and drugged and your body sold to the highest bidder looking to have pups."

Bile rose high along my throat. I forced it back down. "Does he know?"

He shifted on the bed, his body twisting toward me.

"Does he know he never stood a chance?" I asked with more force.

"I don't think so," he said.

I gave a small nod, rubbed a hand around the back of my neck, where dampness had formed, and the first hint of regret swarmed in—that we hadn't got to finish Catherine ourselves. That *I* hadn't. It would never have mattered if

Ethan had obeyed, or not. Not with Catherine's mind made up and her plans in place. She'd played him. And he'd sang.

"He can't ever know," I told Kyle.

To have bitten a human would forever haunt Ethan enough. To discover his reasons didn't mean shit would fuck with his head in a way the pack didn't need.

"You can't ever tell him," I added.

"Dan—"

"None of the pack can know. There's no fucking room for discussion on that. There's no discussing *any* of it." Pushing to my feet, I pulled the bedcovers down, my back to Kyle as I shoved down on the track pants I'd stuck on after my shower.

"You're going to have to talk sometime," he said behind me.

My body tensed at the promise in his words. He could poke all he liked, but he wouldn't get shit out of me. "We done here?"

A long pause ensued, but he stood from the bed. "For now." I tracked his steps as far as the door before they trod back over. "By the way, Nate sent this over."

At a quiet thud, I dropped my gaze to the mattress, and my mobile.

"You should consider answering some of those messages you have," he said quietly and strode from the room.

As soon as the door had shut behind him, I grabbed up the phone, my thumb hovering before I forced it to swipe.

YOU HAVE 23 NEW MESSAGES.

I flicked the list into a rolling scroll. Twenty-three messages. All of them from Liv.

Thickness clenched at my throat. The skin around my eyes pulled taut.

Every fibre in my being wanted me to open the messages. See what she had to say. See what I'd done to piss her off and figure out a way to fix it.

It only took the singular whisper inside my brain to squash that.

Ordering my fingers to shut off the screen, I let a low growl of frustration free, drew back my arm, and tossed the damn device against the fucking wall.

40

An hour out of work, and I had a 'meeting' with Nate. It'd been two days since the vampires' intervention with Catherine, and Dad hadn't wanted me to go to work at all. Just the idea, alone, of sitting at home with my own thoughts scared the shit out of me, though. Hell knew, the first twenty-four hours playing what'd happened on a loop inside my head had been bad enough. If I tore everything up anymore, working through how I could've played it differently, imagining the many ways I'd have fucked Catherine and her dickheads up, if only I'd gotten loose or been stronger or maybe even a little smarter … no wonder the insanity had started to kick in. Luckily, when I'd argued my case, Kyle had backed me. For some reason, Dad had listened to him.

Banking right took me through the gates of Nate's driveway, and I slowed alongside the house before braking. After removing my helmet, I shut the bike down and swung myself free.

Ahead, Beth knelt on a cushion near some planters she'd been working on, her gloved hands pulling bits of green free of the soil despite the light smattering of rain hitting her shoulders. "Young man," she said with a smile, "It's good to see you."

"Good to see you, too." I stretched low enough to drop a kiss on her crown. "Nate inside?"

"He is."

"Guess I'll see you in a little while, then."

I strode for the conservatory, Nate's form coming into view as soon as I rounded the glass. Same spot at usual. Same seat. Same disposition. Although I could hear movement around the house as I stepped through into the kitchen, our Alpha sat alone.

"How're you feeling?" he asked, as I paused beside the table.

Fucked up. Fucked. Anything to do with a whole lot of F's. "Good," I told him instead.

He pointed to the chair beside him, and after planting my gear on the table, I drew it out and sat. For way more minutes than I was comfortable with, he stared at me. Hard. His gaze flickering like he clocked every detail of my face. The intensity in his eyes piercing as hell.

"You want to start by telling me what the hell you thought you were doing when you took that tracking chip and went to meet Catherine?" he said quietly.

Although I'd known the questions would be thrown, I'd hoped for a bit of a warmup first. Something, at least. Leaning back in my seat, I tried to relax the tension in my shoulders, tried to rid my expression of all the shit roiling in my head. "She needed dealing with, and I wanted to do it."

"Catherine being dealt with was something that affected the whole pack," he said, his voice still quiet and measured. "In those cases, personal *wants* have no part in the decisions that are made. In *those cases*, only the needs of the pack should be considered."

"I know that," I said, somehow equally as calm.

"Then, that just makes your ignorance even worse."

I gave a weak nod. "I guess you're right."

His left eye twitched. "Do you have even the slightest comprehension of how angry I am with you over this, Daniel?"

I studied him. The tension in the arms he tried real hard to hold still. The flex keeping his fingers straight under the order not to fist. Even the way he probably curled his tongue upward to prevent the grinding of his teeth could be seen in the careful way he took control. I gave another nod. "I can see how angry you are."

"Do you even care?" he asked.

"Yes."

344

"But you have no apology?"

I inhaled. Exhaled. "I'm sorry." I was, too. Really sorry. Sorry for myself counted, right?

"Is that it?"

"Look, Nate, I …" I shifted in my seat and cursed myself for the weakness. Taking another deep breath, I told him, "If I could do over my decision, I would make it a different one."

"Good," he said, his tone still even. "And that brings us to the next topic." He finally moved, his body leaning forward until he'd rested his forearms atop the table, bringing his face a whole lot closer to my own. "I have Ethan's report for what happened while with Catherine. I have Kyle's report for his version of events. But yours, I have been waiting two days for. I shouldn't have to order your butt 'round here, Danny. You should have been here the moment you got back. Now, talk."

I swallowed as my pulse tripped. "I don't have anything to add to what you already know."

The shrewdness in his blue eyes sharpened. "I *know* what Catherine planned to do with you. Ethan has reported that much."

My head shook before I could stop it. "Nothing happened, Nate."

"I know you were drugged with something when Kyle found you."

My chin jerked up as my brain latched on to something it could share. "I was."

"I also know," he said, his face inching even closer, "that your brother won't meet my eye whenever I ask him what happened to you."

My feet kicked back my seat, but before I could so much as twist away, he'd grabbed my arm.

"Stay where you are," he ordered.

I did, but some kind of fist blocked my airway, and my fingers twerked as if infected with a bad case of Parkinson's. As he stared back me, the steadiness of Nate's calm faltered, the cool blue shifting to the arctic ice of fury—a fury I really hoped wasn't directed at me. Releasing my arm, he sank back in his seat again and rubbed a hand over his face.

As soon as his softened expression turned back to me, his eyes filled with a sorrow I didn't fucking want ... I knew he'd figured out the equation of exactly what'd happened. Not that difficult, I guessed, with what Ethan'd told him combined with my reaction.

"Who're you gonna tell?" I forced out.

"Nobody," he said simply. "It's nobody's business."

I released a held breath, hating that it tremored. Hating that I wanted to throw myself at his feet in thanks.

"But on one condition," he added.

My tongue rolled around my mouth before I unfurled it to ask, "What condition?"

"That, when you're ready—and you will be, someday ... when you're ready, you come talk to me."

Voice hoarse, I asked, "Can I go now?"

His nod seemed a reluctant one. "You can go."

The roads glistened beneath lamplight and rain as shades of grey stretched overhead. Beth had tried chatting again on my way out of Nate's house. I'd pretty much blanked her. Mostly because I'd left the house feeling like I had a noose around my neck that'd only get tighter and tighter if I didn't get the hell away. As soon as I'd hit the road and the wind had swamped my face, my lungs had expanded and the virtual grip on my throat had eased.

I had no plan route-wise. I just rode. Just dipped and flipped and let the cool air fill me with its lightness.

Even so, I should've guessed where my subconscious was leading me way before I halted opposite The Hang & Hide. Parked up on the far side of the road, I stared across at the pitted car park, the worn sign, the guttering that barely clung to the building. Stared at them all like they could somehow tell me if she was inside.

I didn't know why I needed that information. I just did. Just as I knew going in there to find it wasn't an option, because if I did, and I found her there, no way would I turn my butt around and walk back out.

And that'd be a bigger mistake than staying the hell away.

I ordered myself to face the road, but didn't comply.

If I went in there, she'd have expectations. I couldn't deliver on those. Not right then.

If I went in there, it'd just lead to Liv asking questions. Questions I'd refuse to answer because I wouldn't have any to give.

"Move your butt," I whispered.

Because if I went in there and things between us went how I already knew they would, she'd end up wondering how much she was to blame. Much better that she just think of me as some kind of dickhead who'd fucked off after getting what he wanted.

It'd fit well with my usual behaviour toward females, anyway.

Kicking the gears into first, I sent one last glance toward where I imagined Liv to be—then I twisted the throttle and carried my hide away.

41

"So, I spoke to Clem at the weekend," Aunt Maghon said from beside Dad.

Skewering a hunk of liver, I lifted my fork, glancing between the two of them as I shoved it in my mouth.

It'd been a couple of weeks since shit had gone down. About a week longer since Maghon had spied me at the fuel station. Dad could say what he liked about the time he spent with her. Nobody with a set of working eyes would believe they hadn't grown close since they'd begun talking again. I saw it. Kyle saw it. Hell, even Josh saw it, which meant it had to be obvious.

Dad paused chewing, and the glance he sent Maghon's way reminded me way too much of how he used to look at Mum. "Did you mention it to her this time?" he asked.

Sitting on Dad's other side, Kyle studied him a beat before his gaze cut toward me then Josh. Only Brook continued eating like there wasn't some kind of development going on. Or maybe she just thought it didn't concern her.

Shaking my head at them both, I stabbed up a boiled potato and watched the show from beneath my brows.

"Yep," Maghon said.

"What did she say?" Dad asked.

Maghon smiled, something that resembled genuine surprise lending light to her eyes. "That it's great."

"What did I tell you?" Dropping his fork down, Dad twisted toward her and his hand folded around Maghon's shoulder.

My eyebrow arched upward when she hooked her fingers over his.

"Actually, she really wants to see you all," Maghon said, her smile growing like she was on the verge of delivering some awesome news. "She's going to come down as soon as Mike has some holiday."

"That'd be pretty cool," Kyle said, like he knew exactly what to say.

"She said she can't wait to see how much you've changed." She pushed her plate away, suddenly sitting up straighter. I couldn't help but notice she'd yet to let go of Dad's hand. "Said she wants to see for herself that Kyle's still as red as he used to be. And Josh is still as cute. And you …" She pointed a finger across the table while staring at me. "She wants payback for all the times you played hide and seek and left her hiding."

I stretched my lips into something resembling a smile. "Maybe I'll take her out to the forest when she gets here. Show her how hiding's really done."

"Daniel …" Dad warned.

I forced out a laugh. "What? I was kidding."

He shook his head, but my input worked. Maghon laughed. Josh grinned. Brook glanced sideways at me with a badly supressed smirk.

I went back to eating my dinner. Acting like I had my shit together. Like I had it all under control. I hadn't even lifted the next mouthful, though, when a knock came from the front door.

Everyone seemed to freeze, gazes skimming from one person to the other around the table.

Watching us, Maghon let out a small laugh. "You guys have a policy against answering the door during dinner, or something?"

"No," Dad said on a released breath. "We just aren't expecting anyone."

As he pushed back from the table, I could sense Maghon studying us. I scooped up a forkful of onions and bacon, ducking my head to scoff them while tracking Dad's footsteps along the hallway. Listening as he opened the door.

"Hey, Connor."

Recognising the voice, I glanced toward the hallway door, as she asked, "Is Daniel home? I wanted to speak with him."

"Sure," Dad said, and what sounded like heels hit the tiled floor out there. "Take a seat in the living room. I'll tell him you're here."

Stepping back into the kitchen, he nodded my way. "Andrea Hastings is here to see you."

My solicitor. Trying not to let my frown show, I abandoned the rest of my dinner and rounded the table. "Thanks," I muttered as I passed him, grateful that he hadn't brought her into the kitchen to discuss my crap deal in front of an audience.

She hadn't taken a seat when I entered the living room, but sat with her butt propped against the windowsill. "How're you doing, Daniel?"

I sent her a nod. "I'm good. Yourself?"

"Yes, I'm well. Thanks for asking. I hope you don't mind my calling so late, but there's been a development in the case you were questioned about, and I thought you'd like to know about it sooner rather than later."

"A development?" I closed the door on the rest of the house and sank my butt down on the sofa. "What kind of development?"

"Of the good kind." She crossed the room and took the armchair beside where I sat. "Detective Constable Bletchley contacted me earlier this afternoon, to let me know the case has been closed."

Unsure I'd heard right, I stared at her, squinting when a tic flickered beneath my left eye. "They closed the case?"

She smiled. "Yes."

"But … how can they just close a case?" Not that I didn't really fucking like that outcome. I just didn't get it.

She took a breath. "You recall they released you from questioning without reason?"

I nodded.

"Well …" Her gaze seemed zeroed in on my face. "… it was because they didn't have the body anymore."

I shoved my eyebrows up. Worked my jaw a little, like I didn't know what to say. I guessed I didn't, because I should've already put two and two together and realised they'd lost their biggest piece of evidence, the second Catherine had made that first call to my mobile. "How could they not have the body anymore?" I managed.

"She just vanished."

Doing a fast mental rundown of the kinds of details I should've been curious about under normal circumstances, I asked, "Don't they have cameras in those places?"

"They do," she said. "But they couldn't find the footage for the timeframe they needed."

Catherine really had covered her arse—or somebody had. "But they'd already got evidence of the body," I said carefully. They'd had crime scene photos. Whatever evidence they'd have removed from the body, surely? Part of me just wanted me to keep my mouth shut and relish the news of the case being closed. The rest of me needed to be sure I wouldn't be getting picked up again a couple of weeks, or months, down the line. "Wouldn't they have kept the case open on that basis?"

She seemed to be watching me as she said, "Ordinarily, yes."

"What does that mean?" I asked when she didn't elaborate.

The muscles in her face twitched some, her eyes shifting like she couldn't figure out how much to divulge. "They received assurance that the woman they found wasn't actually dead."

That time I didn't have to fake my eyebrows shooting up, nor my heart from pounding. Because Catherine *was* dead. Really fucking dead. Ethan had watched her body burn for reassurance.

"You seem pretty surprised at that," she said.

"Wouldn't you be?" I managed. "I saw the police photos. She looked pretty dead to me." Dad's phone started ringing out in hallway. Ignoring his cutting through for it, the clomp of his feet up the stairs, I kept my gaze on Andrea. "What kind of assurance did they receive exactly?"

"The *victim* is already part of another ongoing investigation, into other cases of bodies going missing from police custody. This isn't the first time she's faked a death."

I could've made dust from stone with how hard my teeth ground as I fought for the right response. The best I came up with was, "That's insane."

"On her behalf, most definitely." She nodded.

Dad's heavy weight descended back down the stairs, and I caught his quiet breathing outside the living room door.

"Who sent the information through?" I asked, a frown creeping in. "Who's investigating her?"

"We don't get to know all of the information—Bletchley didn't have to tell me this much. But I do know the order to close the case as a hoax came through from Shropshire, so they must be dealing with it. Though, like I said, this is good news for you. You can push this behind you and move on."

"Sure," I said, like I could do exactly that. Like pushing shit aside and moving on was a speciality of mine.

"So, I guess this is us finished," she said, pushing to her feet.

I forced my lips into showing some appreciation. "Thanks.

She smiled. "You're welcome. And if you ever need help again, just call. Okay?"

I nodded. "Okay. Though, I really hope I don't need to."

"Me, too." She headed across the room. "I can see myself out."

As she tugged open the door, Dad's face peered in. "I'll let Daniel fill you in," she told him, and I sat staring their way as he let her out, told her thanks.

Once he'd closed the front door, he came into the living room and shut us inside. "She came to tell you the case is closed and you're off the hook, didn't she?"

My eyes narrowed. He hadn't been outside the door long enough to hear everything. "How do you know that?"

"Because that was Nate on the phone. He got a call from the Witchurch vampires. They told him they'd been tying up loose ends of Catherine's, and her body being missing from the morgue was one of them."

"So, what?" I frowned deeper. "They just rang the police and got them to drop it?"

"One of them used their position of power to pull it off."

I let that sink in and swirl around my brain a little before it made any kind of sense—though it still didn't. Not really. It took seconds before I muttered the conclusion I'd drawn. "There are vampires in the police force?"

"Why not?" Dad shrugged, giving a half-smile. "There're werewolves in the building trade."

"I guess so." Raking fingers through my hair, I let out a heavy breath, let my tense shoulders sink down a little. "So, that's that, then."

"Seems like it. It's all over."

"Yeah," I muttered. *So, that's fucking that.*

Too wired for faking more pleasantries, I stuck my head around the kitchen door and made my excuses before heading up to my room for the evening. After snatching up my sketchpad and a pencil, I sank down onto my bed, wriggling until I sat propped against the pillows, my knees bent for leaning on.

The first page I turned to held my latest unfinished piece. I'd already prepped a faint outline of the eyelids, the shape of the irises, the pupils, and I began adding definition along the left upper lid.

About ten minutes in, footsteps approached and my door pushed open. Kyle stepped inside and re-closed the door, heading straight for the windowsill, while I watched him out the corner of my eye.

I'd expected him to turn up. Hassling me had slowly grown into his favourite after-dinner pastime.

Wedging his butt onto the sill, he swung his legs up and sat sideways in front of the window, shoving the curtain back with his shoulder as he rested his arms over his knees.

Pressing down on the paper, I added more shadow to the outer corner of the eye, waiting to see if it was a lecture or random bullshit kind of visit. It never took him longer than three minutes to warmup.

"You're wasted as a builder," he eventually said, breaking into the quiet.

I grunted. Most times, I didn't think he really expected a response, anyway.

"Should've gone to drama college, or something."

Smudging my thumb over the upper eyelid, I stretched the pencil shadows to create the dip.

"Reckon you'd have bagged yourself an award by now."

"And you should've been a politician," I muttered. "They spew a load of crap, too."

"Hell, you almost convinced even me tonight," he said, like I hadn't even spoke. "Those smiles of yours. And that laugh?" He let out a quiet one of his own, but it held no mirth. "Piece of work, Dan. Real piece of work."

"Shouldn't you be off shagging the cat?" I asked without looking up.

"I tried," he said. "But she told me she had to wash her whiskers."

My lips almost curved on their own. Almost. "You just made a joke about the cat."

"Yeah, well." He rested his head back against the narrow inset behind him. "It took less effort than coming over there and thumping you one."

When he didn't speak again, I tended to my drawing, trying to get the shine of the iris just right. To do the tone justice, I should really have used a coloured pencil, but with the right shading, the graphite got it close enough to be convincing.

"More eyes?" Kyle asked, stealing the peace again.

I nodded, darkening the outer ring of the orb.

"Don't you have enough?"

I glanced up to find him studying the main wall alongside my bed, where the last nine sketches I'd knocked out hung in a cluster. Eyes bright and wide with astonishment. Eyes filled with laughter.

Eyes half-mast and so intense, they seemed to be staring straight into the beholder.

"Personally, I like the sexy eyes," he said, like he'd followed where my gaze had settled. "Just looking at them makes me want—"

"Fuck off, Kyle." I turned back to my sketch, ignoring the low laugh he gave.

A couple of seconds passed before he cut the quiet again. "Speaking of eyes. Did you answer any of those texts yet?"

My pencil stilled, my grip of it tightening until my fingertips whitened. Because I hadn't answered the texts. Not a single one of them. It'd taken me over a week before I'd even opened them to see what they said. They'd ranged from mildly annoyed texts like 'Hello, hello, is anybody there?', to angry ones that accused me of dishonesty and messing with people, ending with the last couple to come in, that'd been full of resignation and sadness. All of them had sliced at every inch of the rawness within me and had my entire body aching against the urge to reply. Hell, I'd even *typed* a reply to the last one. A reply filled with '*sorry*'s, and '*it's not your fault*'s, but my head had taken control at the last second and the text had been deleted without being sent.

Not bothering to answer him, I urged my pencil back into action.

He sighed, long and hard, muttering something beneath his breath that I didn't even bother trying to catch.

With Kyle's gob shut off for the next few minutes, I worked on the inner corner of the eye. It was a part I always struggled with, because the required tone needed me to keep my pencil light. Pretty hard to do with my shoulders so fucking tense all the time, like I carried a permanent brick-filled rucksack on my back.

"Quit sticking your tongue out," Kyle said from his spot.

"Maybe you should go see if she's finished cleaning her whiskers, yet," I told him.

"It's good news, the whole case being dropped. What the vampires did." Kyle hopped from topic to topic like a fucking flea lately.

Shifting my butt around to get more comfortable, I nodded. "So long as they're not claiming we now owe them a favour …"

"Nah," he said. "It wasn't done as a favour to us. It was done because they needed it done."

I nodded again.

"One less thing to worry about."

I jerked up my chin.

"I guess that means it's really all over," he said.

Stilling again, I stared down at my drawing, trying to stop the frown from creeping in as I forced out a, "Yep."

Because it didn't feel over to me. Not while crap still swirled through my brain. Still kept me up at night. Still made me want to shower, shower, shower, like I could scrub it all off.

A part of me wondered if the Catherine-sized hurricane of bullshit and destruction would ever truly blow away.

42

My mobile hadn't buzzed in over four weeks. Four weeks of nothing, then, three days earlier, my reprieve from feeling like a lying, selfish bastard had been stabbed to death.

The first text, I'd opened without thinking. It'd been from Liv.

LOOK, DANNY, I KNOW YOU DON'T WANT TO SPEAK TO ME, I'M NOT DUMB, BUT I NEED TO SPEAK WITH YOU.

It'd taken half a day before the next one came in—and until the day after that for my phone to start ringing. After which, texts along the lines of '*Will you stop being a dick and answer your phone. Please*', had begun.

Every noise my phone made with Liv's name as the culprit had my breaths stalling and my chest aching, and my head in a fucking spin it couldn't seem to throw itself out of.

Brushing my teeth in front of the bathroom mirror, I stared at my reflection. The tension that seemed to be a permanent fixture across my brow. The red veins snaking out from my irises. The lies in my eyes. Lies I'd told Liv. Dad. The pack.

Lies I told myself on an hourly basis.

However well I thought I'd been doing in staying away from Liv, her attempt at reconnection showed me just how much I'd been kidding myself.

At a thump against the door, I spat out my toothpaste. "What?"

"Your phone's ringing again," Josh called through the wood.

Yeah, each and every one of my family had noticed the buzzing and ringing kicking back in.

"I *know*," I told him before knocking the tap on and sticking my mouth under it.

After spitting a few mouthfuls out, I shut off the water and headed for the door with a towel hugging my middle.

Josh still stood on the other side, his back propped against the wall. "You should just answer it," he told me. "See what she has to say and get it over with."

"No offense, Josh, but you wouldn't be my first choice as relationship counsellor."

Pushing past him, I ducked into my room and closed myself in. My phone sat on the bed like some kind of fricking taunt, its screen still aglow despite the ceased ringing. Ignoring it, I tugged open my drawers and pulled out a pair of sweat-shorts and cotton shirt.

"Dad said to tell you we're leaving in fifteen," Josh said, before his footsteps finally buggered off along the landing.

Letting out a long breath, I shucked my towel and fed my feet into the shorts. It felt unfulfilling, going through the motions every fucking day. Wake, work, home, sleep, repeat during the week, and then wake, Nate's, eat, home, sleep, repeat every weekend. No matter how familiar the routine, the disconnect I felt from it was too great to not be noticeable. Or maybe it was the monotony of the routine that'd helped me keep rolling. To keep moving forth.

Voices came from downstairs, a couple of bangs, feet padding around the house, while I pulled on my T-shirt and dried the wetness from my hair with my discarded towel.

A knock carried up from the front door, and I stilled, but only for a beat. Was probably Aunt Maghon, anyway. Her latest tricks leaned toward turning up unannounced with pies and shit, and then finding a way to stick around for the rest of the day.

Leaving my towel atop the pile of dirty stuff I had mounting in the corner, I reached for my trainers. In truth, I didn't really need them—they'd be coming off as soon as I got deep enough into the forest to change, anyway—but heavy rain overnight had left small boggy lakes all over the place, and I didn't think Beth would appreciate me walking unnecessary mud all over the joint at Nate's.

"Dan!"

At Josh's yell, I paused in tying my laces, glanced up.

"Door for you!"

My heart banged with unbidden force against my chest, my eyes narrowing as I glanced toward a landing, stairs, hallway I couldn't even see. Finding my voice, I called back, "Who is it?"

After ten seconds of waiting for it, his answer hadn't come, and I shoved up off the bed, tugged open my door, strode along the landing.

As I jogged down the stairs, the scent hit me first, all sweetness woven through with honeysuckle that had my mouth simultaneously watering and drying up.

The vision hit me next, through the entrance glass, all orange and blurry, but orange all the same, and my steps slowed to hesitant compliances at my order to move forward, while battling with the darker ones my brain sent out, to run the hell away.

Almost afraid to, I slowly rounded the door Josh had left half open, and my stomach about bottomed out on seeing Liv there. Right fucking there like she belonged there and who the hell was I to question her presence.

Not quite facing the door, she stood with her head bowed, her hands tucked into the pockets of her skinny jeans as she toed at the driveway with her Converse. Like she'd tried taming it, her hair sat in a couple of bunches either side of her head, their ends poking down toward the swell of her chest, which she'd covered with some kind of baseball shirt.

Feeling like a creeper for staring unawares, I stepped outside. "Liv?"

Her head snapped up and round, the widening of her eyes and parting of her lips making her look more terrified than surprised. "Hey, ah …" She glanced away again, like she couldn't stand looking at me for too long. "I'm sorry to come here, Danny, but—"

"How'd you know where I live?" I asked, feeling like a dick for asking as soon as I had.

"Only two houses in Wild Woodington, right?" Her gaze lifted again, the meagre daylight catching her lenses and obscuring her eyes. "Figured I had at least a fifty percent chance of picking the right one."

Sticking my hands into my pockets, I descended the couple of steps until I stood right beside her. About as close as I could get without giving in to the urge to touch her. Because, damn, did I want to.

Her eyes followed the move. She half looked like she wanted to take a step back. Like she suddenly thought she'd made a huge mistake and what the hell was she doing here.

"What are you doing here, Liv?" I asked, needing to know myself.

She gushed out a breath. Glanced away again. Her whole body language seemed off. Wary.

Of me?

"Why couldn't you just answer your bloody phone?" she muttered.

"If whatever's on your mind is important enough for you to show up here, I'm pretty sure a phone call wouldn't have cut it, anyway," I told her.

She nodded, still staring away, like the bush near the front wall held a whole lot of fascination for her. "I have something to tell you."

Something about her tone had my senses kicking the hairs up along my nape and my fingers fidgeting inside my pockets.

"About the night you stayed over."

My pulse, which'd calmed some in her proximity, upped its beat again as my brain speed-read the details of one of the best damned nights of my life. Scooting over every touch, every sound. Every last image of her body, her skin.

Her head swung back around, and I noticed for the first time the redness of her eyes through her lenses. The shadows dipping down beneath. "Something happened, Danny."

Not even thinking, my hand shot from its safe haven and grabbed for her collar. She barely even flinched as I tugged it down, and I brought my other hand up, smoothing my fingertips over flesh I knew damned well had been bordering on damaged. Damage caused by me and a loss of control.

Not a single scar marred there, though. Not one.

She finally frowned, like her head had only just caught up with my actions. "What are you doing?"

"I—" I heaved out a breath, an almost wheezed sound. "I thought I—I needed to check that—"

"Daniel?"

At Dad's voice, my head snapped up.

He stood staring down from the top step. I hadn't even noticed him come through the door. "Everything okay?" he asked. Anyone who knew him would notice his effort not to frown.

I somehow managed a nod.

"What's going on?"

I glanced from him to Liv, realising I still had my palm spread over her collarbone and her shirt stretched to fuck. "This is Liv," I told him, slowly removing my hands and straightening her clothes. "Liv, this is my dad." I sent a nod his way.

"Nice to meet you, Mr Larsen," she said, but her voice sounded small, unsure.

"Likewise." He looked to me. "Danny, we're leaving in a few minutes."

My skin seemed to tighten across my face. I'd spent weeks avoiding anything to do with Liv, but with her standing in front of me, obviously not fucking okay, I couldn't help but feel that, if I walked away then, if I told her to leave, I'd never get a second chance to hear what she had to say. "Can I catch up with you?" I asked him.

His eyes narrowed, the scrutiny he shot down on me both heavy and stifling. Like he'd found what he needed to, his head made a slow nod. "I'll let Beth know you're coming late."

Shoving my hands back into my pockets, I waited as he stepped back inside, as the shadowy forms of my family made their rambled retreat through the kitchen. Once the back door closing had carried through, I turned back to Liv, not quite able to shift my frown.

She just stared right back, her fingers playing with one another. "Your dad seems nice."

"What did you want to talk to me about, Liv?" Because, although her reaction, the lack of teeth marks, confirmed I hadn't bitten her, I couldn't shake the anxiety that insisted on running through me. "What happened the night I stayed over?"

Her hands dropped, and she wiped her palms over her thighs, her gaze not quite meeting mine as she mumbled words that sounded a whole lot like, "I'm pregnant."

I took a step back even as my body leaned forward, like I hadn't quite heard right.

"I'm pregnant, Danny."

Blood soared past my ears, and as I staggered a little to the side, I threw my butt down onto the steps before I could face plant the drive. My vision might've blurred a little, and I pressed the balls of my hands against my brows, like that'd help.

"I'm sorry," she continued, her voice suddenly thick. "I'm sorry, okay?"

I knotted my fingers around my hair, searched for my breath.

"I didn't mean to show up here like this. I tried ringing you. I tried bloody ringing, and you didn't answer, so I didn't have a choice." The words all seemed to string together like she pushed them all out without pause. "I wouldn't have come at all, but my parents wanted me to get rid of it—"

I bolted to my feet, my head already shaking as I reached for her. Sliding my fingers around her nape, I tugged her to me, lowered my forehead to hers. "Don't, okay? Please," I whispered. "Don't get rid of my baby."

"I told them," she said, her voice thick with tears. "I told them, you had a right to know. I told them I had to speak to you."

"Don't kill my baby," I whispered again, and as her shoulders shook against me, I brought my arms around her back, lifting her until her chest pressed against mine, until her cheek brushed against mine.

Her arms came around and held me right back, as she murmured, "I didn't know what to do. I didn't know."

"It's gonna be okay," I mumbled, as I twisted us toward the house, my feet like a couple of blocks as I carried us up the steps. "Everything's gonna be okay."

Pausing in the hallway, I just stood there, my arms unwilling to let go while I knew she still cried. While I knew what she carried within her was half me, like I suddenly needed to cocoon her from the rest of the world.

Because I didn't, for a second, doubt what she'd told me. Didn't doubt the pregnancy. Didn't doubt that I was responsible. It was the first time my gut had felt sure about something in weeks.

"It's okay," I said again, setting her on her feet.

Tiny tear splatters patterned her lenses when I drew back a little. I slid the glasses from her face and wiped them on the hem of my shirt. Before slipping them back on, I lifted my hem and wiped her eyes dry. "Please don't cry, Liv. You're killing me."

"Do you even care?" She frowned as soon as the words were out, like she hadn't meant to voice them.

"Yes, I care." I cupped the side of her face, my fingers stretching around below her ear. "You have no fucking idea how much."

"But you didn't answer my texts." Her breath shuddered from her. "I tried calling, and …"

I dropped my temple to hers, like crowding her could somehow stop her asking about shit I didn't know how to answer. "You're here now." I let my thumb brush over her cheek, let my nose slide along the side of her face. "That's all that matters."

Her scent seemed enhanced where her pulse beat against her skin, and I paused there. Closed my eyes. Inhaled.

Fuck, I'd missed her aroma. Missed the subtleness of her femininity and the way it flavoured the air. "I'm sorry," I whispered. "I should've answered your calls, but …"

"But?" she asked softly, her breaths tickling my throat.

I swallowed, twice, not once moving my face, as if not having to see her eyes made the half-truth easier to spew. "I've been going through some personal shit, and I wasn't good company."

"And now?"

I sucked in a long breath through my nose, like just drawing her inside me that way could help steady the kick of my pulse. "I'm working on it."

"Okay," she whispered, and a little of the tension slipped from my shoulders.

We stood like that for seconds. Her body unmoving yet relaxed. Mine inhaling a supply of the closest thing to calm I'd experienced since everything had gone bad. My nose nuzzled deeper without order, her breaths grew hotter against my skin, and something resembling contentment moved in.

"I missed you, Liv," I said against her flesh, and her body trembled slightly. Trembled like she'd missed me, too. "I'm glad you came here today."

"I'm glad, too," she whispered, and her fingers found the hem of my shirt. Twisted there.

As I brought an arm around to hold her, her fingers found the sleeves of my shirt. Twisted there.

When my lips parted against her skin, her hands swept inwards, over my shoulders, to my chest.

Except, as they twisted there, I no longer felt the feather light touch of Liv, but the stab-stab-stabbing of fucking fingernails scraping into my chest and clutching at me like fucking talons that wouldn't let go.

My entire body locked up as I dragged my face from her throat to suck in air.

"Danny?"

I hauled in one breath after the other.

"Danny, what's wrong?"

I flipped my eyes open, ordering them to focus on my surroundings, because what played behind my lids was the stuff of my fucking nightmares.

"Danny, look at me."

A hand pressed against my face and forced it round. Until I stared into glassy eyes of the moodiest blue, surrounded by a sunburst of glorious fucking orange wisps. Below those, lips, perfect fucking lips moved, moved, moved, folding around the word, "Danny."

"Danny."

"Danny."

I blinked. Broke past a caught breath and focused.

"I'm okay," I mumbled. Sensing the cinch of fabric still, over my chest, I reached for Liv's hand and unfolded it from there, keeping it in mine as I drew it away. Tugging her in close again, I let my cheek rest beside hers, let her scent lead me back to steadiness with slow inhalations. "I'm really glad you're here, Liv."

A few beats passed without answer, her body more rigid against mine than it hand been moments before.

"Danny, what happened to you?" she asked quietly.

My body stiffened the fuck up again, and I shut my eyes like I could shut out the question.

I took a slow breath in, released it back out.

"Will you tell me?" she asked, when I hadn't answered.

"When you're ready?" she added, and I found myself nodding. Found myself nodding because I didn't know what else to do.

***

After almost an hour of talking, of me sending more pleas Liv's way regarding the baby, I'd realised I had little choice but to go own up to what I'd done. Though to me, it'd felt less like an error with every passing minute. Hell, I'd even got a got a flutter of excitement amid the swarm of *oh, fuck, this is real* inside my stomach.

"Did we just drive around the block?" Liv asked, staring up at the house.

I smiled. Actually fucking smiled. "No, this is the other of the two houses in Wild Woodington."

She glanced at me from the passenger seat of Dad's truck. "Who lives here?"

"Family." I pushed open my door. "But this is where my dad came today."

"Your dad?" she asked, as I hopped from the truck and slammed the door behind me.

She stared at me through the windscreen, while I rounded the front of the truck. Her head was already shaking when I pulled on her door.

"I can't," she almost hissed. "I'm not ready, Danny. I'm not ready for this."

Gripping her hips, I swung her down from the seat until her feet hit the driveway. "It'll be okay," I told her, praying I spoke the truth. "I promise."

With her hand in mine, I deliberated for a moment—whether to just barge into the kitchen and surprise the hell out of them all. It wouldn't be fair on Liv, though, to be hit with meeting the entire pack in one go, especially not under our circumstances, so I led her up the front steps and knocked on the door, more than conscious of the shapes I could see moving around inside through the doorway to the kitchen.

It took about two seconds for one of those shapes to grow bigger as it headed our way, and I recognised its outline before Ethan's face squinted through the glass aside the

366

door. It took way less than that for surprise to show in his eyes and his brow to fold.

The door swung inward, and Ethan stood there, his gaze flitting from me to Liv.

"This is Liv," I told him.

"I know," he said, his gaze lingering on her. "We met."

"You picked him up from the party," Liv said.

Nodding, he stepped back just enough to permit us entry, and I tugged Liv behind me into the hallway.

"Who is it?" Beth's voice called from the kitchen.

"Danny." He shut the front door, still scrutinising the hell out of us. "He brought a friend."

A couple of chair feet scraped over the tiles in there, and Josh's head poked around the doorframe. "A *lady* friend," he said, showing off one of his moronic grins.

Sean's head peered round. Then Jem's, Kyle's.

Beth rounded the doorframe, her smile in place despite the questions in her eyes. "Are you staying for dinner?" she asked Liv.

Liv's mouth opened and closed, and she looked to me like she needed help with the answer.

"Actually, I really needed to speak to Nate and Dad," I said, leaning closer to the older female. "Can you ask them if they can spare a minute?"

Her gaze met mine, her eyes searching, before she turned away like she'd found what she sought. "Wait in the living room, flower. I'll tell them for you."

Ignoring Ethan and his continued staring, I drew Liv with me, to the left, and into the front room. There'd used to be enough seats to accommodate the pack in there. Enough for every single bum. We seemed to have a habit of accumulating females lately, though, and respect insisted they needed the seats at least as much as we did.

Ushering Liv over to a corner seat, I nodded for her to sit down. As soon as she had, my body begged to pace, but her hand tightened its grip around mine, as if telling me not to let go.

I glanced down at her wide eyes, the thin line of her lips. "It's okay," I murmured. "Quit worrying."

A shadow hit my periphery, and as my head swung round, Dad strode over to stand in front of the window. Nate marched in behind him and closed the door before lowering himself onto one of the sofa cushions, his narrowed eyes instantly zooming in on us.

"What's going on, Danny?" Dad asked, folding his arms.

The lacklustre daylight filtering through behind him made it impossible to read his expression. I glanced from him to Nate, taking in the way he'd woven the tips of his fingers together, the way he hunched forward over his knees.

Liv's fingers squeezed mine, and I swallowed. "I need to tell you something."

"So, spit it out." Nate's lips half-curved as he glanced toward Dad. "The last time I saw someone this nervous was when—"

"I had to tell Rob I'd gotten Nadine ... pregnant," Dad finished.

My gaze flitted between the two of them, but paused on Nate.

He no longer smiled as his head made a slow twist back toward me. Not one fucking bit. His frown deep, he simply said, "Danny?"

Damn that fucking ball of stress stuck in my throat. Forcing it down, I nodded. "Liv's pregnant."

"It's yours?" Nate asked.

"It isn't anyone else's," I almost snapped.

Dad's body dropped as he sank his butt down to the windowsill. His face turned to Nate. I still couldn't figure out his expression, his feelings. He glanced back toward us. "How far into the pregnancy are you, Liv?"

Her hand twitched against mine. "About six and a half weeks."

He sniffed before nodding. "And how do you feel about this?"

"Well, I'll probably have to lose some time from classes, but …" She released a shuddered breath. "I feel better since speaking to Danny. I'm okay about it, I guess."

"You guess, or you know?"

"Dad …"

"The girl has a right to be sure, Daniel. You have to give her that, at least." He pushed up and stepped closer, and I finally saw in his face what I hadn't been able to. Fear. Probably an ounce of panic. "This isn't some fad you get to enjoy for a while before you both decide it's not what you wanted, after all. This is for life, and I'm not sure you get the *seriousness* of the situation."

"I *do*," I pressed back. Hell, did I get it. "I'm not stupid, Dad." I knew that what grew inside her held not just a piece of me, but also a piece of my heritage. I *knew* that. It'd been playing through my head since we'd hit the road to see them. Releasing my held sigh, I gave a small nod. "It's okay. I've got this." I glanced down at Liv, meeting her eyes. "*We've* got this."

"I believe you," Nate said, drawing me round, as he peered up at Dad. "I believe him, Connor" he said again. "And maybe you should be focusing on the bigger picture here."

Dad frowned as hard as I'd ever seen him. "There's a bigger picture than this?"

Nate merely nodded. "You're going to be a granddad."

Like the realisation had only just made its way through the bullshit, his eyes scrunched some. His mouth did some weird smirk, despite his funky frown. "I am," he muttered, and a quiet laugh floated out, breaking every bit of tension holding all of us captive. "I am," he said again, and covering the gap between us, he yanked me in for a one-armed hug, his fingers scruffing the hair on the back of my head.

"I think Liv should probably stay for dinner," Nate said, and Dad stepped back.

"That's a good idea." Unravelling her hand from mine, Dad drew her to her feet. "How about you come meet the family?"

"Uh, okay?" Liv said, making it sound like a question as he led her from the room.

"Can you give me a minute, Daniel?" Nate asked, when I went to follow, and I spun back to him. He nodded toward the seat opposite, and I sat, trying to read him even while my brain tracked Liv along the hallway, while I listened in on Dad making introductions. As some exchange went on between her and Brook, Nate asked, "Does she know?"

I didn't have to ask what. I shook my head. No, she didn't know about me. About the pack. No, she didn't know anything.

"Do you trust her?" he asked.

"Yes," I said. I couldn't afford hesitation while being stared at by Nate.

"You're going to have to tell her," he said simply.

"How the hell do I do that?" I asked, fighting against my jaw as it clenched.

"You find a way," he said. "And you do it soon. Because that girl has a right to know what she's carrying. And she better have all her options open to her when she finds out." He studied me for a moment, the slight wrinkles beside his eyes more pronounced. "Do you understand what I'm saying to you?"

Yeah, I understood. I had to fucking well give her enough time to make her own choices, if she ran for the fricking hills on discovering she carried a werewolf offspring. I nodded. "Yeah. I get it."

He smiled like he needed to reassure me. Like he needed me to believe it might be all right, even if I played by his set rules. "You should go and rescue her," he said after a beat.

I pushed to my feet, pausing to glance back when I reached the door. "Thanks, Nate. For being cool about this."

He nodded. "Worse things have happened to this pack than a baby, Danny."

Worse things *had* happened. To me, Liv's news felt like the air I'd been seeking to keep my breaths coming. The jumpstart I'd needed to reboot my heart.

Leaving Nate behind, I stepped into the kitchen and found Liv sat between Jem and Brook. Letting my shoulder rest against the doorframe, I watched her for a moment, ignoring the weight of the stares from the others in the room that told me they all already knew exactly why she sat there.

After muttering something to Beth that earned him a smile, Dad came to my side, his fingers folding around my shoulder as he stepped past. With a gentle squeeze, he made his way back along the hallway behind me, his footsteps softening as he hit the living room carpet. Even as his quiet voice kicked up in there, I couldn't seem to shift my focus from Liv.

Her gaze found mine over Jem's head, like she'd sensed me staring. "I didn't know you knew Brook." Confusion creased her forehead despite her smile as she pointed to her right. "How didn't I know this?"

"Small world," Kyle muttered from across the table.

"I guess it just didn't come up," I said, sending him a warning glare.

"Something definitely did," Josh mumbled.

Smacking the back of Josh's head on the way past, I rounded the table and Ethan and Kyle, and Sean helping his mum over in the corner. I drew back a chair as close to Liv as I could get without kicking Brook from hers. As I sat down, I let my gaze skim over all of those in the room, my family, finding a circle of quiet acceptance and understanding staring back at me, until it'd relocated Liv. Her smile. A smile no longer watery but full of a reassurance she hadn't had earlier.

As I watched her there, amongst my two families like she should've been there all along, it suddenly dawned on me that I was soon going to have another family. One of my own.

One I'd have to take care of, be responsible for. One I'd have to be prepared to die for.

About then, it really sunk in.

I was going to be a motherfucking dad.

DANNY & LIV BONUS STORY

Not ready to say goodbye to Danny & Liv just yet?

Really want to know what happens when Danny tells her the truth about the child she's carrying?

GOOD NEWS!

A Danny & Liv Bonus Story is available, exclusively for readers of the Holloway Pack.

All you have to do to receive it is scan the barcode to follow the below link, and complete the form.

Dan & Liv's extra tale won't be available anywhere else.

Please note: this is not a newsletter subscription; you will be submitting your details to receive the Danny & Liv Bonus Story only.

So, what are you waiting for?

SIGN ME UP!

ACKNOWLEDGEMENTS

Lots of thanks is due to some awesome folk, without whom this book might never have become, so ...

Mr B, The Boy, and Boop. Because they are, and always will be, the most important thanks to give. My kidlets have understood and supported my urge to write from the moment I began back in 2009, and still 'get it', when they try striking up a conversation and get a response of which only a zombie should be capable. And Mr B because he's my everything. My light and my dark, and sometimes the reason I function at all. ♥ you, babe.

And in no particular order:

My street team, for always being so supportive and encouraging, no matter what I'm working on. Denise, Maghon, Lola, Rachel, Carla, Rosemary, Keri, Wendy, Taneesha, Angela, Terri, Rebecca, Stephanie, Louise, Melanie, Jen, Ambur, Sandra, Carole-Ann, Denae, Angie, Renée, April, Janel, Joy, Tammy, Debb, Tina, Pamela, Valerie, Kelly, Paulette, Linda, Eleanor, Jan, Emma, Sandra, Debbie, Jennifer, and Ravannah.

Wendy. You pushed me forth. You spurred me on. You took on my torturous first-draft chapters, one at a time, right through to the very end. And you poked me to keep going, keep going, keep going. I bow to you.

Keri. For reading those difficult to write chapters for me and telling me they weren't poo. For kicking me in the rear when I emailed and said 'I can't do it'. For being there. Always.

Gameboon. Your in-depth input, when I needed help in understanding something I didn't understand, was invaluable. I don't think anyone else could have portrayed the information I needed as informatively as you did, and I thank ye heartily.

The kindly gentleman who answered every question I had (and there were a LOT) on police procedures for arrest and dealing with murder investigations. That section of Danny's story wouldn't have been anywhere near as believable without your help, and I'm wholly and wholesomely grateful.

My full novel beta readers. Wendy (dude, you read this aaaaaallll over again), Terri, and Maghon. Mwah!

To Maghon again – for jumping in and entering an impromptu contest and permitting me use of your wicked name as a result.

To those who entered a different competition what seems like a decade ago, to name a character in the Holloway Pack series. Thank you, thank you to Lola, Pamela & Katherine for helping to birth Olivia Fanella. I think the name suits her well, don't you?

And finally, but by no means least, you, the readers. Without readers, there would be no authors. Without authors, there'd be no me writing the Holloway Pack for others to set their beautiful sights on. So, thank you!

ABOUT J.A. BELFIELD

Best known for her Holloway Pack stories and The Therapist, J.A. Belfield lives in Solihull, England, with her husband, two children, a spoiled dog and a cat who likes to vomit in unfortunate places. She writes paranormal romance, with a second love for urban fantasy. And now she writes erotic romance, too. Because she can. ;)

In 2016, Instinct [now part of Beginnings] earned J.A. Belfield International Bestseller status when it featured in the Paranormal Attractions anthology. J.A. Belfield now hopes to claim that same status solo.

To stay updated on everything J.A. Belfield, join her on Facebook in the Belfield's MotherBookers group.

OTHER TITLES BY J.A. BELFIELD

HOLLOWAY PACK

BEGINNINGS
CALLED
LURED
CAGED
UNNATURAL
HEREDITARY
ENTICED

EROTIC ROMANCE

THE THERAPIST

PARANORMAL ROMANCE

HER MANE ESCORT

www.ingramcontent.com/pod-product-compliance
Lightning Source LLC
Chambersburg PA
CBHW071148100726
47908CB00002B/288